DOG AND DRAGON

DOG AND DRAGON

DAVE FREER

DOG AND DRAGON

A Baen Books Original

Baen Publishing Enterprises
P.O. Box 1403
Riverdale, NY 10471
www.baen.com

ISBN: 978-1-4165-3811-0

Cover art by Bob Eggleton

First printing, April 2012

Distributed by Simon & Schuster
1230 Avenue of the Americas
New York, NY 10020

Library of Congress Cataloging-in-Publication Data

Freer, Dave.
  Dog and dragon / Dave Freer.
    p. cm.
  ISBN 978-1-4516-3811-0 (trade pb)
  I. Title.
  PR9369.3.F695D64 2012
  823'.914—dc23

                                        2011053038

10   9   8   7   6   5   4   3   2   1

Pages by Joy Freeman (www.pagesbyjoy.com)
Printed in the United States of America

This one is for my Old English Sheepdog,
Roland, loyal companion, faithful friend.

═══ Acknowledgments ═══

My thanks go to the many readers who asked for this, and to my editor, Toni Weisskopf, for listening. To my agent, Mike Kabongo, for getting me to write a high fantasy in the first place. As this is my first entirely Australian-written novel: To the Australian immigration authorities for letting us come here to our own enchanted island, Flinders, and to all those who saw our animals (Roly, Puggles, Wednesday, and Duchess, Robin and Batman) safe through quarantine and here with us. To the friends who helped us settle in so that I could write, and the ones (that's you, Jamie) who came up with good ways to kill monsters.

And, as always, most thanks to Barbara, for editing, supporting and driving through Melbourne traffic.

═ Characters ═

Neve	Tirewoman to Meb.
Lady Vivien	Widow of Cormac, the late captain of the Royal Guard.
Lady Branwen	Wife of Earl Alois, not of the House of Lyon.
Owain	Alois and Branwen's son.
Gwalach	Second-in-command of the Army of the South.
Mortha	Wudewasa wisewoman.

— OTHER —

Sir Bertran	A knight of Brocéliande.
Avram, Dravko, Mirko	Travelers who trade between various planes.
Mitzi	Avram's dog, and Díleas's light o' love.

Chapter 1

Back to the sunset bound of Lyonesse—
A land of old upheaven from the abyss
By fire, to sink into the abyss again;
Where fragments of forgotten peoples dwelt,
And the long mountains ended in a coast
Of ever-shifting sand, and far away
The phantom circle of a moaning sea.

—*Idylls of the King*, Tennyson

"WHO ARE YOU?" HISSED THE LITHE, DARK-EYED MAN WITH THE drawn sword.

Meb blinked at him. Her transition from the green forests of Arcady to this dark, stone-flagged hall had been instantaneous. The stone walls were hung with displays of arms and the horns of stags. Otherwise there was not much to separate it from a cave or prison, with not so much as an arrow slit—let alone a window—to be seen in the stone walls.

In Tasmarin from whence she had come, she had known just who she was: Scrap, apprentice to the black dragon that destroyed the worlds. You could call her anything else, but that was who she had been. Now...

"Cat got your tongue, wench?" he said quietly. "Well, no matter, I'll have to kill you anyway."

He swung the sword at her in a vicious arc.

Moments ago, before she'd made the choice that swept her magically from Tasmarin, from the green forest of Arcady, she'd

1

thought she might be better off dead rather than leaving them behind. Leaving *him* behind.

Now she discovered that her body didn't want to die just yet. She threw herself backwards, not caring where she landed, as long as it was out of reach of the sword.

She screamed. And then swore as the blade shaved along her arm to thud into the kist she had fallen over. She kicked out, hard, catching her attacker in the midriff, knocking the breath out of him in an explosive gasp. Trying to find breath, he still pulled weakly at the sword now a good two-finger-widths deep into the polished timber of the kist. Meb wasn't going to wait.

But it looked as if she wasn't going to run very far either. Her scream, and possibly the swearing, had called others, and the great iron-studded doors were flung open as men-at-arms with bright swords and scale armor rushed in.

As she turned to run the other way, her passage was blocked by a sleepy-looking man—also with a sword, emerging from the only other doorway.

There wasn't a window to be seen.

She wanted one, badly.

And then she saw one, in the recessed wall to her left. She just plainly hadn't spotted it before.

She ran to it, and realized it wasn't going to help much. In the moonlight she could see that it opened onto a hundred feet of jagged cliff, to an angry sea, frothing around sharp rock teeth far below.

Some of the soldiers surrounded the man she'd kicked. They'd blocked her escape too, but you couldn't really call it surrounding her. Not unless that included "getting as far from her as possible, while not leaving the other prisoner, or the room."

The man who had looked so sleepy moments before didn't anymore. His sword was up, ready, his eyes wide as they darted from the window to her, seemingly unsure which was more shocking.

"Who are you?" he asked.

There was something weaselly about him that made her very wary about answering, in case her words were twisted against her.

And why did they all want to know something she wasn't too sure of herself?

There was a narrow bridge across the void. Along it walked a black-and-white sheepdog, followed by a black dragon. The dog never looked back at the dragon, just forward, his questing written into every line of his body, from the mobile, pointed ears to the feathered tail.

The bridge itself was narrow—made of vast, interlocking blocks of adamantine—or at least that is the way it looked. Reality might be somewhat different, at least to the eyes of a planomancer. Such eyes would see deeper than the ordinary spectra of light, and could see patterns of energy. Fionn, the black dragon, saw it all as the weave of magics that made the bridge between the planes of existence. He knew the bridge was fragile and fraught with danger. That did not stop him walking along it, any more than it stopped Díleas the sheepdog.

The bridge was barely two cubits wide and had no rail. Far, far below seethed the tumult of primal chaos. The only way the dog could go was straight ahead. He kept looking left though.

That was where he wanted to go. Sometimes he would raise his nose and sniff.

Fionn knew there was nothing to smell out here. The air that surrounded the bridge was drawn and melded by the magics of it, from the raw chaos. It was new air, and Fionn knew that it did not exist a few paces behind them, or a few paces ahead.

He was still sure Díleas was following the faint trail of something. A something which even a very clever dog could best understand as scent...even if there was nothing to smell.

At least he hoped that was the case.

Hoped with ever fiber of his very ancient being.

Fionn had long since given up on caring too much. He was not immortal, as far as he knew. He could certainly be killed. But compared to others, even of his own kind, the black dragon was long-lived. Time passed, and so did friends. His work was never done, fixing the balance, keeping the planes stable. He moved on.

He'd been hated. He'd been worshiped, though it irritated him. He'd been laughed at and reviled. He'd been feared.

He'd even been loved.

He had never loved before, though.

The black-and-white sheepdog was more experienced at love than the dragon, and he was a young dog still, maybe eight months old. Barely more than a pup. But Díleas—whose name was "faithful" in an old tongue, long forgotten by most men—would go to the ends of the world for her, and beyond, as they were now. His mistress was his all and he would search for her until he died, or he found her.

Fionn knew that he'd do the same. His Scrap, his inept apprentice, had been plucked from them by magic. Her own magic and her own choice, made freely for them, and for Tasmarin, the place of dragons. Fionn knew, however, that it had cost her dearly. For him, left here without her, it was a worthless sacrifice.

So now, somewhere, back in some place that she'd been torn from as a babe, they had to find her again.

Fionn had no idea where that might be. A place of magics, where human magery ran strong in the blood, that much he could be sure of. But there were many such places in the interlinking chain of worlds, and they themselves were large and complex places.

It was a good thing that Díleas seemed to have some idea where to go, because Fionn didn't know where to even start, except by trying everywhere. He would do that, if need be. He had time. He would never give up.

The only problem was that she was human and very mortal. And, if he had to be truthful with himself, she was able to attract disaster toward herself, just by being there.

Fionn had never known love. He'd never really known worry either. Pain, and the avoidance of it, yes, fear, yes, but now he was afraid for her. Worried.

The end of the bridge was now visible, if wreathed in smoke or mist.

Fionn wondered if it would be guarded, or if the bridge was too new. The transit points often had their watchers, or barriers.

As the other side of the void came closer, Fionn realized this place would not need such things.

Most travelers would turn around and go back just as quickly as they could.

Gylve was a place of fire and black glass.

Fionn had been there before, and wouldn't have minded if he'd never had to go there again. A planomancer needed to visit such places and straighten things out. Last time, it had glowed in the dark, and he'd had to do some serious adjustment. He was pleased to see that the radiation levels at least had dropped. Still, you could see fire dancing across the sky as the methane jets caught.

On the silver collar on Díleas's neck hung a bauble. A little part of the primal fire, enclosed in what merely appeared to be crystal. It should keep the dog safe from demons and from actually freezing. It wouldn't keep his feet safe on the broken volcanic glass in the place they were coming to; only dragon hide would do for that.

Fortunately, he had some with him, available without the discomfort of slicing it off himself. He could have done that. Dragons were tough... even if they really didn't like making holes in themselves any more than the next creature. But every now and again a dragon died or was killed. If a dragon was sharp about it, they could get a piece of hide before the humans did. Honestly, thought Fionn, for a species that was afraid of dragons, humans had a habit of sticking their necks out.

It was one of the things that he liked about them.

The bridge was beginning to widen... to open onto the jet-black clinkers of one of the fire-worlds. Fionn stopped.

Díleas didn't.

"Díleas, come here!"

The dog did turn and look at him, with a "what do you think you're wasting time at?" look. And then began to pace forward.

"This muck will cut your feet to ribbons. And then you won't be able to walk to her." Fionn had to smile wryly at himself. Talking to the dog. Just like his Scrap of humanity had.

The dog turned around and came back to him. Lifted a foot.

Fionn's eye's widened. He'd have to do some serious reevaluation. And yes, now he could see that the dog was substantially magically... enhanced. Curse the dvergar and their tricksy magics. He was supposed to be the practical joker, not them. His Scrap had *wanted* Díleas to understand her. And she wore a very powerful piece of enchanted jewelry, which bound the magics of earth, stone, wood, fire and worked metals to her will.

Not surprising really that her power worked on sheepdogs. They were clever and loyal anyway, or so he'd been told.

"It won't be elegant," he said, "but then there won't be other dogs out here to see you. He took the section of dragon leather from his pouch and rent it into four pieces, and then made a neat row of talon punctures around the edge, before transforming his own shape. Human form was one of those he knew best, and it allowed him to wield a needle well. It was of course partly a matter of appearances, and a useful disguise. He was far too heavy and too strong for a human—but hands were easier to sew with than clawed talons. A piece of thong threaded through the holes and Díleas had four baggy boots.

Díleas looked critically at the things on his feet. Sniffed them.

"Dragon hide," said Fionn. "I wouldn't show them to any dragons you happen to meet, but otherwise they'll do. And really, scarlet boots match the bauble on your collar."

Díleas cocked an ear at him. Fionn wasn't ready to bet the dog didn't grasp sarcasm, so he merely said, "Well, let's go. The only thing we're likely to meet are demondim, and they like red anyway."

They didn't like dragons, but were suitably afraid of them, so that was the form Fionn assumed, as the two of them walked into the badlands. It reeked of sulphur and burning, and Fionn knew the ground could collapse under their feet, dropping them down hundreds of cubits to white-hot ashpits. Vast coal measures had been pierced by ferocious vulcanism, and deep down, some-where, it burned still. Fionn blinked his eyes to allow himself to see other spectra, patterns of energy, that might allow him to spot such instability before it killed Díleas. But the dog seemed aware and moved with a slow caution that he hadn't showed up on the bridge.

It was, as befitted a fire-creature world, hot and waterless. Fionn noticed that Díleas was panting. He'd have to learn to carry water for the dog, or to somehow carry the dog while he flew, because there were worse places than this, in the vast ring of planes that Fionn had once maintained the stability of. He was a planomancer, made by the First for this task, and there was plenty of work waiting for him.

Right now, it could wait. All he did was to make a few pre-liminary marks with his talon and tail.

And simply because he'd said to Díleas that they would see nothing here but demondim, right now he could hear noises that were very unlike those beloved of the creatures of fire. A jangle of bells, and, clearly, a bark. And human voices.

Díleas, panting, could hear them too. Dogs could hear more keenly than humans, but not dragons.

Fionn changed his form again, becoming human in appear-ance. A dragon would almost certainly be an unwelcome sight. He could, and possibly should, leave the demons to their nasty games. But he had some sympathy for humans these days. She'd taught him that. He would help, simply for her sake. They moved towards the voices and sounds.

The caravan of carts was moving, slowly, along a causeway of blue-black hexagonal blocks. Probably the safest place around here, reflected Fionn, although you had to consider just what had flattened the top of the columnar dolerite dyke into a narrow straight road across the ash fields and lava lands. Bells tinkled from every horse's harness strap. Whoever they were, they were not ignorant of demondim and their dislikes, or quite the helpless lost travelers Fionn had expected. The fire creatures liked to mislead and torment those. But whoever had made those bells knew a thing or two about the demondim. They'd been made either to very precise mathematical formulae, or been shaved very carefully into making an octave.

"Go on, Díleas. We might as well see just who they are and what they're up to and cadge you a drink, panting dog," said Fionn, prodding him with a toe.

Díleas dropped his head and looked warily... not at the advancing carts but at the trail in front of them. He gave a soft growl. So Fionn looked closer. It was a well concealed little trap, the clinker plates hiding the thing's lair. The Silago wasn't a particularly intelligent predator, but it didn't need to be. All it did was to make a bit of a trail and lie in wait. Eventually something—if there was anything—would choose the easiest trail and walk into its maw, just as he nearly had. Half-rock, half-animal, it didn't need to eat more than once every few years anyway. Fionn found a piece of glassy rock and tossed it at the clinker plates. They collapsed inwards and a segmented creature with long snapping jaws reared out, lashing about, looking for prey.

Fionn stepped back, Díleas had already neatly moved up against his side. And then the tossing Silago head sprouted an arrow shaft. And a second. Fionn paused, wondering if he should take refuge behind a rock spike. Any bow that could push an arrow hard enough to penetrate a Silago might even get an arrow into him.

The dark-skinned, white-haired man on the lead cart—with his recurved composite bow in hand, arrow on the string, and perky-eared dog growling from the seat beside him—was smiling, though. A suspicious smile, but better than fear or anger, while he held that bow. And there were plainly others, because of that second arrow. "You ain't one of the Beng," he said, "because they don't like dogs and they don't walk on the ground. And they don't like our bells or garlic. The question is who or what are you, stranger?"

Finn touched his hat. "Finn. I'm a gleeman. A traveling singer and jester. I juggle a bit too."

The man didn't put the bow down. "Not many inns or villages around here. Where are you from, gleeman? Abalach? Annvn? Carmarthen? Vanaheim? The Blessed Isles or...Lyonesse?"

Fionn was an expert on tone. Lyonesse was probably not a good place to be from. He'd been there. He'd been everywhere, once upon a time.

In front of him the Silago still thrashed about. "None of those, recently," he said cheerfully. "A place called Tasmarin. Back there."

"Didn't know there were any Ways over there," said the traveler.

"It's rather new, and I don't think it's going to see much traffic, judging by this charming countryside," said Fionn, waving at the ash lands. "And anyway, Tasmarin is quite full of dragons. They're not overly friendly." The Silago was threshing rather more weakly now. Fionn could simply have jumped over it, but not if he wished them to believe he was human. He slowly, calmly, reached into his pouch, took out three balls and began to juggle one-handed. He'd found it very good for distraction and misleading before. And those little balls were made of osmium, both a lot harder and heavier than observers might guess. Fionn could throw them fast enough to knock an armored knight out of the saddle. "To tell the truth I am a little lost. And my dog could use a drink."

The cartman smiled again. "I think we could probably sell you some water. And the road should see you to Annvn, if you stick to it. You'll have to wait until the Beng-child is dead, though. They usually put themselves in the middle of the only safe path. It's surprising you got this far." His tone said that alone was reason for not putting aside his bow, just yet.

Fionn shrugged, not stopping his juggling. It was good for hypnosis too. "The dog is good at finding safe ways."

"I like his footwear," said the cartman.

"Worn by all the best dogs in the capitals of many great lands. It also keeps his feet from being cut up. Purely as a secondary thing, you understand," said Fionn. He pointed to the Silago. "It's dying, whatever it is." There was no point in admitting to knowing too much.

"Give it a little more time, gleeman. Even half-dead, the Beng-child will have your arm off, and might scratch the dog's boots. When it's dead we'll have the jaws off it. They'll fetch a good price where we're headed."

Fionn nodded patiently, which was more than Díleas was showing signs of. "Where did you say you are bound for?"

"Annvn. Well, if it's there. You never know these days."

Fionn raised an eyebrow. "And where else might it be?" He was a planomancer. There was a logical consistency to where the various planes of existence interlocked. It was not variable. The multidimensionality and subplanes of it all meant it was more complex than a mere three-dimensional ring would be. It was possible that points of departure and arrival could be geographically close. But until Tasmarin had opened up a way to multiple planes, one link point did not lead you elsewhere. Had Tasmarin changed it all?

"Last time we took the giant's road we found ourselves in Lyonesse. If that happens we'll head back," he said, putting the bow aside, and getting down from the cart. He pulled a long metal stake and a hammer from the cart. Looked for a crack, found one and hammered it in. "How far to this Tasmarin place?" he said casually, in an I-am-not-fishing-for-information tone.

Fionn was amused, and used to human ways. "Not far. I could tell you in some detail . . . in exchange for a drink for my dog."

"Ah, you're a sharp one," said the cartman, grinning. "Worth a trading venture?"

"Probably," said Fionn. "What are you selling?"

"Things which are exotic in one place and cheap in another. Peacock feathers and pepper, bottles of mermaids' tears, amber, narwhal ivory, and carved walrus tusks this trip."

"I'd say pepper would sell." It was a game, and Fionn played it well.

"Ah. One of those places," said the traveler. "Magic, and the creatures of it are more common than pepper. Hey, Nikos, Dravko. The Beng-child is ready for you to butcher the jaws out of. You might as well come across, stranger."

Fionn could see things they could not. The Silago was not dead. He patted Díleas. "The dog thinks it is faking, mister. And he's a sharp dog." He caught all the juggling balls in one hand, and picked up another rock and flung it at the open jaws, which snapped closed viciously and sent splinters of rock flying.

The white-haired man looked very thoughtful indeed. "Sharp dog he is. And earned himself a drink, I'd say, gleeman. Maybe worth asking you about the way across to this place."

"I made marks." He had. With a talon. They were not intended as trail markers but they could work as that without undoing his purpose. Energies needed to flow, and the travelers could be vehicles for that. Travelers tended to be a cunning lot though. Over the years he'd known and journeyed with a fair number of these sort of folk, too many to believe them to be easily fooled or used without them knowing.

"Ah. It's a sharp master too. A wonder you don't cut yourself, gleeman. Nikos, come and give the Beng-creature a good poke with that black iron spear of yours."

Someone knew—or had known—a great deal about demondim and the few creatures that survived just what they had made of their worlds, thought Fionn, looking at the spear in the next swarthy man's grasp.

It wasn't iron-edged and had a fair weight of magework about it. Antimony might not be the ideal metal for edging anything, but it was deadly toxic to the silicate sulphur of the Silago.

Soon Fionn and Díleas were able to pass the two traveler men cutting at the dead Silago. The dog on the seat of the lead cart growled and bristled. "Hear now, Mitzi. That's no way to greet a dog with smart red boots," said the lead cartman. Díleas was studiously ignoring her. The cart driver got down, and tapped some water out of a small keg into a bowl. Held it out to Fionn. "Here, gleeman. Best if your dog drinks a little way from Mitzi. It's her bowl."

Fionn gave a little bow. "Thank you, goodman. This place was hotter than we expected. Dustier too."

"Ah well, you've a fair distance to travel in it. Best to be prepared. My name is Arvan, gleeman. I only look like a good man."

"Call me Finn. Most do," said Fionn, taking the water and setting it on the ground. He noticed the watchfulness of the lead cart driver. The watchfulness of the dogs on the seats of the other eleven carts. The fact that they had at least two other men hidden in them, and they weren't watching him or Díleas. The water smelled all right, wasn't bespelled . . . Díleas sniffed it too, and then drank with a great deal of tongue splashing. He had needed that. Well, he was wearing a good thick coat of black-and-white fur.

"And now, Finn, if you'd tell me a bit about this Tasmarin place, I could offer you a mug of beer," said Arvan. Fionn knew the name was a small part of the traveler's true name, which suggested that the travelers knew of the importance of those too. Well, they did accumulate knowledge or fail to survive.

"It's an hour's walk from here. See the double smoking peak? Bear just left of that. You'll find this symbol scratched on the rock here and there." Fionn scratched it with his toe in the dust. "There is a narrow white bridge that you will have to cross. Not much room for a cart on it. And the dragons on the other side are fond of gold, so I'd take care to appear poor."

"Oh, we are," said Arvan, tapping Fionn a small flagon of beer. It was good beer.

"They can smell gold at twenty paces," said Fionn, who could smell theirs, above the beer. It was under the front end of the cart. Probably a hidden panel or something.

"Ah. There haven't been many around for a while. People wondered where they'd got to. Some of us wanted to know."

"There, that's where," said Fionn.

The jaw cutters had finished their work by now, and they carried them back to the causeway and roped them onto the back of the cart, still dripping black ichor. The little caravan set off again, Fionn and Díleas walking alongside the lead cart. It was, it appeared by Díleas's behavior, the direction they needed to go.

A mile or so later the causeway was interrupted by what might have been called a river, if rivers boiled, and did not run with anything anyone could have called water, although scalding water diluted it. It ran through a fresh fracture in the dolerite, and the steam reeked of brimstone and the almond smell of cyanides. Arvan scratched his head. "That's a new one."

Fionn tried to work out the least obtrusive way of changing the situation. Energy and fire magic abounded here. There was even an ancient water pattern. The place had been verdant once. A tweak here and there . . . But it would all take time, and by the way that fool-of-a-very-clever sheepdog was pacing back and forth and bunching his muscles, he would try jumping soon.

The beautiful crone-enchantress, the queen of Shadow Hall, stared vengefully at her seeing-basin. Dun Tagoll—dark stone towers silhouetted against the moonlit sea—seemed to stare back at her. He'd protected it as well as he was able, and she could see no further into the castle on the cliff top. She had stared at it, the same way, for over fifty years now. Eventually, she would win. A few hours earlier she'd felt a surge of magical energy, and wondered if he'd finally died. But no, the tower still resisted her vision—it would not if he was dead, she was sure. So, the fight must continue. She was busy mustering her forces, yet again. She worked with her unwitting allies' fears, and she had the Cauldron of Gwalar. It brewed and bubbled now. Soon she would cast pieces of yet another dead hero in the seethe of it. They had to be boiled apart, or at least finely diced, before she could reassemble them and reanimate them. And then dispatch them . . . to whichever of the nineteen worlds Lyonesse would try to leech off this time.

She stared at the image in the seeing-basin. The tallest tower and its highest window. There was a light there. He would be working away, creating falsehoods and illusions. Working on his simulacra and devices. Bah. Machinery. She had been fascinated by it once, the cogs and springs and the mechanisms for harnessing the tides themselves. The smell of oil, and magic . . .

He was not a summonser, but one who worked inanimate things and the laws of contagion and sympathy. She used that, but drew on higher powers too. The powers of life . . . and death. She learned as much of his craft as she could, of course. In those days Dun Tagoll had been the place to learn and to practice magecraft. He'd stopped that. He didn't like competition.

To think she'd loved him once. Trusted him with their secret. Sworn eternal faith to each other and their secret. Dreamed that some day . . . She spat into seeing-basin, shattering the image.

Death would take him one day.

And it could not be a day too soon for her.

In the meanwhile she had to finish the warrior in her cauldron. And then get onto making more muryans. Shadow Hall would have to walk again, to follow Lyonesse, to raise war and chaos and foes against it. She followed Lyonesse's progression across myriad leagues and subplanes in her palace of shadows.

Her hall moved. It did so on tiny ant feet. Many, many ant feet.

═ Chapter 2 ═

"MY NAME IS MEB," SHE SAID, CLINGING TO A PART OF HER YOUTH.

"Mab?" It was said with a narrowing of the eyes. The sword came up a fraction and Meb wondered if the jump might be more pleasant. She had no idea if her untrained magical skill would work here.

It sounded as if "Mab" wasn't too popular. "No. Meb. E, not A. My real name is Anghared. But I like Meb more." Really, she preferred Scrap.

This had some rather unexpected effects. The oddest was from the man who had tried to kill her—who was now pinned down by three burly men-at-arms: he started to laugh. Several of the soldiers knelt. The sword tip threatening her dropped. "I suppose you can prove that?" said the once-sleep-addled man facing her.

"What proof does she need, Medraut? She is a summonser, able to work in cursed Dun Tagoll itself!" shouted the man on the floor.

If looks were poison, the prisoner would have been dead instantly. "Take him away," said the man called Medraut. "I ask you again, stranger. Who are you, dressed like that, in my outer chamber? How did you get here?"

Meb shrugged. The bleakness of despair was settling over her again. She'd assumed the magic would send her back to the place where she'd been drawn to Tasmarin from. She'd assumed that it would be a place she somehow recognized as home. In truth she hadn't cared. She'd simply known it would mean banishment from all she knew and loved. However, innate caution instilled

13

by dragonkind's hatred of human magic stopped her going too far with explaining. It might be different here. But it might not. "I don't know. I was in Arcady and then I was here. But I'll go away if you don't want me to be here. I think I just stopped you from being murdered in your sleep." She gestured toward the prisoner being dragged from the room.

"It is almost as if she was sent to save you, Prince Medraut," said one of the guards, wonderingly. "The door wardens are dead, the door unlocked . . . and had this stranger not given the alarm, Earl Alois would have killed you. Alois nearly killed her."

Prince Medraut blinked. "You . . . you are the Defender?" and part of the tone said: Why me? But there was hope there too.

Meb wasn't sure who "the Defender" was. But she was pretty sure that it wasn't her, anyway.

"I don't think so," she said, exhaustion, doubt and misery warring in her breast. "I am just someone who is hungry and tired, and going to jump out of this window, if you try anything with that sword."

The prince suddenly realized that he was holding a naked sword . . . and that she was on a window sill. He looked faintly embarrassed. "Your pardon, lady."

How did he know she was a woman? With a cropped head, boy's clothes and tight breastband, she'd passed for a boy for months and months. Well, said her inner voice—the sensible pragmatic voice that overrode village thought, and overrode daydreams too: maybe the name Anghared is a clue. That and the fact that, somehow, her hair seemed to have grown to waist length in the transition here. The clothes remained, of course.

The prince put the sword down, on the floor, as that was the only surface available to him. "We will have chambers and food prepared for you immediately. We are deeply honored by your presence and pray we have not caused you any offense."

She'd trusted him more when he'd been pointing a sword at her. It must have showed in her face. But the soldiers sheathed their swords, and they at least appeared to believe him. "I swear by the House of Lyon that we mean you no harm, lady."

Reluctantly Meb came down from the stone sill. She hadn't liked falling last time, and it looked as if the rocks would get her before a merrow could. Besides, she might as well die well fed. What worse could happen to her than certain death?

She knew some answers to that one, too. But she allowed the guards to respectfully escort her away to a small withdrawing room, where a generous fire burned in the grate and the hangings were rich and old. There was a riven-oak table that must have weighed as much as ten stacks of stockfish, painstakingly smoothed and polished. It was set with two branches of good beeswax candles, with a chair that was more like a throne than the three-legged stool she'd have considered luxury a twelvemonth ago. The guards bowed. "The old queen would dine here, Lady Anghared. They will bring you food and wine, very soon," said a grizzled captain, very respectfully.

If there was one thing that was really intimidating, Meb thought, it was all this respect. But she was hungry, as well as miserable and a little confused. Just where exactly was she? Somewhere called Dun Tagoll? A castle hanging above the sea. The place where she had come from as a baby, presumably, before being magically snatched away to Tasmarin, to a world that had become her own, that she'd loved and had given all to Finn and Díleas. So this must be her world. But, if she'd ever thought about it, she'd expected to return to a fishing village.

She'd never thought of herself as a castle kind of person. That was the place of alvar, after all.

It would seem that was not true here. These castle people were all human. She closed her eyes, and sat back in the chair, remembering. Remembering walking behind Finn in his ridiculous "notice me" lilac and canary-yellow silks and satins, juggling tasseled balls in the palace of the alvar at Alba, with its high arched roof, alv-lights and the butterflylike flitting of the courtiers, as she pretended to be dumb and tossed the balls.

Something landed in her hand. Instinctively she caught it. And the second, third and fourth. The sight of the balls, summoned out of nowhere, was enough to prick her eyes with tears. Someone cleared their throat. There was an elderly man, in neat clothing, but plainly a servant by his mein, with a silver salver, a stemmed goblet, and a chased jug. He was staring, rather wide-eyed, at the juggling balls. At her. He suddenly realized she was looking at him. "Er. I have brought the wine, lady. May I pour for you?"

Meb set the balls down, carefully. They were as precious as... no, more precious than the rubies of the Prince of Alba. She'd helped Finn to salt the sea and the river with those. She smiled at the thought. The servitor thought she was smiling at him and smiled back tremulously. "We're so glad to see you, lady. People were praying for your coming."

It only got more complicated.

He poured wine, looked around quickly. "Don't trust him, m'lady. The old king hated Medraut even when he was a little boy. And I changed the wine Aberinn poured in the cellar," he said quietly.

Prince Medraut had dressed himself hastily, not waiting for his manservant to return from calling Cardun. There were few others he could trust in this place, but the chatelaine would lose her place and probably her life if he lost his position here.

The woman arrived, as he was attempting to dress his hair. "Pellas told me the story," she said, taking over. "I think it is a trick, Medraut." In public of course she gave him the honorifics he was due. In private...she was still his aunt. "One can't be sure, yet, of course. But this is similar to the way Aberinn got rid of Regent Degen. The false feint and the death thrust, if you like."

"It's hard to see just what sort of death thrust a young woman could manage, Aunt. And the sea-window is restored."

"There could be several ways a competent practitioner could arrange that," said Cardun, who was far better at the theory of magic, even if her practice was feeble, for one of the house of Lyon. "The stones have the memory. Aberinn could set it up very easily. So could several others, but with the spells set to suppress magework within the castle, Aberinn is your principal suspect. And you know as well as I do that it is really his voice that stands behind the silence of lords. He is the reason the nobles' houses do not call for you to become the king."

Medraut sighed. His aunt was driven by that ambition. It had its attractions, but being the regent was quite adequate in this dying, riven kingdom. He just wanted to stay that, because the alternative was to lose his head to a successor regent. "I was there. If it was trickery, Cardun, she must be the greatest actress in the world. She might be this Defender, and in some ways that might a relief. And now, I'd better go. Some fool will have called Aberinn, and I'd rather be there when they meet."

Few guards were courageous enough to go and disturb the mage in his tower, no matter what had happened. And thus the guard sought his peculiar out, telling her the story.

Vivien was just as afraid of Mage Aberinn. And she had even more reason to be afraid, for with Aberinn, that which she knew,was worse than the guards' imaginings. Part of her hoped, though, that what the man-at-arms said was true.

She went to the tower. Knocked on the heavy door.

It opened by itself. He liked those sorts of small displays of power. He was sitting at his workbench...but he had been waiting, she was sure. "So Prince Medraut is dead. And they sent you to tell me. There are no secrets in Dun Tagoll," he said, smiling his humorless smile.

"No. Prince Medraut is alive. The Defender has come! The first part of the prophecy..."

"What?" He stood up, disturbing the model he had been at work on. "The royal chamber..."

"The sea-window is back. And a young woman calling herself Anghared has saved Prince Medraut."

"Anghared! Who would dare use a name like that? Don't tell me—our all too clever manipulative regent. The commons will assume that the royal names are worn by the royal house," he walked to the door, shooing her out in front of him, like a hen. "What has happened to her?"

"They've taken her to the old queen's withdrawing room. They fetch her food and drink. She said she was hungry."

"I'd better see this convenient miracle," said the mage. "A neat ploy by Medraut. I wonder if she has any real skills? You are to watch and befriend her."

"But the queen's window..." protested Vivien.

"A trick that could easily enough be done...once. She could even merely spring the spell, without any skill herself."

There was a sound from the doorway and the servitor straightened up, bowed, as Prince Medraut entered with another man in once-white robes and a beard that he should have washed after eating egg, and of course the obligatory couple of guards. Meb sipped the wine. If this was good wine...she'd had worse in her travels with Finn. But not much worse.

More servants came in, carrying platters. It did look something of a feast.

Medraut bowed his head politely. "Ah, Lady Anghared. May I introduce myself more formally. I am Prince Medraut ap Corrin,

Earl of Telas, and Prince Regent of Greater Lyonesse. And this is our court magician, Aberinn. I trust you are enjoying your wine?"

Meb had always been a poor hand at lying. So she stuck to a nod and a smile.

"Allow me to cut you a piece of this bird," he said, slicing into what appeared to be a plump roasted pheasant and placing it on the trencher that another servant had set before her. Meb knew it was a high honor to be served with choice portions cut by the lord of the hall, with his own dagger. And besides she wasn't sure she still had one to eat with. Mostly a rough hand-carved wooden spoon would have done for the pottage of most inns and fingers and a knife for the meat they might have grilled on the way. Here...there were platters and silver salts.

They were watching her rather carefully. She picked up the slice of breast and ate...

It wasn't pheasant. It wasn't even bird. It was bread. And stale, at that. Fortunately, she eaten a fair amount of that in her time. The pickings as a gleeman's apprentice had often been slim, but they were still better than they'd been growing up in Cliff Cove. There was always enough fish, of course. But bread was quite a luxury at times, and a girl-child often got the stale crusts. She washed it down with some wine.

The magician and prince relaxed visibly.

"If we might ask, lady, where did you come from?" said the magician.

There seemed no harm in telling him. "A place called Tasmarin."

They looked blank at the name.

"Ah. A far-off realm, no doubt?" said the prince.

Meb was tired. The stale bread was better than nothing, as was the sour wine. But her stomach, and temper, were set up for more. "How would I know? I don't even really know where I am now."

"You are in the Kingdom of Lyonesse, in the great fortress of Dun Tagoll, the crowning-place of the Kings of the West," intoned the magician as if reciting a poem.

"Never heard of it, I am afraid," said Meb with a yawn.

"Er. Perhaps more wine. Some of these little cakes?" asked Prince Medraut, into the awkward silence.

She had no doubt, now, that those too would turn into stale bread. "No, thank you," she said curtly. "Why are you doing all this?"

The two looked at each other. "Because it was foretold that the return of the sea-window would come with the guardian against the sons of the Dragon," said Prince Medraut.

Meb decided not to tell them that Tasmarin was a place ruled by dragons, or just how she felt about a specific dragon. "What do you mean 'the return of the sea-window'?"

The magician shrugged. "There has not been a window in the antechamber since Queen Gwenhwyfach leapt from it with her baby son. She was the greatest of the summonsers, a powerful mage and much loved. The king was heartbroken, and had the window walled up. The masons closed it off, and then, when that was not enough for the king, they knocked out part of the wall, tore out the lintel and the sill, and built it again so there was no trace of the window."

"Oh." It seemed a very inadequate response. But Meb couldn't think of anything else to say, so she sipped her wine, and thought about it instead. She didn't want to tell them that their prophecy was wildly inaccurate and the window, she now realized, had been something she needed to escape through, and that the magic of the dvergar artifact on her neck obviously still amplified her own magical skills, even here, far from Tasmarin. She didn't want it! A hand went to her throat. And then Finn's words about the dragon necklace with its wood-opal eyes came back to her. It wouldn't stay lost, not even if she buried it or threw it into the sea. And would it be better used by the likes of either of these two men? She already trusted neither.

Someone knocked on the door. It was a warrior, in a dripping cloak. "Prince Medraut. The enemy have been sighted from Dun Argol. They look a great host, burning and plundering as they come."

The prince tugged his hair. Sighed. "M'lady. We will talk further, later. I must consult with my war leaders and wizards. The women will come to escort you to your chamber. You have not come at a time of peace, I am afraid."

It looked more like she'd come at a time of murder, war and conspiracy. She sipped the wine. Looked at the "feast" she had largely ignored. Out of the corner of her eye she realized the far items looked like hunks of bread. So she turned her head. Yes . . . on the periphery of vision it was all various shaped lumps of coarse bread. She had to wonder why, and about the wine.

Was this what they had? Was it just for her? She hoped it was the latter, if they were facing war and probably siege. So...this was where she'd come from as a baby, was it?

It made Cliff Cove seem quite attractive.

A stiff-looking matron came in, her washed-out blonde hair done up in tight coiled braids and disapproval written on every line of her plump face. She had plenty to write the disapproval onto, but the application of powder and paint plastered over some of it. She looked Meb up and down as if examining a side of stockfish from a not-very-reputable dealer. "You are the Lady Anghared?" she said in a chilly voice. "Lady" was definitely questionable. "I am the Lady Cardun, the Chatelaine of Dun Tagoll. I was told that you would require a bedchamber and water and suitable attire."

Given the matron's attitude, it was clear she felt Meb should be sleeping in the attic on a straw pallet with three others and a lot more fleas, and given a kitchen trull's castoffs. Meb had already begun to think she might be better off leaving, even via the window that had once been blocked off, no matter the sharp rocks below. Maybe her face showed it, because one of the two women in the chatelaine's wake, the one with the spare, lined face smiled sympathetically at her, and said in a quiet, much kinder voice. "Oh, Lady Cardun, she looks about to fall over. And so young too. Come, child. We'll see you safely bestowed."

Obediently Meb stood up. Tears pricked at her eyes. She hadn't had much female sympathy, or company, since the raiders had destroyed her home. And even there...she'd been an outsider. "Thank you," she said gruffly. "I am very tired. It's been a long and awful day."

"With Prince Medraut and Mage Aberinn at the end of it," said the sympathetic one.

— Chapter 3 —

A CHEMICAL BRINE STEAMED AND FROTHED AS IT GUSHED THROUGH the new tear in the black road that crossed the shattered ash lands. Something hissed up from a fissure, taking shape into one of the elemental creatures of the smokeless fire. Díleas backed away, barking. So did the travelers. "Back on the carts, men, it's one of the big Beng!"

Fionn had spotted what he had been hoping for, deep down. This dolerite dyke had blocked it, and now the creatures of smokeless flame had cracked that. The bells that were ringing from the carts helped to hide the sound he made, as he sat down next to Díleas and scraped rock-sign onto the stone.

The fire-demon was less easily fooled than the travelers. "What does one of your kind want here in our demesnes?"

"Yours? I thought you liked places of ash and smoke and flame," said Fionn mockingly, answering in the creature's own language. "Not such a place as this is about to become. I am one of the advance surveyors."

"Surveyors?" hissed the creature.

"Yes, that is what they call those who make accurate measurements and determine the boundaries. Those are busy changing," said Fionn, with exaggerated patience, as if explaining to a simpleton.

"We changed them, in order to stop this endless incursion into our lands!"

"You did, did you?" mocked Fionn. "I was of the impression you liked incursions. Devoured their essences or fed them to your pets."

"These have protections. We seldom get one. So we have broken their road."

"And that has broken your land. You should have guessed that when you got the brine-boil instead of the lava," said Fionn, with all the confidence in the world.

"We frequently have fumaroles," said the creature of smokeless flame.

"Do they usually get cooler?" asked Fionn, his voice even. He had redirected sufficient heat downward for that to start to happen. All that heat was cracking the dome far below now. When there had been tiny fissures...the water had boiled and picked up minerals on the way up. But, if those fissures grew, more water would flow from the strata below. Water that had been trapped down there for millennia, under increasing pressure. A lot of water. Fionn chuckled to himself. The fire creatures would hate it, but it might help their ashpit world regenerate. They were running out of coal measures, and once, after all, it must have been wet and warm here to grow the forests to make the coal. It would ease the balance of forces here. So good to achieve two things at once. And seeing the look of startlement on the creature of smokeless flame's features—you couldn't really say "face"—was a joy.

Ah, he'd forgotten the pleasure of being the trickster in the last little while. The wider worlds *needed* him. Aside from rebalance, there was the pure delight in overturning the expected and changing the order of things.

The creature of smokeless flame left hastily, with no further words, not even of farewell, or of threat. No doubt it had gone to consult with its superiors. They had a habit of doing that, whenever confronted with something different. They were so hierarchical they struggled with independent thought. It was their weakness. Which was just as well, really. They needed some weak points.

Fionn watched its departure with some satisfaction. And went on talking. He did the fire-creature's speech part too, while he backed up to the cart, and felt for the catch to their hideaway with his foot. The travelers would be hiding their heads from illusions, most likely. And anyone peering out could see his head and hands. He was just as dexterous with his feet as with his hands, and he'd a lot of experience with hide-aways. He deserved a fee for this, besides the sheer pleasure of doing it.

In a way, he thought, he had taught his Scrap of humanity,

and she in turn had taught him. He told her that there were many ways of solving a problem. She'd showed him that his ideas were still quite constrained to maintaining the status quo. His purpose was retaining the balance, but it didn't have to be same balance—just so long as it was balanced.

A few moments later he was back at the edge of the flowing, fuming stream through the blue-black stone of the causeway. It was running stronger and fuller now, and definitely not as hot. He put his hand on Díleas's head. "Wait. It will get cooler."

So what was it about him, and her, that would have unbalanced Tasmarin, that meant she had had to go back to where she came from?

It didn't make much sense to the planomancer.

There was a need for balance, but why the two of them? In terms of energy all things were different, but not that different that they could not be balanced out.

The traveler Arvan emerged from the cart. Fionn noticed he had his bow again, arrow on the string. "What were you talking to the Beng about, stranger?"

Fionn had spoken in the tongue of the creature of smokeless flame. There was no need of course. They were nearly as adept linguists as he was, but it unsettled them to have someone address them in their own tongue. He wondered how the Scrap was coping with a language that would be strange to her...only that dvergar device might just help. She'd learned to read fast enough with its help. He grinned at the traveler, cheered by that thought, and pleased with his bit of work here. Force-lines were realigning already. "I just ruined his day. What did you want me to say to him?"

"Nothing. They're tricky, those ones. You know his language, though." That was outright suspicion.

Fionn shrugged. "Rather a case of he knows mine. They have the gift of tongues, those ones. All the better to lie to you with. So I told him a truth, and made him very unhappy."

"And what was that? You have a spell against them?"

"I wish. But they have a dislike for water. The merrows could sell you a few charms, if you had goods they were interested in. I've a protection I bought from them for a song and some entertainment. The Beng tried me, and the merrow spell has brought a counter to the demon. I pointed out to the creature that water is wet. Wet, and cooling down, and spreading out. It didn't like that and has probably gone to consult with its master. We'd best be away before the master comes here too. They can put powerful compulsions on people, and the bigger they are, the stronger they are. We'll have to contrive a bridge of some kind, but we'll be able to cross it. The dog and I can swim it if need be. By now it'll be like a very hot bath."

Díleas growled and shook himself. Looked suspiciously at the water.

"He doesn't like baths," said Fionn, grinning.

The traveler burst out laughing. "Same as most dogs. Usually when the Beng find us here, they torment us. Send their creatures to attack us. We've got the bells and other protections on the carts, but the best we can do is to stay in them and keep moving until we get out of the local lordling's territory. Never seen anyone chase one off before."

"I wish I could chase them off. It was just the merrow spell doing it, and a lucky happenstance. But the chances are next time I won't be near a lot of hidden water, and the merrow spells need water. You don't happen to have a plank about those carts of yours? And maybe a rope? I could get you a start on a way across the water. It's cooling, but I wouldn't swim it for a while."

"Plank?" asked one of the other travelers, curiously.

"Yes," said Fionn, pointing. "There is a rock there, see. I could put the plank out to it, and then another—or maybe a long jump and I'll be over. I can take a rope over and tie it off for you. There is some rock on the other side you might make something of a bridge with. Or you could take a cart apart and make one. But you probably don't want to hang about here too long. The Beng will come back."

In a place where time ran slowly enough to at least sustain the illusion of immortality, where even free energy danced slow minuets, and the beings called the First dwelled, occupied by and large with passions of immortality, beyond most mortal ken. The First were not a matter for easy understanding. The dragon Fionn was one of the few beings that actually remembered them, which was...less than desirable. They had become distant and disconnected observers of their immeasurably vast creation.

It had taken a human glimpse within their roil of energy, interconnected as all energy was, to let them know that after millennia there might be a problem that they had not foreseen. That they had taken no steps to prevent. That a group mind made of the descendants of fractions of themselves could exist briefly. That something rather like their own power could be exerted by it—temporarily, it was true.

They didn't like that.

But there was a worse possibility. And they always looked at possible futures.

The situation could become permanent.

Food did not interbreed with its predator. They had designed it like that for that precise reason.

Paradoxically, the very powers they had built into Fionn made him quite immune to their manipulations, and near invisible to them as a result. The same could not be said of the dog.

But if they destroyed the dog, they would be blind to Fionn's doings and movement.

The dragon would not be easy to destroy, and the human had taken a part of them into herself. That made her difficult to deal with. The energy that flowed into her had been supposed to take control, not become a slave itself.

It would have to destroy all of them, by proxy.

Fortunately it had an almost infinite supply of proxies.

Unfortunately, the planomancer would be able to detect and counter their movements. They would need to be subtle.

"Right," said Fionn, looking at the rocking plank he'd set up. "Come, Díleas. I'll have to carry you."

"You're out of your mind, gleeman," said Arvan.

Privately, Fionn agreed with him. But he knew humans too well. When they stopped to think about it, they'd start getting even more suspicious about his dealings with the fire creature. And they had weapons that could hurt the dog. He could kill them if they tried, of course. Had he been any other dragon, he would have been free to devour them anyway. Had he been any other dragon he might have desired to do so. But he was Fionn: the last of those who were made first, to see intelligent life flourished. Best to get on the narrow board and away. The water running through the gap would not kill him. Not now. The acids and toxins were already much diluted. But it might still be too hot for the dog. He'd have to throw Díleas if he fell.

"Ach. I was something of an acrobat in a traveling show once."
He looked at the plank. It was twelve cubits long and none too
wide, or thick. It came from under the canvas of the cart, from
the arch where it helped to spread the load. Now it stretched to
a rock in the middle of the flow. "Let's put it on edge, and jam
it. It'll be narrower, but stronger."

"You're definitely mad. Leave the dog here. He's a good, valuable dog," said Arvan.

Díleas growled at him, as if to prove he might be valuable, but
he wasn't good, and danced onto his hind feet. Fionn reached
down a hand and said "up," and Díleas jumped up, putting his
front feet over one shoulder. He really still was a pup with more
fur than body.

"It's like he understands every word you say!"

"You wouldn't say that if you knew how long it took me to
teach him that trick," said Fionn, sticking out a hand for balance
and stepping out onto the narrow plank. And falling off it. He
was still above the rock so no harm was done.

"Give up, gleeman," said the caravan leader, shaking his head.

"I have hardly begun to try and you want me to give up!" said
Fionn. "No. I can do it, I'll wager."

One of the younger travelers snorted. "How much?"

"Well," said Fionn. "I haven't got much." He stuck his free hand
into his pouch, felt about, past the nine golden coins he'd removed
from their hidden trove. They had plenty more. Never pluck a
peacock bare naked, and he'd give you plenty of tail feathers over
time, was Fionn's feeling. He fished out some coppers. Counted
them with great show. "Nine. I'll give you nine coppers if I fall
in. What do you dare wager? A silver for my copper?"

"Huh. Gold, I reckon," said the traveler. It was Dravko, one of
the men who had been discussing what price he'd fetch as a slave
in Annvn. "But what's the point? You fall in there and you're not
coming back, you fool."

"I'll set the coins on the rock here," said Fionn, suiting the
deed to the word. "Then you get them if I lose. Give me a coil
of rope, and I'll tie it off and toss the two ends back, and you
can tie them onto your cart. With one line for my hands and
one for my feet I can walk across easily."

"And then we lose a coil of rope when you fall in," said Dravko
scathingly, but looking at the coins.

Fionn shrugged. "No entertainment for nothing."

"A coil of rope is worth nine coppers," said Arvan. "Give him one, Nikos."

So Nikos did. It was a finely braided rope, and worth, Fionn reckoned, at least eight coppers.

Fionn took a few dozen steps back and measured it all carefully with his eye...and sprinted at the plank. It was only three long strides to the rock, with a bit of a wobble in the middle, and he was on the midstream rock. The tricky part had not been crossing, but stopping in time to avoid landing in the water beyond—or dropping the twisting dog, who squirmed loose and bounded around on the lump of rock. Fionn leaned out and levered up the plank—a feat of strength most humans could not have managed, and swung it over. The other bank was not as far off—a mere nine cubits or so. Fionn laid the plank on the widest edge, with a good overlap.

As Fionn inspected it, Díleas ran over it, nearly but not quite falling in. He stood on the far side, and barked at Fionn. Fionn shrugged. Walked along it. It bent quite alarmingly, but did not break.

On the far side, Fionn, not quite off the plank, did an artistic stumble and jumped for the rock, kicking the plank off its rest and into the water, but gaining the far side, rolling. It was pure showmanship, but the fool dog was not proof against arrows. Someone could still decide they were demons. He stood up and dusted himself off. "Now I just need somewhere to tie the rope to, and I can come back and fetch my coins, and my winnings. Come, dog."

They walked off. They must have been a good seventy yards further along the causeway when one of the travelers said: "I don't think he is coming back." Fionn had keen enough ears, even at this range, to hear them, just as he'd heard the quiet talk on the price that he might fetch as a slave.

Fionn whistled cheerfully and lengthened his stride. "I'd run ahead, dog," he said quietly. "They might not have gone through with selling us, but soon someone is going to work out that I didn't leave nine copper coins for no reason. They didn't cheat me too badly for the price of a rope though. It might be useful. And you nearly fell in, you fool dog."

Díleas looked at the red, dragon-hide boots as if to say, "they have poor grip," and then bounded away along the hexagonal stones. Fionn walked still faster. He did hear distant yells, but there were no arrows.

And it was comforting to have a little gold about him again. It always made a dragon feel good, in a way that coppers did not.

The causeway was an interesting thing. He'd never run across it in his many earlier wanderings across the multidimensional ring before, and yet it apparently led to places he once used to visit, and visit quite often.

Had the structure changed? And what would reintegration of Tasmarin do to it all?

If Fionn had not had to walk the worlds looking for his Scrap of humanity, he'd have been dead keen to find out. He rather liked changes, after millennia of the same.

= Chapter 4 =

MEB AWOKE TO THE SOUND OF SOMEONE IN HER ROOM. SHE HAD only vague, exhausted memories of how she got to this bed. Of the women, talking around her. But the sound of someone there, now, trying to keep quiet was enough to make her instinctively nervous. She opened her eyes just a crack. Unless she was due to be murdered with a ewer by a young, scared-looking female, she was in no danger. There were towels and a basin set on the tall kist already, and a wisp of steam suggested that the water was hot. It brought back to Meb that her last wash had been in a horse trough, and that had not had warm water in it.

Once, not so very long ago, washing herself all over had been something undertaken only when unavoidable. Usually in spring. Now she itched to do so. Well, maybe just itched. The bed linen was fine, but there was undoubtedly a flea in bed with her.

Her doing something about that itch nearly had the young girl pour the ewer down her own front. "I am sorry, your ladyship. I didn't mean to disturb! Only, Lady Cardun said..."

Meb blinked. Your ladyship? "I don't bite. I've got a dog who does, but he's not here." She swallowed. Díleas. How she missed his unswerving, unquestioning loyalty. But he couldn't be here. She'd told him to look after Fionn, when she'd hugged him farewell. It was almost as if he understood. Obviously, the distress must have showed in her face.

The serving wench forgot her own fear in seeing it. "Is...is something the matter, lady? Can I do anything?"

"Just missing my dog," said Meb, her voice cracking a little.

The serving wench nodded. "We always had a dog, too. And then, when I came to take service...he ate a blowfish and died. You'd think a dog living on the foreshore would know better. But he always was eating some rubbish."

Meb nodded. "There was always trouble with Wulfstan about dogs and the stockfish. I grew up in a fishing village."

The serving wench gaped. "You, my lady? But you've the power!"

"I'm not too sure what you're talking about," said Meb, although she did indeed have a very good idea. It struck her that it might be a reasonable idea to find out a little about this world she had exiled herself to. The misery of that exile struck her again. Best to distract herself. "Tell me about this place."

The servant wench looked puzzled. "What place, lady? Dun Tagoll?"

"That's this castle, right? I know that, but it means nothing to me. I've never heard of it."

"But...but it is the greatest castle in all Lyonesse!" said the maid. "Everyone knows that. Even the forest people."

"I'd never even heard of Lyonesse until last night. And now I am here," explained Meb.

"So, where are you from, my lady?" asked the maid.

The "my lady" was beginning to irritate her. "I was from the island of Yenfar, the demesne of Lord Zuamar—but he's dead and no loss. Tasmarin was my world. And my name is Meb."

"Oh. They said you were the Lady Anghared. That's one of the royal names, lady. They don't use it anymore after Queen Gwenhwyfach died. Only the royal line were called that. It's usually used by...by the daughters of kings."

"Oh. Finn said that was my birth name. But no one ever called me that."

"Not even your mother, lady?" asked the maid.

"Hallgerd called me Meb," said Meb resolutely. "And she was the only mother I ever knew. The sea spat me out on the beach at her feet when I was a baby."

The girl wrinkled her forehead. "But your father Finn knew your name was Anghared?"

The very thought of Finn as a father made Meb laugh. Not that he hadn't helped her grow up a bit. "I think you should put the ewer down. What's your name? Are you needed elsewhere?"

The girl shook her head. "No, my lady. I'm to wait on you. I've never attended a lady before."

Someone didn't think much of the "Lady Anghared" then, thought Meb, sending her a tirewoman who was so new she still had fish scales on her hands. Well, the girl suited Meb better than someone she couldn't talk to. "So I am supposed to give you orders, am I?"

The girl nodded, looking worried.

"Well, my first order is to put the ewer down before you spill any more of it. And then to tell me your name."

The girl set the ewer down, carefully. Curtseyed. It was plainly not something she had done often. "Neve, m'lady."

Meb smiled. "Now come and sit down on the bed and answer my questions."

"Oh, I can't sit on the bed, m'lady!" said Neve, horrified.

"You can. I just told you to. And I also told you my name was Meb."

"But... but I'll get into terrible trouble from Lady Cardun."

Meb got up. The stone floor was strewn with rushes, but still cold on her feet. The door was heavy and had a bar. So she closed it, and put the bar down. And took her cold feet back into the bed. "Now she won't know," said Meb. "Sit." She'd hold off on the "m'lady" a little.

The girl giggled nervously and did, at the very foot of the bed. On the very edge. "I... I'm very new to this work, lady... um, Meb. I don't want to lose my place. Times are hard."

"I'll do my best not to lose it for you. I promise I won't tell anyone you sat on the bed while I asked you questions," said Meb, smiling at her. "I just... I'm just lost. I don't know anything at all about this place. I should be doing your job if anything. I'm not a lady. I can't dance, or play music, or do embroidery or even ride. I rode a donkey once. I fell off that. I should be a kitchen maid, if they didn't turn me out. I don't know why they're doing this to me. Who do they think I am? I... I don't want to be turned out either. There's an army out there." Armies had a certain reputation. Meb decided that if she couldn't have Finn... they wouldn't have her either.

The girl shrugged. "Ach, there is always some army. Every few months, it seems. They'll be gone in a week or two when the moon is full. Or we will. Then we try and get our lives back together. The nobles send messages and play at politics and we try to make a living again."

That seemed a rather fatalistic acceptance of war. "You're always at war? Who are you at war with?" No wonder they were enchanting stale bread. Growing crops and farming during a war were going to be difficult.

The girl, her round face serious, started counting on her fingers. "Albion, Brocéliande, Albar, Annvn, Vanaheim, the Blessed Isles. There are more...My gamma said in Queen Gwenhwyfach and King Geoph's time it wasn't so, but it has been almost ever since. And there was much magic then, and there was peace and plenty."

"Hmm," said Meb. "I bet she also said us young people don't know how lucky we are."

The girl giggled so much that it shook the bed. Nodded. "It was all rich and wonderful and we're soft and disrespectful, and don't know what hard work means. I love my gamma Elis, but if you believed her, there were spriggans in every pile of rock, piskies in every field and bog, muryans everywhere, knockers underground, and even dragons on the hilltops. Dragons, I ask you!"

Gradually Meb began to build a picture of the place she had ended up in. A craggy coastline to the west, with Dun Tagoll in its center, with a fertile plain bounded by mountains to east and north, and the shifting sand coast across the bleak moorlands, to more mountains in the south. Ruled by men—not the alvar, or the dragons. Under almost constant attack from the forces of darkness itself, cursed because the kingdom had to be ruled by a regent, and its magic needed a king. And the king needed its magic...not Prince Medraut.

"Him? No, m'lady. He's scarcely noble enough to raise a mage-fire on his blade. Without Aberinn the wizard, Dun Tagoll would have nothing magical. You'd barely think the prince was of the old blood, but he's good at turning troubles to his advantage, as they say."

"Why?" asked Meb. "I mean why would you say you'd barely think he was of the old blood?"

The girl looked puzzled. "Because he has the magic, m'lady. Only the House of Lyon has that. That is why they rule."

Men ruled. Meb shook her head. It was just so different from Tasmarin. And then the fact that magical ability marked the noble house. On Tasmarin the use of magic by a human would have gotten one killed. Here...It turned out that even the court magician was a royal by-blow. A very ancient and much feared by-blow.

"He's awful, m'lady. Been here through three regents. They say he keeps dead men's bones in that tower of his. It stinks enough, and no mortal ever gets in there to clean, unless it's the prince himself sweeping the floor. You be very careful of him, m'lady. You can't lie to him. He pounces on you the minute you offer him falsehood. He has the power. It's his great engines that keep Lyonesse free."

Meb avoided saying she didn't think much of the freedom. "Engines of war? Great catapults?"

"Oh no. Magical engines. They defend us from the magics and the enchantress of Shadow Hall and her dead creatures. And it's there the great engine of change is, m'lady. We hear it clanking, but it's few who have seen it."

That all left Meb none the wiser. Dead creatures and sorceresses were something they accepted as sort of normal here. So was magic by humans. Dragons were not. "So what's this bit about the sons of the dragon? This prophecy?"

The girl looked at her, openmouthed. And then recited:

> Till from the dark past, Defender comes,
>   and forests walk, the rocks talk,
> till the mountain bows to the sea,
>   Till the window returns to the sea-wall of great Dun Tagoll,
>   beware, prince, beware, Mage Aberinn, mage need.
> For only she can hold the sons of Dragon,
>   Or Lyonesse will be shredded and broken and burned.
>   Only she can banish the shades,
> and find the bowl of kings.
>   Mage need, mage need.

"Er. So who are the sons of the Dragon?" asked Meb.

Neve shrugged. "It could be the Vanar—that's who I think it is—in their dragon ships, or the Saxons under the white dragon banner or there are princes of the middle kingdoms who call themselves the sons of the dragons, whose banner is a red wyrm. No one knows. Not even Aberinn. They say he fitted and foamed at the mouth when he spoke the words."

"I wish I could have seen that. I didn't like him much. He had egg in his beard."

Neve snickered. "My father says men with beards should only eat boiled eggs. Or have a wife to watch them."

Someone knocked on the door. A sort of perfunctory knock... and pushed it. And then knocked harder. "Lady Anghared. Lady Anghared, are you within?" By the look of terror on Neve's face it could only be the chatelaine. What was her name? Cardun. She was nearly enough to frighten Meb, and best on the far side of the door.

"Who is it?" said Meb, grabbing Neve's arm as the girl wanted to run to the door.

"It is I. Lady Cardun," said a chilly, haughty voice from outside.

"I am busy with my ablutions," said Meb, very proud of that word. She'd heard it on their journeying, and had to ask Finn what it meant. And then she realized...it wasn't the same word by shape or sound, coming out of her mouth. It was not the language she had spoken all her life. Neither was the rest of what she'd said. And in this language, Díleas actually meant "faithful." How...how had she learned another language? Learned it as if she had spoken it all her life.

There was a moment's silence from outside the door. "Do you need any assistance? A message has come that we are to take you to Mage Aberinn's tower."

Meb looked at the window. It was far too narrow. She touched her throat, and the hidden dragon that hung there, and courage came to her. "Thank you. But no. I have my tirewoman to attend to me. I shall be out when I am finished," she said, doing her best to sound like a spoiled alvar princess.

It must have worked. Cardun sounded slightly chastened. "The girl is new. Is she satisfactory? I could send some of my women..."

"She is exactly what I want, thank you. A perfect choice. I would like her to continue to attend to me," said Meb, trying not to laugh at Neve's expression. "And now, I will need to finish washing and robing, if you do not mind."

"Oh. Yes, my apologies," said Cardun from outside the door, sounding as if the words would choke her.

It was a good, thick door. Meb was at it, listening. No footsteps. Huh. She motioned Neve—who looked like she might just burst—to silence. She tiptoed back to the bed and poured water from the ewer into the basin. "Next time," she said loudly, with a wink to Neve, "see the water is hotter."

"Yes, m'lady," said Neve. "Do you want me to fetch more?"

"No. Just remember in future," said Meb, in what she hoped was a suitably long-suffering manner for a noblewoman, putting up with inferior service.

Meb washed, and went to see what clothes she had. And then she was truly glad of Neve, because she had absolutely no idea of how to put the garment on. The woolen cloth was fine-woven, and while, as far as she was concerned, gleeman colors were her colors, not this pale blue, and breeches were more practical than skirts, and anything was more practical than this dangly robe thing, it was still rather nice to have fine new cloth against her skin.

Neve brushed her hair. "How would you like it put up, m'lady?" she asked, nervously.

Meb had absolutely no idea. She had a feeling her fisherfolk plait and pin would not do. Anyway, she'd lost the wooden pin to the sea, before the merrow took her hair. And she was willing to bet Neve was not much of a hand at it either. She needed something like that combination of comb and hair clip the alvar women had used at the Alba soiree she and Finn had walked through disguised as elegant alvar butterflies. It was something that could look beautiful and keep the hair out of your eyes. She'd truly envied one. She recreated the filigree curlicues of it in her mind, thinking of the details.

It would appear she could summons small items to her; she marveled, looking at the intricate, ornate piece of silver in her hand. She hoped the alvar that had owned it would forgive her. She also hoped she wasn't unbalancing things too much, as Finn said her magic did. She'd never understood that aspect of the black dragon's work. She handed the pin-comb to the startled Neve. "It's worn at an angle." She shook her combed hair forward. "Slide it from the front, to pull the hair away from my face, and then slide the pin in, once the back corner is past my ear."

Neve did. "Oh, it's beautiful, m'lady," she said, holding a mirror so that Meb could see. "But...but it's not how it is done here."

Meb looked closely at the reflection. Of course she'd remembered it perfectly, capturing the details in her mind's eye. But she'd not really realized that it was filigree dragons—very Tasmarin alvar. The silver of them showed bright against her dark hair. Looking at Neve's tight braids, here at least she was no longer the wavy-haired brunette among the straight yellow thatch heads of the fisherfolk of Cliff Cove or Tarport. "I am not from here. I don't think I could pretend to be."

She stood up, and Neve held the mirror. She wasn't sure she recognized the stranger in it. "Well. That will just have to do. What do we have for footwear, because I don't think my water diviner's boots will do, will they? They're the best boots I've ever owned."

Neve looked at them, critically. "They're good boots. But, well, they look like, well . . . men's wear. Lady Vivien—she sent the clothes and the combs with me, sent some lachet boots for you. They're good boots."

Meb tried them. "They'll do. But they're too narrow. I have wide feet. Finn said it was from going barefoot. He had to get the cordwainer to change his lasts to make them for me."

Neve looked impressed. "Specially made just for you? This Finn, he was your father?"

"My master," said Meb quietly. "I love him very much. But . . ."

Neve nodded understandingly, although Meb was absolutely sure she did not even start to understand. But Meb wasn't going to try to explain. Instead she walked to the door. "Do you think I get to break my fast before going to see the mage? Or does he feed me on the bones of dead men?"

Neve shuddered. "I don't know, m'lady. No one goes to his tower. I told you. I don't know what is in there."

Meb took a deep breath. "Time to find out, I suppose. Can you show me where I have to go?"

"Well, there's an inner door, but it's locked. I'll have to take you into the courtyard."

Meb let Neve lead her down the flagged passages and up the stone stairwell, onto the battlements and up the stair to the door of the mage's tower. It faced the narrow causeway of land that linked the almost island of Dun Tagoll to the rest of the lands beyond. Meb looked out at those, across fields and forests toward the distant high fells tinged purple with blooming heather.

The door swung open abruptly, before she'd even gathered herself to knock. Neve squeaked and retreated behind Meb as Mage Aberinn loomed out at them. His beard, in daylight, was longer and less clean than she'd realized the night before. "I didn't know I had sent for two of you," he said curtly.

Meb knew she ought to be afraid, but instead, his manner just made her angry. "My mother told me not to go alone into strange towers with men I did not know," she said coolly. Actually, Hallgerd had not ever quite said that, but variants of the same usually involving bushes, huts or fishing boats. And she hadn't been too concerned about whether Meb knew the men or not. But it would do.

Aberinn raised his eyebrows. "Your mother. And who was your mother? Do you remember her?" he seemed to find that very important.

Meb remembered what Neve had said about not being able to lie to him. She thought . . . well, she should try it. "I ought to. I lived with her for seventeen years," she said.

It seemed to take the wind out the mage's sails a little. "Ah. Well, I suppose your reputation should be considered. Yes, bring her along."

Neve looked as if she might faint in pure terror. "Me? I was just showing m'lady the way." she squeaked.

"Just think what stories you'll have to tell the others," said Meb, smiling an unspoken "please" at her.

"Of course, she'll do as she's told," said the mage, an edge coming back to his voice.

The fisherman's daughter took a deep breath. "For you, m'lady."

The first interior room of the tower, reached after climbing a short stair was rather a disappointment after all that. It was a large and comfortable room, with a fireplace, and a number of tables, and book- and equipment-filled shelves lining the walls. It was, unlike the magician's beard, very tidy and ordered. No spider webs, no dust, no disorder. The tables were full of various items being worked on, but even the tools were set out in very precise neat rows, and components tended to be set out in what almost seemed geometric patterns. There were no dead men's bones. In fact, Meb couldn't even see a thing made of anything that was not metal, let alone human remains. The nearest to "human" anything was a model—a very precise and carefully made model—of part of the castle. It was opened so she could see into the rooms, with every item in them exact. It looked like a child's—a very rich child's—dream dollhouse.

That was not to say that the room looked like anything but a magician's workshop, because it didn't. The objects being worked on were strange. Some glowed with their own inner light. Odd clicking noises came from somewhere. And some things looked as if they might almost be alive. There was a bird in a gilded cage. A crow. Only it too was gilded, and appeared to be made entirely of metal.

Meb had seen dvergar artifice, and that was finer. But the magician was better than most humans at mechanical contrivance. She identified the source of least some of the clicking—a device with a series of globes suspended from thin brass rods. As it clicked, the globes moved. "What is it?"

"An orrery. It allows me to predict the positioning of certain celestial forces for my work," said Aberinn. "It is essential for the Changer. Unfortunately I have found certain inaccuracies in the movement. There may be factors outside of my knowledge operating on the spheres."

"How...how does it move?" Part of her was impelled by the peasant fisherman fear of the unknown, to not want to know, to fear the worst, to believe it demonic and evil. The other part of her mind was already imagining small imps on treadmills, or perhaps magical recitations of spells that would command it to move...

"Springs, counterweights, and various cogwheels. My magic is confined to working on things of a higher order," he said, as if reading her mind. "But I asked you to come here to establish some of your own history."

Which, thought Meb, I don't think is a good idea to tell you too much about. But she smiled. "I will be glad to answer the questions of the High Mage of Lyonesse." She wondered how much of alvar life in Tasmarin she could get him to swallow. Finn, gleemen and fishing villages seemed good subjects to avoid.

Oddly, she didn't need to. His questions seemed designed to catch her out. To betray a knowledge of Dun Tagoll or the people and politics of Lyonesse. He asked about the view from home and the plants there. Meb was happy to describe the cliffs of Cliff Cove in loving detail. He asked about the rulers of Tasmarin. Meb didn't think it necessary to point out that the dead Lord Zuamar and Prince Gywndar were a dragon and an alvar princeling. Or even that they were both now dead. And then someone came knocking on the door. In obvious irritation Aberinn went to open it. "What is it?" he asked the wide-eyed page.

"A message from Prince Medraut, high mage. The prisoner... Earl Alois, has escaped. Magic, the prince believes. And the woman has vanished from her chambers!"

Aberinn sighed. Shook his head. "The young lady—and her maid—are right here. And it was obvious Alois must have had some accomplices to get so close. This is not magic. It is treachery." He sighed again. "Tell the prince I am coming. Send messages to the other Duns. He won't get far on foot."

═ Chapter 5 ═

FIONN AND DÍLEAS WALKED ON DOWN THE HEXAGONALLY PAVED "causeway." Now out of sight of the travelers, Fionn stuck to being a dragon. While it was fun to tempt the creatures of smokeless flame into folly, they tended to see too clearly to be easily fooled. Besides, he had other things to do.

It was inevitably hot. Fionn began wondering if he should have relieved the travelers of some water as well as some of their gold. The smoky air was still and thick, and Fionn traced more flows of energy rushing through it. It felt like a thunderstorm—not just dry lightning, but a real cloudburst of rain—was coming. It even looked like it, with black thunderhead clouds forming. The creatures of smokeless flame would not like that! They'd be exerting all their power to stop it. Things were definitely in a state of flux here, although the causeway itself did not seem to be a problem. The weather could always be a side effect of Tasmarin rejoining the great planar ring of worlds. That would have an effect on all the planes and all the sub-rings that spun off those. Had others of his kind kept the energy of the planes balanced, while he was trapped in Tasmarin? Would Tasmarin itself remain truly stable without him? That could be awkward, as his hoard was hidden there. The few pieces of gold he had with him were a poor replacement for that.

Just when Fionn thought he'd have to carry the drooping dog, who was still determinedly pushing onwards, two things happened: firstly, it began to rain, in thick hot drops; and secondly,

they came to a large stone trilith set over the causeway, which
had narrowed down and become stones in the dust here. The
trilith—made by hauling a huge megalith onto the top of two
other upright megaliths—was big enough to have required several
giants to move the vast, shaped stones. There was considerable
magic about it, but yet it did not disrupt the flow of energy.
Either the builders had consulted another planomancer or this
was a relic of the First.

The dog wasn't waiting to examine it. He found the energy to
scamper towards it.

And did not emerge onto the causeway beyond. Fionn could
see that. It was singly devoid of dog.

So he lengthened his stride to walk though himself.

On the other side there was still a trilith. It was just much
lower and entirely surrounded by forest. And darkness.

It was also cold, and wet. Fionn's dragonish eyes saw further
into the various spectra, and also rather well in the dark. He could
spot the white patches on Díleas. The dog was sitting there, looking back at the trilith. Waiting. Plainly not with much patience,
by the way he stood up. There was obviously a time difference
here. That happened in transitions between the planes. It was
usually more gradual though.

"I am so sorry to keep you waiting," said Fionn. It occurred
to him the dog probably did not understand irony, even if he
understood entirely too much speech, by the way Díleas butted
his hand with his nose, and started to walk down the rough track.
The dog seemed to know where he was going, and there wasn't
much to keep Fionn here, even if he might be tempted to have a
closer look at that trilith. Human worlds had once abutted those
of the demondim, so that was not that surprising, but to find a
path he did not know . . . worried him.

Also, he was sure, just by the feel of the place, that this was not
the cool damp of night in fair Annvn, but the cold terror damp
of night in Brocéliande. Mind you, in the dark it was hard to tell.
If they were attacked by monstrous beasts or wolves it would be
the vast primal forest of Brocéliande. If it was mere bandits, it
was probably Annvn. The beasts or bandits were more likely to
attack a human, and Fionn had nothing against helping himself
to their booty, so he altered his form accordingly. If it turned
out to be Brocéliande, he'd probably regret that. It was, either

way, one of the Celtic cycle. His Scrap's true name suggested she might have come from one of those.

They walked on, the wood even darker than the cloudy night sky, with trailing branches drooping over the track. A sliver of watery moonlight peeked out from the cloud as they came to a stream with a shallow ford. Díleas ran forward to drink as if there was no other water ever to be found.

Fionn was beginning to wonder whether he had been wrong, and this was somewhere else entirely, or that times had changed for the bandits or wolves or monsters. He was also thinking about the trilith-gated road, and wondering about the mathematics of joining planes thus, and how it could be that the outcome was uncertain. He was so deep in thought he almost didn't see the afanc slithering closer to the dog. He barely had time to yell and leap as the crocodilian jaws clashed shut...

...On Fionn's cloak and the arm rolled in it, giving Díleas a chance to utter a startled yelp as he leapt back and pulled his head aside. Without Fionn's yell the monster would have had the dog, and even with it, the afanc would have had Díleas by his nose, except Fionn had stopped the jaw closing on the dog with his arm.

The downside of this was that the water monster had Fionn instead. And while dragon skin is tougher than human skin by several orders of magnitude, and the thick woolen cloak would have stopped a knife thrust, the afanc still had a truly viselike grip, and it was using all of the strength of its massive legs and beaverlike paddle tail to haul its prey back into deep dark water to drown him.

Dragons are not easy to drown, and the afanc would need more than just patience to manage that. But no one told Díleas that. The crazy dog latched itself onto the afanc's nose, burying his sharp teeth inside the sensitive nostril.

The afanc was now trying to get away, shake off the agony attached its nose, and deal with Fionn. And Fionn knew that he wouldn't drown, but there was no such guarantee for that obstinate dog.

So he stuck the fingers of his free hand into the afanc's eye, and at the same time hauled with all the strength of his legs.

And got wet. Fell over and got showered. The afanc did not like having its eye poked out. It loosed its grip briefly and, with a ripping of cloth, Fionn pulled the arm and cloak free, and dealt the afanc a wallop alongside the head that would make the monster regard anything bigger than a field mouse as hard chewing on that side for a month. As Fionn fell backwards he grabbed Díleas by the scruff of the neck and flung him back up the bank, before scrambling that way himself.

A minute later he was sitting high above the stream, wet and a little wary, with a sheepdog nearly on top of him, inspecting the damage to himself and the dog. Fionn could feel Díleas's heart pounding. Fionn realized that under all that fur, he was still not a very large dog. He was not too sure if the dog thought he was defending the dragon, or seeking a safe spot. "I think," said Fionn, "that we're in the forests of Brocéliande, dog. Which makes that thing one of the nicer creatures that inhabit these dark woods. I think my dragon form is probably wiser and safer. The blasted thing has half shredded my cloak and given me a rather sore forearm. But that could have been the end of you. And I do not want to have to explain that to your mistress. So, could you cope with riding over the water on my back? And I should probably take those boots of yours off. You've got them full of water."

Díleas held up a foot in the moonlight. The thongs were wet, easier to cut than untie, but the dragon-leather hide was still good.

Fionn became the black dragon, and was sure that the eyes watching from the water, and quite possibly the woods, would sheer off. He wondered, as always, just what happened to his clothing and gear in such changes. For years he'd set them aside. He still was wary about a pack, but it appeared that somehow all his clothing and gear were with him, yet not with him. He could still feel the ghostly touch of them, as a dragon.

The logical answer now was to fly across the water, but he had no idea how the dog would deal with that. And it was unlikely the afanc would seek a second encounter just yet. "Up on my back," he said, wondering what would happen. The answer was readily supplied. Díleas jumped up. Stood between his wings. "If I have more trouble with the afanc, you're to jump off and make for the bank. I can deal with it, but not if I am trying to stop you getting drowned or bitten."

Díleas growled at him.

It was a good thing, reflected Fionn, that he'd taken the dragon-skin foot coverings off Díleas. The dog was getting far too big for his boots. Fionn walked slowly into the water of the ford, trying to keep his back even and steady.

He was prepared for Díleas to fall off, or even for the afanc to make another try. They really weren't very bright. What he wasn't expecting—and it nearly had him lose his footing on the slippery rocks—was for Díleas to bark at the water the whole way across. A sort of "come and get me if you dare" bark.

Fionn had to try and ignore it and concentrate on keeping his balance on the slimy, shifting, round rocks.

On the far side, having had enough of barking in his ear, Fionn said, "Off."

"Hrf?"

There was definitely a questioning note to that bark. Or was he beginning to imagine speech from the dog too? "Yes, off. You enjoyed that, didn't you? You were taunting him. Well, I suppose he did very nearly snap your nose off, and possibly would have eaten you. But—although this advice may seem odd coming from me—make sure the beast you taunt is not merely making you advertise yourself to the rest. Because unless I am very much mistaken, those are wolves howling a reply to you. You had better stay up there after all. But no barking in my ear unless you're warning me of something. My foreleg is somewhat tender from the last effort."

They walked on, and the only sound Díleas made was an occasional low growl. Looking behind himself briefly—one of the joys of dragon form was that he could, while humans could not without turning their entire bodies—Fionn saw that the dog was alert, questing, tasting the air with inquisitorial sniffs. The white fur made him quite visible, as did the glowing red bauble at his throat. There might be a need to do something to hide it.

The wolves, and anything else watching from dark woods—and there would have been things there, Fionn was certain—left the dragon alone. At length, after perhaps an hour's walk, dragon pace, they spotted a light. And smelled a more welcome scent than that of a manticore or wolf—woodsmoke.

"I think food and sleep, indoors, is called for. If you sleep outdoors in the forests of Brocéliande, something digestive, or even nastier, can happen you. The trick is going to be persuading anyone to let us in at this time of night. I think it is time for me to become a gleeman and you a gleeman's dog rather than a dragon rider. I don't think those are much more welcome than dragons. Of course in these parts you never know just who might own the farmhouse. They could be just as keen on eating us. And finding space can be an issue out here. Even the cows have to sleep indoors."

Díleas received this speech by lifting his leg on a roadside bush, from which something sneezed and retreated, making Fionn laugh and Díleas growl. "Even half the trees in Brocéliande have some sort of awareness. And many are not going to enjoy that kind of shower, dog." They walked on.

As it turned out it was not a farmhouse, but an inn at a cross-road, catering to travelers who didn't want to chance spending the night out in the forest. In these forests men traveled in groups and, as none had arrived at the inn, it had plenty of space. The crossbow-armed innkeeper wanted a vast sum to let them in, which as far as Fionn was concerned, was both iniquitous and, worse, up-front. "I should have slept under a bush," said Fionn, grumbling as he counted out silver. Copper would have been more appropriate and normal.

"You're welcome to, and the dog'll be extra," said mine host. "They make work."

Fionn sighed. "And not much chance of juggling for my supper, I suppose?"

"Supper will be another silver penny. You can juggle all you please, but half your takings will come to me. Anyway, there's no one here but a pack-peddler and a pot mender, both waiting for a group going West. The rest of their party was going to Carnac."

Mournfully Fionn fished out a coin from the corner of his pouch. Rubbed the edge of it, with a good imitation of regret. It was larger than the pennies, and gleamed. "I only have this. I'll go hungry before I give you all of it. Make change for me."

The innkeeper took it. Looked at the unfamiliar face stamped onto it—the silver pennies were so thin and worn, it was hard to tell what they were. "Where is this from?" he said suspiciously.

"How would I know? Some drunken merchant gave it to me in a tavern as payment for my juggling. The light was bad and he probably thought it was a copper. I did, then. I didn't go looking for him in the morning to ask. It's silver. Worth at least twenty pennies. Give it back if you don't want it."

The innkeeper slipped it into his pocket. "I'll give you ten for it."

"Eighteen I'll take. No less," said Fionn.

"What's money to a corpse? You're lucky to be alive out there, on your own in the dark. Wolves or monsters get most such fools."

"I didn't plan it," said Fionn. "The others ran the other way when we had our little run-in with the afanc at the ford. It ripped my cloak, curse it."

"You're lucky it was just your cloak."

"Ach, the dog gave me warning. I sleep sound enough knowing he's there," said Fionn. "Now either give my silver back or give me eighteen silver pennies for it."

For a moment it looked like the innkeeper was weighing up whether simple murder would not solve this dilemma. Then he sighed. "Seventeen. And that's merely because the dog looks hungry."

"I haven't let him eat a rascally innkeeper for weeks," said Fionn, sardonically. "Seventeen. Provided you feed him too." Twenty silver pennies was still far too little for the weight of the coin—had it been silver, or going to be staying in the innkeeper's pouch.

The beer was good, the squirrel stew adequate. Fionn found the quarters less so. The window was thoroughly barred with heavy iron bars and a fair amount of magework too. In fairness, Fionn had to admit it did seem directed less to keeping him in than to keeping the various forest denizens of Brocéliande out. Only he had thought a little fly-around would help to orientate himself, and quite possibly make the denizens of the forest a little more wary. With self-mocking virtue, Fionn laughed at himself. There was nothing quite as easy as performing a public service, while actually looking for the sort of magical chaos his Scrap of humanity would be generating, just by the way she was. So he sat down and took out a fragment of the coin he'd given the innkeeper, and called it back to itself to be whole again. He was rewarded a few moments later by the coin squeezing itself under the door, and rolling across to him. The dvergar coin would follow its heart piece for miles. Fionn had once thought he'd lost it, when it had been trapped in an iron strongbox. But sooner or later, someone had opened the box. Besides, it wasn't silver, but actually a great deal harder. Dvalinn said it would burrow its way out of anything in time.

Díleas growled at the coin, as Fionn put down a hand to allow it to roll up to his pouch. Fionn shook his head at the dog. "Tch. After it paid for your dinner, too."

The dog informed him—by jumping up onto the bed—just where he was planning to sleep. Fionn suggested he try curling up under his tail. Díleas thumped the bedclothes with said tail, and ignored him.

Later that night—by the feel of it, approaching dawn—Díleas woke him with a nose in his ear, and a low growl.

No human would have heard it...or smelled it. But someone was talking, and there was a faint smell of wolf. An odd smell of wolf. And it wasn't coming in through the window. Fionn got up. So did Díleas.

"I think you should wait. Those claws of yours make a noise on the wood," said Fionn quietly, and slipped out. He moved as quietly as only he could, through the dark building and down to the landing of the stair to the main room and kitchen. From here he could hear them, and smell them. Ah. Mine host was talking to something that smelled...both like a wolf and a man. That was worrying enough without the faint smell of decay too. Fionn had dealt with enough skin changers before to know how those smelled. They were dangerous, in that they had the strength and skills of their beast side and the cunning of men. It was fortunate that men were not always particularly cunning. He listened.

"...too much money for what he pretends to be. He gave me a silver coin, from a realm I've never heard of, worth five times what I gave him for it. Also there were no other travelers on the Malpas road. Leroy would have let me know, and I would have let you know," said mine host, the innkeeper.

Fionn had to swallow his snigger at the mention of the coin, now safe back in Fionn's pouch, and go on listening. So the innkeeper—and his friend along the trail—kept the skin-changers informed of good targets. Such things were always useful to know, eventually. The wolf-man's voice was gravelly and deep. "We saw no men on the road between here and Hunger ford. Just a mighty wyrm and a dog."

"This one had a dog. A sheepdog."

"A black-and-white dog. It rode on the wyrm. I think you have a magician here. Our mistress will reward you well for such a one, Gore. Let us see the coin he gave you."

Fionn did not wait. It was time to leave. He moved quietly upstairs, picked up Díleas and was back down the stairs while the innkeeper was still searching and swearing. Fionn took himself into hiding next to the fireplace breastwork. A few moments later, the innkeeper, candle in one hand and club in the other, exited from the kitchen with his companion—heading upstairs for the room Fionn had just vacated. If Fionn had waited, he'd have met them on the stair. As it was, he was able to duck into the kitchen, and close the door. Most conveniently, it had a bar, perhaps for when the food displeased the patrons. In the light of a bunch of rag wicks in an oil jar, Fionn scanned the shelf, and helped himself to a jar. The travelers must bring the spice here, as it would have been too precious and rare for anyone but royalty otherwise. He put Díleas down, tipped an oily crock of olives onto the floor, opened the outer door and left.

Of course at this stage, like most slick plans, it went awry. There was a pack of wolves waiting only a few yards outside the door on the roadway.

Fortunately, they were as surprised to see Fionn and Díleas as the dog and dragon were to see them. Fionn had a moment, as Díleas barked, to fling the fired-clay spice jar at the roadway just in front of them.

Fionn flung the jar with all his considerable strength, so it literally shattered into flying fragments, releasing a cloud of the precious pepper within.

He grabbed Díleas and ran the other way. The sheepdog was blinking and sneezing and trying to rub his eyes with a paw, so Fionn had a feeling that the wolves would not be doing too well in pursuit. Nonetheless, he preferred to deal with them in dragon form, so he underwent the short discomfort of changing his shape. It was not ever something particularly pleasant to do to one's body, especially in a hurry, but...needs must. Thus it was that the first angry, sneezing wolf got a bat from Fionn's tail that sent it thirty yards back down the road. The others retreated hastily and Fionn realized that Díleas had not waited on an invitation but had leapt up onto his back and was now barking defiance at the chastened pack.

"Enough, Díleas," said Fionn. "It's time to leave before this escalates into an angry innkeeper with crossbow bolts. We'd better go." He started down the trail. And Díleas leapt off, ran ahead and turned and barked at him.

"Not really playtime, boy," said Fionn, pushing on. Díleas growled at him and stood resolutely in his path. And then, when

Fionn would have snagged him with a foreleg, he grabbed a talon with his mouth, but gently, holding, not biting, and pulled Fionn back the way they'd come. Whining anxiously between his teeth. Wagging his flaglike tail furiously.

"I don't think we should . . ."

Then it occurred to him that he'd already seen enough evidence of his Scrap's magical meddling in this very intelligent dog's nature. "You're trying to tell me something, aren't you? Do you know where your mistress is?"

Díleas tugged at his arm again. And then let go and sat down. There was little light—it was still grey predawn. But Fionn would swear the dog was nodding. Then he got up, danced a little circle and darted back down the road. And then ran back. And whined.

Fionn sighed. "Up on my back then. I can't chance flying with you. But my skin is more proof against arrows than yours. At close range, crossbow bolts could still be a problem."

Díleas leapt up, and they turned back toward the inn. The innkeeper, when they met him at the next bend, did have his crossbow, but Fionn had learned how to fling rocks with his tail, years ago. The result was very bad for the crossbow, and Fionn simply barreled past, down to the inn at the crossroads. And here Díleas leapt off his back—a flying leap that had him doing a somersault—before running a little way up the left-hand fork, and then coming back to make sure Fionn was following. So he did, into the dawn and off toward the distant sea at Carnac, because now that it was light, Fionn recognized this trail. He'd been down it before, many years back, before there had been an inn at that crossroad.

As it grew lighter Fionn could see more of the ancient forest surrounding him. The trees there must have been old when he'd last been free to walk this road. He looked for signs of imbalance, and also back for signs of pursuit. He could—and often did—change his appearance to avoid that sort of problem. The dog however, well, that might be a bit more tricky. Of course, this being one of the wildest and most dangerous of the Celt-evolved cycle of worlds, Fionn was also cautious about the road ahead. There would almost inevitably be wood dwellers who would try anything once, especially with a dog, although probably not on a dragon.

The road could provide problems of its own for walking dragons, though. The Brocéliande knights would probably not respond well to sharing the road with him. And they fought monsters of various sorts here.

Well. He'd deal with it. Right now the one problem he was most troubled by was breakfast, or rather, the lack of it.

So when he saw a knight in full armor, barring their way, he regretted the conditioning set on him by the First. His kind of dragon could not combine moving the obstacle with having breakfast. Knights apparently broiled well in armor. It kept the flavor in, or so he'd been told. Armor being what it was, and having epicurean tastes, Fionn suspected that knights were probably too gamey for his liking anyway.

The knight was no coward. Well, in a place like the forests of Brocéliande, cowardice might let a knight survive, but did poorly at making them acceptable to potential mates.

It was selective breeding that made the knight lower his lance and put his spurs to his horse.

It was the sight of a black-and-white sheepdog on the dragon's back that made him pull up the horse and stare.

"I am a knight under an enchantment," said Fionn loudly.

The knight almost fell off his horse. But he was a superb horseman, and recovered himself. "Which one of you spoke?" he asked.

"I did," said Fionn. "And I am afraid if you bar my path I must fight you, although I have no quarrel with you. I need to go to my lady's rescue. She was plucked from me by magic, the dark workings of the same enchanter that bound me to this form. I must free her, and then I can be free of this curse."

The knight stared. "Is having a sheepdog on your back part of the curse?" he asked, still not entirely putting up his lance.

"Considering the dog barks in my ear, you might think so," said Fionn. "But no. He was my lady's loyal companion, and he guides me in my search."

The knight shook his head. "I have seen various monsters and fearsome creatures. But never a dragon. There has not been one seen in all Brocéliande for many a year. I thought great honor had surely come to me this day. But I had not heard that the fell beasts could speak or, well, that they would put up with a dog. Methinks it is an illusion."

At which Díleas leapt down and trotted over to the knight. The horse paced warily, sniffing at it. "Your horse does not think it is an illusion. And to be honest with you, I could flambé you, right now, before that lance got near me, should I wish to. Actually, all the dog and I wish is to go on our quest, and to find some breakfast."

Díleas had by now walked around to the stirrup and stood up against it, reaching his nose up. The knight reached down and his chain-link-covered gauntlet got a lick.

"If he's an illusion, he's a remarkably friendly and touchable one," said the knight, somewhat more mildly. "What is your name, Sir Dragon? And where are you from and whence bound?"

Anything rather than another fight on an empty stomach, thought Fionn. And besides the wolves and monsters, Brocéliande was known for the ideals of chivalry. Fionn had found these often crumbled when closely examined, but there were exceptions. "Might I know yours, Sir Knight? I hail from a far land, and I am bound I know not whither, because I cannot speak the language of dogs. The dog knows, but I do not. I merely follow, but will follow until I find and rescue my lady. My name is Fionn of Tasmarin, and my style, Earl of Laufey." Which was true, in a manner of speaking. It was one of the advantages of having assumed many personas and having been a fraud for so many years. It was unlikely that the knight would know Laufey, which was in the Nordic cycles somewhere.

The knight raised his lance in salute. "Well met, Earl Fionn. I am Sir Bertran, son of Ywain, guardian of the fountain of Escalados. I had hoped this day to fight a great battle against some foul creature, to gain honor. But instead I have met something so passing strange that I can at least have a tale to tell my grandchildren one day. It would be ignoble for me to fight someone on such a great quest. Is there some way I can aid you?"

"Breakfast, and to allow us free passage, would be good." Fionn never forgot geography. Escalados fountain was a place he'd had occasion to visit. It was a pinch point for water and electromagnetic energies he'd had to adjust before. It was close enough to here.

Díleas barked in agreement, and danced on his hind legs. Fionn had realized that the dog was quite good at the manipulation of humans...and dragons.

═ Chapter 6 ═

"I THINK, M'LADY," SAID NEVE FIRMLY, ONCE THEY WERE OUT OF earshot of the tower, "that I am going to faint."

"Must be the lack of food," said Meb, grinning. "I'm hungry enough to fall over myself."

"Oh, I am sorry, m'lady. I'll run to the kitchens..."

"You'll do no such thing, Neve," said Meb, grabbing her. "Without you I'm lost. I'd probably end up down the well or wandering in on Aberinn and Medraut in counsel and get executed on the spot. Show me the way instead."

"But...but you shouldn't go there, m'lady. The nobility don't. Only Mage Aberinn goes down to the kitchens and cellars to magically replenish supplies."

"He does?"

"Yes," said Neve, cheerily. "Otherwise we'd be eating our shoes, m'lady. The wars have been that fierce. And the Vanar raiders have burned most of the fishing boats. That was why I came to the castle seeking a place. At least the food is wonderful. There are times that it looks better than it tastes, though."

Meb was willing to bet that those were the times that it really was old boiled shoe. "Well, if I can go into his tower, I can go into the kitchens. And if anyone asks I will say he told me to, and I'll bet not one of them will ever check."

Neve giggled, which, the sensible part of Meb knew, was just the sort of encouragement she did not need. Without Finn to keep her out of trouble...That nearly made her cry again, so she resolutely thought about other things until they came to the kitchen of Dun Tagoll—with spits and hobs and great cauldrons...and most of them idle. There was, however, new bread. That much her nose told her. There was also a sudden shocked silence at her presence there.

The cook, large ladle in hand, approached tentatively. "What can we do for you, Lady Anghared?" he asked.

So even here they knew who she was. "I have just been speaking with Mage Aberinn in his tower." Someone would have seen them going there, unless castles were vastly different from villages. By the gasps and nods she could tell that the two weren't that different. "I came to see the state of the provision of the castle. And also to get a heel of that new bread." Neve's struggle to keep a straight face definitely made her worse. "And a jug of small beer."

"The...mage put a stop to brewing. There is wine..."

Meb didn't need to be a mage with great powers to tell that that hadn't happened. "I won't mention it to him. Or to those in the hall," she said with her mouth as prim as possible.

She got the bread and small beer. And smiles as the two of them retreated to her chamber.

"I'm not eating or drinking this alone," said Meb. "And small beer is the only kind of reward I can give you for coming into the lion's den with me. He didn't seem to know that I wasn't telling him the whole truth all the time, either."

Neve shook her head. "Eh, my lady, I had a friend back in our village like you. Always up to some mischief."

"Oh, dear. What happened to her?" asked Meb, already expecting a homily.

Neve shrugged. "She got into a fair amount of trouble, got a few beatings, but mostly got away with it, I suppose. And then she got pregnant."

"Ah." It had to end badly.

"Yes, she married the miller's boy. She was the strictest mother in the village," said Neve. "You wouldn't think she was the one who got up to mischief. Or led the rest of us to do such."

"I was a mouse back in my village most of the time. I was too different. Then the pirates burned our boats, and, well, I had to learn," she said quietly, trying not to think of who had taught her. Never do the expected...

"I just came here when that happened," said Neve, equally quietly, helping herself to some of the bread without thinking.

"Well, that's learning too. So you'll help me? Tell me, quietly, when I am doing something too crazy? I just don't know. I don't know where I should be, and what I should do."

Neve nodded. "When you've eaten, m'lady, I'll take the plate and jug to the kitchens. You should be in the bower. The ladies would be sewing and weaving there now. Maids too. I'm not very skilled."

"Oh good. That's two of us." Meb ate another piece of bread and tossed her tasseled juggling balls in the air, doing a simple one-hand routine, keeping all four balls in the air while Neve stared. "I think this is about all I'm really any good at. Will that do? Mama Hallgerd also showed me how to set stitches and weave flax, and tie netting knots."

"Don't show them the juggling! They'll think you're...I don't know, m'lady." They won't like it. I think it's wonderful. Like magic. Can you do other things?"

"A few," said Meb, taking a drink and wiping her lips with the back of her hand. Grinning she said: "I can belch pretty well, too," and she demonstrated, "but I don't think that'll impress Lady Cardun."

Neve looked as if she might giggle herself into apoplexy as she shook her head.

Aberinn attempted to look at Prince Medraut without his contempt showing. Medraut was a schemer and plotter. That was normal for the House of Lyon nobles. But it also normally went with courage and mage-power. Aberinn had kept vacant the throne of Lyonesse through two other regents, and seen that the old king never had any heirs to claim it. The mage had kept it for his own son or no one. And as the spell from the cord-blood showed, the child still lived. Aberinn had devoted an entire table to drawing-spells to call the boy back here to claim his own. And he'd seen to it that no one could be anointed as the new king ever since the old king had died. Only those of Aberinn's line could ever find the ancient font now, for all that it was in plain view.

All of the regents had planned to take power, of course. But none had been as eel-like about it as Medraut. Aberinn was even more certain now that this woman had been Medraut's plant. The window was a simple trick and could easily have been hidden. And at a stroke, Medraut was free of Earl Alois—his worst enemy from the South—and the royal mage. Aberinn knew there were no other mage-workers of his ability in Lyonesse—but that was unlikely to worry someone as shortsighted and power hungry as Medraut.

"Do you think she's really the Defender?" Prince Medraut said, plainly attempting to cover his tracks.

Aberinn wondered just where the regent had found her. She did have some power, he suspected. There were Lyon-blood children conceived on the wrong side of the blankets all over the kingdom. His mother had been one, which had made Queen Gwenhwyfach his cousin. Well, if Medraut wanted to play this game, so could he. "It is possible. Magic will find a way. Of course, if she is, your regency is over, Medraut."

Medraut shot a quick glance at the royal mage. "That...would depend on the rest of the prophecy coming true. Or of her being the true Defender. The real Defender was supposed to come from the past, not this...Tasmarin place. Everyone knows that. And anyway, she did not come to be king." He laughed at his little joke. "She could hardly be that, eh?"

Aberinn decided it best to ignore that attempt at humor. "It is possible that she deceived us as to where she came from. Her accent speaks of the south."

"She hasn't got much of an accent," said Prince Medraut, confirming the mage's suspicions. "And anyway, I thought the wine was bespelled to make her speak the whole truth?"

"It is possible to magically proof someone against enchantment," Aberinn did not add "as you know, full well." After all, who would know better than Medraut about that? The man could lie like a flat fish.

"Yes, but why?" demanded Medraut, with a good show of puzzlement. "Alois would likely have killed me, without her."

"Really? You had no other safeguards?" asked the mage.

"Yes, but he had already got through the outer ones. If he had that much knowledge, and that much skill...and look how he escaped from the dungeon before the torturers could put him to the question. You said you had proofed that cell against enchantments and magics. You told me it would hold the sorceress of Shadow Hall itself. You told me I was safe!"

That was nearly a scream. Perhaps Medraut really was worried? If the girl were not Medraut's plant...maybe she was Alois's tool? But surely that was too extreme. She could, of course, be the tool of the enchantress in her Shadow Hall. The woman was mad. "No crowned head is ever safe, Medraut. No regent either. I'll watch her."

"I think we should kill her quietly," said Prince Medraut.

"It would have to be subtly done. The commons are already very full of the story. Your hold on Lyonesse is not a strong one, Prince," said Aberinn.

"Tell me something that I do not know," said the prince, sourly. "And now they expect me to lead the troops against this latest foe. Can we not change earlier?"

Aberinn shook his head and got up to leave, not trusting himself to speak. Thinking about it with the benefit of hindsight, perhaps his freeing of Earl Alois had been a mistake. Or premature.

The ladies' bower was all Meb feared it would be. For a start, it was a-buzz above the clicks of weaving shuttles—like an angry beehive—with woman talk when she came around the corner, following Neve. She grabbed Neve's shoulder, and they stopped. And Meb proved that eavesdropping is a sure way to prove that you do in fact never hear anything good about yourself.

"...she has the magic, but she is not noble. Look at the way she was dressed."

"And she did not even put her hair up or cover it. Wanton, I tell you. She was in Aberinn's tower this morning."

"She does seem very young."

A gentle voice. The one who had been sympathetic the night before.

"Hmpf." That was Cardun. "I have never believed that prophecy of Aberinn's. He's never done the like before or since. It just came when Prince Medraut had the Royal Council and the earls ready to agree to the vote."

"Oh, no one could have faked that, Lady Cardun. Why, there was foam coming out of his mouth. It was terrible."

"It was as real as this 'Defender.' She's a common trollop who was wearing a man's breeches!"

Meb took a deep breath and walked on into the room. The comments about Aberinn's fit or the reality of the prophecy—or her—died. Vanished into silence and false smiles.

She gave them one which matched theirs very well, and did her best to look down her nose at them, which was difficult, because she was not very tall. "So this is what the ladies occupy themselves with in Dun Tagoll. How nice." She hoped that sounded condescending. She'd never really had a chance to do condescension before. There were tambour frames, a bigger loom than she'd ever seen, women sitting and stitching where the light was best. Meb loved fabrics and loved fine embroidery. They just weren't things that had come her way. She was saved from deep embarrassment, or finding some way to squirm out of this, by a call from outside. It was a panting page. "The prince's troop is about to ride out, ladies."

So they all went out to the collonaded cloister above the court-yard to see the brave colors hoisted above the cream of Lyonesse, before they rode out to do battle. The little woman who had been kind to Meb the night before looked as if the sight of it cut her to the quick. She did not go down and bestow favors on the men of the troop. Instead she looked as if she might start crying.

Meb had no one to cheer on either, so she just stayed looking out from between the pillars too. "What is wrong?" she asked, looking at the tight face.

The woman made an effort to smile. "Nothing, Lady Anghared. It just brings back old memories. Painful ones. Cormac, my hus-band, rode out like this, with my favor on his sleeve... oh, more than ten years ago."

"And he never came back," said Meb quietly.

"Yes. They say they saw him fall... but they also say he's been seen with the hosts of the Blessed Isles."

Meb did not know what to say.

"And with the armies of Ys. He was a very recognizable man. But he was as true as steel. He would never betray Lyonesse."

The "he would never betray me" was left unspoken. But she did not have to say it. "I have two young sons. They too will ride out one day," she said fatalistically. The "and maybe fight against their father" was also left unsaid.

Desperately looking for something to say, Meb came up with: "You chose my clothes, didn't you? I'm sorry... I don't think I know your name."

The woman nodded, looked her up and down. "You were so pale last night I thought the blue might suit you. I think yellows and greens would bring out your color better, dear. I do like the comb, even though I imagine Lady Cardun won't approve. I'm not surprised you don't remember much from last night. My name is Vivien. My husband was once captain of the Royal Troop."

"I think if I wound my hair up just like hers, she'd still say that it didn't suit me." said Meb, looking down at the chatelaine in the courtyard, a safe distance off.

Vivien shrugged. "She's worried about her place. She's the prince's aunt.

Meb wrinkled her forehead. "What does that have to do with me? I am sorry...I just don't know what is going on here, lady. I'm...I'm out of place. I was...living in another land. In what nearly was a war to end all of it...we...Finn and me, stopped that, and then suddenly I was here."

"It sounds a rather momentous history for someone who looks...How old are you, Lady Anghared?" It was asked kindly, with a gentle concern.

"Um. I think eighteen. It was rather hard to keep track this last while. Might be nineteen," said Meb, who was better at dealing with outright conflict than this. Was it a trap of some sort?

"They say you're too young to be the Defender. But at nineteen I had two children. They're saying a lot of...things about you, dear. Don't give them fuel."

It was actually meant kindly, Meb decided. And Vivien was plainly more careworn than actually old. "I don't know if I am this 'Defender.' I don't think so. I think I am just an unhappy person dropped here, far from everything and everyone I love. I don't want to be here. I don't want to be your Defender."

"You saved Prince Medraut from death, and you brought back the queen's window, a great magic, and Dun Tagoll is defended in every way against those. You frightened Prince Medraut into giving up his sword. You spoke of dealing with dragons...The men-at-arms...well, I heard about it from my boys. They are both squires. But the haerthmen and the men-at-arms are full of it. So are the servants. Also you've been into Aberinn's tower. Almost no one does that. Don't let...spitefulness hurt you."

Meb realized that Vivien, too, believed. Or wanted to. She feared for her sons. "I don't...Lady Vivien. I can't *be* a lady, let alone your Defender. I don't want to be."

"What do you want?" asked Vivien.

Meb sighed. "Something I can't have, either. Ever. I am not even sure I want to be alive, half the time."

"I think I understand," said Vivien, holding her. "I'm sorry."

"I've lost everything I ever had. Everything I ever loved," said Meb quietly, tears starting to form and flow. Vivien said nothing. Just hugged her. There were others weeping and being comforted, so it was not that very obvious. Somehow Meb found herself being taken back to the bower and shown embroidery stitches. She was given an ivory frame, and she concentrated fiercely on it. Trying to lose herself in it. She did love the threads' silkiness and the bright colors of them.

A little later someone looked at what she was doing. "I thought... you said you had never done this before?"

Meb looked at the picture that had started to form out of the tiny stitches. There had been a carefully drawn pattern there, but after a while she had somehow lost the simple flower pattern, and gone on setting stitches according to a pattern in her head, not on the stretched fabric. The dragon was perfectly detailed on the white lawn, and his flame was orange and red and bright, almost seeming to burn out of the material.

The dragon was black, and its eyes were wicked with mischief.

Meb got up and left, her eyes blind with tears again. Neve and Vivien led her to her room.

"When I saw the stitchery... I thought you were making a fool of me, getting me to show you the basics. That you knew far more than I could ever learn. But that was magic, wasn't it?" said Vivien. "Magic here, in Dun Tagoll."

Meb nodded.

Vivien shook her head, eyes wide and worried. "I thought that maybe Cardun and the others were right. I thought maybe you were just here by accident. But Anghared... that is magic, and straight out of the prophecy. Now I think you are the Defender, whether you know it or not. I think you have come to save us, even though you didn't know it, and don't want to do it." The woman paced a little. "Anghared. I know... I can see you are heartsore. I remember my own heartbreak when they told me Cormac had joined the fallen. But, please... there are so many of us. Others who see their men ride off to a war we can't escape and can't win. Can you not... try to spare them the heartbreak too? We need you."

"She's right, m'lady," Neve said quietly. "The boy I was, um, sparking with. The Vanar killed him when they burned our ships. Lyonesse is..."

"Dying slowly from a thousand cuts," finished Vivien. "Every time there is a little break, people try and plant crops, messengers go to the outer marches. Life starts. And then the next invasion comes."

Meb sighed. "I don't even know where to start."

"By washing your face," said Lady Vivien, practically. I don't think you need to know. I think this is a sign. You will defend us against the black dragon."

Meb started to laugh, maybe a little hysterically, but laugh, all the same. Eventually she stopped. Smiled a little at Vivien's worried face. "Whatever I don't know, I know I won't be defending you against that dragon. And even if I wanted to, I couldn't." She got up from her bed. "Let me wash my face. And then let's see if we have dry bread and sour wine again."

"We eat well here, Anghared. Not quite siege rations yet."

Meb pulled a wry face. Well, maybe this was not the right time to tell them. They needed her, or something. And she needed something. Anything. This would do.

— Chapter 7 —

"I HAD NOT," SAID THE KNIGHT, SIR BERTRAN, "BEEN AWARE OF
the usefulness of dragon fire in kindling a fire in these wet woods."
He was eyeing the dragon with a little more respect.

That was a good thing, probably, Fionn thought. He was a nice
enough lad in a society where the nobility had to prove themselves with deeds of courage. Ignorance of dragons—and some
might leave Tasmarin now—could be rapidly fatal. It was small
repayment for the fact that Bertran was sharing a hind he'd shot
earlier with them. Besides, the dog approved of him. Of course,
Fionn admitted to himself, Díleas was a shameless beggar from
anyone who had food, but he had gone trotting over to the knight
before he'd known about the knight's nearby camp and the deer
carcass strung in the tree next to it.

"I had hoped," said Sir Bertran, "that it might serve as bait
and bring the fearsome beasts to me. They are more numerous
in the woods than in my father's time, but still, they are wary
of an armored knight. But if not bait, then food, if I can get a
fire to kindle." Fionn had been happy to oblige. Díleas had been
perfectly content to eat it raw, and had been provided with a
few slices of meat to keep him going while it cooked. If Fionn
understood soulful doggy looks, a little drool, and the occasional
hrrm noises, it had been wholly insufficient, at least in Díleas's
opinion, and "cooked" should be a relative term.

And then, of course, something scented the bait. The knight's
horse gave first warning, before the distracted dog. But even

without that whicker of fear, they would have known soon enough.

The giant broke trees and shook the earth with his tread. The forest life fled before him—birds, deer, a unicorn, foxes, a cockatrice, squirrels and an ogre.

The giant wasn't interested in them. It was hunting, in Fionn's opinion, a dog and a dragon.

In Sir Bertran's opinion, it was hunting him, and thus the company he was in.

There was nothing wrong with the young knight's courage, or the agility of his horse. He did manage to place his lance tip in the bellowing giant's eye, and the horse danced aside from the giant's club—a ripped-up tree—as the lance tip snapped. Unfortunately it had five other eyes—as it had three tusky heads.

Fionn had yelled at Díleas, "Run!" before taking to the wing himself. Dragon fire singed the giant—as he kicked over their fire and sent the partly cooked hind flying.

Dragon fire carbonized the club, but the giant itself merely bellowed in anger and lunged at him. It didn't burn. It was a siliceous giant...A rock giant, as opposed to the frost and fire ones Fionn knew for their bad temper. Normally the rock giants were slow to anger, and slow of reactions. This one was neither. In fact, thought Fionn, as his wings bit air and pushed him higher, this one was a rock giant in its resistance to dragon fire, but looked fire-giantish, with its three heads and brutish nature. And it smelled...odd. Like something had died and it had stood in it. That was always possible.

The fool dog, however, was not running. He was standing and barking. And the fool knight wasn't running either. He'd drawn his sword—which was not going to be a lot of use against the giant. Fionn swooped down and slapped the left outer head with his tail. It might be a rock creature, but a blow from a dragon tail was enough to make it stagger. And bellow again, and plunge towards him.

The dog and the knight, instead of running, followed.

So Fionn had to taunt the giant again, because it narrowly missed seizing the teasing dog. Spiraling up again, Fionn looked for answers. He could lead it off and lose it—if the knight and dog would back off. The dog might...possibly. The knight wasn't going to. Which meant that he had to deal somewhat more permanently with the giant. One could poison them—the silicate organic chemistry was quite susceptible to arsenates, and to some of the powerful acids. Heat would not work. One could bog them down, sink them in a lake, but they'd just keep walking, or toss them over a cliff. Or he could smash the giant apart with a hammer bigger and heavier than itself. Or bespell them. Looking at the energy flows, Fionn thought he saw another answer. This was Brocéliande, and this young knight was, after all, the son of the guardian of the fountain of Escalados. Escalados, the red fountain that drew the storms . . . and the stone giant dragged his feet as he blundered through the trees.

Fionn swooped down. "We must lead him to Escalados. To the fountain."

"I must defend that! And my mother, the Lady Laudine, is within the manor there. There are no tall walls . . ."

"He's a stone giant. It is the only way to kill him. He wants us, not the manor or anything else." The giant proved that by ignoring a small herd of deer that bolted from in front of it, and by plunging after the three of them.

The knight nodded. "It is the better part of half a league!"

Brocéliande's ancient, ferny, mossy forests, full of vast trees and twisted branches, were no place to play catch-as-catch-can with an angry, hunting giant. The giant was capable of going straight, rather than around. Still, the trees slowed him, as they might a man pushing through thick brush.

The giant had by now decided that the knight, sheepdog, and the dragon were all part of its target. And it had three tusky-mouthed heads to feed. It must want one each, Fionn decided. The knight was at most risk, as Fionn had the open sky and Díleas could dart through gaps that were too narrow for a horseman. Perhaps it was the color, but the giant was fixated on the dog . . . who in turn was determined to prove that he was as capable of herding giants as he should be of herding sheep, darting behind it—even between the tree-trunk legs, to snap at the giant's heels. Of course his teeth could not make any impression on the giant's flesh, but the giant itself seemed far more interested in trying to reach the dog. On several occasions when the knight was trapped, the dog drew off the giant before Fionn could flame its eyes or bat its heads.

Then they broke from the woods into what was obviously the

home farm of the knight. They'd cleared a bit of land since Fionn was last here. You could see the thatch of the walled manor house, low down along the shallow swale that ran from the standing stone against the ridge. There was a good reason for the house being low down and far from the standing stone, Fionn knew.

The magic fountain was at the base of the standing stone, some half a mile across the fields. The knight's tenants were in the fields—or at least running from the fields. Someone had the ability and courage to flight an arrow so Fionn took to the ground, making it very obvious—with shouts and cooperation—that the dog and dragon were working with their overlord, dealing with—or at least taunting—the three-headed giant. It would seem to Fionn that the giant had no understanding of human speech, which was odd, as most other giants did. It was either that, or it was very stupid, because they kept it away from the mill and away from the barns and away from the cattle, leading it on—on towards the bleeding fountain. The bleeding fountain was once nothing more than iron in the rock the water oozed through—but superstition and magic often built on each other, and Fionn wouldn't be surprised if it really was some kind of blood now, with all the belief in it being that.

It was a numinous spot, with the squat misshapen monolith and its altar stone above the old stone-carved basin into which the ruddy water seeped. It was surrounded by blackened and dead oaks. That, Fionn knew, had nothing to do with mysterious powers, but everything to do with the energies channeled here.

"It's your fountain, Sir Bertran," he yelled. "You'd better scatter the water."

The knight leapt from the saddle of his steaming, tired horse as Díleas and Fionn teased and taunted the giant. It was, Fionn knew, a dangerous game. They were still faster than the giant, but they were both tiring.

The siliceous creature was not. He would pursue them relentlessly. Fionn was willing to bet he now had the scent of their essences, and would follow, no matter how fast or far they fled. Eventually it would catch them.

This smelled, and not just faintly of dead things.

Sir Bertran scooped a handful of the red water and poured it out on the altar rock, respectfully. He ignored the giant as he did this.

And then he mounted again and charged back towards the fray.

Above, already, the thunderheads built, as with a magical speed the sky darkened. The air seemed to thicken.

"We need that idiot in the iron suit off the horse and further away from the giant," said Fionn, sotto voce, to Díleas. "Because any minute now..."

Then lightning, blue-white and so close there seemed no pause between it and the terrible rattling boom of thunder, carved a ragged, jagged line to the tallest point.

The giant.

Sheeting rain began to fall.

But that was of no concern to Fionn because he was under a shivering dog, and he had to pick up a knight who had fallen from his horse, as more lightning hissed down, hitting the giant again and again.

Nothing, not even siliceous proteins, could survive the lightning bolts. Dragons had found out the hard way that lightning could be survived in the air...but not when they landed.

Now Fionn just had to deal with minor problems—an unconscious knight and a dog that really, really didn't like thunderstorms. And he had torrential rain to cope with, of course.

That was still a better deal than the three-headed giant had gotten. Fionn was fairly sure it was now dead, the neural circuits fried. It was probably a large lump of glassy rock now, for people in later years to laugh at the superstitions of their ancestors.

The rain began to ease off, and Sir Bertran sat up. "What happened?" he asked muzzily.

"I think I'd tell your adherents that you struck it a thunderous blow. Some of the braver ones are approaching now, and I'd appreciate it if you told them that there is no need to pinprick this particular dragon with arrows and that the quivering sheepdog is no threat. It's all right, Díleas, the storm is over."

Sir Bertran stood up. "My mother," he said resignedly, looking at the palanquin approaching. "Sir Fionn, you and your dog strove bravely with me today. I give you thanks. I am in your debt, as I am aware the giant could have caught me on several occasions had the two of you not drawn him off." He patted Díleas. "Seldom has the world seen a braver, cleverer dog, Sir Fionn."

"As long as there are no thunderstorms," said Fionn. "Anyway. One of your grazing paddocks now has a new rock formation,

I think. Let's go and inspect it before they come and fuss about you. You took a quite a toss there. Got something of a shock, too, I shouldn't wonder." Fionn didn't point out that he thought the knight had got off quite lightly, all things considered.

They walked across to the late three-headed giant, now a vast tor of blackened glass, with the evil tusky faces distorted and twisted into something even uglier. The giant glass statue was somewhat the worse for having suffered multiple lightning strikes, but that didn't stop the peasants and men-at-arms approaching cheering their lord, or Díleas lifting his leg on its foot. He was still rather new to this lifting of a leg instead of squatting puppy- or girl-dog fashion, and nearly fell over in the process. That could have been awkward, as the foot was still cracking with internal heat.

Maybe the loyal retainers might have been approaching a little less fast than they might . . . if their lord was not being supported by a dragon. And even from here Fionn could hear the hero's mother. He was a brave lad, this Bertran. Best to leave him to be brave alone, decided Fionn, but it appeared he was not going to be that lucky.

═ Chapter 8 ═

ALOIS, THE EARL OF CARFON, HAD BEEN RIDING SOUTH BY NIGHT, hiding by day for more than a week now. He was exhausted and hungry and he was in a better state than his horse. He knew he should be grateful for the horse. Grateful for the magical intervention that had plucked him from the cell, while waiting for the torture chamber, and dropped him next to the horse in a half-ruined stable, a good fifteen miles from Dun Tagoll, where months of planning had all gone so wrong.

And he was glad. Glad that he would see his son and wife again. Glad, in the last few miles, to see signs that he was returning to farmed lands and not anarchy and banditry. Only Dun Tagoll had wholly abandoned any effort to farm the lands. Only they could. All of the Duns tried to keep at least some agriculture and livestock farming going. It was usually limited to fields just outside the walls. Too few fields, feeding too many mouths. Only in the South had they managed to keep a reasonable amount of land under cultivation, and that by building a great many more forts and having as nearly as many men-at-arms as neyfs working the land. And as he'd said to Branwen when he'd rode out on this venture, the Gods above and below alone knew how much longer they could survive. That was why he'd taken up the offer from the plotters. They'd be dead for their pains, he had no doubt.

So close. So very close to seeing Medraut dead.

And then...He mulled it all in his mind, as he had a thousand times since.

69

He rode slowly along the lane. It was muddy, but at least not overgrown too. And bandits were rarer here.

"Halt. Who rides after the curfew bell?" demanded a voice.

"Earl Alois. And I am truly glad to see my own land and my own men!"

Six hours later, after a sequence of fresh horses, and with a troop around him, he rode into the gates of Dun Carfon—he'd never thought to see it again—and then into the arms of his wife, and to gaze on the sleeping form of his son. "We'll have to wake him," said Branwen. "I'm afraid...like most of us, he believed you were dead, Alois. It's...its been hard for him."

She was a jewel. A mere local chieftain's daughter, not even of the House of Lyon. He'd married her against the politics and calls for alliance. Married her just because he was a headstrong young lord and he'd looked at her and known what he wanted. In earlier years it would never have been permitted. But if one good thing had come out of this chaos of endless war, it was her. "Yes. Hopefully he'll see a better Lyonesse before he grows up."

She blinked, holding him, as if to reassure herself he was real. "I thought Medraut still sat on the throne?"

"He does. But the Defender Aberinn forecast in his prophecy has come. I was there. I saw it. She made the sea-window reappear."

"Really?"

Earl Alois sighed. "Yes. I saw her appear from nowhere, I saw the sea-window reappear. And I heard her name herself as Anghared. I believe it is her. That was magic of no low order. She has come to set things to rights. She even looks like the old queen in the tapestry hanging in the banquet hall. But the bad part, Branwen, is that she will want my head. And if that is what it takes to put Lyonesse back together again, I will go to the headsman."

"No!" she said, clinging to him. Clinging as to someone whom she'd loved, thought dead, and now had to face the fear and uncertainty again. Which was true, of course. "Why would she do that? It's Medraut who has brought Lyonesse to ruin. Not you, Alois!"

The boy woke up and stared at his parents, and rubbed his unbelieving eyes, as his father said: "Because I tried to kill her."

Meb wondered how long the state of tense waiting would continue in the halls of Dun Tagoll. Wars could go on for years. This one had, it appeared. But the answer this time was: not too long. The prince seemed to have developed a hit-and-run strategy, simply designed to hurt the foe, irritate them and make them plunge after the army, toward Dun Tagoll, rather than ravaging the countryside.

That might be good for the countryside, but right now it meant that the attackers were setting up siege engines on the headland. "Last time they threw everything from dead horses to rocks at the castle," said Neve. "It looks like they're making bigger ones this time."

"And ... will it break the walls?" asked Meb.

"No, m'lady. The walls are magical. Even if they break, they just pull together. But a dead horse ... oh, the mess. And the rocks can kill people."

The causeway was too narrow and steep for a charge, but their foes had sent brave men across in the darkness, under their shields, carrying a brass-headed ram. So Meb woke to the pounding of the ram and a sudden, inhuman yowling and screaming. In the darkness of her room, it was terrifying. She'd never been in a castle under siege before. Had the attackers broken through? What should she do? Fight back, obviously. What was there in this room that she could fight back with? She needed a sword. Or better yet, an axe. You needed to have some skill with a sword, but an axe—one of those metallic-handled, narrow, wicked-bladed ones that the alvar gate guards used—surely didn't need much. She was afraid and imagining it in detail ... and it was a great deal heavier in her hands than she'd thought. Summoning magic again ... it seemed to work when she was absorbed enough and afraid enough ... neither of which were easy to switch on at will, she thought as she wished for a light ... and failed. She couldn't even find the pricket, let alone light it. So she went and opened her door by feel, alvar axe in hand. There was a tallow-dipped brand of rush on a metal wall sconce at the end of the hall. She walked down that way. To find a bored guard walking down the passage ...

He was a lot less bored seeing a woman in her nightclothes with a silvery, two-handed spatha-axe in her hands. "M'lady," he took a grip on his own sword handle. "What's amiss?"

"The noise. That screaming. What happened?" she asked.

He looked a little startled. "Oh, just the Angevins getting a snout full of hot pitch, m'lady. Never man the ram. Aye, first at the loot, but also first at the hot pitch."

"Oh ... I thought they'd got in," said Meb, feeling faintly foolish.

"No, m'Lady Anghared. We're safe enough within the walls of Dun Tagoll. Siege engines and rams won't do naught. Starvation neither. It'll take more magic than the Shadow Hall can throw against us."

Meb went back to her bed, leaving the axe next to it. It was a long while before sleep came again. What was this Shadow Hall? And why did the Kingdom of Lyonesse seem to have such an ample supply of enemies and, apparently, not one ally? Finn had said magic use inevitably made work for him, distorting energies. What was happening here? Were there other dragons, planomancers like Finn, moving in their shifted shapes, fixing things? Her dreams were troubled. Full of screaming and silver-handled axes with narrow, curved slicing blades.

She awoke to a troubled squeak. It was Neve, staring at the axe, looking as if she was about to drop the water she carried and run. Meb yawned. "Thank all the Gods you're all right, m'lady! What's that nasty thing doing in here?"

"I thought I might need it if you spilled all the water on the floor . . . I'm only joking, for dragons' sakes. I thought we might have to defend ourselves. And I don't think I can use a sword. I've split wood with an axe, so I have an axe."

"Dun Tagoll is safe enough, Lady Anghared. It's those poor people outside who need defending. Where did you get it? I've never seen anything like it. It looks very sharp and dangerous."

Meb decided it was better not to answer that question, and began washing. She thought it looked just about sharp enough to slice stone, let alone armor. It wasn't a subject so easily avoided when Lady Vivien came in a little later.

"How did it get here?" she asked, warily, looking at the axe. "It has the look of a Finvarra spatha-axe . . . what are you doing with such a thing, Anghared? It's no weapon of the men of Lyonesse. Where did it come from?"

"Oh, um. The alvar guards use them back in my homeland. I was afraid in the night and wanted something to defend myself with."

"But you couldn't have had it with you. You . . . you had barely the clothes you were wearing, when you came here, Anghared," said Vivien, troubled. "I was there. I helped to put you to bed."

"Sometimes, when I'm really scared or just dreaming . . . imagining things deeply, they come to me. Fragments of things . . ."

"Fragments...aha! Summonsing magic. Here, in Dun Tagoll? You can't," said Vivien.

"I didn't mean to. I just heard the screaming. I was scared."

"No...I mean it is not possible. The Mage Aberinn, by his craft, protects the castle. But while we're guarded, it affects us too. Only those of the greatest of power can manage the smallest working. That...that is a vast object for a summonser. It would take preparation and skill..."

"I don't know what I am doing or how I do it," said Meb, knowing this to be slightly less than the truth. The dragon-shaped dvergar device around her neck, the thing that carried some of the magic of all the species of Tasmarin, the device that would help her be what she wanted to be...tricky little dvergar! That would affect things. But...well, she summonsed far larger things, wanting to, needing or just...wishing to. A black dragon, once. And she'd needed him. She still did. She just hadn't known it, then. "I do summons big things sometimes. I summonsed a dragon once."

"Gods above and below. Well, I hope you don't do that again!"

"I can't," said Meb flatly. "Never ever again, although I want nothing more. It would kill him."

But that seemed to have washed right over Vivien. "You *are* the Defender, Anghared. Oh, thank all the Gods. I must tell..."

"No. Please, no," Meb grabbed the fluttering, excited hands. "Please. I want to help. But...well, Prince Medraut. Aberinn. Do you think they'd like it much?"

"The prince has honored you and respected you so far. And the mage called you to his tower. I should have known when we heard about the sea-window. I thought it must be stone memory. The embroidery...that was a small thing, and I was amazed. But, but summonsing magics. And so powerful. I'm Lyon, on my mother's side, and I can call things from across the room. Small things. A brooch like this one." She pointed to the thumbnail-sized one at her breast.

Meb sighed. "Vivien. I don't trust Prince Medraut, or the mage. I don't know how to make magic happen every time. And, and it goes wrong. My master said...he'd teach me. But now, I just feel it would be a very wrong thing to do. I am going to help. I promise. I swear. I swear by the black dragon."

"That...binds you?" asked Vivien.

"It binds me more than anything else ever could," said Meb.

"And I think I'd better hide that axe before anyone else asks awkward questions."

"I could wrap it up in something and take it to the armory," said Neve, coloring slightly. "There's, there's a man-at-arms who might do me a favor. If I asked."

It made Meb smile a little, determined to find out just who this armsman was, and let him know that someone would make his life very unpleasant if he was anything less than good to little Neve. She could do that. Finn had taught her quite enough for that. "I think I want it a little closer. Lady Cardun might decide to do my hair. Stop laughing, both of you. It would make a wonderful mirror. We can slide it under the bed."

"They're very full of your embroidery in the bower, by the way. Even Lady Cardun was saying she didn't know how you worked so fast and set such precise and tiny stitches. Of course she said it showed a lack of discipline not to stick to the pattern, and you were a flighty, moody young girl; that the regent's guidance would be needed for many years, even if you were the Defender, which she didn't for a moment believe."

"I need to ask some questions about this regency," said Meb, who didn't see why it was up to her, but would not have left shifty Prince Medraut to look after a tub of jellied eels, let alone a kingdom. "Who is the prince the regent for?"

They both looked at her as if she'd suddenly started dribbling and gone simple on them. "The true king of Lyonesse, of course," said Vivien.

"Oh. And who is he?" asked Meb.

"He is the king anointed with holy water from the ancient font of kings. He alone can bind to the land and draw its strength to himself to destroy our enemies," explained Vivien.

"But who is he?" Meb pursued. "Does he have to be found or something?"

"No. It is the ancient font that must be found. It vanished just after Queen Gwenhwyfach and her babe plunged from the sea-window. It is believed that the enchantress of Shadow Hall summonsed it, somehow."

"So...do I get this right...the prince is not the regent for someone specific. It could be anyone that finds this font, and gets dunked in water from it?"

Vivien nodded. "Prince Medraut is regent for the Land, because the Land is the King and the King is the Land. Of course the king would have to be of the blood of the House of Lyon, because they have the magic. Normally the old king would take his son or chosen heir to the font and hand on the power. But the old king died before it was found. That is why the Shadow Hall has been able to raise everyone against us. That is why the Land will not destroy the invaders."

"So where do the women fit into all of this?" asked Meb.

The other two looked at her, faintly puzzled. "They say men make kings. Women make babies. We carry the bloodline. Some Lyon women are powerful magic workers too. Queen Gwenhwy-fach was."

"They were wondering down in the kitchens if you were going to marry Prince Medraut," said Neve.

Meb snorted. "I'd rather marry a midden. I'm not..."

"But they were saying he was considering speaking for you. And he's a prince of the blood." By the tone, that was obviously all that was required. Well, it wasn't going to happen. She'd take the axe to him first. And the little logical part of her mind said, well, it happened to women here. And Fionn...she'd never see Fionn again. She should accept that and move on.

There was an enormous thud and the walls shook.

"What was that?" asked Meb, fearful.

"They've set up trebuchets and have started flinging rocks from the headland. Be easy, Dun Tagoll can withstand anything they can fling at it. And besides, Mage Aberinn has said he had something planned for them. Don't worry, Anghared. It wants but three days to the full moon."

And what did that have to do with it?

They seemed to assume she'd know. She hated showing her ignorance, but she needed to know. "So what happens at full moon?"

"The full tides power the Changer. Lyonesse moves."

"You mean...an earthquake?"

Vivien stared at her. "I forget, Lady Anghared, that you are not from here. You know that the land is linked to other places? Places which are not our world? We call them the Ways."

Meb knew that from Finn's talk of other planes. She supposed that was what was meant. "Yes."

"Well, back in the time of King Diarmid, the magic of Lyonesse grew much weaker. Magic flows in across the Ways. The king and his mages built a device, a magical device, that moves Lyonesse around the Ways. When we move, our magework is refreshed. It takes a great deal of power, and so the device was harnessed to the tide in caves beneath Dun Tagoll. It stores power from every tide, but it takes a full tide, usually the equinoctial tide, to do the change."

"These enemies outside...are they from these other places?" asked Meb, a light beginning to dawn.

"Of course," said Vivien. "Yes...I suppose you wouldn't know. They come storming in across the Ways to attack and ravage. It wasn't always like that, of course. When we had a king...and then it took a while for them to realize we were unprotected. The mage says the sorceress of Shadow Hall has turned them against us. But it could as easily have been the raiding."

Meb did not need that explained to her. And to be honest she could understand and sympathize with the army out there. Lyonesse had come and drained out their magical energy...and Lyonesse's raiders had gone out, and come running back to a land that the victims could not attack to punish. No wonder Lyonesse had no friends. She said as much.

Lady Vivien nodded. "King Geoph forbade the raids, but there were always some. But this land was also a refuge. Defeated tribes, persecuted people. They knew they could find shelter and safety here. The other lands hate us for that too. Then when the invasions began...well, Prince Medraut began counterraids. We needed the food. They burned the fields and ran off our kine and sheep."

And now they were left with a situation where everyone hated their guts, wanted to kill them, and they still could not farm, and had to eat ensorcelled scraps or rob their neighbors, thought Meb. And I promised to help them. I thought taking on the dragon Zuamar was crazy. This is worse. And they don't even seem to see it will just gets worse, every time.

There was another shudder, and a hollow boom, as a trebuchet-flung rock struck the castle...and a spectacular flash of violet light through the high window, and distant boom. It didn't rattle the walls but she felt that it should have. All the women took cover, diving down next to Meb's bed.

"What was that?" asked Vivien.

Meb managed not to say "how should I know?" but instead, "Maybe we need to find out?"

"Could we leave the axe?" asked Vivien, beginning to recover her calm. "I think we'd hear the call to arms if they'd breached the walls."

So the axe was placed under the bed again, and they went out. It seemed a fair number of others were doing the same thing. There were definitely no vast crowds of fighting men, or even the sounds of battle.

They went up a flight of stairs to be met by a bemused guard. "The stone," he said. "It flew back."

"What do you mean?" asked Vivien.

"They threw a stone at us with that big trebuchet of theirs. And it flew back from the castle with a big purple flash. Go and have a look."

Peering over the battlements, Meb could see the enemy encampment on the headland short of the narrow causeway to the castle on its peninsula. The camp had probably been set up in good order. Right now it was in chaos, with that chaos centered around the huge, smashed wooden structure of the trebuchet and the plowed-up remains of tents beyond.

There were three other large trebuchets... but no one was near them. They were all—along with half the camp—plainly damaged by flying shards. The foe's engineers were busy seeing just how far from the camp they could get, and the soldiery looked to be, in part, joining them and, in part, under their knights' orders, trying to stop them.

Somewhere on the wall of Dun Tagoll, a cheer started.

Meb was walking back, deep in thought, when she came, abruptly, on Mage Aberinn. He stared narrow-eyed at her. "A word, young woman." He looked at the other two women. "Here in the courtyard. So you do not need a chaperone."

Meb didn't know how to avoid this so she walked a little way with the mage. "Did you interfere in some way with my working?" he asked abruptly.

"I wouldn't know how. I didn't even know you were doing anything. What am I supposed to have done?" asked Meb, alarmed by the ferocity of his tone.

He seemed mollified by hers. "I had built a device to mirror back the energy of their projectiles. To return them."

"But it worked, didn't it?" said Meb, puzzled.

"Yes, it worked. It worked far too well, with far more power than such a working could harness. Not since King Diarmid has such a thing been reported."

"Well, it had nothing to do with me! Ask the others. We hid behind the bed when it happened."

He sucked his teeth. "I do not like or trust this. Or you." And he turned on his heel and walked off without another word.

In the Shadow Hall, the queen stared at the viewing bowl. Where had Aberinn acquired such power? Lyonesse had been crumbling, slowly. Onslaught after onslaught it had lost more men, lost more ground. Once it had taken troops months to fight their way anywhere near Dun Tagoll. Now the borders were unguarded. West Lyonesse had become, effectively, a few fortresses along the seaboard, hated by its neighbors, with even the peasantry turning from their Lyon overlords.

Even if magically he had barely remained able to hold her out of the castle itself, it was failing.

Nothing was simple or quick. She'd learned that. And now to add to her irritation, the muryans had brought her hall too far while she had slept. So many years of working her magic on them, and they'd never been less than precise before, and right now she was not in the deep ravines of Ys, but somewhere near a noisome town in the lowlands.

She had her cauldron-men to send out. With the colors of Lyonesse flying at their head they'd go raiding and pillaging and burning for her. But was there any point in doing it here? The great Changer would not open these Ways this time. She knew its pattern. Aberinn had never guessed that.

Meb knew her curiosity about the Changer would have to wait. She'd done some subtle questioning and the answer to what it was and how it worked was simply that the women of Dun Tagoll did not know. Her attempts at being a good lady were being met with very mixed success, and she'd been getting the feeling that leaving the castle might still be the easiest way to help. Or at least, easier for her. They accepted that she could embroider. Her skills at the rest of the womanly arts, Meb knew that they considered as far below the salt.

Maybe this Changer would bring other changes? It was inside the mage's tower, she was told. It had always been, from long before Mage Aberinn. Yes, it was a device of some sort, which he worked with. And no, when they changed, nothing was really that different within Lyonesse...except that the attacking army could not return to its own country. Nor could they get supplies from their home. Their supply chain was cut, the country was picked bare, too bare to live off, and chances were good, any other invader would attack them too. And back in their own country, the people would know: attack Lyonesse and you are lost, forever.

Once that had been enough.

Now it wasn't.

When the change came it was silent and sudden.

Meb knew it had happened.

She could feel it. It was a little like some strange scents carried on the night air. Scents of faraway things, and of spices she knew the smell and taste of...but did not have a name for.

The association was not a pleasant one though; it somehow also smelled of cold, salt, decay, and other nasty things.

— Chapter 9 —

"YESTERDAY, ALL YOU WANTED WAS TO GO WEST," SAID FIONN AS Díleas danced around him, barking. Darting off southward, and then running back to see if Fionn was following. Doing everything but to bite the dragon's heels to get him to follow. "You'd have been well served if I'd had have left you there for the plump lady to pamper, forced to sit on a satin cushion, and be fed sweetmeats for saving her precious boy. It wasn't easy getting you out of there, but the last thing we need is a young knight traveling with us as well. He's probably trying to track us, and we're a lot harder to follow moving down the roadway than fighting our way through the forest."

Díleas was paying no attention to his eloquence, so Fionn gave up and followed. He wasn't prepared for the sheepdog to turn around and give him a lick on the nose.

He also was not prepared for another trilith, some three hundred yards into the forest. A low, squat one, barely five cubits from the forest floor to the balancing stone, and covered in enough moss and fern to blend into the woods.

"Now just how did you know that was there? And I'll warrant it leads to elsewhere," said Fionn.

It did. They came out in a long grassy dale, with the hills rising all around them. Fionn smelled the air. And then turned his back on the dog and went to have a long hard look at the trilith . . . which wasn't there. He walked back up the track past where they had stepped into this place. It did not take him back to the forests of Brocéliande.

"A one-way gate. And another I did not know existed. Either things have changed in the wider planes while I've been trapped, or I knew very much less than I thought I did." Fionn used his vision to peer into the currents of energy around the spot, ignoring the dog and his "come on" bark. There was very little sign of the vast flow of magic and other energies that such a displacement should cause. Someone or something very skilled had set up this gate.

Fionn preferred to be the one who knew more than others, to being the one who was still trying to understand. Why had the dog come this way? How did it know where the gate was?

And . . . did it really, somehow, as he hoped desperately, know where his Scrap of humanity was? He missed her fiercely.

Up the slope some white-grey shapes ran away. "Sheep. Yes, Díleas, I am coming. I don't entirely like it, but I am coming. And you should be a very happy sheepdog as there seem to be a lot of sheep, rather than wolves, afancs and giants . . . not to mention the mother of knights here. Lead on. Here I think the appearance of being human will lead to less problems."

It felt like Albar or Carmarthen. Which was illogical. Ys and Cantre'r Gwaelod abutted Brocéliande. But as the trilith-gated way had proved, there were places and things that he had known nothing of, linking places, obviously by some sort of different mechanism. Well, Groblek could be anywhere . . .

They walked on. Díleas seemed determined that only one direction would do, taking them cross-country and through a muddy stream, over several dry-stone walls and into some conflict with a shepherd and his dogs on the steep hill-path they were following. "What are you doing in this pasture?" yelled the shepherd standing astride the path next to some large boulders. "Here, Strop, Cam. See them off, boys."

Two black-and-white sheepdogs, remarkably like scruffier versions of Díleas, hurtled towards them, barking, dividing at the last minute, to flank them, and then suddenly getting the smell of dragon.

They weren't stupid dogs. They were a lot brighter than the shepherd, Fionn decided. Brighter than Díleas, who was regarding the two suddenly halted dogs with a display of fur, a curled lip exposing his teeth and a deep burring growl. "We're just passing through, fellow. Call off your dogs, and we'll be on our way."

"Not over my master's land you're not! Strop, Cam, gettim."

The dogs advanced. Not in a hurry.

"Díleas. Put your head between my legs," said Fionn quietly.

The sheepdog did, and Fionn whistled. He'd found dogs—and animals who heard higher frequencies—did not like that whistle. People didn't even hear it.

The dogs did. So did the sheep on the hillside and quite a lot of mice and a fox. They all wanted to leave.

The shepherd did quite a lot of yelling and then some whistling. And a fair amount of swearing. "He lacks originality, Díleas," said Fionn, addressing himself to the sheepdog. "And you're a young dog. I don't think you should be listening like that," because Díleas plainly was listening, head cocked to one side, tongue a little out. Looking at his expression, Fionn was fairly sure Díleas was laughing in doggy fashion. "Now, shepherd, we're tracking someone we've lost. Will you get out of our way, or shall I repay the favor by letting Díleas bite you? Or I could toss you down this hill? I've no real desire to fight, but I'm in a hurry."

One of the sheepdogs had returned to behind its master, nearly crawling on its belly, tail between its legs. The other was staying a lot further off. "What have you done to my dogs?" said the shepherd, backing up himself. "I can't let you walk over here. My lord said I was to keep people off. They're stealing his game, he said."

"Don't be dafter than you have to be," said Fionn, his sympathy, as usual, with whoever was stealing the odd pheasant. "Firstly, you can see I'm not stalking or hunting anything, and secondly, I'm not going to tell him I met you if I happen to run across him. And who else will tell him? I'm just passing through."

"But ... but there is nowt up there. Just devil's leap."

"Then maybe I'm the devil, going there."

The shepherd looked at him, wide-eyed, and then jumped down the rocks on the edge of the path and ran away as fast as his legs could carry him, followed by his dogs.

"Come on, Díleas. Barking at him is just rude," said Fionn. "I think we've started a new legend, which is enough chaos for one day. And it should make poaching up here a bit easier too. I do like doing public service, especially when it involves a mischief. And something tells me you're taking me to this 'devil's leap.'"

Indeed he was.

It was well-named, if you were human. A great plate of cap-rock had been eroded into a narrow tongue, while the softer underlying rock had been eaten away. It hung above the wrinkled valleys of the lowlands a thousand feet below.

To a dragon, of course, it looked like it could be prime real estate, especially if there was a cave somewhere close. The difference was that dragons had wings, and dogs and humans were a little short of those.

And that fool dog was simply walking towards the drop. It did seem to be giving him pause . . . well, he was slowing down. "Wait. Díleas, this is a better task for a dragon than a human. And better too for a dog to have a dragon for company. I really need to rig you some kind of harness. Aha! I have it. The coil of traveler rope. Let's tie it to you, because my talons might have a bad effect on a fast-falling dog."

So they stopped, high above the world, where along a distant roadway a cart toiled. Fionn could detect a minor perturbation in the energy flow here, but he would never have found it without getting so close. Whoever had built these Ways between worlds had been adept at hiding them from planomancers, also from others here, if reaching them involved walking over a cliff.

The dog got a long harness, which, Fionn could tell by his pawing at it and sniffing, was less popular than the red boots had been. "I haven't got you on a lead. You've got me on one," said Fionn taking the end in a dragon talon, and wrapping it around his leg. "So lead."

And Díleas did. One cautious foot at a time . . . stepping out into the air. And then, he leapt into space. Fionn followed. Either the dog knew more or could sense more than a planomancer, or it was just a really crazy dog.

They did fall.

But not far enough for Fionn to unfurl his great wings. Actually he had to do a frantic roll in the air so as not to land on the dog. And the turf they landed on was springy and covered in thick moss. There were trees—gnarled, huge, ancient trees—overhanging the dell. The air was sleepy, warm, and full of the gentle background sounds of bees.

Fionn was attuned to the use of energies and magics. He knew this for what it was. He turned to Díleas, who had flopped down, panting. "Come, dog. Don't even think of lying down. Think of rats, or rabbits, or better still, busy beavers. Or you'll end up like that."

He pointed to a green-white curved dome, lying in the shade. It might have been a rock, except for the eye sockets. Díleas got up and walked with leaden feet, still with the rope leash on, too tired to even protest that indignity. There were other bones here in the forest. A rotten femur nearly tripped him. Fionn could feel the lethargy affecting him too. Dragons were not as much affected by the magic of other species, not even the magic of the tree-people. How many desperate humans had walked to the devil's leap to jump . . . and found themselves here? Spared to become plant food. They walked towards another long-dead human, with shreds of faded clothing and a rusted sword and hauberk. Fionn picked up the sword in his dragon talons. The dog was swaying on its feet. "That's enough," he said. "Stop this now or there will be trouble."

The dog sat down. Yawned. And Fionn threw the sword as if it were a knife, to peg in the nearest tree. The branches swung lower over them. "Dragon fire is next," said Fionn grimly, hauling Díleas to his feet by the leash. "Onwards."

The sleepiness lifted as they moved on. Fionn searched out the patterns of the working. It was a deep and old enchantment, that the trees had merely enhanced. But it had been intended as place of rest, not a final resting place. A place to comfort and allow the wounded in heart and spirit who fell into this place to recover.

Kindly meant. Not predatory.

The sprite-trees who had moved in had found it a good way of obtaining fresh nitrates. That irritated Fionn. Well, the tree-people irritated him quite easily. The First had created vegetative intelligence, but wood had shaped it. Fionn wondered if he should burn the place. But there was real beauty all around, so he settled for collecting together a small mound of skulls that could be seen from the entrance, and scratching a little symbol on each. The sleep spell did not work on insect life, but merely on vertebrates. And now it would still be a wonderful place to sleep . . . if not for the mosquitos that would infest it henceforth, and make it impossible. Fionn chuckled quietly to himself as they walked on. He saw Díleas stop and scratch furiously and attempt to bite at the base of his tail.

He looked anything but asleep. "Ah. Fleas too. They are an irritation, but at least you can get rid of them with a bath, Díleas. Those blackhearted old trees there wanted all of your blood, not just a few drops."

Díleas scratched and wrinkled his nose at Fionn. "You'll live through a bath. You would not live through that place. Let's move on."

A half a mile further and they merely had the fleas and not the tiredness. Fionn knew that that was a good bargain, even if the trees would not have thought so.

Díleas rolled and rubbed his back, and Fionn kept a lookout for fleabane plants. Dragon hide was hard for a flea to get through, but these ones were hungry and determined. It was a pity they didn't eat sprite. A little later Fionn and Díleas came on a stand of silver birch—with a sprite. There was something familiar about them. It was Lyr. All the tree-sprites on Tasmarin had been Lyr, part of the one tree that was Lyr.

The beautiful tree-woman bowed. "Fionn. We bear fruit."

"Ah. So he is still fertile, is he?" Plainly the sprites who had been trapped in Tasmarin were either leaving there or merely spreading back to other sprite places. His Scrap had given them back their male sapling, and brought the long-dead stick back to life. Male sprites had no intelligence, but plenty of sprite-pollen.

There was a joyousness in the "Yes."

"Good. He is growing well?" asked Fionn, out of politeness. They made bad enemies, the sprites. The sisterhoods—and there were various forms, each associated with its own tree type, and some were more talkative and friendly than others, although all of them poorly understood animal life, and did not tolerate it very well. Lyr had been one of the worst... until his little Scrap had given them what they needed.

The sprite nodded her gracious head. They were beautiful. Humans, and alvar, found them almost irresistibly so. Dragons, and it appeared dogs, could take them or leave them. "The human chose well. The soil there is rich."

"I think she made it like that for him," said Fionn. "She had powers over earth, and she's, well, kind by nature. It's not something you sprites understand, but it is something humans possess from time to time."

"We had not understood humans. We need to cultivate more such. Where is she who gave us back our mate?"

"We're looking for her ourselves. She is no longer on Tasmarin."

"Lyr has not seen her. She has not been near living wood since the day the towers became bridges and some of us could return to sprite lands."

That was worrying. The sprites weren't everywhere of course. But they did have ties to forests, and all trees communicated. Mostly they did not say anything very interesting, except to other trees.

"Well. The dog is getting impatient, Lyr. It seems to know where it is going, and I am hoping it is to her. But if you find her . . . well, a bit of dragon gratitude would be good for the trees."

"If we find her, you will be told. We understand your role too in saving our beloved. We have learned the value of that."

"The tree-women learn gratitude and wisdom," said Fionn. "Well, you'll have mine, if you help me find her and keep her safe."

"Word will go out."

Fionn and Díleas walked on. And on. As far as Fionn could establish, the dog walked as straight as it was possible to walk in the forest. That night they slept in a pile of dry leaves under the trees. It was warm enough for sheepdogs and dragons, anyway. Both of them would have preferred a comfortable bed, and a meal that consisted of something other than the remains of the food from Sir Bertran's feast. There was no other animal life, and Fionn had not seen any fruit. Like Díleas, he thought fruit was all very well for herbivores and omnivores. Not for dragons, unless it was a slice of melon wrapped in salty ham.

Drink was supplied by a stream. Díleas eyed it very suspiciously, and looked at Fionn a couple of times, before coming to drink thirstily. He was a very intelligent dog, to have learned the danger of afancs (and other water creatures he hadn't met) but he seemed to prefer walking in the stream and drinking downstream of himself. Perhaps he liked the flavor of the mud. Fionn wondered if they would be reduced to eating that before they got out of this Sylvan world.

The next day was more of the same. Fionn found flows of unbalanced energy to put right. There was a newness about them. He wondered if they'd come about as a result of Tasmarin rejoining the great ring. That had to have had an effect. Magic would grow a little stronger in places. Much had been tied up just in keeping Tasmarin isolated. That magic would flow now.

It should change a great many dynamics. It might well even change the way magical forces worked.

Most mages performed their arts by rote. They'd find this interesting, thought Fionn with a nasty laugh, imagining the consequences. Undoubtably, what he'd just done was going to make their lives difficult.

It was a full hungry day and a night later that they came to what Díleas had plainly been aiming for. As a way out of a Sylvan world, it was appropriate.

It was a row of trees... well, it had been a noble double column of lance-straight firs, standing in what could only be a planted line to the top of a round hillock. A mound, Fionn guessed. An ancient one, that trees had long since covered. Díleas walked up, until he got to the last pair of trees... which were different. They had been the same, but now they were just blackened stumps. That would put off the sprites, Fionn thought. They feared fire. Didn't even like its old sign. Just as the people of Brocéliande would superstitiously avoid triliths...

There was a pattern here.

Mysteries like this teased Fionn. He'd get to the bottom of it, just as he'd eventually work out how the dog knew where they were.

The other mystery was that, having got there, Díleas just sat down. He'd been eager to go through the gates to other places before. But now he was just sitting. Looking intently ahead. In a way that was worrying. The Sylvan worlds were slow-time worlds, not as much as the alvar ones, but still, a month might pass in human worlds while a day slipped by in the tranquil Sylvan forest.

Fionn tried walking past him. Díleas growled at him. A real growl. A "don't do that even if you are a dragon" growl. So Fionn sat down, and waited. He stared into the energy patterns around him. Most of the time he confined his vision to the ordinary spectra and a few others. Otherwise it simply became too much for his brain to process. Now he looked deep, trying to learn more. Trying to learn how to find these gates to other planes. They were magical workings, and yet... and yet showed little sign of their presence. The trees were centuries old at least. Had this been here when he'd soared over this forest looking for things to put right? The planes he patrolled were huge. He went to areas where the balance was disturbed. They often seemed to be the same places. That too was unsurprising.

Díleas suddenly got up, turned and barked at Fionn, and walked forward. The dog vanished from view as he stepped past a certain point. And there was quite a vortex of energy between the trees, right now. It hadn't been present, earlier.

Fionn followed...

... And was not surprised to find that they were elsewhere. And, pleasingly enough, in an elsewhere where he might find food for the two of them. That was undoubtably peat smoke on the air. Of course hearth fires had their own downsides, but it was better than hunting worms and bugs in Sylvan.

The problems the First had with the bauble of energy that hung from the dog's neck were twofold. For a start, it gave a limited view of the world that the dog experienced. It was not impossible to track the dog and dragon by their energies, but it was harder. It had been many eons since the First had exerted themselves, and the time dilations and contractions were confusing and very rapid. Logically they lived where time passed slowly. Very, very slowly. Some of the movements of the tiny gobbets of energy seemed absolutely microscopic, to the First.

But this was better than the Sylvan worlds. Annvn was a slower world, and they could move plenty of pawns here. They were easier to move than trees.

Chapter 10

"THE KITCHEN WORKERS HAVE IT THAT WE'RE GOING TO HAVE A bit of a rest. Gather fresh food. Ys is slow to arm and their Eorls are too busy fighting and robbing each other to send much of an army," said Neve, "and Queen Dahut does not care."

"And what of the army at our gate?"

Neve shrugged. "They go or are killed."

It was outside her knowledge, obviously. So Meb asked Vivien. She had, with her contact with her sons, and her dead husband's position, a far better grasp of the military.

"Some of them fled after the rock thrower was destroyed. But most of them are trapped here. Obviously their mages thought they had at least another month before we could accumulate enough power to change. It can take up to six months some-times. I know Prince Medraut was surprised. He expected it to be another month or three. Anyway, the ones that are left . . . the prince will offer them terms in a week or two. These days they always refuse them. It's a pity. The Angevins make good soldiers, my husband said. The army used to recruit most of its men like that. My Cormac's father was a gallóglaigh himself, trapped here with the armies of King Olain."

Meb shivered. Trapped, far from home, with no way out but to accept service in the army of your enemy. She felt a little bit like that herself. "It's cold this morning. Is it always this cold here?"

"No. In summer it is often too hot!" said Vivien with a smile. "It is only the start of spring. We still have bitter nights and occasional cold snaps if we have a cloud front come in from the ocean. You can usually see the warmer weather coming from the outer parapets, with the blue patches forming across the sea. Take your cloak and we will walk up there and have a look. You are looking a little confined."

"It'll be even colder up there," said Neve. "There is a fire in the bower."

Meb shuddered. "I'd rather freeze than face the bower right now," she said.

So they walked across the courtyard to the outer parapet on the western side. Here there was no cliff, but a steep green slope down to the foam-laced edge of the dark ocean. That was deep water. "You could get a line out to some big fish from there," said Meb expertly. She'd caught fish, along with all the Cliff Cove children at the foot of Cliff Cove's crags. She'd missed fish, she suddenly realized. She'd never thought she would.

Neve laughed. "They'd never lower themselves to fishing here."

Looking out to sea there was no sign of blue-sky patches in the slate grey. Instead there was a wall of cloud, right down to the water, stretching across the horizon. "That doesn't look good. If I saw that back home, in Tasmarin, I'd expect a sea mist for days. Cold and clammy and useless for fishing," said Meb. "The fishermen would stay home, drink too much and get morose."

Lady Vivien gave a little snort of laughter. "I thought you said you had no experience that would help you to live in a castle. It sounds like winter. We get freezing fogs in the winters. But I have never seen anything like that before."

It was apparent that not many of the castle people had, as others had come up to look at the cloud wall. Someone had even called the prince.

And the mage was called too.

His face became as bleak as a winter storm as he looked at it. He sent a soldier running along the battlement.

To fetch both her and Prince Medraut.

He turned to the women accompanying her. "You are not needed. Go." Before, Aberinn had made some pretense of abiding by the conventions. Now he plainly was simply too angry. "Prince. I do not know what meddling you are attempting, but you have led us to the very brink of disaster."

Medraut first looked guilty—which Meb had decided was his

normal look—and then puzzled and worried. "What are you talk-ing about, High Mage?"

Aberinn waved a hand at the western horizon. "That!" he snarled. "The Changer was set to take us to Ys. This is your doing somehow, Medraut. Ever since you brought this woman here, nothing has worked as it should."

"My doing? MY DOING?!" Prince Medraut snarled, roused to fury like a cornered rat. "I nearly got murdered in my bed, Aberinn. The assassin escapes, and we still do not know how he got in in the first place, although I've put the suspects to torture. You are supposed to guard me. To guard Lyonesse. Your pre-cious prophecy says I need you. You brought this woman here, not me. Admit it. She could not lie to us without your magic supporting her."

"You fool!" shouted Aberinn right back, inches from his face. "There are records, ancient records of all the places the Ways link Lyonesse to, even the non-human places. This Tasmarin creation was a mistake. There is no such place. I do not know which of the Lyon have allied their magic to this prop of yours, but I will find out. I have means denied to you..."

Meb looked at the two madmen...and walked away.

"Where are you going?" demanded Aberinn.

Meb shrugged. "Away. Away from that," she pointed at the horizon, "and away from you two. Even that army out there has to make more sense than either of you."

"The gates are closed," said Medraut, tersely.

Meb shrugged again. "Then I'll go as far as I can. You're killing this place, both of you. And neither of you care, except about yourselves."

Aberinn snorted. "Well, you'll be glad to know that you have brought about its final destruction, you and this prince of plots. The Ways are not open to Ys. They are open to the Fomoire. And they come."

It looked like a wall of cloud to Meb, but it was enough to make Medraut's blood-suffused face go from red to white. "It can-not be. After the last time the Changer was set so that it could not link us to Fomoire lands."

"So see what your meddling has brought us to!" yelled Aberinn.

Meb did not stay to listen to them. She kept walking away.

Vivien and Neve hurried to her. "What is it? What do they say?"

"They say those are the Fomoire. They both accuse each other and somehow it is my fault too. I don't even know who the Fomoire are."

Vivien stopped dead. "In King Gradlon's time, when Lyonesse was near the peak of her strength, the Fomoire came. They nearly destroyed us."

"Who or what are they? It just looks like a cloud to me."

"The sea people. They come from under the sea and have much magic."

"Under the sea . . . the merrows?" Meb felt a shred of hope. She knew and got on with merrows. She knew she had to watch them, but she could trust them, deal with them. She'd liked them, for all their tricky ways.

"No . . . not water-creatures. They live in a land beneath the waves, and the waters are magically held at bay. They're human . . . well, giants, but deformed." Vivien shuddered. "And they are powerful and evil. They built great bridges of ice and came with their war chariots and mages. They don't have ships, so they must freeze the sea into a bridge to attack us."

"Um. What do they do when they get here?"

"It was said they brought disease and bitter cold, but I suppose that could just have been the ice. Their chieftain had the evil eye. He only had one eye, but if he looked at a man . . . he turned them to stone. Not that that is possible."

It was. Meb knew that. She'd done it once. But that had taken touch, on her part. The news was obviously spreading around the castle, by the frightened looks on many faces.

And a cold, stinking wind was blowing from their ice bridge. It reeked of staleness and of old smoke. Meb wondered for the first time if she could bring some kind of magical power to bear on these attackers. This was not her home and these were not her people. But they were so afraid.

The next weeks were fraught with fear, tension . . . and helplessness. They could see the ice bridges now, although the cold meeting the warmer water tended to swirl up a sea mist. The Fomoire mages were pushing them in three long tongues toward the shoreline. When the wind—bitter cold and dry—came blowing off the ice, the people of Dun Tagoll could hear the chanting and the drumming coming out of the sea mist. When the wind blew the other way they could see the black huddles of the mages walking circles on the ice tongues. And day after day it grew closer. And colder.

Aberinn had retreated to his tower, and although sounds of industry, hammering and metal shrieks came from inside, he did not.

The Angevins had broken camp and fled inland.

Meb wondered if they should not all just follow.

She did, finally, get out of Dun Tagoll herself. Hunting parties— those included the ladies, and the dogs and the hawks—sallied out on horseback to see what food they could gather in. She was invited to ride out with them.

Meb decided she liked the country a great deal more than the castle. And riding, which she'd been more than a little terrified of, she actually found she loved. She hadn't dared to tell anyone, except Neve, that she'd never even been on a horse before. A donkey wasn't quite the same, and she'd feared the derision that would bring. But like the language, riding came easily. So did being sore afterward, but the horse liked her as much as she'd liked it. She'd treated it rather like Díleas. She'd watched covertly as the other ladies had mounted, and realized she was being watched herself.

Either she was more athletic than most castle ladies, or she was mounted on a good mare, or her magic worked as well on horses as puppies, but those who expected her to fall off, or cling to the saddle, were disappointed. Meb spent a fair amount of time petting the dun, and talking to it. She had no idea if she was supposed to do that, but she wanted to, and did, leaning forward to whisper in the horse's ear, telling it quietly where she wanted to go. It seemed to work, which was just as well, because the reins were something she was less than sure about what one did with.

"You have a fine seat, Lady Anghared," commented one of the noblemen. "You need to watch that mare. She's nasty-minded."

Meb thought the seat could do with a bit more padding, if it was supposed to be so fine. And the mare seemed the sweetest-natured animal. But she knew very little about riding, so she settled for smiling.

The country near the castle showed signs of the devastation from the armies, but Meb could see it could be rich and fertile. There really wasn't much game left on it though, and of course the farmhouses had been burned and there had been no crops in the fields for years, by the look of them.

The day's hunting tally had been one feral pig, some songbirds and some rabbits. And, oddly enough to Meb, a glimpse of a nasty little grey-mottled alvlike face from among the rocks near a hilltop, grinning wickedly at her. No one else seemed to see it, but having seen one once, Meb saw several others. They vanished when they realized she was looking. Were they so normal here no one spoke about them? Or did no one else see them?

She wasn't ready to ask.

They dismounted in the blackened ruins of a village—something that tore at Meb, remembering Cliff Cove before the raiders. This was long gutted and burned though, and the wilderness was reclaiming it. There remained, however, a fountain that bubbled out of a central rock and down into a stone bowl set among the winter-dead ferns. It overflowed into a long horse trough. The hunters went to drink, as did their horses. And, leaning against the stone, being sniffed and nuzzled by the dun mare, Meb saw something walking across her hand. She'd stripped off her gloves to drink, and had not put them on again, as she was rubbing the mare's nose. It was quite a large ant. She nearly brushed it off but something made her pause at the last moment and peer closely at it.

It had an oddly human face, and it was staring at her as intensely as she was staring at it.

"Excuse me," she said to one of the nobles walking past. "What is this?"

"Your hand, Lady Anghared." He seemed to find that funny.

"I mean walking on it." Her tone told him she did not.

"It is an ant." He reached out to flick it off.

She pulled her hand away. "I mean it has a face. Look."

"It looks like an ant to me, lady. Mind you, the neyfs believe they're little people. They won't harm them. Call them muryans."

Meb put her hand against the rock and the ant walked off.

"Your steed has behaved?" asked the knight, seeing it reach out to nuzzle Meb.

"Oh, yes. She's lovely."

They rode back to the castle. That felt like oppression, even if it was not a devastated ruin. Up on the seaward walls there was a great deal of construction going on. By the robe, Aberinn had finally emerged from the seclusion of his tower. She would have gone for a closer look, but for the thought of meeting him up there.

"She's either ridden from an early age or we were misled about the horse," said Prince Medraut to his aunt. "Aberinn has it fixed in his head, or at least he claims to believe, that she is from the South, and it is somehow my doing to upset his prophecy. I think he is going mad."

"He's been mad for years," said Lady Cardun. "You need him, though, Medraut. There is no one else with his knowledge or skill in the working of magic. You know that as well as I do. As for that...woman, he plainly dredged her up as an excuse to seek changes. She's no lady. She has no knowledge of the feminine arts. She dresses her hair like a trollop and walks like a man. She cannot hold a conversation. The lower orders are fascinated with her, of course, just as Aberinn intended."

"I had heard she had some skill with a needle," said Prince Medraut, mildly.

"She couldn't even follow the cartoon, Medraut. Trust me, it was merely some magical trick of Aberinn's. Still, she is being watched all the time. She's no lady, whoever she is. I would guess at a Lyon by-blow, but maybe from one of the other worlds. The product of rape on a raid out on the Ways somewhere."

"I wish I could see just exactly how Aberinn plans to use her. Of course, the other possibility was that somehow she was a plant of Alois's faction. But I don't know how she dealt with that mare. That horse is supposed to be a killer. It even bit the groom bringing it to her."

The queen of Shadow Hall had stared into her seeing pond, still seething with rage. She had put in so much effort to get the Angevins into a treaty with Ys. Queen Dahut was an insatiable slut, and it had been almost impossible to get her to cooperate on anything that wasn't bedding her latest victim. Dahut killed them, which was something the queen of Shadow Hall could see the sense and value of. And then, just when Ys was seething with rage at Lyonesse, with the Eorls all demanding war, and not even fighting each other, which had taken her years of work and planning...Aberinn had somehow not opened the Ways to Ys.

But when she saw the cloud wall and the tongues of ice, she crowed and cackled and danced with glee.

What the mage had been setting up on the inner wall was a series of huge lenses. In the morning the men-at-arms were trying to aim the weak sunlight at the ice tongue, which was barely out of bowshot now. He was painting patterns around each of the devices, and in some way, they must be working because the chanting and drumming stopped, and what could only be swearing had started. Meb braced herself for the possibility of meeting Aberinn and went back to the wall.

The ice was dazzling with the brightness of the sunlight reflecting off it. It might just be spring here, but it was midsummer out there. The water around the floe was actually steaming, making the black-cloaked army on it look even more monstrous than nature had managed. Even from here she could see that they were somewhat bigger than most men. Not giants as Meb thought of giants, but eight or nine cubits tall, she would guess. And even from here she could see that they would not win any contests for handsomeness. Their shapes were just wrong. Arms too long, or they were too squat and broad in the torso.

The ice was black with them and their chariots. They were drawn up under various banners—here a severed head, there a blood-dripping axe, and in the center, a large eye.

The floe cracked. It sounded like a whip crack, but right in her ear.

The Fomoire broke ranks and retreated with as much speed as possible.

It still wasn't quick enough for some of them. The floe calved off the tongue and deposited half a dozen huge, black-cloaked warriors into the ocean with much bellowing and yelling.

And much cheering from the wall of Dun Tagoll.

That worked for the morning. But by the late afternoon, the chanting had returned, and the good work of the morning was being undone. Now the archers had begun firing at them. Only those capable of the longest of shots, true, but the Fomoire archers, bigger than the defenders of Dun Tagoll, had drawn mighty bows and were launching their heavy black-fletched arrows back at the defenders.

And the ice-making did not stop for darkness either. The

chanting went on all night. By early morning, Meb could stand it no longer. She'd barely slept. She went out to see how close they were.

There were plenty of other women up already. In fact Meb wondered why she'd been left, until she was told that Neve was in the infirmary. "She'll have been overlooked by the eye, lady," said one of the other servants, fatefully. "By tonight we'll all be dead of it, I shouldn't wonder."

Meb made her way across to the infirmary. Already the women were carrying wooden buckets, and ewers, and bowls and anything else that would hold water from the central well to higher points. The buildings within the outer wall were almost all thatched, and plainly fire was a threat. So they labored up from the well with water. Meb wondered why they didn't take water from the worn rock-bowl next to the outer wall. That was still full and trickling its water into a clay pipe. But perhaps it was for some other purpose. It was a very scruffy spot in the otherwise tidy courtyard. There must be some reason it was ignored. The water was probably brackish or something. It would still put out fires, surely?

Neve was looking pale and wan, and had apparently been carried in from the battlements about midnight. "We're going to die, m'lady. I shouldn't have done it. But she told me I'd lose my p-place." Tears streamed down her little face and Meb could get precious little sense out of her, or little comfort to her. Somehow she must use her magical skill to get rid of these attackers. She knew she still had the power that she'd wielded on Tasmarin, only . . . only most of the time there it had gone wrong. She'd had Finn to fix it for her. She actually really had no idea what she could do, or what she should do. She knew she was a summonser. She could call things to her. What would turn the Fomoire back? A dragon? A troop of centaurs? It sounded like everyone had reason to hate Lyonesse. She wouldn't bet that that would not be true of anyone she summoned too.

So she went up to join the bucket teams. Like the men-at-arms, they were trying to stay out of direct sight of the Fomoire, but judging by the chanting, the ice bridge was not there yet. But the sky was slate-grey, and the sunlight through Aberinn's devices would not help today. Meb bit her lip. Well, there was no point in hiding the axe under the bed at this stage. And she could summons it . . . but best to save that. She went and fetched it instead.

It remained the most deadly, sharp-looking thing she'd ever seen. She imagined she might cut a hair by dropping it on that blade.

No one questioned her taking it with her to where a row of women huddled below the stone and mortar on the inner bailey with their buckets.

After a little while Meb's curiosity penetrated even her fear. The chanting seemed to have gotten far louder. She'd have to risk a peep soon. And then the idea stuck her: she had a perfect alvar-silver mirror in her hands. She held it up.

No wonder the chanting was louder. The Fomoire host was nearly at the least-steep edge of Dun Tagoll's peninsula. The monstrous, shaggy warriors had their big ovoid shields up to protect their chanting mages from the arrows being fired from behind the battlements without looking over—with their errant aim, quite a few were landing in the water. And lined up on the chariots just behind them and under the huge eye banner was a row of gigantic, misshapen men...all with only one eye...staring at the walls, from behind their shields. Meb changed the angle of the alv axe a little more to get a better view of them. Saw one stagger and fall sideways off his chariot.

And then someone knocked the axe down. "What are you doing, woman?" demanded the man-at-arms.

"Using my axe as a mirror."

"The evil eye will overlook you just as well in a mirror! Do you think it hasn't been tried?"

"It's as bad reflected as direct?" she asked.

"Yes, of course. Everyone knows that."

It was like a candle in a great darkness. A bright spark, in dry idea-tinder.

Meb picked up the axe. The blade was bigger than her face... she held it in front of her face, and stuck her head up above the parapet. She couldn't see anything. But she'd bet some Fomoire's baleful eye was hurting. And she was rewarded by a reverberating groan from outside the walls. She was aware that the women—a mixture from both the bower and the kitchen just here—were staring at her. "Every one of you! Quick. Go fetch a looking glass. Any looking glass. Anything that reflects. We'll give them their own back. Let them enjoy it."

Women looked, gawped, and then began scrambling away to run down the stairs.

Within fifty heartbeats, mirrors—everything from ladies' hand mirrors, with gold foil behind the glass, to polished pieces of copper sheet, to a shiny piece of plate—were being held up above the battlements. And even the chanting outside the walls had stopped.

Meb had to risk a peek. By the cheering from the walls of Dun Tagoll she wasn't the only one. The chariots which had held their one-eyed starers were being hastily driven back, pushing through the mobs. The eye banner had fallen. There was chaos in the Fomoire ranks, and quite a number of their men were down, and now archers on the walls of Dun Tagoll began aiming their shots at the rest.

Meb saw Aberinn come out on the lower battlements. She could recognize him by the robe, but his head was encased in a glassy, spiked helmet of some kind. He took in what was happening. Took in the mirrors. Spoke to some people.

Soon he was up on the inner battlement himself. "This was your idea?" he asked Meb, with no pretense of ceremony or politeness.

"Yes. Someone said the evil eye affected you even if reflected . . . so I thought we'd give them their own back. It seems to have worked."

"You are either cleverer, or more powerful, than I had realized." He turned on his heel. "Sergeant. Get me four men-at-arms and carry that lens down to the tower. We'll give them a mirror to avoid. I'll tin one of the lenses."

Even Meb's dealing with the baleful eye did not stop the Fomoire mages. They were back by late that night. And by morning the Fomoire warriors were assaulting the walls. But now it was just warriors against walls. And gigantic though the Fomoire were, they were as scared of hot pitch, and as easily killed by a dropped rock, as the Angevins had been.

What wasn't better was the sheer volume of warriors they had to fling at the task. Fomoire would climb dead Fomoire to get up those walls. If the sun shone in the mornings the mage's lenses poured heat at the ice bridge. The Fomoire mages tried to build the ice bridges, and when the sun did not shine from the east, turned the cold of chanting onto the castle itself.

It was bitter. So was the siege. The part that Meb really didn't understand was how it affected her. It seemed to have merely deepened the infighting among the women.

And Neve wasn't dying. She just wasn't getting much better either.

═ Chapter 11 ═

THE PEAT SMOKE FIONN HAD SMELLED CAME FROM A SMALL VIL-
lage. It appeared that Fionn had reached the travelers' destination
of Annvn.

The travelers might have wanted to go there for trade, but it
was not one of Fionn's favorite places. Its hereditary rulers had
always had something against dragons. That was not abnormal or
unevadable. It just meant he'd have to stick to human or some
other form. Fionn could, with sufficient study, do a passable
imitation of most body forms that he could cram his mass into.
Some, like human, he was so at ease with that it took little or no
effort. Others were barely worth the effort it took. But for Annvn,
human would be best, although an alvar would be respected.

On the other hand, it wasn't even the best of places for a
human. Slavery was still widespread, and the law was petty and
very carefully enforced. There were licenses required for almost
everything—including being an entertainer.

In most planes silver was silver and copper copper, and the
locals weren't too fussy about the coin's imprint. Annvn really was
picky. Fionn had none of the local currency and a very hungry
dog and a fair degree of hunger himself. It was late afternoon,
not the ideal time for him to be doing a gleeman routine for his
supper, beside the fact that, no doubt, some officious little man
would demand to see his license. Anyway, there seemed to be
some sort of contest on. Annvn was sheep country, like quite a
lot of the Celtic cycle. And right now, several of the locals were

showing off their dogs' skill at herding sheep to the locals. By the looks of it there were some considerable sums being wagered. Fionn was a competent pickpocket. He just had a moral objection to it, and would in general only relieve thieves of their ill-gotten gains. He'd pushed the line of who were "thieves" to certain merchants, lordlings and tax collectors, too—and to the dvergar, simply because it was part of the game. You always paid them for what you stole or tricked them out of afterwards, or they'd get really nasty. But they liked the game. So did Fionn. "If you want to eat, you'll have to work," he said quietly to Díleas.

Several of those taking bets had the look of professional gamblers doing their best to look like passing farmers. Fionn relieved one of them of a silver penny. He'd give it back later, if the man proved honest. "I'd like," he said, assuming his best village idiot look, "to see how my dog would do."

He could feel the eyes of the "prosperous farmer" take stock of him. Apparently he looked enough of a rube. "Hey, Lembo. Stranger says he wants to try his dog at the sheep work."

"Aye," said what plainly was a shepherd. "He good with sheep, mister?"

"Well," said Fionn. "He's never worked with sheep before. He's young, see. But he's a really smart dog. He understands every word I say. I reckon he could be a champion."

"He looks like a sheepdog," said the shepherd.

"Well, his mother was. But his father was one of my lord's grazehounds. He's but a pup. But you should see the size of his feet."

This provoked laughter. "And you reckon he can herd sheep? He'll be more inclined to eat them."

"Oh, not Díl!" said Fionn, patting Díleas' head. "He's a good dog. Sharp as a whip."

"It takes a lot of training."

"I'll bet my dog can do it," said Fionn. "Sharp as a whip, I tell you." He dug out the silver penny. "Here. Bet you my dog can get a sheep into that fold," he said, pointing at an enclosure made of hazel-withy hurdles.

"I'll take you on that," said the shepherd—who had not been Fionn's intended target.

Well, he could return it, once he'd worked over the money men fleecing the crowd. Fionn shrugged. "Which sheep, mister?"

The shepherd shrugged in turn. "Any one. But just one, mind."

So Fionn bent over Díleas and said quietly, "One sheep, in that pen. But don't make it too easy. We want to get the others to bet." He'd found Díleas could hear him perfectly at a pitch humans could not. He'd realized it could be useful some day.

Díleas trotted off as if he was the most obedient and smartest dog in the world. Started nosing one of the punters, pushing him out, with a wicked look in his eye at Fionn. Really. That dog. Showing off. "Sheep, Díleas, sheep. Not a man," said Fionn. "One sheep. Up there. He hasn't had much to do with sheep before," he explained earnestly.

"Neither have you," said the shepherd with a laugh.

That was true enough. As a dragon, Fionn had regarded sheep as needing to be well seared to get the wool burned off, or it might stick between his teeth. When masquerading as a human he generally had it served to him roasted or stewed.

He rapidly began to appreciate that they really were best that way, and that he'd just lost the silver penny he'd wagered. The problem was twofold. Díleas was smart. Perfectly capable of understanding what was needed of him. The first problem was, of course, that sheep were stupid, and not capable of understanding his canine orders, and he'd never had any experience at herding them. The second problem was that sheep...didn't separate. They really, really did not like it. The minute Díleas managed to get one out of the bunch, the sheep would either desperately try and rejoin the others, or the others would try and join it.

Díleas was seriously unimpressed with the sheep and their lack of cooperation. He barked and told them about it, and they ran away. He had to run after them. The crowd, on the other hand, were delighted with the performance. Several of them were laughing so much they had to sit down.

Fionn sighed and relieved the pickpocket, who had thought to take advantage of the distraction, of a few coins, and gave the probing hand a squeeze that would put the thief off for a while.

"You'd best call him off," said the shepherd, wiping the tears off his cheeks. "He's chasing a month's grazing off the sheep. I'll not hold you to your bet. He's got potential, that dog of yours."

Fionn knew when to admit he was beaten or, at least, when Díleas was, and called the dog, who came back panting, looking hangdog. Ears down, and his self-esteem somewhat lowered. Well, it might be a stolen coin well spent, for that. "A bet is a bet," said

Fionn, and handed the shepherd the silver penny. "I've learned something and so has Díleas. Worth the money."

The shepherd slapped his back. "Ah now. I'll buy you a mug of ale with it. Best laugh I've had for years. Here now. Watch and learn." He whistled up his dogs, and gave Fionn a lesson in how sheep should be handled. Fionn noticed Díleas studying the proceedings with intense care, head slightly to one side. "He's a bright one, that dog of yours," said the shepherd, noticing. "If you'd care to sell him, I'll buy him."

"Oh, I can't do that," said Fionn. "He's the lass's dog, really. And she'd eat me alive if I didn't come home with him."

"You watch some of those fellows then," said the shepherd, jerking a thumb at a pair of apparently well-to-do farmers. "If they think he's good, they'll try and steal him and sell him. Did it to one of my dogs a year or two ago. I got him back; he must have come halfway across the county to find me, and he was in a terrible way. But straight as an arrow he came to me. Don't know how he knew the way, but he did."

Fionn marked the two men down, and pondered what the shepherd had said. So dogs were known to have this ability, were they? She'd probably enhanced it without knowing.

They went across to the alehouse and the mug turned into two, and Fionn used some of the copper to buy a mess of pottage for both himself and Díleas. The shepherd's dogs were at least amiable—and also at his heel constantly. They, of course, were aware of the smell of dragon. But they were also fiercely loyal and very obedient. When told to shut up, they had. "You're a good man. Many's the fellow that might have sat quaffing and eating and left his dog hungry. Bella and Sly here, they eat in the morning. I'll not be running to a bowl of stew for them, Finn! I don't win silver every day."

"Well now," said Fionn thoughtfully, "it's possible that we could win some more of it. Those fellows who stole your dog are over there. Did you ever get your own back on them?"

The shepherd scowled. "They are talking to Barko. He's a gambler and a fixer. I have my ties to Old Persimmon. He's as straight as a corkscrew, but he's a fine man compared to Barko. They'll be drinking some fellows into the army tonight. You be careful with them, Finn. You can't touch them."

Finn smiled wickedly. "I thought they might like a little easy money. A bet with a drunk who is far too proud of his dog to have any common sense."

"Not your Díl and the sheep again!"

"Oh, he's not good with sheep. But I've taught him a trick or two with numbers. Enough to fool people he can count. Here, Díl. What's two and two? Tap your paw for the number of times." And speaking too high for the human to hear he said, "Tap each time I say 'now.'"

So Díleas tapped out four. The shepherd nearly fell off his stool. "Now, that's clever. He really is sharp as a whip, Finn."

"Good," said Fionn. "Now all you have to do is tell me and the alehouse in general, loudly, what a fool I am. No dog can count."

"But he can," said the shepherd, puzzled.

"You know that. And I know that. But our friends over there don't. All they know is Díl and I made fools of ourselves earlier. If I'm willing to put my money down, they will be."

And indeed, they were. And oddly, simply because Díleas had made many people who were now in the alehouse laugh, some others were prepared to bet on him getting it right. "Any sum," said Fionn, slurring his words. "Shmartest dog inna world. Sharp, sharp as whatchamakillit. Whip. Whip. Bet you a piece of gold, he c'n add or shub ... subtrac. As long answer's not over twenty-one. He only got his toes an' tail ter count on, see."

"It's a trick," said a skeptical individual.

"S'not. You make up the ques ... questi'n. Smartes' dog inna world. Worth a fortune, see."

Fionn ignored the comments about how smart his dog had been at handling sheep.

Bets were taken. The alehouse silenced. "Make it up," said Fionn to the sceptic.

"Uh. Seven add three add four, minus nine, minus two."

"Ach. He can't count on his toes that fast. Write it down. Say it again slowly. An' then you count his barks."

"Seven ... add three ..."

There was a gasp. "He's looking at his toes."

Díleas was nothing if not a showoff. And it appeared that he could count, at least well enough to fool a rural alehouse. When he barked three times, and then looked at Fionn expectantly, Fionn's "good boy" was lost in the roar. And quite a few people intervened to stop Barko and his friends hastily leaving before paying their bets. For the price of a few more bits of addition and subtraction from the smartest dog in the world, the shepherd's Bella and Sly got mutton bones, as did Díleas. And Fionn could have had enough beer to float in. Fortunately alcohol had almost no effect on dragons. He simply liked the taste and the company.

The shepherd, however, was a lot more worried than Fionn was. "They'll have marked you down, Finn. They'll not like you having taken money off of them. You'd best come with me. I'll see if I can sneak you and Díl out the back."

It was at times like this that Fionn knew why he preferred low human company to high dragon company. They'd bet on the underdog, and they'd help out a stranger. At least, some of them would. "I've decided I don't like them taking dogs off people either, my friend. Neither Díleas nor I are easy to catch. He's cleverer than most and I am nastier than most. Unless I am much mistaken they'll wait until Díl and I stagger out to sleep somewhere. And then I think they'll plan to relieve me of my winnings and of my dog."

"But there are two of them. Maybe Barko too," said the shepherd.

"Don't you worry," said Fionn. "I've got a little surprise for them."

"You're a thief-taker?"

His Scrap had once come to just that wrong conclusion. "By the First, no! But I have nothing against taking from thieves, and I have decided I really don't like people who steal dogs. Díleas doesn't either."

Díleas had started out very doubtful about the other two sheepdogs. But now that they had all finished the bones, and it appeared that the other dogs were now used to the dragon smell, and the treats that came with it, he was quite enjoying being one of the pack. They were all peacefully snoring together at the dragon and shepherd's feet. How to gain social acceptance with animals you were designed to eat: via the dog, thought Fionn, sardonically. He really would have to try it with horses, someday. It made traveling incognito very difficult in some areas. He prodded Díleas with a toe. "Come, boy. It's time to be bait."

"They'll likely use drugged food. There is a piece of meat from down the inside of a horse's hoof that dogs find irresistible. I've trained mine to only take food from my hand, now," said the shepherd, still looking worried. "They're bad men, Finn. Best to leave them alone. You've hurt them enough with the money."

"Oh, it's best, I'd agree. But we've come a long way today, and have a fair way to go tomorrow. And you might say I have a little training in fighting."

This plan was rather turned awry by a shout from the door of the alehouse. "Recruiters!"

There was a frantic press at the door, and they were a long way from it. Fionn's shepherd friend was very pale, and rapidly sobered by the situation. "Do you have a chit from your lord? Or are you a freeman?"

It was clear that the press at the door were only getting out one at a time. Fionn would bet the kitchen door was guarded too, but probably with a club rather than a demand for papers. By the way the shepherd said it, being a freeman was anything but free...or good. It appeared that Annvn hadn't gotten any more pleasant since Fionn was here last. Well, he worked on the energy flows of planes, not their social evolution. He'd seen plenty slip downhill. "No. And you?"

"Mine's out of date," said the shepherd, tersely. "And what'll happen to my dogs if I'm taken?"

"Well now," said Fionn. "The answer is you can't be. This is the work of our friends that we tricked out of robbing a drunk who was too proud of his dog. So now I'm going to work another trick or two. I will get us out of here. You call your dogs close, make for the hills, and I'll organize a distraction."

"What...?"

"Hush. Close your eyes. Cover your dogs' eyes with your hands. Díleas, eyes closed, boy."

Dragons were good with fire. The alehouse was fairly badly lit with tallow rush dips. The recruiters had lanterns—and they included the two who had been dealing with the gambling fixer. Fionn concentrated on the energy flow of tallow dips and especially those nice iron-bound lanterns. Iron oxidizes...usually as rust, but in the presence of sufficient oxygen, finely divided iron will burn. And when you can direct energy and focus heat, and speed chemical reactions...

The smokey tallow dips exploded into a bright flare, burning up instantly. So did the iron lanterns. Fionn could have made that reaction hot enough to consume the hand that held them too, but he cut it short, settling for sudden darkness and some burns. He could still see perfectly well, but he was the only one in—and probably outside—the building who could. A lot of people decided that this was the perfect time to panic and leave. Fionn held back his shepherd friend, who was all for joining them. "Wait."

When the bulk of the stampede had gone out the front door, they walked through to the kitchen. There was a burned-out lantern and an iron-bound club there, but no sign of any other watcher, so Fionn, the shepherd, and the three dogs slipped out. By the sounds of it there was an almighty fight going on in the village green. Fionn was quite tempted to go and join in, especially as it appeared that, having had the tables turned on them, a fair number of people were for tossing the recruiters into the river. Fionn and the shepherd instead skirted the backs of kitchen gardens, and cut onto the road just beyond the town.

"Finn, my dogs and me owe you," said the shepherd, looking back. "That'll teach me to come to town without a chit from my lord. But they were in town recruiting barely two weeks back. There was no reason to expect them here again, gods rot them. Ach, that was a neat trick with the light. Magic worker, are you?"

"Not really. I've picked up a few little spells." Fionn gathered by the tone that that, too, was something to be cautious about in Annvn these days.

"My grandmother had the sight. And she had nowt to do with Lyonesse, either," said the shepherd.

Lyonesse again. "Me neither. But people think that," said Fionn.

The shepherd shrugged. "If you're the demon himself, I'm grateful not to be a foot soldier and to leave my dogs to starve. I've no wish to be a soldier. And I'll say nowt if they come looking for you."

"Well, if they come looking, I'd stick to saying you fell in with me at the ale-house and claim I borrowed money from you, and left without paying it back, if anyone asks. Who are they fighting with that they need to use such harsh recruiting methods?"

The shepherd stopped and looked at him incredulously. "Where are you from, stranger?"

"Further than you can imagine, friend. And I have further to go. I'm just passing through. No real interest in your wars, I just need to know where to avoid going."

"We go to war with Lyonesse. They raid our lands, rape our women and steal our sheep. The mage has foretold the Ways will open soon, and we must be ready this time, to strike hard and fast before they do." It was plainly a recitation of a speech he'd heard, rather than a deep-held belief that could make a shepherd volunteer.

Given that the paths between planes that Fionn had once known were poor places to try and take armies through, Fionn had to wonder just how they did that. And just how this mage knew all this. But he was human. Probably therefore a charlatan. Fionn was one, himself. But he avoided starting wars.

That night they slept under a haystack. And the next morning they came to the coast, and the next of the spots that the dog seemed to know just where to find. This one involved swimming.

The dog could do that without any alteration or teaching, even if he still tried to bite the waves that splashed his face.

Fionn decided there were better forms for the ocean here. There were sharks big enough to try their luck with humans, and certainly dogs. And besides the water looked cold. Form gave some protection. It took him a few moments to change into that of a large sea lion and plunge after the dog.

It was nearly a few moments too long. The dog wasn't paddling his way across the surface anymore. Heart full of terror, he plunged down, looking for Díleas, his eyes wide, staring, twisting over and over in the water to look all around him. Then he shot to the surface, propelling himself out of the water to look around.

There was no dog. No triangular fin cutting the water and no trace of blood either.

Forcing himself to calm down, to be systematic and sensible, Fionn began looking for telltale energy patterns, and, on the third pass, found them.

It took five more dives to find the exact point of transition, to somewhere beneath the waves.

In the strange dapple-shadowed world, Díleas greeted him with a bark and by shaking all over him.

"So kind of you to share," said Fionn, "but I was wet enough without your help." He wished that transformation did more than hide his clothes. They were wet. And it was cold here.

"This may be the way to your mistress," said Fionn, "but it's an awkward place to pass through," said Fionn, looking at the water-dappled "sky" above. "They don't have dogs like you, and it's not exactly a friendly place. I am hoping that we are just passing through, Díleas, because this would not be an easy place for her to survive. If anyone has harmed as much as a hair on her head, I am going to extract a vengeance that their great-great-great-grandchildren would remember. But I'd rather find her alive and well, and generating chaos."

"Hrf."

"So the issue is just how to travel where we need to go, without it turning into a running war. Fomoire lands are, shall we say, interesting: the effects of magical ideas meeting real physics. The locals aren't friendly either." He shrugged himself into a body form that would pass local muster. Díleas, who knew his smell, and was accepting of dragons, and of Fionn shifting to human form, still backed off and barked. Fionn was not that surprised. It was the extra head that did it, as well as the withered arm and the extra height and bulk.

"It's me, you fool dog," growled Fionn through his snaggled teeth. "Smell. I smell better than most Fomoire. The problem with most of their 'blessed plain' of the land beneath the waves is that it is abyssal plain. Cold and dark. And the magic needed to keep off the weight of the water produces some very strange side effects.

"You need lead underpants if you're going to live here rather than just pass through in a hurry. Besides that, they're inbred, which is why they look like this. I think you will have to be my fur. There are places where dogskin cloaks are very fashionable on people, not just on dogs, and this is one of them. I doubt if they'd realize, with you sitting on my shoulders, that you aren't a dead dog. They don't always bother to skin their cloaks here. They figure they can always eat the contents later. My glamour might affect you too. I look the part, thanks to learning a thing or two from the alvar about their magics."

Díleas stared at him. It was a disconcerting, intent stare. "And I know you were studying those other sheepdogs, but it's no use giving me the eye. I am a dragon, not a sheep, and I'll go with you without being herded. Up on my shoulders, and you can point me with your nose."

Fionn bent down, and the dog jumped up. It was rather odd to be that trusted. It was rather odd having his ear licked, too.

They began walking. Mag Mell, the blessed plain, or the joyous plain, or, as far as Fionn was concerned, the blasted plain, sloped steadily toward the dark depths. The sunlight that did penetrate down here made everything a twilight blue. The only fertile areas of the land beneath the waves were those parts which lay in the shallows, and the entire thing had a bad effect on marine life. It was a good example of how a need for security could blight a people, thought Fionn. Yes, the Tuatha Dé Danann could not reach them here...but that was all that was good about it.

It did not take Fionn long to realize that something was seriously amiss with the land beneath the waves. It was the first of the places he'd been recently where the energy flows were seriously adrift and in trouble.

The other thing, of course, was a lack of Fomoire. They farmed— as much as they could—the shallow lands, where the water-filtered sunlight still fell. Mostly they grew seaweeds, watered with salt water—the freshwater springs of this place were few and far between. Too precious for plants. And rain could not fall from their saltwater sky. They lived as much by hunting—harpooning fish and whales and other creatures in the sea above them, spearing them through the magic curtain that kept the sea off and dragging them through—as they did by cultivation. But the sea was wide, and seaweed could be nutritious, and fish were abundant, and one could feed a fair number off a whale, and most things washed into the sea. Some things were pretty dead and ripe by the time they got into the depths, but the Fomoire had long ago stopped being fussy.

Now they were not around. Not even their women, for which Fionn was extra grateful. They had ideas about the hospitality owed to visitors. Curiously, they hadn't been gone long. Fionn came upon a still-smouldering fire. Fires were precious down here, for all that they made the air hard to breathe.

He could simply fix a few things as they went. And it seemed like it was going to be a longish walk. It was cold here under the ocean, but not, Fionn realized, as cold as it should be. Nor was the air as foul as it usually was. It smelled of the upper world, and not just of salty damp.

That might be an improvement, but it meant something was not as it should be. And by the traces of the crude magic they were using it was easy to spot.

So he made a few changes.

Their mages were not going to enjoy that.

— Chapter 12 —

EARL ALOIS AND HIS MEN WATCHED FROM THE HEADLAND. OF course the water was warmer down here, and it must be taking the Fomoire ice tongue more time to reach here than it would in the colder waters near Dun Tagoll.

That was scant comfort. Well, the ice would spill Fomoire onto the land and those ill-formed giants would fight their way south—if there was anything to fight against—once they'd overwhelmed Dun Tagoll. If they did, which, considering history, seemed likely.

In the meanwhile they had to be stopped here. Straining his eyes, Earl Alois could only make out the outlines of their banners. His engineers were busy building siege engines, and he would add his art to their strength and accuracy shortly. But he wanted a better view. "I am going up there to have a look, Gwalach," he said to his second-in-command, pointing at the rock spike above the bay. There was nowhere up on it flat enough for the catapults, or they'd have been building them there.

"Supposed to be a spriggan up there, my liege."

A few months ago, Alois would have laughed. No one had seen a spriggan—outside their imaginations—for many a year.

The last while . . . it had been different.

"I've a mail shirt and a good steel sword, Gwalach."

He scrambled up the rocks and was staring at the ice on the sea, at the banners, when someone said, "One standard with the eye. I make it seventeen of the one-eyes under it."

"You've better eyes than I have," said the earl, still staring. "With any luck we'll land a rock on them."

"If the catapult doesn't break and drop it on you," said the the other observer with morbid satisfaction. "Mind you, I'd throw a sheep or two. Fomoire haven't seen fresh mutton or decent fleece for a long time. And they're loot-hungry. They'll fight each other for it."

Alois turned to look at just who was telling him how to wage war, and nearly fell off the rock he was sharing with a spriggan. Its skin was the same color as the etched limestone he stood on. He reached for his sword. And it stepped back into a crack and . . . vanished.

Alois stood staring at the rock for a long time. And then swore. Long and hard.

At himself.

Drawing his sword! That was nearly as stupid as trying to kill the Defender because she stood between him and Medraut.

Since she'd come, the land's fay had been waking. Scarcely a day passed without some neyf being piskie-led. Other creatures too had been reported—including the spriggans. He should have realized. Worked out the connection. The spriggan hadn't been there to kill him. It had been watching the Fomoire. Advising on what could be done.

Well, they'd have to drive some sheep up here. Slaughter a few ready for flinging. And drive the rest into the Fomoire horde, when they came ashore. Hopefully without their seventeen evil eyes.

Further north, the siege of Dun Tagoll dragged on. Meb was the only one unfortunate enough to be tasting and seeing just what the feasts consisted of. It was curious that no one starved on the food. It was real enough though, just not the rich fare it appeared to be. Meb decided that somehow Aberinn must multiply it from some little stock he kept somewhere, rather than making it out of nothing or summonsing it from elsewhere. That had puzzled her at first: if all the blood of the House of Lyon were skilled in magic, well, why then did they not use it? Finn had said it was a poor idea because it distorted the other energies, but firstly, she wasn't too sure what that meant, and secondly, she couldn't honestly see the castle people caring unless it hurt them. But it seemed that was Aberinn's price for the magic he guarded the castle with. Other magic was suppressed, only barely possible to the most powerful with great effort. And it seemed their magics were very different from hers, all tied up with long complex rituals and symbols and appeals to Gods. Well, at least they knew what they were doing.

She didn't. And she really didn't have anyone she dared ask about it.

Neve was still pale, weak, barely able to swallow gruel, and very inclined to weep whenever Meb was there. She didn't seem be able to speak anymore. That left Meb with Lady Vivien, as no one else in the bower was even speaking to her. It appeared there had been considerable trouble about precious mirrors being used without their owners' permission. Mirrors were valued and expensive items in this society.

On the other hand, she'd found that the kitchen servants, the stable hands, and the common men-at-arms all were, to varying degrees, her partisans. They would bow, and give her a smile and a greeting.

Meb also found she was desperate for space. Dreaming space, if nothing else. Space away from the cold fetid breath of the Fomoire host would have been good. Her room felt too...watched. Too small. She took to walking in among the buildings and along the inside of the outer wall. It was a much older wall than the main keep, built of precisely fitted dry stones that had later been plastered over with mortar. It had cracked in places, and, because it was sheltered from the wind and caught the morning sun, the inside of the west wall had some tiny plants growing in those cracks. Periodically they were scrubbed off, except down by the fountain and the rock-bowl. For some reason the neyfs left that area alone, and Meb liked to go and sit there, on the edge of the basin. No one had told her not to, and it seemed that when she was there, they ignored her, and left her in peace. It was the one place the reek of the Fomoire invaders didn't seem too noticeable. The water was sweet, and she'd taken to having a drink there and dribbling some off her fingertips onto the ferns. Even in the cold Fomoire winds, they'd put out some little curled green shoots.

She had a drink and washed her face. It had been another restless night. She sat and thought about happier times. Before she'd known too much. When she'd had a dog and Finn to follow. And had slept rough and been nearly killed...and had been happy.

At last she decided there was no use moping, and she needed to go and do something. Anything.

She got up. Bent down, had a last drink, washed her face, and walked away, away from the little oasis next to the wall.

She was passing next to the washhouse when an uneven stone made her stumble and fall headlong into the muck. It saved her life. The arrow would have spitted her otherwise. She sat up and saw it quivering in the wooden washhouse wall. For a second she stayed still. And then she scrambled on hands and knees behind the nearest wall. And another arrow hit that.

Someone was trying to kill her. And it wasn't one of the crudely fletched big Fomoire arrows either. Those, she'd seen, had long multibarbed points. This was a normal arrow, with the single barb of the Lyonesse arrows.

Meb wondered just what she should do now . . . besides get out of there. "What's wrong, Lady Anghared?" Anxious voice, male . . . it was the elderly steward who had changed her wine from the one Aberinn had bespelled that first night. Was that why she saw and tasted what the food really was? She didn't care. He was help.

"Are you all right?" he asked, kneeling next to her.

"Someone shot at me. Someone tried to kill me."

"Are you hit?" he asked.

"No. I tripped over a stone. It saved me," she replied.

"The Fomoire have not managed to get many shots over the wall. Come, my lady. Let me help you . . ."

"It wasn't the Fomoire. It was someone in the castle. Look." Meb pointed at the arrow in the washhouse wall.

Only it wasn't there anymore. There was just a narrow hole where it had struck.

Having someone try to kill her was bad enough. That had her on her feet and sprinting for the shelter of the main keep, with the elderly steward running behind. She didn't stop until she had barred herself into her own room.

Panting, she sat on her bed. If magic was that difficult inside the castle—unless one was Aberinn—it could only be the castle mage who had had a hand in trying to kill her.

It took her quite some time to settle her nerves. She had to get out of here. She would have to wait until the siege was over, unless . . . well, she had no idea how to get herself magically anywhere else. And if mere wishing would do it, well she knew where she would have been now...except it would kill Fionn. And she'd rather die herself. She took a deep breath. Stood up. Well, she'd brave the bower. At least there, if anything happened, she had some kind of ally.

Walking down the passage towards it she met that smiling ally.

"Good news! I've just heard that the Mage Aberinn has nearly enough power for the Changer. We'll be able to escape the Fomoire, months before anyone could have expected it."

Several other women came down the passage. Now was no time to tell Vivien that she was going to flee this castle just as soon as the siege was lifted. Instead she made her best effort to smile and said, "I must talk to you later, but first I will go and see poor Neve."

She made her way down to the sickroom. The news had plainly got there too by the looks on the faces of the injured. She made her way to Neve's bedside. The poor girl looked, if anything, worse. Meb had heard that others—those who had not died—recovered. The only thing holding her here in this castle was this faithful girl.

Holding her hand, she said. "Neve. Someone tried to kill me. I..."

Neve squeezed her with a clawlike little hand. And then spoke in a little dried-up whisper. It was the first thing she'd said for two weeks. "I didn't want to do it, m'lady. They said I'd be turned out. Left to starve and be raped." She sobbed convulsively, wracking her little body. "So I told them. I...hate myself."

Meb looked at the weeping woman in puzzlement. "But you've been here in the infirmary for weeks."

"I...I told them about the donkey. That you couldn't ride. So they put you on the killer. I tried to run and warn you, but Methgin, he held me, put his hand across my mouth when I screamed."

Methgin was one of Prince Medraut's bodyguards. And some of the comments about the horse now made sense. "I didn't get killed. The horse liked me, and I liked it. So all their plans came to nothing. Stop worrying about it, and get better."

"I never told them about the magic. I told them things I thought would make you seem safe. They'd be scared by the magic, and want to kill you. But it didn't work. They told me I'd have to poison your wine. Prince Medraut sent the order... I couldn't. So...so I went and looked at the evil eye. You must flee, m'lady. You must go."

Meb hugged her. "I am not leaving you here, you silly goose. You didn't have to do this to yourself."

"I'm dying, m'lady," said Neve. "You've got to go, as soon as you can. As soon as the Changer takes us from the Fomoire."

"Firstly, you're not dying. If you were going to die, you'd have been dead within hours. You've just been wishing yourself dead and starving yourself to death. That stops right now. I am going to need you to help me get out of this place," said Meb firmly. "I'll talk to Vivien..."

"She reports to the mage."

"What?"

"She's scared for her place and her children. Besides, her family are old queen's men. Aberinn is too," said Neve.

Meb swallowed. Friendship? All she'd had was spies. And Aberinn had to be behind the latest attempt, surely. And then she got a grip on herself. One of those spies had tried to kill herself, rather than go through with murdering her.

She hauled Neve upright, sitting her against the wall. "Let's get some food into you, dear. You'll need your strength, because we are going as far as possible from this nasty little nest of vipers."

"Me?" asked Neve, puzzled.

"Well, unless you'd rather stay here and starve yourself to death, while we could go and take a chance on just starving to death."

"You...forgive me?"

"There's nothing to forgive, and everything to be grateful to you for," said Meb, kissing her. "And I probably would have done the same if it had been the other way around. Now, let's get you some food."

Neve ate, very little, but she ate. But one-handed, as the one skinny little claw hand held onto Meb. And Meb knew that the mending had started.

Now all she had to do was get the two of them out of here, which was going to be more complicated than just going missing during a hunting ride, which had been her half-formed plan up to now.

It did have one positive effect. Meb was so absorbed in thinking about it that she forgot to be afraid. She decided there was no point in trying to go through the motions with the bower—they knew who she was, and what she was, by now. Instead she went to the stables, something ladies did not do. The expression of the stable hands would have told her that, if she hadn't known already. "The horse I rode."

"Yes, Lady Anghared," said the chief groom, who had hastily swept up to see what she wanted. He had looked very wary before the mare was mentioned. "Leia. Um. a good bloodline."

"Can I see her?" asked Meb.

"Um. Yes...she's got an unchancy temper." The groom looked as if his own entrails might melt out of pure terror.

"She was lovely to ride," said Meb. "Who was kind enough to suggest her for me?"

"The...the p-p-prince's groom."

But you all knew, thought Meb. They'd arrived at the stall. And the mare rolled a liquid eye at her, and whickered softly and pushed her nose at Meb. Meb stroked it instinctively. "I wish I had an apple for you," she said, putting her cheek against the side of the nose, horsey whiskers tickling her neck.

And of course, she then had one. She just wished, earnestly, that she really understood this and could do it with intent—but that wish was not granted. And it was only right that she took a bite of the apple first. It was real food, not old castle food. The mare thought so too.

The chief groom shook his head in amazement. "They said you were a good rider, lady. Not that you were the Horse God-dess herself." Obviously she had stepped up several leagues in his esteem. "If you need anything of us, my lady, you just say."

There was a murmur of assent from around the stable. "Just look after her," said Meb. She couldn't ask them for what she'd need. Horses, and a way out of here. But...step by step. "You could show me how you put the tack on properly. I have never learned."

If she'd wanted to be shown how to fork dung they'd have shown her, even if she was supposed to be a lady. When she left the stable, she was floating on a sea of goodwill and feeling oddly happier than she'd felt since parting from Fionn and Díleas. Horses were not as clever as dogs, or certainly not as clever as Díleas—but they had some of the same kind of trust for humans.

Of course it was all too good to last. She had horsehair on her dress, her hair less than well ordered, and she found Lady Vivien waiting for her, worry written all over her face. "Anghared. You look a fright. You mustn't go to the stables. You mustn't wander around without an escort. The women are in an uproar about it."

Meb wondered if now was the right time to challenge Vivien about being a spy for Aberinn. She decided she just couldn't face dealing with it right now. "What does it matter? They don't like me anyway. They won't like me, and won't accept me."

"They're saying you must be some kind of lowborn imposter."

"Well, I am, I think. I'm not what they thought I was, anyway. And the minute I can get out of here, I will leave. I know...I promised to help Lyonesse, but I can't do anything here. There must be somewhere else I could go."

Vivien shook her head. "Anghared!" she sighed. "Yes, there are some fortresses to the north, and down to the south where Earl Alois still has some following. But, well, they are leagues away. You can't just 'go.' Even the regent's messengers go with an armed escort of twenty men. There are the tail ends of armies out there. You can't feed yourself and there is nowhere safe or dry to sleep. And anyway, judging by the talk, they're more likely to throw you in a cell and question you than to let you go. You have to try to fit in, and you have to show them your power."

"That will probably make them want to kill me instead," said Meb crossly. As if they hadn't been trying to do that already. It was obviously no use asking Vivien for help in escaping. "I'll wash and change, and come and smile and try to be nice. And tell them I had left something in a saddlebag, and as I don't have a tirewoman to send, I went myself."

The queen of the Shadow Hall peered in puzzlement and anger at her glass. Not only had Dun Tagoll withstood the evil eye, but they were thinning the ice bridge. She'd worked hard, feeding pieces of the dead to her cauldron, mixing, blending and making her creatures. Filling their minds with her orders and sending them out. Spreading the fear of treachery across Lyonesse. She'd been able to preempt the false, treacherous Aberinn, because she'd known the patterns of the Changer. Known that the Ways between would open when next the mage used the ancient device in the tower. He did not understand it fully. His strength lay in protecting, cloaking and hiding. Who would have thought he could turn that against her skills? Of course he did have the legacy of the devices and the books in the tower.

She had the cauldron, her muryan slaves and the vision. He could stop her looking at Dun Tagoll, but that was the limit of his power. She sighed to herself. She'd fought this war for such a long time now, she would not let a little check stop her. There was work to do, the cauldron to be fed. The muryans brought a constant stream of material for it. She'd been getting behind, and some of it was quite ripe. Of course, when the muryans brought it in, some of it was overripe already.

═ Chapter 13 ═

IT WAS INEVITABLE, FIONN THOUGHT, THAT THEY DIDN'T MEET just one Fomoirian, but a good fifty of them, All waiting as they came out of the mouth of a defile, so there was no avoiding them. And they were in a filthy, fight-picking mood. In other words, their normal selves.

"What are you doing here?" their leader demanded. A number of them, Fionn noted, were walking wounded.

Fionn stared at him as if he was a large salad at a carnivore dinner. "It's more like what are you doing here? Here of all places."

"Why shouldn't we be? It's our hunting territory," said the burly, misshapen leader, scratching his vast paunch.

"Where have you been?"

"Killing Tuatha Dé children with the magic-stealers. But they've melted the south bridge, and the priests say they can't find the cold to send out."

"Ah. That explains it. Part of the sky is going to come down," said Fionn, pointing at the dark water above their torch flares. He got suitable expressions of terror from the Fomoire. It had happened, occasionally. "They've drawn too much cold out. It got too warm in here, and that's making the sky fall. I'm supposed to be looking for fires. You better put those out."

"But . . . it'll be darker than the inside of a whale's belly if we do."

"It'll be wetter than one if you don't," said Fionn. "Keep one lit, and head out for somewhere higher."

"And you?" demanded one of the warriors. He was quite well

made for a Fomoirian. Could almost have passed for a large, pallid man with very big ears and horns.

"I can see in the dark. Been sent by my clan chief to smell out fire. So that's what I'll do." And he walked on past them, aware that his neck piece was twitching. The dog was behaving as if it was going to sneeze.

"Who is your clan chief?" demanded one of Fomoire.

"Balor." There were always at least twenty Balors in the evil-eye clans. And they had the most power and the most respect as a result of the status of the evil eye.

"Huh. The Tuatha Dé children taught you lot a lesson, didn't they?"

Fionn could only hope they had. The evil eye gave him a headache, which of course was nothing to what it did to creatures less robustly built than dragons. The dog wouldn't survive it, even if it was about to sneeze in his ear. "Yeah. But we'll make them pay," Fionn grunted and walked on. Fomoire were, because of where they lived and because bathing was not a cultural practice they'd ever been that keen on, always a smelly bunch. But this lot had a real taint to them. Dead meat. Rather like that giant.

"I don't think he is what he claims to be," said the fellow with the horns.

Most of them had been good little Fomoire and put out the torches. Fionn helped the surviving two to go out, and loped off.

They wouldn't manage to find him. But word would get around. That would cause panic. The Fomoire had retreated here to be safe from the cheerful genocide of their successor people. They had made repeated attempts to take their old lands back, in the earlier days anyway, secure in the knowledge that they had a place which was safe. Which could not be reached, let alone invaded, by others. It had meant that they didn't even have to try to get on with their neighbors. It also meant no one could get away, and they had to live with their own fire smoke and mistakes. The place didn't even have decent beer. Fionn hoped that the dog was leading them out of Mag Mell, and soon. They'd been walking in this direction for several hours now.

And then, abruptly, the dog sat up and barked in his ear. Fionn looked around. It was pitchy dark of course, but planomancer dragon eyes could still see a little. They were alone, in the darkness.

The dog nosed at his face.

"What do you want?"

Díleas jumped down and began walking...back. He turned around and gave his little "come along" bark.

Fionn wanted to sit down, put his head in his hands and use some very descriptive terms in several long-forgotten languages. "We just came from there," he said between gritted teeth. "Look. I followed you, principally because I didn't want you to get hurt. You're important to her, and one place is much the same as the next for starting a search. I'll spot her magic easily enough. When you started taking me through gateways between worlds that I didn't even know existed, instead of the usual transitions, *and* you brought me to the Celtic cycle...well, I assumed you had some way of knowing where she was, just as the shepherd's kidnapped dog found its way home. I'd heard of lost dogs tracking people who had moved before, but this is insanity. This is the second time you've just changed direction. Do you have any idea where you're going?"

"Hrf."

"Two barks for yes. One bark for no."

"Hrf. Hrf." A pause. "Hrf."

Fionn closed his eyes. "That's either 'yes and no' or 'maybe' or just me imagining things. Well, the only way I know out of here is a good two weeks' walk away...so is it back the way we came?"

"Hrf hrf."

So they began the long walk. That was one of the major drawbacks, as far as Fionn was concerned, of Mag Mell. The land beneath the waves had a magical "roof" a mere ten cubits up, which made dragon flight impossible there. It was shank's pony or nothing. Anyway, he had the dog to look after. He needed to see how he could fly with it.

Fionn was careful to avoid Fomoire. It was easier, because night had fallen above the water, and even in the shallows there was little ambient light. Smoke drifted up here and was trapped, polluting their best lands. One could, to some extent, understand why the Fomoirians were such a charming bunch, even if it was partly self-inflicted injury.

Fionn was glad the dog knew where to find the way out, because there were absolutely no marks on this side. Just gravel that had once been seabed and dead scallop shells in the water-filtered moonlight. Díleas jumped down and danced around him on his hind legs. So Fionn reached down and picked him up and held him above his head. Díleas jumped through the "roof" of dapples. Fionn, determined not to lose him again, used all his strength to jump up and follow. It was pretty much, Fionn decided, exactly where they'd entered Fomoire lands, only it was not dark out here, but late afternoon instead. Well, time ran at variable speeds in these planes. Fionn and Díleas swam back to the beach. The rocks provided some fresh oysters, and a driftwood fire dried them, and while Díleas did not deign to dine on raw oysters, he did eat them cooked; a small, slightly brackish trickle provided their drink. It wasn't ale and a good roast dinner, but Fionn was tired, and tomorrow would have to provide those.

They were woken in the morning by cockle pickers. Fionn had time, barely, thanks to Díleas's warning growl, to assume a human form. By the reaction of the cockle pickers he might have been wiser to let them confront a just-awakened dragon. It didn't help that one of the cockle pickers threatened to beat Fionn for poaching and trespassing, so Díleas bit him. Matters only went downhill from there, as there was a small army of cockle pickers arriving. And the terrain of low-sand hills and marrams did not lend itself to running away.

"Look, I'll go along with you to your lord. Just don't lay a hand on my dog." It was usually easier to talk his way out of situations than to fight or to run.

"He bit me," said the aggrieved cockle picker, carefully not coming close enough for Díleas to have a second try. "He'll have to be killed."

"No," said Fionn, patting Díleas, who was working on giving the cockle pickers the intimidating eye, as he had seen the other sheepdogs do to the sheep. It seemed to be working on cockle pickers too. "He should be fine," said Fionn. "I don't think he ate enough of you to poison him. Dogs have tough constitutions."

Fortunately—in a way—for both parties, an overseer came riding along to see why they weren't at work. He defused the riot by escorting Fionn and Díleas back to the lord's manor and promising his master's retribution.

Their overlord was faintly puzzled at the demands for summary justice. "How many bags of cockles did you catch the varlet with, Velas?"

"None, milord. He was trespassing in the bay, though," said the overseer.

The lordling turned to Fionn. "Well? Don't pretend you didn't know that it's my land and my rights. Where are you from?"

"Well, my ship was from Dun Arros, but it's sunk now. So I am from nowhere, I'd reckon," said Fionn slowly, as if this much speech was a chore.

"Your ship?" asked the local lord.

"Aye. She ran onto the sands last night. The dog mostly hauled me ashore, led me out. Was not my idea to trespass, milord. Just to stay afloat."

"You mean you were shipwrecked?" The local lord was sharp for an aristocrat, Fionn had to admit. Only had to be told twice, and not the usual three or four times.

"Aye, look at my clothes, all salt-stained," said Fionn, doing it for the third time anyway, just in case. "We ran onto the sand and tore her keel off. Lost her masts . . . She was heavy laden, poor old thing."

"Where?" demanded the local lord, a predatory light in his porky eye.

"Out in the bay. I reckon that bunch of corpse ravens are all over her by now. Fine woolens she was carrying. That's why they wanted to be rid of you," he said, jerking a thumb at the overseer, who had been unwise enough to hurry Fionn along with his whip.

"Wreck rights are a lord's rights!" said the noble, his jowls quivering at the indignity of it all.

"You had better go and claim them then," said Fionn laconically, and sat down and put his head between his knees.

"Velas! Get what men you can. Damn this levy for the war. We need to get down there before they steal me blind. What's wrong with this man?"

"I'd guess he's half-drowned, milord. I think he's faint," said the overseer, shaking Fionn. Díleas snarled at him.

"Well, leave him. Let's get down to the beach."

And in a flurry of shouting and yelling, they did. Before the dust had settled, Fionn got up, walked to the kitchen. "Your master said to feed the dog and me," he cheerfully told the cook.

Well breakfasted, they were on their way a short while later. Fionn wished the cockle pickers and their masters the best of a miserable morning, and walked really fast. It would take the local lordling a few hours to establish he'd been gulled, but he was not going to be very pleased when he failed to find the wreck, or the sailor.

"The question is, Díleas, where we should go now? And don't suggest 'back.' I think 'back' is going to be a bad idea for some years," said Fionn as they stopped to take a breather at the top of a hill a few miles from the bay. "You appear to have an instinctive idea, which I've been following. But I am reaching a few conclusions after a bit of thought about this. If she went back to where she once came from . . . well, that would fit with the Celtic cycle. Anghared was her name, and that could be from anywhere, with Annvn, Carmarthen, Abalach, and possibly Lyonesse being the more likely places. And she has the ability to stir things up around her, and to be in the very center of all sorts of trouble, and yet she's shifted from place to place. So right now my bet—if I was a gambler, which I am not, as I only bet on certainties, except where I am wrong about innate sheep-herding ability—is Lyonesse. On the other hand, your sense of direction indicates that either she is moving, or her world is, and as the latter is impossible, perhaps she is with an army that is moving? Or maybe some more of those travelers are with her."

He prodded Díleas with his toe. "Of course, I am open to your canine guidance."

The dog yawned, rolled onto his back, and exposed his belly.

"That's either a statement of trust or an invitation to scratch you. I think I should have investigated those travelers more closely. At least they would have been able to answer my questions," said Fionn, obliging Díleas with a scratch.

— Chapter 14 —

THE ONE POSITIVE THING WAS THAT NEVE, NOW THAT SHE'D started eating, recovered very rapidly indeed. It wasn't her body that had needed to heal. The other advantage was that Meb, having decided that she was going to leave Dun Tagoll, knew now that her purgatory was temporary. She smiled mechanically at the jibes and ignored them. She found there were several women in the bower who were mere general servants and she took one with her to visit Neve, or to take some air in the courtyard. They didn't like going with her, of course. But they didn't have to like it. Just be there. Ideally, Meb decided, between her and any cover an archer could shoot from. She did discover one odd thing. They all skirted the rock basin and its little weedy patch of wall. It was obviously a local shrine or something.

She had more important things to do than worry about that. She had to work out a way to escape from the castle for the two of them. And that was proving difficult, especially as she couldn't discuss it with anyone.

Vivien, in the meantime, kept pressing her to show the bower her magical power. Somehow Meb felt that would be a very poor idea. "It comes when I need it. Not when I want it," she explained. And that was partially true too.

Lady Cardun folded her hands in her lap and shook her head. "I don't know. She just does not say much, Medraut. And she's either a very good mimic or she was leading her maid on. She

131

Dave Freer

makes faux pas, she hobnobs with the servants, she wanders about without any chaperonage. Yet...she does some things in a manner well-bred. I'd suspect she was raised in a noble household. The daughter of a favored woman, maybe."

Medraut tugged his beard. "I think she may be cleverer than we suspected. Look, it turned out that she could ride. To ride that well...she must have had a great deal of practice. I know you said she was stiff and sore the next day, but that is still possible, if she had not ridden for some time. She claimed never to have ridden a horse. And she's been very close to Vivien. We know she reports to the mage." He sucked his teeth. "Having her fall from a horse or become sick and die would remove her from the situation. That was my thinking. Yet Aberinn appeared genuinely angry and distrustful of her. And she's immensely popular with the men-at-arms for some reason. To act openly to get rid of her would be foolish until I have more information, I think.

"There are those who believe she made the queen's window reappear. But the more I think of it, the more certain I become that the entire scene with Alois was contrived. It was Aberinn's doing. They may have fallen out since. I have spies in the south, still. We may hear something."

"Her maid is recovering. She has returned to work. She will tell us what we need to know," said Lady Cardun confidently.

"It would seem to me that she's guessed that the maid is a spy." The prince pursed his lips. "I may have to trump something up, to at least put her to the question."

"You cannot deceive me, Vivien."

The eyes bored into her. She wished the mage was wrong, just this once. "I've told you," she said, wringing her hands. "She did the embroidery as no mortal could. It's *sídhe* work. It's some kind of glamor. Some kind of deception, but I don't think she knows she's doing it. It's not like our magic at all."

Vivien hated this. Hated being in the tower. Hated being given orders. Hated reporting to the mage. Hated his touch. But she was trapped here. Trapped by chains of fear and her children. Trapped by the shreds of hope. Hope that had breathed in her when she'd seen that spatha-blade axe. She'd thought Aberinn would be pleased at the time. It would spell the end for Prince Medraut and his pretensions.

Aberinn rolled his eyes. "There is no secret magic. There is no unknown magic."

"I've tried to get her to use her magic again, so you could trace it. So you could see," said Vivien.

"She probably can't. There are ways around the protection on Dun Tagoll. But it is self-healing. Such tricks will work only once."

He toyed with the models on his workbench. The interior of the royal chambers, perfect in every detail. He was building a model bedchamber. The shape of the chest showed that to be that poor child's room...she looked away, at anything else. A miniature of an Angevin crossbow, a tiny thread on the arrow, a trebuchet... she had been taught some of the theory behind symbolic magic and scalar spells. The magic of Lyonesse had, especially among the males, always been tied to mechanical symbols. But she had no idea of how the compulsion on her worked or how to break it. She stood, silently. Waiting for the orders. Finally, she could endure no longer. "Maybe she is the one you prophesied. Maybe she really is the Defender."

Aberinn snorted. "That she cannot possibly be. She may even be less than human, as you suggest. But put one idea from your mind. She is not this 'Defender.'"

"But how do you know?" asked Vivien.

He laughed. "She is the third fraud we've had. And soon she too will be dead. Now go."

He walked away to the piece of bench with the symbols and careful patterning as she turned away. She knew, from her training as a child, what some of those symbols were. She wished she dared stay and make it permanent. But he would have his protections. And she had her children, hostages to fate.

The mage had cheated death for so long by being one with the dead for most of the day and night. She'd recognized the symbols, even before she'd seen him lying there, unbreathing.

Weeping to herself, she fled the tower.

From its cage the gilded crow watched her with a jewel eye.

Meb sat in her room as Neve brushed her long, wavy hair. Hair that at least was like the hair of the locals...she felt the dragon neckpiece of the dvergar gold, heavy, magical and yet invisible, its links cunning and perfect, full of what magic the dvergar had been able to bind into it, designed to enhance her own power, designed to draw on the magics of wood, fire, gold, earth...She must still have some of the courage of the centaurs' windsack about her...centaurs? Maybe that was why the horse had liked her? What was it that the dvergar had said about the piece of magical enhancement she wore about her neck? It would help her to be what she wished to be. Well, at one stage she'd wished to be dead, and it had nearly helped her there! Only she'd changed her mind. It had helped her, and Fionn, to travel unseen and unsuspected into Albar, she was sure.

So could it help her to get out of here? Just how would her master have done it? Besides outrageously? Well, maybe that would have to work.

"Is it a full moon tonight?" she asked.

"Yes, m'lady." Nothing Meb had done or said had ever been able to shake Neve from calling Meb that. Not even discussing gutting and gilling techniques.

"So tonight will be the night for the Changer?"

"Yes, m'lady. The Fomoire will have their ice melt under them," said Neve with grim satisfaction. "Except those ones already ravaging the country. They kill just because they can."

"I hope the next change is something better."

"Can't hardly be any worse, m'lady," said Neve.

Finn would have said that that was a sure guarantee that it would be.

He would also have walked into the stables and demanded that they saddle a horse for him and Neve. Meb didn't think she'd quite get away with that. But a little glamor...If the alvar could do it..."How do I look?" she asked, thinking of Hallgerd, dressed in her best go-to-market-in-Tarport clothes.

Neve dropped the brush. Backed away, fright on her face. "M'lady?" Her voice quivered tremulously.

"It's just me," said Meb, wondering if her appearance would stay like that. It didn't, it appeared. Neve hugged her. "Oh, m'lady. I'm sorry. I...I just got such a fright. There was this wicked old crone here. An old fishwife..."

"It was me. I just took on a seeming."

Neve shuddered.

"Tomorrow we will use it to leave," said Meb. "Or as soon as some ordinary women walk out of here. They must, sometimes."

"Once the troop rides out to clear out any last foes, m'lady.

Could be a week or two. But the Fomoire will know something is wrong quick when their ice bridge goes. Then, usually after the men have gone, the kitchen women go out and collect rock samphire and birds' eggs on the cliffs with a couple of guardsmen."

"Excellent. Once we're among the cliffs and rocks we can slip away."

"Yes ... but ... those are the kitchen drabs," said Neve. "And you're ..."

"A fishing village brat. Like you. How did you end up in the bower?"

Neve blushed. "My granny was a bower woman in the old king's court. Not to say anything, but my mother was born something like seven months after the wedding, which happened soon enough after she left service with a fine gift. She must have taken the fancy of one of the lords here, because it was enough to buy a house and boat and a cow, and to keep a bit for spoiling us. The Lady Cardun, she remembered my gamma. Took me for the bower. Didn't take her long to find out that I didn't know much, though."

"Well, at least you know who your mother was. Which is more than I do. Or my father," said Meb. "Anyway. A seeming is easier with some props. Can we get some baskets?"

"Easy," said Neve. "They're hung in the corner of the kitchens. But, m'lady. I'm quite scared. And it won't be safe for you out there ..."

"I could probably look like a dragon, as easily as a fishwife."

Neve squeaked at the thought.

It was hard to sleep that night, and then when she did finally get to sleep, Meb woke abruptly again. It was ... different. The last time the air had held the smell she'd come to realize was Fomoire. This ... this was a melange of new scents. Just hints of them, as if carried by errant breezes from faraway places. Some were of forest, mushroomy and moist, some of gorse flowers, and some of Tarport on a hot day.

It wasn't all pleasant, but it was a lot sweeter than the Ways to the Fomoire had smelled. She slept well now, for the first time in weeks. She had such sweet dreams too, dreams that involved her kissing Fionn and didn't, in a rather confused fashion, entirely stop there, so that being wakened was anything but welcome.

Neve was too full of the news to even wait until Meb's eyes were properly open. "Oh, m'lady! The Changer. Something is wrong. It didn't work properly. The mage is up and in a rage. The prince is going to ride out with his troop soon to try and work out which of the Ways are open."

"And somehow it will all be my fault," said Meb. "We'd better go, and quickly."

She'd tried to think, last night, just how she could take the axe with them. Could she tell it to look like a stick? Could she rely on summonsing it again? She rather wanted it with her. She tried making it look like something else. An old stick.

It seemed to work, at least while she was holding it. Put it down, and it reverted to being an axe.

"M'lady! You can't take that!" said Neve, shocked, seeing her pick it up.

"But it's just the thing for cutting rock samphire," said Meb, swinging it about. "Anyway, it changes appearance with me. Look."

They made their way down through the passages of the castle. No one questioned the old woman, with her stick and one of the castle maids. Collecting two baskets from outside the back of the kitchen where Neve had stashed them, they walked down to the great gate, to sit and wait in the sun on a mounting block.

"The other women will be along presently. They were talking about it last night," said Neve.

"And best we got down here early. Mage Aberinn will be sending for me again," said Meb. "And somehow it's always someone else's fault. I'll be glad to be out of here."

"But... m'lady. Just where are we going to go? What are we going to do?" asked Neve.

And then Prince Medraut and his troop rode up, and saved Meb from answering something she had no idea of the answer to. Because things went badly awry, just about immediately. Medraut didn't recognize her. But he did recognize Neve. "You. Wench. Where's that mistress of yours?" he demanded, jigging his horse up closer, reaching down and raising her chin with his whip.

She dropped onto her knees. "P-please, your Highness Prince, I don't know. I just got told to go and collect samphire this morning."

"By whom? Your mistress?" demanded Medraut.

"N-no. Lady Cardun sent me to the kitchen. I'm not to work in the bower anymore."

The whip slashed at her unprotected face, and Neve screamed as it cut her cheek. "Don't lie to me. I spoke to Cardun not two minutes back. She said she had no idea where you were." He raised the whip again.

"Stop it," said Meb, standing in front of her. "Don't you dare hit her!"

The whip halted. Prince Medraut stared. "So that's where you've got to."

Meb realized she'd stopped concentrating on the glamor. She was no alvar, able to just to set a glamor in place and have it stay in place.

"Yes. I am leaving," said Meb.

"No one leaves Dun Tagoll without my permission," said Medraut. "Aberinn is blaming the latest disaster on you."

"Everything that goes wrong is my fault," said Meb. "What has he done this time? Just so I know what my fault is supposed to be, so I can be very sorry for it." She was seethingly angry now.

"We are not in the right place to intersect to the Ways," said Medraut, tersely. "Some form of sabotage is suspected. And you are the stranger in our midst, Anghared, as you call yourself."

Meb sighed artistically. "He got it wrong, and now it's my fault again. I think he is going senile. Or your machine is not right. It's the second time it has been wrong, and it has nothing whatever to do with me. Maybe he just needs a little more effort or more power. Magic is like that."

Medraut looked at her strangely. "You came here, and were granted a place for appearing to have performed a major magic. Yet...you don't seem to me to understand the rudiments of magic. It can't be wrong, young woman. The very rules of sympathetic magic are scalar relationships. They are very precise. One grain of weight becomes seven or seventy-seven or seven hundred and seventy-seven. One hair width is multiplied by precisely the same measurements. Not somehow some arbitrary number! Magic would be chaos then!"

His eyes narrowed. "You've claimed to be a worker of magic, but yet you do not appear to know the very most basic principles. What is the law of contagion?"

"If you get sick it spreads?" said Meb, who honestly had no idea.

The prince rolled his eyes. "How were we ever fooled by you, woman? I was shaken, I suppose, by Alois. But even the newest of adepts learns the principles of 'once together, always together.' You claim to be a summonser and do not understand how the basis of it works. Lady Cardun was right: you are simply a fraud."

"I never claimed to be anything," said Meb. "You all said I was. And anyway that's not how summonsing works. If I need it and want it badly enough, and can imagine it clearly...it comes."

That provoked scornful laughter from the prince. "Yes, that is how the commons think it works. Well, you've had a good time imagining you can live as your betters do. And I'll be first to admit, you were a quick imitator. Well, you seem to have a taste for the neyfs and kitchen trulls, by all reports. You will make an excellent one. But first you can have some time at the posts and a good whipping. Afterwards I will be back to ask some questions and finally get some straight answers." He gestured to one of his bodyguards. "Methgin. Take the two of them to the posts. And you, Captain, get them to open that gate so we can go and try to establish just what sort of mess we have to deal with this time."

The gate swung open and the press of horses rode out. For a mad moment, Meb thought of trying to run with them.

But Methgin was in the way and she still had Neve with her, and besides, they would have to cross the causeway single file... there was no point in even trying to run.

Methgin grabbed Neve roughly with one hand and then reached to twitch Meb's "stick" from her with the other, plainly thinking two women no match for his burly frame.

"Haaaa!" he screamed. Fortunately there was still a lot of noise outside. He let go of Neve and clutched his partially severed finger. And found himself staring at the bloody edge of the spatha-axe he had just grabbed. "I think," hissed Meb, "that I am going to cut you in half right now. I forgot I had my axe with me or I would have cut your prince in half. Neve. Take that sword of his, and his knife. We're going to walk out of that gate. And if you try anything, Methgin, I'll kill you."

He was a braver man than many. "Where...where did the axe come from?"

"Magic. Real magic," said Meb. "Not your feeble magic. It's an alvar axe. It'll cut through that armor of yours like thin parchment. You've felt how sharp it is."

The three of them walked out past the gate...which swung closed behind them. The last of the troop of horses was still about thirty yards away, waiting their turn to ride the narrow causeway path over to the main cape.

Meb was wondering just what to do, and what to do with the prisoner when Neve solved part of her problem for her. She hit him really hard, two-handed, with the back of his own sword on the back of his head, just below the helmet. Neve was not a large woman, and she'd been sick and was weakened by that. She made up for it in fury. The big man fell like a poleaxed steer. Neve kicked him. "And that's for trying to kill my lady. He was about to call out, or try something, m'lady. I could see his shoulders tense. What do we do now?"

They were just outside the gate, with two baskets, an unconscious bodyguard and an axe. There were guards on the gate towers, but presumably, as no one had yelled out, they were watching the horsemen on the causeway. There was no way that Meb and Neve could get across that causeway unseen, though. "Let's just walk along the wall. There might be somewhere we can sit down until dark or something."

"There's the cave..." said Neve, doubtfully, "but surely they'd look there?"

"It's better than standing here."

So they walked slowly and calmly along the narrow track directly below the castle wall, along to the seaward side, where the peninsula sloped into the water. Then down over some rough ground and a few scraps of half-rotten shale and down onto the sea shelf. As they walked along this, Meb was trying hard to project "you can't see us" thoughts at the ramparts above.

The sea raced and fumed into the dark, steep-sided zawn. Above was just cliff, now, and above that...

"That's the queen's window up there," said Neve. "Poor dear. They were some who said he pushed her rather than that she jumped. I don't believe it myself, because they say he was a broken man afterwards. Never went to bed anything but dead drunk ever again for the rest of his days. He had lost both his son and heir and her."

"We'd better get down in the gully before someone spots us from it," said Meb. It was a long fall from that window.

And the water looked deep and cold, and laced with rocks.

"There are bats in the cave, m'lady," said Neve, wrinkling her nose in distaste, as they advanced towards the point where the cliff on both this and the foreland overhung, to join in a dark hole where the water surged and gurgled inward. They must be under the edge of the causeway now. Someday the hungry sea would eat through here and make an arch, and then collapse the causeway. Right now it offered a dark refuge, if a smelly one. But part of Meb's apprenticeship with the gleeman-dragon didn't like it. "It's the place anyone would hide. They'll look there."

Neve shook her head. "They say there are knockers down there. It's a place that the haerthmen, let alone neyfs, won't venture, not without ten of them, and then if they hear a squeak, they'll run. I wouldn't go down there myself, except with you!"

Meb wasn't sure what a knocker was, but it was a heavy load to bear. "What's a knocker?" she asked as they walked forward into the ammoniacal gloom.

"They live underground..."

Her voice died as they came face to face with the current occupants of the sea-grotto.

Not all of the Fomoire had escaped or been drowned. A few of them had been left behind. The five broad, huge, shaggy men with their long iron swords came running, whooping, for the bounty that had suddenly walked into their hiding place.

Meb swung the axe, trying to defend herself, as one of the others was throwing Neve down and tearing at her skirt. Meb had plainly forgotten to tell it not to look like a stick. The lead Fomoire warrior batted it away with his round whale-hide shield as he tried to both grab her and hold a sword.

The axe cut through the shield, through the arm and through the hide-coated body behind it, nearly jarring itself out of her hands. She wrenched it free of his body as the other Fomoire—the slower ones—turned and ran. The one who had been about to rape Neve rolled frantically away, as Meb's next clumsy axe stroke took the horn off his helmet and a slice off his buttocks. He rolled on and screamed and somehow rolled into a staggering run, diving into the churn of the water after his fellows.

Something behind them cheered and clapped. Meb turned to deal with whatever this new menace was.

High on the rock next to a fissure in the wall were a new crowd. They were not tall and aggressive...the biggest was only about two cubits high. There were half a dozen of them, though.

But the worst thing they were doing was to clap. So why was

Neve clinging to her, gibbering in fright, seeming even more terrified than when she was going to be raped?

"Nnn Na..." was all Neve managed to get out, pointing a quivering finger. Meb patted her, and tightened her grip on the axe.

The tallest of the shaggy-haired, bright-eyed dwarfish gang
bounced down. Bowed. "Ah. The Royal House of Lyonesse has
decided to pay us a visit," he said sardonically. "To what do we
owe this unexpected pleasure?"

Meb knew and had liked and got on with the dvergar back on
Tasmarin. These looked similar. "I had heard of the hospitality of
the knockers," she said, for that, she decided, was what they had
to be, "so we thought we'd find some refuge with them. Seeing
as we're being hunted."

"No orders? No commands? No demands for jewels?" asked
the hairy little man. He carried, Meb noted, a mattock rather
than a sword or axe.

"No. I have all the treasure I could desire," said Meb. "And
most people don't seem to listen when I give them orders."

The knocker chief grinned, teeth white in a dark face. "Eh. I
see the treasure. Dvergar work. Worth a good few kingdoms."

So he could see the necklace. No point in denying it then. She
nodded. "It's made of dragon gold, and has eyes of wood-opal,
made with the cunning and virtue of the dvergar. It was made
for me by Breshy, also sometimes called Dvalinn, at the order of
his father Motsognir."

The knocker nodded. "Names of powerful cousins. Not us. We're
just miners for silver and tin. And how did you make them give
you such a talisman? Or did you steal it from them?"

Meb looked at him crossly. "Breshy is nice, not like you. Anyway,
only a fool steals from the dvergar. It was a gift. I wished for him
some fish when he needed them. Finn said he would get them."

"Finn?"

"He...he's a dragon. Called Fionn sometimes." They were non-
humans themselves.

"A black dragon. We've not seen him for many centuries,"
said the knocker. "Nor any other dragons, mind you. Not a bad
thing. Fionn was something of a joker, but he usually paid for
what he took."

Meb's heart leapt just at a mention of the dragon. "He always
paid, just not always in the coin you expected," she said defensively.

That actually got a snort of laughter. "Sometimes in mayhem."

"That's . . . fair enough," admitted Meb. "What is your name, knocker?."

"Names are tricky things. But you can call me Jack."

The others seemed to find that funny. "And we're all Jack, too."

"I am called Meb," said Meb, thinking to not even start the Anghared business. "Now we need to hide or get away from here. Could you show us where to go?"

"Getting away from here at your size, by our ways, that could be a bit tricky," said the chief Jack, tugging his beard. "You'd be like a stopper in most of our tunnels. We could widen them, but it would take time. And the only human audits would not be taking you away from the castle. Mind you, the human tunnel would be a fair place to hide for now, at least in the entry to it. It's hidden from human eyes, it seems."

"That'll do. Thank you."

"Polite too," said the chief Jack. "Well, well. Come along then."

It was near low water, and they walked along a splashing path, part of which must be underwater at high tide. The knocker Jacks lit their lanterns and led them deeper into the grotto, to where the sea and the back wall came to join each other in a gurgling corner.

"Just to the side there," said the chief Jack.

Meb saw a small door, and beside it, a coracle.

"Where does it lead?" she asked.

"Where does what lead?" asked Neve, still clinging to her.

"The door," said Meb.

"What door?"

"That one," said Meb, pointing.

"But . . . that's just a rock."

"It's bespelled," said the chief Jack, chuckling. "Leads to the tide caves for the great machine above."

"Can we go in?" asked Meb.

"It's locked," said the knocker, shaking his head. "We can break it open, but that'd tell the mage. And we're banished from in there. It's part of the castle and we can't go there anymore. Will you set that to rights? It was ours before it was theirs."

"Um. How?" asked Meb.

"Now if we knew that, we'd be doing it ourselves," said the chief Jack. His smaller fellows bobbed their heads in agreement.

"But you could sit on the doorstep with the little round boat and be hidden with it."

"I still don't see the door," said Neve.

So Meb led her up to it.

"I can feel it . . . but not see it. It looks like you pushed my hand into a damp rock," said Neve, incredulously.

"There's a cockle shell of a coracle there too," said Meb. "Here. Come closer."

"Oh. I can see it now," said Neve, puzzled.

"'Tis because you're inside the illusion," said the chief Jack. "Anyone coming down here would not see you."

It was chilly, clammy and dark. And, Meb thought, quite difficult for anyone but Aberinn to find. This must be his bolt-hole. She looked at the coracle. "Could we use that to get across the gully?"

"At low water, probably," said the knocker.

"Well. Our thanks, again." Meb wished she had some kind of payment, some small gift to give them. Her time with the dvergar had taught her that that could pay handsome dividends. Well, the dvergar had loved to watch her juggle. And it would help to pass the time and keep her warm. "Would you like me to juggle for you? A small entertainment in thanks for your help?"

There was a moment's silence. Almost breathless. Then the chief Jack said: "Indeed," followed by a chorus of "Yes," and "Yes, yes!"

So Meb dug out her precious tasseled balls and lost herself in their rhythms. She made her strange audience gasp and she made them laugh and clap.

And then the chief Jack held up his hand. "They come."

In the silence Meb caught the sound of men's shuffling feet. "I swear I heard something down here," said a nervous voice.

"Maybe the rest of the Fomoire," said another, sounding no less nervous. "That one was barely cold. Not more than two hours dead, I'd reckon."

═ Chapter 15 ═

FIONN WAS BACK TO FOLLOWING THE DOG. IT WAS SOMETHING HE was used to doing by now. The trouble, in a way, was that the dog was intent on the straightest line to his goal. Fionn had a slightly wider world view, which included being able to see obstacles which they could not simply go through. Where it might be faster and easier to go around. Unfortunately, all he could work out about "where" was somewhere more or less directly in front of the dog, because the dog would follow a path or road . . . if it didn't deviate too much. Díleas was bright enough to know that straight was not always fast.

Obstacles, like meals and drinks, were Fionn's responsibility to deal with.

"I think we're going to need to try some flying, young dog. At night, perhaps. This country is as stirred up as a hornet's nest," said Fionn as they emerged from the ditch where they had just watched a troop of soldiers—and a troop of new-pressed recruits—pass. "If they'd been less noisy calling step, we might have walked into them and they'd probably have wanted me to join the army, which seems odd, because I have never wanted the army to join me. Also, I don't think they take dogs, and they were going the wrong way, and they'd object to my not going the wrong way with them. Sometimes it would be very convenient not have this inbuilt prohibition on taking intelligent life. Unfortunately, that is the way I am made."

Díleas nosed him behind the knee. He'd come to understand that by now. It meant "get a move on, that direction," in basic overintelligent sheepdog language.

So Fionn did. It involved some trespass in various fields, including one with a bull who felt quite strongly about trespassers. "Next time," said Fionn to Díleas, surveying the bull, who was now convinced the far corner of his paddock was very interesting and that if he ever saw a trespasser again, he would rapidly retreat to it, "Try not to run behind me when you've made the bull mad."

At length they spotted a huddle of buildings, and as the day was drawing to a close, Fionn informed Díleas that they had the prospects of supper and a basket. "If I can find a suitable one, we will try you on being a flying dog. I hope you do that better than you herd sheep."

The cluster of buildings proved to be a farmhouse, with a farmer's wife, three small children and another due all too soon, and a sheepdog. The sheepdog was less than pleased to see them. The farmer's wife was more than pleased to see a man, of any sort.

"My man's been taken for the army and I've yet to get the hay in," she said, "and there's two dozen sheep to be crutched and sheared still, and I've got the children to cope with. I see you have an eye dog there." Díleas was staring intently at the other sheepdog. Who was staring just as intently back.

"He's young yet," said Fionn. "I'll help with the hay, ma'am. You can get on with what needs be done here, if you'll feed me and the dog tonight. He'll only take food from my hand, and if I am taken for the army, as my lord wanted, well, he'll starve." It was too good a story not to reuse.

The woman nodded. "It's the paddock just behind the hedge. Tom had it scythed and drying. But do you think they'd give him another day to get in?" she spat. "Damn them and Lyonesse too. Now it'll rain for sure before I can get half of it stacked. What we'll do in winter for feed, I have no idea."

The field had a high surrounding hedge. And days of work, forking the hay into a handcart and gathering it to stack. Days for a man, anyway. Not quite that long for a dragon with talons that did a fair job as four outsize hayforks, and a tail that could wield the actual hayfork. "It'll ruin my reputation if this gets out," said Fionn to Díleas. "Why don't you watch to see if the farmer's wife—or anyone else likely to be alarmed by a dragon doing farm chores—is coming, and give me warning. It's that or collect hay in your mouth."

Díleas seemed to prefer keeping watch.

The job still took a good three hours. Fionn then thatched the rick in the only manner he knew, which was centuries old and cultures away. But it was a fair method for keeping the water off.

He then walked back to the house, with the hayfork, having thoughtfully thrust a few haystalks in his hair.

"You're not much of a sticker," said the farmer's wife. "Three hours' work and you'll be looking for me to feed you. There's still a good bit of daylight left."

"Well, I've done the hay, and I came to see what else you could use a hand with. Looks like the woodpile could use a bit of splitting."

"You've never raked up all the hay!" she said incredulously.

Fionn shrugged. "Come and have a look."

She did...obviously ready to exercise a shrewish tongue. And gaped at the field and the neat stacks with their plaited caps. "And stacked! Well...well, I'll be..."

Looking at her, Fionn was fairly sure she had been.

"I've never seen stacks like that," she said.

"Old custom in my parts. Holds the stack together and keeps the rain out as well."

"You've earned a good feed, shepherd. That lord of yours was daft to let them take you," she said.

"I'll split a cord or so of wood for you. That green wood needs to dry or those babies will get cold this winter."

Fionn enjoyed splitting wood, so it was not a chore for him. Also, he'd been aware of the fear, bordering on desperation, in her eyes, for all her brash talk. His Scrap had had something of the same feeling about her when he'd first met her, trying to rob him and nearly getting drowned. Perhaps it was a human thing.

The farmer's wife had plainly been feeling the isolation as well as the fear. She talked almost nonstop. Partially about the farm, but more about the war.

"I'd like to know," she said belligerently—a tired woman who had had a little more cider with supper than usual, seeing as she was feeling just a little better about winter and surviving—"just how this Mage Spathos knows when the Ways will open. You ask me...he's in with them. Letting our men be taken for slaves."

Fionn subtly found out a little more about Mage Spathos, who it appeared was driving war preparations and recruitment to fever pitch. He was based in Goteng, and lived very well.

Later that evening the farmer's wife indicated that there was other work the farmer wasn't doing.

Fionn had to wonder at his desire to get too closely involved with this species. Fortunately they weren't interfertile, even if other dragons had mixed with them. The thought of dragon-human crosses with the proclivities and abilities of both was quite alarming.

He left early the next morning, before cockcrow, with the deep hop-picking basket he had bought from her the night before. He left a little extra silver on the table, because winter would probably be harder and longer than she guessed, and having a baby seemed to be something humans found harder than dragons found laying fertile eggs.

A few miles down the road he came upon a placard nailed to a tree. Obviously they had some sort of rudimentary printing press now in Annvn. Fionn was all in favor of cultures learning to print. It meant more books, which he found entertaining, and it tended to make for a broader, more entertaining society in time.

He didn't approve of it being used to reproduce pictures of himself and Díleas, and offering a reward.

The farmer's wife could have earned a lot more than the paltry amount of silver he'd left her.

Paid by one Mage Spathos.

"It's time," said Fionn, removing it, "for us to experiment with flight and dogs. I suggest you climb into the basket, and I will try a short, low hop. Try to stay in the basket. Climbing out while we're flying will probably kill you, and I am trying to avoid that. Your mistress would get upset with me, and against all logic I am becoming fond of you myself."

They did a very short few hundred yards of quite hard work—wing muscles and magic and no thermals, keeping very low and slow, in which Díleas decided that sitting up in the basket was a bad idea and curling uncomfortably into the bottom was a better one.

The landing, where the basket touched ground first, spilled Díleas out into a somersault or three. The sheepdog did appear unhurt, but very unimpressed.

"Yes. All right. A slower landing and keeping the basket up. And stop looking at me like that. I've seen you do somersaults when chasing your own tail. I'm sorry, right? It's just going to be faster and safer. And I think putting some distance between here and us is called for. Now, exactly which direction are we going?"

Dìleas showed him with his nose.

"Well, it wants a half hour to sunrise. It'll be hard work, but fast. Into the basket again, young dog. We'll go a fair bit higher this time. And I'll take great care setting you down."

They took to the wing again. Fionn noticed a poacher fleeing the woods, dropping his pheasants. Too bad. He probably would talk and wouldn't be believed. And it was good to be above the world again, where a dragon belonged, watching the sun lip the far horizon.

They flew for less than half an hour, as Fionn wanted to set down in a good spot, where they could land unseen. And there was a town not half a league ahead, so Fionn picked a field and actually slowed to a hover before setting down the basket as light as thistledown.

Dìleas did not emerge from the basket. Fionn peered anxiously into it. Had he dropped the dog without knowing?

Dìleas was there. Shivering. Uncoiling from his tight ball slowly. "By the First . . . I had forgotten how sensitive to cold you mammals are. I was generating lots of heat, flying."

Fionn took the basket and the dog at a run to the edge of the woods. Dragon breath kindled a fire. He could even make rocks burn, if need be. He cradled Dìleas against his still-flight-hot body and in front of the fire. Gradually the dog emerged from his tight ball and stretched.

"I am sorry. It was more complicated than I realized. It's cold up there, and the basket lets the wind through. And you couldn't exactly tell me you were freezing."

Dìleas stuck out his tongue and licked Fionn on the dragon nose. They sat there. Then Dìleas got up, stretched, shook himself and did a little tentative bounce.

Never had a dragon been so glad to see a dog bark at him. "Yes. All right. We'll walk though. And I will change my appearance, which is harder work, as I am used to the Finn visage. Blond and a beard, and a little shorter and broader, I think."

Dìleas watched intently as Fionn's visage and appearance changed. "I know you're an eye dog, but this staring is quite disconcerting," said the new Fionn, tousling the dog's fur. It was a good thing, he thought, that it was so thick. It had probably stopped him from actually freezing up in the cool, thin air. Fionn would never have forgiven himself for that.

They walked on to a minor road, heading towards the town. A pair of bored soldiers were checking papers as people crossed a bridge, but as Fionn had heard them well before, he and Díleas were able to go around and swim the river. It was deep and fast, and fairly cold. Not, as Díleas's look informed him, anything like as cold as flying.

They dried off and then walked on. The town offered a chance to relieve a thief of some loot—a merchant who had thought to doctor his scales—and to use some of it to purchase some black hair dye, and a loaf of good bread, a sheepskin with the wool still on and a couple of fine blankets. It was amazing how easy it was to spend other people's money. And there were plenty of posters and several agents of the local military in plain clothes, looking for draft dodgers. They were rather obvious and inept at it, to someone of Fionn's experience, and so it was his pleasure to pick their pockets and acquire their papers.

Fionn was quite skilled at altering documents subtly.

He left the walled town cheerfully just after curfew, by means of a little private door from the house of ill repute. Some things are very predictable.

Díleas was very impressed with the sheepskin basket liner and the warm, thick blankets for sleeping on that night. Less so with the idea that they might be used to keep warm in flight. But he braved that again, somewhere the wrong side of midnight. They did not fly so long or so high, and Díleas was actually panting a little from heat when they landed, gently, to have another snooze before dawn. And walked on again...

There were more wanted posters.

These showed a blond man with a beard, and a black-and-white sheepdog. And a reward, payable by Mage Spathos.

Dead or alive.

═ Chapter 16 ═

THE KNOCKERS HAD ALL SLIPPED AWAY INTO A FISSURE IN THE rock, far too narrow for humans. Meb gripped the axe, and they waited. There was nowhere to run.

The search party from Dun Tagoll was twelve strong—and by the way they pressed together, swords out, lanterns held high, they felt they were still twenty too few.

They came on cautiously. Soon they were shining their lights onto Meb and Neve, sitting huddled, holding their breath...

And were not seeing them. "Well, we can get out of here," said their leader, relieved. "It wasn't to be thought they'd really still be here."

"But by the dead Fomoire and the blood trail to the sea, she must have come that far."

"Did you see what she did to that one? I'm glad we didn't find them. I don't care what anyone says, the prince made a mistake."

"Shut your face, Hwell," said another warningly as they began to walk away.

"I reckon that the Fomoire must have had a boat and taken them. It's a pity. She was a good lass, and that Neve was a game-some little kitty. I fancied her."

Neve snorted, but they did not hear.

A little later the knocker Jacks came back. "Ahem. Lady Meb," said the chief Jack. "We...we was wondering...if you'd mind doing a few more tricks for us? A couple of the younger ones will fetch the little ones. It would be something for them to see, I reckon. It's not entertainment that has come our way before."

Meb had seen Fionn work the crowd before. She smiled. "I'd love to. But look at poor Neve. She's so cold and hungry. I'll have to hold her to keep her warm. And I am so famished I might fall over if I tried. Besides, they might come looking for us again."

"We'll post a watch, and give plenty of warning. Anyway, the tide is coming in. They won't be able to get here without getting their feet wet, soon enough. Besides, we'll pelt them with rocks. Drop a piece of the roof on them. And we'll bring hot soup and hot food and hot apple wine and honey for you. And a good blanket of mink fur for the young lady."

Meb smiled. "Bring them."

She really enjoyed the next hour or so. She stretched herself a little too, performing a trick Fionn had done—but she'd no idea how he'd done. She cheated and did it magically—making the juggling balls glow as if lit internally by different-colored lanterns. The knockers—at her order—put out their lanterns, and watched, spellbound, the dance of the lights, as she made patterns in the darkness with them. She noticed, in the light of the balls, that Neve's face was every bit as delighted and rapt as the smallest knocker child.

"Ach, it's better than a piskie dance!" said the chief Jack, when she had finally stopped, lanterns had been lit again, and the clapping had stopped. "You'd best not tell them I said that, though. They're inclined to be spiteful."

A smaller Jack popped his head out of a fissure. "There are men coming along the sea trail. They got dogs a-smelling."

"Illusions won't hide us from dogs," said Meb, worried.

The chief Jack laughed. "But the water will. Tide's in enough. And so will we. Lend us your shoes . . . and we'll lead them there. If the dogs smell us and try and climb into our holes, it'll be the worse for them." The expression on his face said that the dog that tried to eat a knocker was going to regret it for the rest of his life.

"Try not to hurt their noses too much," said Meb.

"It's their ears we hurt. The little 'uns can let out a squeal that no man can hear, but it surely upsets the dogs."

They sat and waited in the darkness. Faintly they could hear the mournful baying of the dogs. And a yelping.

A little later the knockers came back, cheerful. "They're thinking you went into the water. And they're fair afraid because the dogs won't go more than under the first overhang."

"Still," said Meb, finding a very small knocker tugging at her skirts and looking hopefully up at her, and picking it up and putting it on her lap, "I think we'd better leave when we can."

The chief Jack shook his head, looking at the littlest knocker babe happily sitting on her lap. "Now they'll all be wanting to do it."

"One at a time they shall," said Meb, doing a single-handed toss for the small one. They had hours to darkness, and longer still to the low tide.

The chief Jack looked at her with what could only be respect. "You've the gift, to turn what is yours to command into a pleasure for us to give. We're long-lived and we don't have that many young ones."

"When I was very little, a gleeman sat me on his knee and did a few tricks. I never forgot it. How could I not do the same?" she paused. "And it was another gleeman who saved my life, who taught me to juggle. That gleeman was your black dragon."

"Aha. Well, he did a fine job," said the chief Jack. "Although, like most of the things he did, we'll be cursing for months as these young cloth-heads all make the tunnels and shafts echo with dropped pebbles and rocks that they'll be trying to juggle with."

By the time darkness and the low tide came, Meb was very tired of small knockers. She noticed Neve had gone from terror of them to cuddling and rocking the smaller ones to sleep. The coracle, never the largest of vessels, now had sufficient food for a few days: oatcakes, a small crock of honey, some dried meat, some dried apples, a metal flask of apple wine, a blanket sewed of mink strips and a knocker lantern, with a magical flame that came when you tapped three times on the metal, a couple of small bags—to knockers they would have been very big bags—and a very good supply of good will. They paddled out cautiously, edging between the rocks.

"Can you swim?" asked Meb.

"No, m'lady."

"Well, that's two of us then. We'd better not tip this up or our drowned bodies will wash up with the Fomoire after all."

"No, m'lady. The current will bring the bodies into Degin bay. Always does with those that drown around here," said Neve.

"That's so cheerful. Let's just paddle carefully."

"Yes, m'lady," said Neve, dutiful as ever. "The knockers are quite different from the stories, aren't they?"

"Some things are," said Meb, paddling. "But at least we know we can get food and shelter if I can find an audience who don't just decide to kill us first. And the knockers will help us and hide us if they can."

"So where are we going to go and what are we going to do, m'lady?" asked Neve.

"Well, I'd thought getting away from where they were trying to kill me—where they all hated me, spied on me and were willing to make you murder me—was a good start," said Meb, yawning. "We'll need someplace to rest later tonight, hide for the day, and then get a bit further away. Then we need to find some breeches, because it'll be hard enough for men traveling in these times. Then I thought we might go north, just because Prince Medraut's demesnes are east, and the South is where that earl who tried to kill me came from, the sea is to the west, and I know nothing about the north. Vivien said there are other Duns. We can find ourselves a better place than Dun Tagoll, even if it isn't as magically protected and fed."

"The north parts...it's wild, m'lady. Forest and mountain and forgotten people up there," said Neve warily. "I've never been there, of course."

"Wild and forgotten sound good to me right now. Mind that rock."

Despite their inept paddling of the loaded little vessel, they got across to the shingle on the far side of the narrow inlet without any mishap. They pulled it up, and at Meb's insistence, carried it to under the cliff, tripping over rocks in the darkness. They left it between two boulders and covered it in dried seaweed. It took time, but there was no point in telling some sharp-eyed guard, first thing in the morning, just where the prince's men should start looking with the dogs. It took more time to move around the cliff edge in the darkness, lit by a bare sliver of moonlight. They found a gully that took them up to the top. Then they made their way away from the coast, where the salt wind kept down the trees, to look for forest and shelter. At first they walked through the dew-wet grass, and then, with wet shoes, and wet clinging skirts and cold legs, through heather and gorse. Finally they came to a little V-shaped valley with a thick stand of trees and the gurgle of a stream.

"Enough," said Meb. "We're probably not more than a mile from Dun Tagoll, but I am so tired that I don't care if they catch us. Let's light the light, make a fire and try and dry our shoes a bit and eat something."

So they did. Meb had had her experience of living rough with Fionn to turn to...and poor Neve fell asleep, wet feet and all. The axe was better, Meb thought, for carving up anyone that tried to molest them than for cutting firewood. It didn't have much bevel on it. But there was some dry deadwood, and using the knocker lantern, and splinter to take flame from it, she managed a respectable fire. She ate some of the dried meat the knockers had provided—she had no idea whether it was dried miner or rabbit, and couldn't care right then—put their shoes to toast a safe distance from the fire and snuggled in next to Neve, blessing the knockers for the fur. Their skirts, however, were too cold and damp. She managed to remove Neve's and hers, and hung them on a branch near the fire. And tried lying down again, wrapping the fur around numb, cold legs and toes that she'd tried warming at the fire. The axe she kept in her hand.

And then sleep came.

She awoke to the sound of a rather nasty snigger.

There was something up the tree...with their skirts. A tiny blue-green-skinned man with a little tuft beard and narrow eyes all dancing with mischief. He was wearing nothing more than a hat of new leaves pinned with a hawthorn spike and a ragged cloak, so perhaps he didn't consider skirts as necessary.

Meb leapt up, axe in hand. "You drop those! Or I'll...I'll chop your tree down!"

"Ach. Mean and spiteful. Then I'll toss them in the stream. You'll be lucky to find them at all, and they'll be even wetter!" said the little green fellow, sticking his tongue out at them.

Bribery might work better. "You just woke me up suddenly. Come down and have some breakfast. We've got oatcakes and some honey."

"Oh, changing our tune, are we, fine ladies. Fine ladies without skirts," he said, wrinkling his pointy little nose at them, but coming down.

"It's a piskie...just like in Gamma stories," said Neve warily.

"Aye, and she had her skirts up or right off often enough, too," said the piskie. "Now you promised oatcakes and honey. We're fond of honey. Doesn't come our way too often, because bees are not fond of us."

"It's only a very little jar of honey," said Meb.

And in the distance—but not too great a distance—a horn sounded.

"What's that?" said Meb, relieving the piskie of her damp skirts. He wasn't worried by his nakedness, so she didn't see why she should be, although Neve stuck under the fur and struggled with hers.

"Just the soldiers from the Dun. They probably saw the smoke of your fire," said the piskie disinterestedly.

"We must find somewhere to hide," said Meb, looking around.

"But you offered me oatcakes and honey," said the piskie, sticking out his lower jaw, plainly angry, his little tuft of a beard wobbling, his cheeks flushing green.

"No time to find them now." said Meb, grabbing the little knocker bag. "If they don't catch us, you can have the whole jar as far as I am concerned."

"Now that's a bargain. Just you wait right here!" said the piskie, and let out a shrill whistle. Other whistles answered, and he bounded off, up into the tree.

"What do we do?" asked Neve nervously.

"Move. I haven't been through all of this to get caught without at least trying to get away," said Meb, pulling her to her feet.

"Ouch. Blisters," said Neve, hobbling.

Meb's own feet were not in a much better state. They'd been cold and numb the night before. Now the sun was up and it was looking to be a glorious spring day. "As far as those rocks. Let me see if I can manage some sort of glamor to hide us there." If she could look like Hallgerd, and make the axe look like a stick, surely she could make herself look like a rock.

And it seemed she could. There was a little niche and, with Neve inside it, Meb sat against her legs and thought rock thoughts. The axe she made into a flying holly sapling. So they sat, Meb wondering if this could possibly work, and thinking "don't see me" thoughts.

No riders came. She heard them in the distance, several times. What did come was a little naked blue-green man, in a green hat and a ragged cloak—with half a dozen of his kind, some male, some female, and all wearing little more than leaves or acorn-cap outfits.

"Ach, tricksie humans. Cheated me," said the piskie crossly. "She promised me a whole jar of honey."

"I don't cheat," said Meb.

Piskies vanished in the twinkling of an eye.

And then the little leaf hat reappeared, followed by the piskie wearing it. "You gave us a fright," he said crossly. "We trick humans. Not you trick us. Not unless you want us to curse you."

"I can hide better than you. Maybe I can curse better than you, too," said Meb.

That took a moment to sink in. "Ah. Well now, no offense, but if you can hide better than we can, why did the horsemen worry you?"

Meb did not say "because I didn't know I could, and I am not sure it would work on Neve." She had a feeling telling the piskies that would only lead to more trouble, and a fair amount of mischief directed at her companion. "Because I knew you could lead them astray better than I can. And last time the castle people came hunting... let's put it this way: I should have hidden from them the first time, because ever since Earl Alois tried to kill me, they've tried."

"Aye," said tufty beard proudly. "That we can. We're the best. They're so mazed they'll never be home before nightfall. Earl Alois, eh? He went through our woods a while back. We didn't know or we'd have made him so lost he never got home."

"A pity you didn't," said Meb as she dug through the bag and came up with the little crock of honey. "Here you are. As promised. We'll have our oatcakes without it."

"Ach," said the piskie generously. "I daresay we'll spare you a little."

So they broke their fast on little knocker oatcakes with a circle of largely naked—bar leaf and wood scraps—piskies. Meb reflected their food would last far less time than she'd thought, at this rate. On the other hand, not only had any form of pursuit failed to find them, the men of the troop would probably be blaming her, and far less keen to try again. For once, being blamed for something she hadn't done was going to work in her favor. That made a change.

After they'd eaten, lighter by some oatcakes and their honey,

Meb and Neve took their leave and hobbled on. After a little
while, Meb stopped and took her shoes off. "I'll try barefoot for
a bit, Neve. My heels and toes are raw."

"We'll look like poor peasants then, m'lady."

"Well, that'll be a good thing," said Meb.

And it was easier walking. Yes, it still hurt when the grass
touched raw flesh, but they came on a path quickly enough. All
of these lands must have been farmed—and probably still would
be, if Lyonesse stayed free of invaders for any time. The path must
have been a cart track once, between fields and hedges and forest
patches, all overgrown and beginning to show spring signs. It was
too early in the season for most food plants, but they gathered
asparagus shoots from the banks as they walked, and ate some of
them raw. It was a long day, and warm. "Oatcakes and asparagus
are not as fine as castle food, but they taste fresher," said Neve.

"That's because the castle food was mostly stale bread, bespelled
and stretched," said Meb. "And this might be simple, but it's real.
But by the look of the sky, food and shelter are going to be real
issues, and soon, too, not to mention piskies."

"You should never mention them," said the ugly pile of misshapen rock fallen from the lichen-cloaked drystone wall on the
corner. It stood up, and Neve tried to pull Meb into joining her
in running away.

"It's a spriggan! Run!" shrieked Neve.

The spriggan was growing before their eyes and was now considerably bigger than they were. It still looked like it had been
badly carved out of granite. "You run. I'll hold it back," Meb
said, swinging the axe.

"I can run faster than you," said the spriggan, showing square
teeth. "And your axe is not cold iron, but some faerie metal. 'Tis
sharp. Magic sharp, I'd grant."

"If you want to try it out, I'll help you," said Meb, looking it
in the eye. She couldn't think of what else to do, really.

"I thought I was going to help you," said the spriggan, shrink-
ing and changing before their eyes. Meb knew where she'd seen
that sort of triangular alvish grey face before—when she'd been
riding with the hunting party. They'd been watching her then.

"What are you planning to help us with?" asked Meb.

"Food and shelter were what you sought, I thought," said the
spriggan. "Shelter is easy enough. Food is a bit more difficult. Not

food for the likes of you, anyway. Simple fare is easy enough. But the noble ladies of Lyonesse wouldn't want to eat that."

"Given a choice, I would," said Meb. "I've had enough of fancy food that tasted of stale bread for my lifetime. Give me stale bread that tastes like stale bread and I'll be happy."

"Ah. Stale bread is a challenge. We've got fresh, but it'd take a few days to make it stale. But if that's what you want..."

"No, fresh is even better."

"Well, it'll make you sick, I shouldn't wonder," said the spriggan.

"They're dangerous, m'lady," said Neve timidly. "Spirits of old giants, so they do say."

"Spirits of the rocks and tors actually," said the spriggan. "And we're dangerous all right, but not to you. Sadly."

"The knockers and piskies did us no harm, Neve," said Meb reasonably. "You even had knocker babies on your lap."

"Probably piddled on you," said the spriggan with a kind of gloomy satisfaction. "They do."

"They were good little things," said Neve defensively. "Nice to me and m'lady."

"Ah, should have been suspicious then," said the spriggan. "I daresay they gave you food which turned your insides to wax or something."

"You're a grumpy so-and-so," said Meb.

"We have that reputation, yes. Now if you'll follow me, I think we've got a few rabbits and some wild onions in the pot. Won't agree with you, of course."

Meb shouldered the axe, stepped forward and took the rather surprised-looking spriggan by the arm. Grey-skinned and touched with lichens, he was still warm, she noticed. "Lead on. Come on, Neve. He won't eat us, or he would have, because there is another one at the start of the lane. We're between them."

The spriggan blinked. "My brother will give you a hand with the bags, if you like," he said, escorting her in as courtly a manner as any of the haerthmen of the prince's retinue.

They walked up the hill, to where the abandoned walled fields gave way to grazing lands and to the rocky tor at the top. Meb recognized it from her day's hunting, and realized just how close to Dun Tagoll they still were. "It was you that I saw, watching me, wasn't it?"

The spriggan nodded. "We weren't too sure how to talk to you in all that press around you. Too much cold iron. It won't kill us straight off, but we don't like it."

He tapped a rock and it slid aside to reveal a passage down. "An old tomb," he said cheerfully. "Gloomy, but clean and dry."

Meb suppressed a shudder. "Just don't mention the tomb part to Neve. She's...she's lived a bit of a sheltered life, compared to me. Can we leave it open?"

"It'll let the spiders in, I daresay."

"For now." A glance showed Neve was almost white with terror. Meb winked at her to tell her it would be all right. And Neve managed a smile, and appeared to relax slightly.

They walked down stone steps and into what should have been the cold of the tomb. The spriggans plainly didn't have much regard for these ideas, as it was pleasantly warm, and scented with...not dust and decay, but the smell of onions, garlic, wild thyme, and cooking meat. It might once have been a tomb, but the current occupants had scant respect for funerary furniture or the dead that might have lain there, having used the central sarcophagus to make a table, on which they had laid a cloth, and around which they'd placed several three-legged stools. A fire burned in a grate in the corner, with a pot hanging from a hob, from which the smells were plainly coming.

"Welcome to our lair," said the spriggan, rather formally.

Meb wasn't sure how one answered that, but she had a feeling that formally would be best. "Our thanks to you. May it remain dry and warm and safe," she said.

"What...what are you cooking?" asked Neve, warily.

"Rabbits. We have to make do. We can't get enough unwary travelers these days," said the spriggan tending the pot.

"Stop teasing her," said Meb sternly, hoping she was the one not being naive. But they were just enough like Finn, when he was being outrageous, for her to recognize it. "The fay here seem to delight in mocking people."

"But there is so much to mock," said the spriggan who had escorted her. "I suppose it is that you humans are more numerous, more powerful than us in many ways. It's that or kowtow to you. And we'd rather mock."

The cook looked thoughtful. "The muryans are hard-working, serious and not given to practical jokes, if they understand jokes at all."

"Yes, but there are more of them than humans. And look where it has gotten them."

Meb looked at the stone-coffin table. Five places laid, trenchers ready. Three spriggans and the two of them. "Either you were expecting us, or you're expecting some more spriggans."

"Ah. It's what they said. She's so sharp it's a wonder she doesn't cut herself. Probably will, with that axe. Or her brain will overheat with all that thinking," said the spriggan cook.

"Don't you say nasty things about m'lady," said Neve, straightening up. "She's had enough of that."

That seemed to amuse the spriggans. "Wouldn't dare, your majesty, wouldn't dare. Now, if you want to put your things down and take a seat, the food has been ready awhile, but you're slow."

"Who told you to expect us?" asked Meb.

"The knockyan—what you call knockers. Very full of it they were. But their tunnels are a bit tight for your kind."

That was reassuring. Meb knew the knockers had liked them, and if they were willing to trust the spriggans, then presumably the rabbit stew wasn't a first course to fatten up two women as the main roast. The stew was very good indeed, so good that it didn't worry either of them that one of their hosts got up to close the front door to keep the rain out.

"To think," said Meb, stomach full, warm, and sore feet up on what could easily be the treasure chest of a dead king, "that I worried about food and shelter on our journeying."

"Tonight is well enough," said the spriggan, "but they'll be looking for you. The mage has tools in his tower and he'll have traces of you. Best to go further off, and to keep moving a while."

"The piskies seemed to think they could stop us being followed."

"Ah, but that's piskies for you," said the spriggan. "They're not great on the understanding of things. We can't really shelter you indefinitely, any more than the piskies can mislead the prince's troops indefinitely. Neither we nor they can stand cold iron, and their misleading and mazing can be dealt with by turning your clothes. Once the prince's men realize that they're being piskie-led, they'll counter it. Our kind are weak and small here, for all we seem frightening. There are places where it is otherwise, where our kin rule. We are kin to those you call alvar, just as the knockyan are distant cousins to the dvergar."

"Um. You're nicer than a lot of the alvar I've met," said Meb, thinking of the faintly supercilious attitude of even Finn's friends Leilin and her sister. Finn had told her that the alvar were of many different groups, but this degree of difference had not occurred to her.

It amused them, and seemed to please them.

"It's not a reputation we need among humans. We've changed too, with being here. The underlying magic of the worlds shapes us."

Meb juggled for them. It seemed the least payment she could offer for shelter and food. The spriggans enjoyed it. Not with the childlike delight of the knockers, but with an appreciation of craft. They slept on a bed of heather in the corner of the tomb that night, and Meb slept better and longer than she had since she'd lost Finn and Díleas. Tiredly, just before she slept, she wondered if there was some kind of magic that would at least allow her to see them. It would make such a difference to know they were safe and happy and that all was well back in Tasmarin.

The next day brought a gruel breakfast, salve and leaf plasters for their feet, and a quiet, friendly but firm escort further from Dun Tagoll. "We are tied to the tor. We cannot go more than half a league from it. You'll find that's true of all of the spriggans and piskies here. They have their place, and they're quite strong in it," said the spriggan walking along with them. "The knockyan can travel but don't like to. The muryans, well, they do move, but it's war when one tribe meets another."

Neve coughed. "I didn't ever believe in the muryans either." She turned to Meb. "Do the magic creatures come to see you, m'lady? I mean... I lived all my life in the village and people talked of these things... it was stories. Some you believed and some, well, you mostly didn't. Never saw any myself, never saw one in Dun Tagoll either... until with you. Now, it is as if they're everywhere. Even," she colored, "when I went to relieve myself, without you. There was this little blue-green man looking at me."

"I hope you were very rude to him!"

"I was," admitted Neve.

"The piskie have no sense of privacy," said the spriggan. "Now if it had been one of us, you could have known it was to laugh at you. But they barely understand clothes. They wear them for pretty, when they feel like it. And of course we come to see you. We've always been here, but many were in a kind of hibernation.

Like bears in winter. Now the fay of the land are waking as the magic pours back in. Like the equinox flood tide it's been, after so many years."

Tasmarin. Magic and energy confined there for so long must be flowing back here. Suddenly Meb knew exactly what the problem with their Changer was. In a way, she was really the right one for the mage to blame. It was her, her and Fionn, back in Tasmarin, that had started this. Mind you, it could have been worse, had Fionn succeeded in his original aim of destroying the place and returning all its parts and people to where they came from.

"And, of course," said the spriggan, "we can't go to the Old Place on the headland, where the castle now stands. It's been bespelled against us for many a year. But even that weakens."

"Fleeing certainly confirms her treachery," said Lady Cardun.

"It may, but how was she able to do so?" asked Prince Medraut. "My man should easily have been able to deal with two women. And yet they disarmed him, cost him a finger, and frightened him into gibbering superstitious nonsense at half of the men-at-arms in the Dun. And the troop that was out this morning managed to get lost. Lost! A good half of them were born around here. They couldn't get lost in a thick fog. But they claim they blundered around country they've never even seen. And I've been shown it myself—they're black and blue from something. They're claiming it was bewitchment or a curse. And half of them are blaming Shadow Hall and the other half are saying it was Lady Anghared punishing them. If it wasn't for Aberinn and the fact that he keeps the Dun safe and provisioned, they'd desert."

Earl Alois had been relieved to see the moon full, hoping the Changer would bring some respite. Perhaps he'd been wrong about that girl being the Defender. But no. He'd seen it with his own eyes. It had been grim fighting the Fomoire, but the earl and his men had dealt them some doughty blows. More by luck than judgement, some of them. A sheep carcass landing in one of the chariots of the evil-eye men had been one such. It had caused a fight among them. There had only been nine by the time they got ashore. And the men of Carfon had laid traps that didn't involve looking, had the archers drop shots in a valley, had fired from ambush once the chariots had passed. The evil eye was terrifying, but there were few of them, and they had to look at you for a good few moments.

If Dun Tagoll and the North had held them off too, and there were no more coming south...they'd won.

And of course...if there was no next army. But there would be, and a next. And a next.

═ Chapter 17 ═

FIONN WAS BOTH WORRIED BY THIS PLACARD, AND SERIOUSLY quite put out by it. So he was a spy from Lyonesse, now. How had this human mage—they were fairly inept generally—found out this quickly and not only found out but also got more posters out?

And the dead or alive part was . . . interesting.

It was quite a generous sum. In gold, too.

That had to be very tempting.

"I think you're going to get your fur dyed, and I am going to have to change yet again," he said to Díleas. "This is getting tiresome."

A little work and he and Díleas had different appearances and, according to the documents he carried, Fionn was an agent of Prince Maric, the local panjandrum. He and his agents plainly commanded a great deal of respect and fear, by the way that they passed through the checkpoints. Fionn was able to glean a fair bit of information about himself in the process. He'd been seen in an amazing number of places. Fionn could imagine there were any number of very upset shepherds. Well, as the city of Goteng seemed to lie directly in their path, Fionn thought he'd do some reparation. Fionn and Díleas made their way through the streets peacefully, with a brief contretemps with some butcher's dogs who thought they owned the streets of Goteng, and not this black upstart who was passing through. The smell of dragon gave them pause, and Díleas delusions of grandeur.

Mage Spathos lived in a sumptuous tower within the grounds

of the military barracks—where even the parade ground was now full of tents.

It was near evening anyway, so Fionn found a tavern, fed himself and Díleas, avoided trouble with some bored conscripts on a pass out of their camp, before he went to the military barracks. As was usual with taverns near military camps, this one was something of a freelance brothel too—except that the women were very wary. Spathos's guards had apparently taken to collecting fresh meat for him every night, and payment was not part of his equation. Fionn decided that the man was due a call. Besides putting a price on the head of a dragon, such conduct deserved it.

As with most military establishments of the kind, the barracks were designed, really, to keep bored soldiers in, rather than determined dragons out. Seeing as dogs did not climb as well as dragons, they used the forged documents to enter the barracks and Spathos's tower, and to pass all the guards, except for the last two. With those ones he used the documents to distract, before cracking their heads together with calculated force—calculated not to kill, but to stun. After which he tied and gagged them and put them into a storeroom.

He did lock and bar the mage's door for them, but it was probable that they had been supposed to do this...with him on the outside.

He then stopped and examined the passage quite carefully. It was likely that any self-respecting magic worker would have a few other defenses, besides guards. Fionn's vision helped him to spot such disturbances of natural energy. He was not disappointed. They were there.

They were also inept rent-from-a-grimoire-I-don't-understand-properly spells. Spells written into that grimoire in the first place by someone who barely understood effects and had no real grasp of the causes. Not quite what he'd expected after the wanted posters. He was able to erase a little of the pattern and proceed to the wizard's workshop, where Mage Spathos was hard at work...eating supper. Most of the paraphernalia, Fionn judged at a glance, had no purpose and had not actually been used. It looked good though.

"I thought that I had given orders I was not to be disturbed. Or have you brought the girl here early? Take her to my bedroom. It had better be a younger one this time."

"I am so sorry to disturb your meal," said Fionn, who had

taken the liberty of changing his appearance in the antechamber. He was blond and bearded now.

"Not as sorry as you will be," said Spathos.

Díleas growled and that finally got the man's attention. "I've come to claim the reward," said Fionn.

Spathos's face would really have looked far more entertaining on those posters, decided Fionn. It was an interesting shade of white almost tinged with green. "The food obviously hasn't agreed with you," said Fionn with mock sympathy. "Now you promised fifty golden pounds, or twelve thousand silver pennies for me, dead or alive. I am here, alive. I want the reward. And the gold will be easier to carry."

His dragonish senses said that there was in fact a considerable amount of gold in the desk at which Spathos now quivered. "And it's not much use calling your guards, as they will not be able to help. And screams from your tower are what the soldiers regard as quite normal, I gather."

Spathos opened the upper drawer and reached inside. Something about the way he did it cried warning to Fionn. "Slowly," said Fionn. "Very slowly bring your hand out. Otherwise you may... regret it. Or worse, not live to regret it. I am not planning to kill you, you know. But I could change my mind."

That was a lie, but Fionn could lie quite cheerfully. It was just often more entertaining to tell the truth in ways that would not be believed. He couldn't intentionally kill.

The hand came out with a single gold coin. "Here!" shrieked Spathos, and flung it at Fionn.

Dragons will instinctively catch gold. Even bespelled gold.

Unless of course a sheepdog jumps up and catches the coin... and deliberately swallows it.

Díleas had seen that trap used before. It wasn't going to happen again.

Fionn had Spathos by the throat and hauled across his dinner before Díleas even burped. "This will need some very good explanation," he said in a quiet hiss. That act implied that the man had known that Fionn was a dragon merely passing as a man. And that in turn carried many other implications, none of which Fionn liked. And all of which he intended to get answers to. "Just what was on that coin? If the dog suffers any ill effects, I'll sit you on your own flagpole. After I sharpen it."

"A spell...just a spell. He said it would knock you out. I swear, nothing else. I made him hold it in case it was poisoned. He said...he said I should have it ready. In case you came. He said it was the kind of thing you might well do."

So whoever this foe was, he not only knew enough to try what seemed likely to be dragon-trapping magic, but also knew enough about Fionn to predict the course he might follow. "So who is this 'he'?" asked Fionn.

"I don't know! Truly I don't. I thought he came from the witch of the Shadow Hall."

Fionn was very good at detecting the change of inflection in human speech. It was not infallible, but it did help to split the liars out. This "mage" was little more than a hedge-magician. But it appeared that Annvn had very little magic or practitioners of the art, these days. It had once been quite a rich place for the magical arts. Fionn had had to come and fix things here. Not as often as Brocéliande, or some of the others, but often enough.

Before the eyes of the horrified "mage" he changed into his dragon form. He went on asking questions...now there was such naked fear in Spathos's voice that Fionn was fairly sure he was getting straight answers. He learned of the hedge-magician's source of information on Lyonesse—a crone in a house that moved.

"You won't find it unless she wishes you to," the terrified Spathos assured him.

Fionn was not some hedge-wizard, so he doubted that. However, it soon became apparent that Spathos's power had been built on the drip feed of information about Lyonesse raids from this source. And it told him when the next "Way" would open to that land, and where.

Yet he earnestly believed that the order—and money—to kill Fionn had not come from her, but from someone else. He'd lied when he thought he'd had just a man to deal with.

The questioning was interrupted by a pounding on the outer door. "Doubtless your entertainment for the evening arriving," said Fionn.

For a moment hope bloomed in Spathos's cheeks. Then he looked at the dragon and it died.

"Yes," said Fionn. "You guessed right. It won't help to save you from a dragon. And I wouldn't call to them because that could be worse right now." He wrapped Spathos in his tail. It wouldn't kill to be that constricted, but Spathos would not scream much either. He rifled the desk where his senses said that there was a substantial amount of gold. There was quite a lot. Quite a lot of silver too. Too much to carry... along with this Spathos. It would take the soldiery some time to brave breaking in here, depending on how soon someone got to asking about whether the agent who had come in had left. It was a good, solid, iron-reinforced door, too. Fionn gave Spathos the sort of squeeze that would probably crack a rib or two and certainly render him malleable. It would not be wise to leave him here. He knew too much and, what was more, dragons—including Fionn—had no tolerance for those who could bespell dragons, or even knew it was possible. At the very least, a salutatory lesson was called for.

Fionn stripped him, tied him up thoroughly. Blindfolded him and gagged him with his own clothing. Fionn then took fifty pieces of gold, and a handful of silver, and added it to his pouch. The dragon then moved himself, the victim and the remaining four bags—two of gold and two large ones of silver—onto the balcony. Tied them onto the other end of the rope. "Watch him. I'll be back in a few minutes," he said to Díleas. Because it was easier, he used human form to haul himself up onto the roof. Pulled up the bags of loot. He poured gold in a nice flat layer into the gutter, enjoying touching the gold, however briefly. He picked up the silver bags. Selected his targets—a handsome statue of one of the local robber barons in the town square two hundred yards away, neatly lit by two oil lamps; and a harder one, a flagpole on the parade ground a mere eight-five yards off. They were also some five stories down. The tower doubtless gave the so-called mage status, as well as giving Fionn good throwing practice. He pitched at the flagpole first. It snapped, but not before the bag ripped and showered coins onto the tents of the conscripts.

Fionn tossed the other at the statue. The stone copy of the local robber baron was so excited by the money that he completely lost his head, and coins sprayed far and wide, splattering against buildings and even in through windows.

By the sounds of it, the conscripts had discovered their pay had come from above, thought Fionn, as he dropped onto the balcony.

The guards were trying to pound down the door. He wondered how long it would take before the mayhem in camp got to them, but thought it might be fun to watch... "Time to fly, Díleas."

Díleas climbed into his basket. Fionn carefully put the blankets around him, took a firm hold of the basket and the end of the rope, cut the blindfold and gag away with a talon, and launched into the night sky. The weight of the screaming mage strained his wing muscles and they dropped before the dragon began to gain height.

The fighting and looting and destruction happening in the army encampment was briefly stilled by a near miss of the tent canvas by a hurtling, screaming wizard.

Fionn flapped on, having checked that Díleas was secure. The gold revived him a great deal, and his target was near enough. The slave vessels berthed on the river just outside the city opened their hold lids to allow a little air to their pitiful cargo.

Fionn considered the possibilities of dropping the man into the hole from the air...but decided that he might hurt Díleas, with yards and spars and ropes to crash into. So he landed on the quayside. Spathos got a little dragged and bounced, but he was beyond complaining and screaming, and merely at the whimpering stage. The slaver vessel was showing signs of readying itself for sea, with men on the foredeck. Fionn could quite see why the city appeared to be in something of an uproar.

The only watch on the hold was looking at the city. Fionn dropped him—and Spathos—into the hold, before jumping ashore. Once he and Díleas were back in the shadows, Fionn yelled. "There's a rebellion! They're coming to free the slaves!" and the two of them walked off into the night.

A little later they took to wing again. From the air Fionn could see that there were several fires in the city of Goteng, and there appeared to be some burning vessels on the river. Tch. Humans did get carried away. He hoped that Spathos's tower survived. He had gold to collect from that gutter. It was too heavy and flat to easily wash out.

In the meanwhile, traveling by day, as a man and a dog on their own, could become difficult, no matter just what the man or dog looked like.

Fionn looked for an alternative. And found it in a small group of carts, going in more or less the right direction. Travelers. Mostly they had a very poor relationship with authority. It could be worth looking into.

✧   ✧   ✧

The ancient energy beings pondered the situation. Annvn had seemed an ideal trap. The planomancer dragons were incredibly rare, and had been constructed far more robustly than the messenger-errand-beast kind. They were neither easily nor lightly killed. Merely putting him into some form of suspended animation in a slower time plane would have been preferable, but Annvn had good pawns and he was there...and now, it was likely he would deduce the role of a conspirator of greater reach than mere local humans. Possibly realize that it stretched as far as the Tasmarin pseudoplane. Possibly even deduce the existence of their hand in this.

That was most undesirable.

Worse than letting him interbreed with their creations. Those were—at least in major forms—not interfertile. Quite a lot of them simply physically could not do it, and even those that could tended to produce offspring that were either less fertile or sterile mules.

But shape-shifting dragons...

Fionn studied the carts from a safe distance. He was almost sure that they were the same brightly colored ones he'd encountered back in the lands of the creatures of smokeless fire.

There was a chance they'd be less than pleased with him, he had to admit. But on the other hand he knew things about them that might make life awkward with the local authorities. If they had papers of any sort, they were almost certainly forgeries or bought for a backhanded payment.

And, in a pinch, he could pay them. That, of course, would be a last resort. He had a feeling that if he was ever going to get to the bottom of these pathways between worlds that he had known nothing about, he was going to have to get the information out of the travelers, as Díleas was limited to yes-and-no barks. Besides, he had a feeling that Díleas did not know where, or understand how, the Ways between worked; he just was following his mistress, by the shortest possible route.

"I think," said Fionn, "that I'll have to alter my appearance and yours a little, my dog. I can change shape, but the best I can do for you now is to hide that flame bauble of yours. We're less likely to meet creatures of smokeless flame here than in Tasmarin, but protection is still a good idea. They don't have to be seen to work, though."

He sat and fashioned a tube of cloth and put it around the collar of silver and crystal. Funny, people assumed it was a cheap chain with a bauble on it. People saw what they wanted to see. The chain was of alvar manufacture and probably valuable. And the glowing little crystal bead, probably priceless. The creatures of smokeless flame would certainly give their entire stock of gold for it, rather than have it in the possession of another.

He walked closer to the carts. The travelers were lighting a fire and busying themselves with morning chores. It was indeed the same group of travelers, but somewhat less wary in Annvn than they had been traversing the flame-creature lands of Gylve.

Their dogs let them know he was coming. Díleas ran straight up to the cart of their leader and was wagging his tail very fast at Avram's Mitzi. She wasn't barking at him . . .

"Better call him off, mister," said Avram. "I don't want puppies this trip."

"Here, dog." He should have arranged a pseudonym for Díleas. He slapped his leg and whistled.

Díleas paid absolutely no attention.

Fionn hauled him off by the hair. "Sit! Or else!" and he took ahold of the collar.

The traveler laughed. "I reckon you'll have to tie him up. Our lot are. What do you want, stranger?"

"A place to hide," said Fionn. "To be something other than a single man and a dog. The authorities are looking for one of those."

Avram's eyes narrowed slightly. "We've seen the poster. Didn't look much like you." There was definite suspicion in his voice.

"Fortunately, yes. But they're still giving men on their own trouble. I've got some good papers and a little silver to pay for being one of the band for a few days. I'm going the same way as you are."

"Papers? What excuse do you have to travel? We've got war materiel."

"I'm supposed to be an agent of Prince Maric. I'm not, but it looks good," said Fionn. "And I can tell you Mage Spathos had a tragic accident and isn't paying any rewards right now. I'll give you ten silver pennies to travel along with you for the next three days."

"Let's see the color of your money," said the traveler.

So Fionn produced and counted out the silver.

Avram tested and smelled the coins. Pocketed them. A couple of the others had wandered over from their chores and were watching. Fionn scented something that could be trouble. But there was cover nearby and not a bow in sight. "You can travel with Nikos. He lost his dog, but you'll have to tie yours up," said Avram. "You still got that rope we sold you, Finn?" he asked, grinning.

"How did you know?" asked Fionn.

"Heh. It was the first poster. Dravko took one look and said he had no idea having a sense of balance could make you so valuable. He was quite proud of having been gulled by a man that could make himself that unpopular. And it's the way you speak and the way you stand. In our trade it pays to notice those things. What did you do to them?" There was serious admiration in that tone.

"The annoying thing," said Fionn, "is that I don't know, and I want to know. I know exactly what I've done to Mage Spathos since. He's not going be paying any rewards, but he could only tell me someone was offering to pay him a great deal for me—dead. I have a description, but not a name. And I have been told who he thinks it isn't . . . but that leaves a lot of people—and things which are not people—that I could possibly have made very angry over the years."

The travelers laughed. "We're making breakfast," said Avram. "Come and eat. We can swap lies easier over bread and salt."

"I'll need to tie this dog up," said Fionn, as Díleas was sniffing the air hungrily and just about turning his neck all the way around to admire the come-hither look in Mitzi's eyes.

"Let him go and get friendly with Mitzi," said Avram. "He's a smart dog."

"You have no idea just how smart," said Fionn, letting go. Díleas charged off, and leapt up on the seat of the wagon, to indulge in some more stiff-tailed fast wagging and some very personal sniffing.

Avram led Fionn to the fire, where bacon was being sliced into the long-handled skillet. "Ah, but when that starts thinking," he said, pointing at his groin, "the brains stop."

"Never a truer thing was said," said Fionn, thinking that it might almost apply to him. But there was heart there too, which he had noticed actually made it less logical and more intense.

They ate rosemary-scented pot bread and salt, and drank ale.

When the bacon was done, they all speared pieces of it on their knives and rubbed their bread in the grease as they passed the iron skillet around. Fionn was aware he was being watched carefully. They were friendly, but watching. When he handed the skillet on, Avram asked, "What are you, Finn? You're not one of the Beng. You're too at ease with iron to be one of the alv, although I thought so because of the glamor. You're too big to be one of the Dueregar. And the water-people don't like rosemary."

"I could be a giant," said Fionn, trying to weigh this up, "that's washed himself too often and shrunk."

"Bit sharp-witted for one of those. But men don't handle hot iron that easily either. And that's not glamor. Simon has a special bespelled mirror for spotting that. He checked when he was fetching the salt."

"I would have thought it was pretty obvious," said Fionn, reading posture, preparing himself, trying to work out just how he would get Díleas, who was far too busy to even notice possible trouble. They had just shared bread and salt with him . . . that was not usually a precursor to treachery. "I'm a dragon."

He was surprised to see them smile and relax.

"Welcome," said Avram. "You are the kind that works the balances, I think? The others don't change shape happily and don't think as fast from what I have heard."

"You don't seem very surprised," said Fionn guardedly.

Avram shrugged. "You said you came from a plane of dragons. And we have met your kind of dragon before."

"Oh? There were never that many of us. I thought I might be the last. It's been a long time since I met another one. We each had our planes and subplanes. I was trapped in Tasmarin for a long time. Like you, I used to travel around. Which is what I need to ask you about. These paths between planes . . ."

"The Tolmen Ways, yes."

"How do you find them? I didn't know they existed, and I think I need to know, to . . . do what I have to do. To go on with the balancing. I am not going to close them. They seem well made, very convenient, and magically near neutral."

"The dragon Corran made them and showed us. He helped us with the protections against the Beng and alv, and the tree-people too. We regard ourselves as his people."

"Oh?" This was possibly dangerous territory. Some dragons

could be quite possessive. The last thing he needed was a fight with another planomancer. That could be ugly. And he should have guessed that the Ways between planes were planomancer work. No wonder they were stable and hard to find.

"Yes, the legends said he was very rude about the idea," said Dravko, "which we like too. We don't do very well with overlords. But we are the friends of the dragon."

Fionn bit his knuckle. "Take my advice on this. Don't be. Most of them are not our kind of dragon and would eat you and steal your gold."

"Not just trick us out of it?" said Avram cheerfully.

"That was a fee, for teaching you a valuable lesson, and organizing water and a safe spot in future in Gylve," said Fionn. "And as a lesson to not sell other travelers into slavery."

"We only talked about it," said Mirko. "We might have changed our minds."

"You might have ended up being sold instead," said Fionn.

═ Chapter 18 ═

EARL ALOIS WAS GRATEFUL FOR HIS OWN MAGICAL SKILLS, WHICH included the ability to divine a way home. That was how they finally got back to the Dun—the troop had blundered through places he would swear were not in Lyonesse, let alone his familiar Southern Marches. He'd been aware that his people had been encountering the various non-humans more and more frequently. But suddenly they seemed to have turned inimical, to him in particular.

And now, thanks to rude piskies who had misled them, and pelted them with pine cones, he knew why. Somehow they'd heard that he'd tried to kill the Defender. And the fay—at least the piskies—were taking it out on him and his. He needed help. Allies. Not this.

The spriggan escort handed Meb and Neve on to a fair of piskies. "They're flighty and troublesome," said the spriggan as the piskies stuck their tongues out at them. "But they'll see you further north."

"Thank you. I'd like to be further from Dun Tagoll, but north was a direction chosen for no good reason. I'm really not too sure where we should go," admitted Meb.

The spriggan smiled wryly. "So now you're asking me for advice, and my thoughts, beyond that it will all end in tears, I shouldn't wonder. And if I know humans, you want more than that. Go north. We don't really believe in chance or coincidence.

There are forces pushing you north. Powers in the land itself. The humans believe the King is the Land and Land is the King, and it's been without one for too long. Humans, of course, have a poor understanding of it, but that's no surprise. Anyway: the forest people in the deep woods are closest to the Land, of all those in it. They could give you refuge. And they have a freedom of movement across the country that we don't."

Meb thought of her brush with the sprites—Lyr—for they were all, effectively, the same vegetative intelligence. They hadn't liked people much. "Oh. You also have sprites here?"

"Sprites?" asked the spriggan.

"Tree people...sort of like trees but people too," explained Meb.

"Ah," said the spriggan, nodding. "The dryads. This is far from their realms. We've had a few once, long ago. No, I speak of the Wudewasa, the wild people of the deep forest. Lyonesse was once all theirs when it was also almost all forest. They're touchy and dangerous."

"And that was supposed to cheer me up, was it, as well as help?" said Meb.

The spriggan smiled. "Can't have you getting too enthusiastic. May the Land stay with you." And he turned and left.

So they were left to travel on with the piskies. They were flighty travel companions, needing to be reminded that they weren't actually here just to play little practical jokes on the two humans with them. The idea that humans might not like their hair tweaked, and that it was a bad idea to do, took a while to get into their heads too. Neve finally did it, catching one shrieking with laughter in her ear as he did so, and holding him up in front of her. "It's being put over my knee for a good spanking that you'll get if you do that again. Go and tweak the squirrels' tails instead."

"They bite," said the piskie, looking sulkily at her. "It was no harm we were doing. Just a bit of fun."

"And it's no harm I'll do to your tail end. No worse than you did to my hair."

"Then you wait and see what I'll do to you next," said the piskie crossly.

Meb thought it was wise to try for a distraction. She'd started to try and learn the cartwheels and tumbling and flick-flacks that Fionn used as part of his gleeman showmanship. She wasn't particularly good at them, in skirts...but then the piskies seemed totally unaware of clothing's purpose being to cover nakedness. "Can you do this?" she asked, managing a credible cartwheel... and resolving never ever to do it in a skirt again.

They didn't seem to notice that part at all, and next thing they were all cartwheeling and tumbling and spinning. From there it was natural enough for Meb and Neve to start singing. And the piskies found that a good reason to weave dances around them, and between their legs, rather like cats. It was noisy, but it beat having your hair tweaked and ears pulled by bored piskies. It was a relief to come to the point where the fair said: "Thus far and no further," and left them with capers and cartwheels and a raspberry or two.

"You know, m'lady," said Neve tiredly, when they were out of sight of the little people. "They're like little children. There's never been anything quite like piskies to make even spriggans look very nice."

"I had always wondered what they were good for," said the spriggan, who had been doing a good job of looking like an old milestone. "But they're not always or all quite such flighty fellows. They're fast workers, when it takes their fancy. Of course they'll usually leave you in the lurch just when you needed them most."

"And spriggans do a good job of frightening me out of a year's growth, and you can rely on them to come up with the next glum prediction," said Meb.

"Yes. Those are the things we do best," agreed the spriggan. "I'll tell you there is a group of Angevins prowling the lanes in the next few miles, along this way. They're best avoided, I would say. They're hungry and mean. If you detour a bit west, that trail has got nothing particularly nasty that we can't discourage."

That night was their first full night beneath the stars, sleeping rough. Meb had the feeling they were being watched but no piskies or spriggans or knockers or even Angevin mercenaries disturbed their rest. It was cold, but survivable, thanks to the fur blanket, and a layer of bracken to keep them off the ground, fire and a bit of shelter from the wind with an old stone wall and a tree. Food, however, was getting sparse. They had some of the dried meat they'd got from the knockers, and some fiddlehead fern shoots that they boiled in a bark bowl, and a last oatcake divided between them and washed down with what the knockers probably considered quite a lot of apple wine. It didn't really go very far. Meb was seriously thinking magic was going to have to be employed to find them food, soon.

Except that morning brought food. Food laid out neatly in precise rows next to their bed...nuts—some squirrel had plainly not eaten his winter store—and a pile of sulphur-yellow bracket fungus neatly laid out on some young leaves. Meb recognized that from her time with Fionn, mushroom hunting. "Chicken-of-the-woods! And there are two small bird's eggs. We have breakfast."

"But who brought it?" asked Neve. "The grass—look, it's full of dew, but there isn't a sign of a footprint in it."

There wasn't.

"Maybe piskies?" suggested Meb, yawning, looking around.

"I don't see them laying out the food precisely. It'd be tossed in a heap and probably tumbled in the grass. And look how neatly the fungus is cut," said Neve, pointing. "My ma is...was a fussy housekeeper. And she was never that picky."

"Well, let's make a little fire and cook the chicken-of-the-woods. I'm just grateful for it. We should have got a cooking pot from the knockers," said Meb, suddenly thinking of mushrooms and bacon. "Finn always had a little iron skillet."

"He must have had a pack horse to carry everything he had... I am sorry, m'lady. Didn't mean to make you cry."

"You didn't," said Meb, sniffing determinedly and rubbing her eyes. "Something just got in my eyes, that's all." And out of my memory box, she thought. It was the mushroom smell and the mention of that skillet. Determinedly, she thought of where the food could have come from rather than dwelling on happier times. It was good to have food, at least. It seemed they'd better hang on to it, because a determined team of ants were rolling one of the walnuts away...

And then she looked again. They weren't rolling the nut away. They were bringing it to add to the rows. She peered closely. The ants all had remarkably human faces. And they stared back at her.

"Neve," she said quietly, as the young maid picked up twigs from the leaf litter to start the fire, "I think I found out who brought us the food. Look."

Neve followed her pointing finger. Clung to her arm.

"Muryans. As I live and breathe, muryans!" said Neve, incredulously. "Whatever you do, m'lady, don't make them angry. They're small but there be millions and millions of them."

Meb looked at the tiny creatures positioning the nut, which was far bigger than they were, with meticulous precision. "Right now I'd rather work out how to thank them. The spriggans said they were very serious and hard workers. I don't think juggling or tumbling will have much appeal."

"They say they are ruled by a queen," said Neve, "and she looks just like a person, only tiny. They say if she's your captive, they'll serve you."

It brought to mind the doll's house stuff that Meb had seen in Aberinn's workshop. Well, why not? She'd been fascinated enough to study it, to remember it in detail. The queen's chamber with its little mirrors and brushes and combs... She called them. Wanted them. It produced a very strange feeling... and an entire little room in her hands. Meb put it in the basket, but picked out the tiny silver comb, which was smaller than her pinkie fingernail. It was perfect and must have taken some artificer many hours of painstaking labor to make... or some form of magic. She knelt down and looked at the laboring muryans. They stopped, little ant antennae twitching at her. She held out the comb, balanced on a finger. "A small gift. For your lady, with thanks for your breakfast."

One, and then a second of the muryans approached her finger. They had antlike, sharp-biting jaws—doubtless what had cut the tough bracket fungus. They took the comb—it was still big enough to need two of them to handle it—and ant-handled it back to the wall, and down between the stones.

A little later, just as they'd got the fire lit, a small sea of muryans came pouring out from between the rocks. Then came several hundred larger muryans, with jaws like scimitars, nearly an inch long. And then, carried on a litter made of grass stalks with highly polished seed handles... their queen. The soldiers arrayed themselves watchfully. Meb was sure that if either of them made the slightest move toward the muryan queen they would attack with suicidal ferocity.

The little queen was human-looking. Her clothes—probably woven from something like spider web—were remarkably fine, and bright colored. She was perhaps six inches tall—big compared to her subjects. And she had the comb in her hands.

Meb and Neve stared at the perfect, doll-like little woman. Her skin was porcelain white and her hair long and dark and intricately braided. There were little sparkling lights set in it. "My subjects are very worried about me being aboveground," she said in a piping little voice. "But I wished to thank you for the gift, Land Queen." She admired the comb, delight written on tiny features. "You did not have to do that."

"It seemed only polite to say thank you for breakfast," said Meb. "Fionn said that only a fool takes without giving something in exchange. Even if it is only his gratitude making the giver feel good."

"That is wisdom. We struggle to fashion metals. And the knockyan work is not so fine as this. They are miners, not artificers. Thank you," said the muryan queen.

"It is our pleasure. We appreciate breakfast."

The queen nodded regally. "My workers want to know if you can spare them an ember on a stick. They struggle to kindle fire, and it has been damp and cold and we lost ours."

"Nothing easier," said Meb, taking a smouldering stick from the fire. Was Lyonesse full of such obliging fay? It was very different from Tasmarin, then. "All of the non-human people here seem so...helpful. Generous. Thank you."

"It is our duty to serve. We have waited a long time for you," said the queen muryan.

Meb blinked. What? Then it struck her. It must be this prophecy. She did *not* want to be their "Defender." Although, she admitted to herself, it was easier to have to defend the knockers, spriggans, muryans and even the annoying piskies than the nobles of Dun Tagoll. "I don't know what I am supposed to do," she admitted.

The muryan queen toyed with the comb. "The Land knows. And you do it in a better fashion than the last one. He took it as his right. Never gave anything or thanked anyone for anything."

One of the soldier muryans clicked his mandibles.

The queen nodded. "He says there are large birds coming. I must go back to my palace."

The bearers literally whisked her away just as she was finishing speaking, carrying her back down into the mound.

"Large birds?" said Meb looking around. They were under a tree, and the un-farmed countryside was returning to woodland. A bird, she supposed, especially a bird of prey, could be a grave danger to the muryans, to their queen.

"You can see them over there," said Neve in an odd voice, pointing. "I think we need to hide, m'lady."

They gleamed golden as they caught the sun. It was a reflection off metal, but they flew and tumbled through the sky like a murder of crows. Even from here you could hear their harsh cawing cry.

"Aberinn's crow." She'd seen it, in his tower, in the gilded cage.

"Yes, m'lady. One is the same as many. And what they sees, he sees," said Neve, fearfully.

"Let's put that fire out, and think hidden thoughts," said Meb.

So they did, sitting tight, staying under the tree and cracking nuts.

The golden birds scattered across the sky. Hunting.

On the ground the piskies could maze and mislead, and the spriggans could give warning. Meb had a feeling that up close the muryan could deal with any attacker, just by sheer numbers. But the metallic crows stayed above, in the sky, and Meb honestly could not think what to do about them, except to wait them out.

They had to sit for a good hour, as the day grew warmer, before they could start walking again. It had given Meb a chance to think about what the various fay had said, and she'd perhaps not really understood. She had no desire to be some kind of savior. She'd just wanted . . . well, she knew what she'd just wanted, but as she couldn't have that, she'd just wanted somewhere quiet to be relatively miserable and peaceful about it all. Then she'd said she would help . . . and found that she'd promised a spy. Vivien had been kind to her. She'd been grateful. The castle's "little people" had been good to her. The non-human denizens of Lyonesse had been helpful . . . and in their ways, generous. Well, the piskies had helped rather than just generating mayhem, their most frequent habit. The spriggans had as much said they thought the whole process was using her. If it had to be that way, and she wasn't sure why it should, she'd shape it to her, not the other way around. And why her? Neve said only those of Lyonesse's noble ruling house had magic—but that just meant one of her parents had to have been. And she was a realist enough to know that could have been on the wrong side of wedlock. She was no lost princess: the last king had been dead more than fifty years, and the queen nearly sixty years. No one else at Dun Tagoll had been leaping up and claiming a child lost eighteen years ago. Or no one who was willing to admit to it, which put her as likely to be the love child of a servant. It would have been some small consolation for losing

Fionn and Díleas to have loving parents waiting for her. She had never had a father. Hallgerd had at least been a kind of mother.

And then her type of magic was simply so different from the way they seemed to do things here. Did it really mark her as from their royal house at all? They knew precisely what and how they were doing what they were doing, and followed precise methods, but were quite weak in their degree of success. She had no real idea how she did what she did, had no real clear method, except that of a clear image and real desire or need, and a sort of day-dreaming focus seemed to help. But she was far more successful than most, she gathered, excluding the likes of Aberinn.

She was still deep in thought as they began their walk. Eventually she asked Neve, "What would fix Lyonesse? If you could, I mean, just could...wave your hand and it happened."

Neve blinked. Meb had decided a while back that it wasn't that Neve was stupid. She just hadn't ever done much thinking and wasn't too eager to start. Meb understood that too. In a village, being smart or daydreaming weren't things that helped you to fit in, and it was easier to fit in than not to. "I'd stop the fighting. Stop the armies coming along the Ways. Never mind the Changes. Just leave us alone."

"But Vivien said it was needed to keep magic going in Lyonesse."

"Aye. It is," agreed Neve. "But no good that's been to burned villages and burned fishing boats, and killed people."

Meb suspected that the nobility of Lyonesse, whose power rested on that magic, would not see it that way. Well, she had no reason to care how they felt. But she did have reason to care for the spriggans and knockers, and the muryans and even the piskies. They needed magic. They were "wakening" because of the magic...then it dawned on her. They were wakening because the flows of magical energy had been restored because of the reintegration of Tasmarin, not because of the device in the tower. "So all we need is a bit of peace."

Neve nodded. "Mind you, stopping fighting usually takes some fighting." She swallowed. "I had...two little brothers. Only way to stop them fighting was to spank both of them, my mother said."

Meb suddenly felt overwhelmingly guilty. She'd never really found out much about Neve's family, beyond stories of her grandmother. "What happened to your family? Your village? Could I take you back there?"

"It isn't there anymore. No one along the coast near Dun Tagoll after the Vanar's last raids. M'mother and the boys...they were killed. Later, in Dun Telas, my Gamma...Well, she had money and my uncles, they moved to Dun Telas. I am not going back there." There was a terseness in her voice that said "don't ask me any more."

But Meb wouldn't have anyway, because just then a javelin spiked the trail in front of them.

═ Chapter 19 ═

"SO, FINN. HOW FAR DO YOU TRAVEL WITH US?" ASKED AVRAM, as the carts made their way along the track. Fionn was sitting up on the box with him, and Díleas was fast asleep just behind him. He'd growled at Mitzi a little earlier, and she was still bright-eyed and eyeing him with interest. Fionn had been keeping an eye on Díleas for an entirely different reason. He was aware of gold, and had known just where in the dog's digestive tract the bespelled gold coin was. The spell probably wouldn't survive stomach acid, but the coin might do Díleas some harm, Fionn feared. He was relieved to know the coin wasn't in the dog anymore, but had been deposited somewhere. Díleas had obviously made sure it was a long way from Fionn, and that was one piece of gold Fionn had no interest in finding.

"Until the dog tells me it's time to go elsewhere. And right now he's too tired and his mind seems elsewhere."

"You're following the dog?" said Avram, incredulously.

Fionn nodded. "I told you he was smarter than you realized. He's following his mistress. He's taken me straight across four planes and back across a fifth. He takes me to these Tolmen Ways of yours, which are shorter, straighter, and less dangerous than the planar intersections that I know. Right now I believe you're going in the right direction."

"What are you seeking?" asked Avram.

"I said: the dog's mistress. She is very important and special to me."

Avram nodded. "She is a very desirable dragon, then?"

"She's a human," said Fionn.

Avram nearly dropped the reins. "There are some very fair young women among our people," he said cautiously.

"She's rather special, and to be honest with you, given all the time rates out here, I am not too sure if she'll be a young woman by the time I find her. The planes are extensive, although her magic use tends to make her stand out like a bonfire on a dark night," said Fionn.

"She's a mage?"

"Of sorts, yes," replied Fionn, smiling, thinking about it. "More like an accidental mage with more innate power than most dedicated and trained practitioners."

"Has she enchanted you, Dragon?" asked Avram. "We've got a few back home who are good at undoing those things..."

Fionn shook his head, knowing it wasn't entirely true, but preferring matters the way they were. "In theory, anyway, it is very hard for one human to use magic on our type of dragon. We are mostly proofed against magic for good reason. I think I love her in the same way and for the same reason the dog does. Because she is what she is, and she loves us."

"So...how did you lose her?" asked Avram, in the fashion of someone who knows this a bad question to ask, but is going to ask it anyway.

Fionn shrugged. "She used her power to go, and we don't know exactly where. I believe she was misled by...by something. And I intend to find out, and I intend to find out why."

"We have a saying that if there is one thing more determined than a man led by his testicles, it's one led by his emotions."

"It's true of dogs and dragons too," admitted Fionn.

Now that he was accepted as a dragon, there were no major secrets, and Fionn had built up something of a picture of the travelers. Their base was on the Blessed Isles, and there were ten carts in this venture, making it a small one. There had been eleven but one had had to be cannibalized to make a bridge. Twenty-two men, no women or children this trip; Annvn was considered too dangerous, as were the shifting gateways or Tolmen. There were several that the travelers never quite knew where they would come out. Some outcomes, like Brocéliande and Finvarra's kingdom, were merely dangerous, and places they visited in the normal course of business anyway. But Annvn, despite being profitable, was so full of regulation—and corruption—that travelers had had major problems, entire parties being sold into slavery, and needing expensive rescues.

"We're officially going to the assembly point to the way to Lyonesse, with supplies for the army," explained Avram. "Actually, in two days we slip off the pike road for a mile or two and there's a Tolmen Way to Alba, and then about two weeks' travel and back to the Blessed Isles. Alba's none too bad. We're not going to Lyonesse. Not with or without an army. It's a bad spot, even if it didn't have the habit of raiding its neighbors. The land is unfriendly."

They showed Fionn several maps, indicating the Tolmen Ways, which he faithfully copied. He was pleased to add some extra points to their maps, too, with notes. Díleas had taken him places they either didn't know or didn't go to. Some could be awkward with a cart. Horses probably wouldn't enjoy being driven over a cliff.

He was still musing ways to get around this when they came to one of the inevitable checkpoints. Mind you, Fionn thought, this one was in more chaos than check. The soldiers were busy dismantling their camp. Avram waved his papers at them.

"Oh hell, check them," said one of the sergeants busy packing his kit. "You, soldier."

So the soldier came over and looked. Snorted. "You might want to turn back. They'll probably not pay you," he said as he returned them and took Fionn's papers.

"Not pay us?" said Avram, looking suitably horrified.

"We're not even sure if they'll pay us." He looked at Fionn's papers and began laughing. "You're out of a job, scumbag. They hung Maric last night."

"I can't tell you how pleased I am," said Fionn, beaming at him. "Finally. Tell me what happened."

The soldier, who, in Fionn's judgement, had been about to haul off and punch the supposed agent in the mouth, paused. "What?"

"I bought the papers from a pickpocket," said Fionn cheerfully. "Do I look like an agent? What happened to Maric? I can go home now!"

"I'll have to arrest you..."

"For what and for who?" asked Fionn, grinning and slapping his back. "If Maric's dead, who is paying you and who is giving you orders? So who is the new prince going to be?"

"Who knows? Sounds like there is a civil war going on. Slaves broke out, half the town in flames, looting, rebellion..."

"I think," said Avram, "that we'll keep going a bit, and let it all settle down."

He flicked his whip and the horses began to trot. They didn't stop and the soldiers didn't bother to try and stop them.

They slowed up about a mile further on. "That, Finn, could have been ugly," said Avram.

"The law of unintended consequences," said Fionn, "and how all things are interconnected and balanced always amazes me. I tossed a spark in there, I suppose. Didn't expect a wildfire. Yet, I couldn't have made as big a one if I tried."

"Still, it makes getting ourselves and our goods on the trail to Alba ever more important. Civil wars are bad for trade and bad for travelers. I'll be glad to get there."

"I'll be glad to be going with you if I am," said Fionn. "Let's see what Díleas says."

Díleas informed Fionn by leaping off the cart—and away from Mitzi—that he was going straight on, on foot toward the staging post of the army, not on by cart towards a stone arch—a Tolmen which opened a Way to Alba—but to one which intermittently led to Lyonesse. There were a couple of other possibilities beyond that, but that was the closest. And what could be more likely than that his Scrap of humanity would be in the middle of a war, in a place which everyone seemed to detest?

The countryside became hillier and intermittently wooded as they walked on. Fionn had rather expected it to be full of troops heading back to their homes or to the city, but it wasn't. In fact the road was deserted, as were most of the farms. He did see smoke coming from the two chimneys of an odd, shadowy, angular building on a hilltop that had some magic-use problems which he would have gone to deal with normally, but that was the only sign of human life he saw. There were signs of devastation, though. Reading the map, late that afternoon, Fionn decided they had barely a mile or two to go, and was about to press on, when he realized they were being approached. By a tall, graceful tree-woman.

"Fionn. The black dragon?" She asked as if she were some messenger, checking she had the right person.

"Yes," said Fionn. There seemed little point in denying it.

"You move fast and far. My sisters have sent me news for you," she said. "The trees pass word slowly from tree to tree, plant to plant, growing thing to growing thing. The planes are not a divider to them, because they do not understand them or comprehend them, and thus are not limited by them. They bring us word, in time. The woman you seek," said the tall tree-sprite, "is in the land humans know as Lyonesse. She walks among the new-leaf oaks there. And at her side and following behind her are the myriads."

Fionn took a deep breath. He'd found her, and his secret, never-voiced fear had not been realized. The wilder worlds out there had not killed his precious Scrap of humanity. "I owe you... your kind...a debt. And I never forget," he said, his voice thick. "Hear that, Díleas? We know where we're going now. It sounds like she has a big army."

"It is not a big army. Just very numerous," said the sprite. "Or that is how the trees see it."

She gave him a swaying bow, and turned away. Fionn knew her kind better than to waste his time running after her and asking for clarification.

At least he knew she was alive and where she was.

"Come on, Díleas. Let's go."

So they went.

But their way was blocked by an army that was both numerous and big. And which had rather effectively blocked the gate, even for a dragon in a hurry.

The gate looked rather like a castle gatehouse, and was—unlike the ancient triliths—an obviously recent construction...so much so that there were still construction materials piled near them. It was quite different too in that it smelled of oil and human magic to Fionn's senses. Quite unlike the other Ways.

The gatehouse still looked imposing. Complete with solid gates, and a portcullis. And an army camped outside, and a formation of pikemen at the ready.

"The Annvn invasion force might not be going through at the moment," said Fionn to Díleas, inspecting it from a nearby hill with a convenient forested gully for cover, "but nothing is coming out, either." Fortunately, it appeared that the army was looking for trouble not from within Annvn but from elsewhere.

He inspected the gate as carefully as he could at this distance. Breaking into places was, after all, very much his stock in trade.

Normally over, rather than through, would have been his chosen method.

Only he doubted that would help here. "Over" would merely get him to the other side of the gate, not to another plane. The same probably applied to "around" or even to "under."

It would have to be "through." And while dragon fire would deal with their gate, and even with the portcullis... That rather depended on no humans being in the way to get incinerated.

Fionn scratched his head in irritation. "The answer might be to frighten them off. But every now and then, they can be very hard to frighten. Their unpredictability makes planning interesting. Normally I enjoy that."

He fished out the maps while Díleas stared curiously. "On the other hand... It's late afternoon now. How about if we try a two-pronged strategy here. Come dusk, a dragon will drop on the army with as much tumult and hair-searing flame as I can muster. If they run, the dragon's dog guide will be sitting ready on this hillside in his flying basket for me to pick up. Are you with me? Two barks for yes."

"Hrf, hrf."

"Then a bit more dragon fire and we're into Lyonesse, and we go hunting for your mistress's magical pyrotechnics."

"Hrf hrf!"

Fionn held up a hand. "But if they stand... well, the Tolmen Way to Vanaheim is close, and then from that, it's a flight out to sea, and we come to this islet, from which we can get to Lyonesse."

Never had a wait seemed quite so long to Fionn. He was used to exercising patience. Energy was about alignment and flow, all in their proper times... Right now he would have moved the sun itself, if he could.

At last the sun touched the far horizon in a crimson blaze of dying glory. Fionn readied the basket for Díleas, made sure it stood securely. The dog was pacing, plainly impatient too. The moment it was ready he jumped in, but he didn't lie down. Instead, he sat, looking at the gate.

"I can understand you wanting to do that, I suppose," said Fionn. "If we get through, we can stop. If we don't... we can stop in a mile or two." He took on his dragon form, spread and stretched his wings. Warmed them up with a few flaps. All good things for a dragon to do, but seldom done. He was putting this off, he knew. He leapt upwards into the purple sky spattered with the first stars and still with the memory of red on the western horizon. He flapped his way upwards, and then dived, spreading wing tendrils and talons to make the loudest possible air-shriek.

As pale faces turned upwards, he gave their wagons and mess tents a brief wash of flame. And then began to climb again, to arc around, letting his claws rip canvas down one row of tents, sending men diving into the mud. Then he climbed again, looking down at the chaos he'd stirred.

The camp was scattering. Parts of it were burning.

But, to his annoyance, the pikemen assembled before the gate had not joined the chaos. They'd turned their formation to defend the gate. Their officers must be made of stern stuff, and the pikemen, hard men.

Normally, with dragons, that would have meant crisp men. Fionn climbed higher, and dived again, this time coming from behind the gate that they had just turned away from.

Dragon fire seared over them, melting pike points, causing considerable blistering.

But they held. Fionn flapped upward. Someone even managed to loft an arrow at him. He burned it midair, to discourage that.

"Hold hard, the forty-fifth!" bellowed a voice that would have done a bull mammoth proud. "About . . . turn! Face the gate. They must be planning to break through!"

Fionn sighed. It was cook them or give up and go around. So he flew back and picked up Dìleas, and flapped off into the night.

The glorious forty-fifth would remember their night of triumph. By the looks of it, half of the rest of the army wouldn't. From a bit of altitude and in the infrared spectrum, Fionn could see them scattering. He dropped down and encouraged a few to keep running, and then flew onward, to the gate into Vanaheim.

He stopped a few miles down the road, to tuck Dìleas in, and apologized. "I can't just cook them, Díl. It'd be easier if I could."

"Hrf." A resigned sort of "Hrf."

"There is no point in your getting out of the basket. You'll get killed back there. We'll just go around them. It won't take any longer than your walking would."

They flew on. Fionn had the feeling that his status was a little dented. But when they landed at the little stone Tolmen, Díleas gave Fionn a lick. On the nose.

They walked through together. Into sunlight and a crackling breeze.

The queen of Shadow Hall was tempted to spit into her seeing pool. She knew it would not make her vision any better or sweeter, and they would not feel it on the other side, but it might make her feel better.

She'd worked so hard on Annvn. And now, when an army twenty times the size of anything Lyonesse could possibly manage, with siege engines and good maps and wagonloads of provisions, and more and more reserves pouring in...

A revolution. A slave uprising too. The army dispersed and their stores demolished, and half their war machines burned. And the survivors were all very pleased with themselves for holding off the dragon. Why had the fools not let it through to ravage Lyonesse?

With an exasperated sigh she turned her attention to the next place the Changer would link Lyonesse to. Or should. She looked to Vanaheim. She'd kept them from their normal happy pastime of butchering each other for the last few years and goaded them into building a vast fleet to attack Lyonesse instead.

It seemed, on looking at the empty harbors in West Vanaheim, that the fleets were at sea.

Sweeping her gaze around, she found them to the southeast, heading for shelter...

Loaded for war and conquest.

Only the wind wasn't helping.

Where did they think they were going! She'd prepared them for her use against Lyonesse, not their own petty wars. She had her cauldron-men among them, of course. She would find out.

And she did. They had their own seers and seid-women, the völva. Ones who were as capable of finding the Ways and when they were open.

They were sailing to attack Lyonesse. Just as soon as the wind cooperated.

The queen set her muryan slaves to work, moving Shadow Hall to Vanaheim.

It was late that evening that it occurred to her to check on the gate in Annvn. She might as well start the slow process of reorganizing against the next cycle.

Out of habit, she checked the Way.

And it was open too.

Then she began feverishly checking the others, cackling with glee. Rubbing her bony hands in delight. How had he botched so? Ha ha ha.

At last. At long, long last! She began sending out messengers to her cauldron-men, to those she had implanted as counselors and advisors to the kings, queens, princes and chieftains of the nineteen worlds.

Someone was at her outer door.

How dare they interrupt her triumph? And how could they? Shadow Hall was moving steadily. It was not easy to see. And it had its defenders. She used the seeing bowl to look.

The creature of smokeless flame, which the locals would probably call a demon, had no trouble keeping up with Shadow Hall, or with seeing it. And it could probably devour her cauldron-men, if they succeeded in attacking it.

She'd done business with them before, so she went to see what it wanted. She had some defenses on hand, but theirs was a mutually beneficent arrangement. She could kill this one, if she needed to, but she would rather hear what it had to say.

The hooded creature bowed respectfully. That, of course, was something it would do, and she was not fooled. They had scant respect for any other life-form, except where that was reenforced by fear. Among their own, of course, they were hierarchical to the extreme. Other life-forms were theirs to use... if they could. If vanity was the key, they'd use it. She did not bow back. "Well. Why do you interrupt my work?"

"My apologies, great queen of Magic Workers. My master's masters... offer great rewards for a simple service."

They paid. They paid in whatever form she asked and without any form of haggling—no matter how ridiculous her asking price. The entire funding of that Spathos had come for the hire of one cauldron-giant. Giants were hard to make, being so large, and needing thus to be assembled in sections, but still... "What do you need?" She had a list of raw materials for the cauldron needed from other planes. She'd had difficulty getting them before.

"My master's masters require the disposal of two beings. One is in Lyonesse, and one is proceeding there. We think he is in Vanaheim now. We believe you will be in the best position, with your seeing device, to find them and destroy them. I have images of both." He handed her a crystal into which a three-dimensional image of a young woman with an axe sprang into existence, sitting in a little coracle.

"A little warrior princess," said the queen of Shadow Hall, faintly amused. The child had a determined chin. But, as she had found out when she had tried her own hand at armed combat, those many, many years ago, men were physically stronger. You had to defeat them more subtly.

"She goes by the name of Meb. We believe she fled Dun Tagoll. Briefly she was on the water but she has returned to land."

"If she fled Dun Tagoll she is hardly an enemy of mine."

"She is one girl-child," said the flame creature dismissively. "There are many such, but my master's masters have concerns about her associate. She must die, to control him. Name your price."

"Tell me about the other one," said the queen.

The flame creature produced a second crystal. In it was the image of a black dragon.

"The dragon that thwarted me in Annvn," said the queen.

"He's a shape-changer. Turn the crystal over, and more images will show. We had a very good visual trace on him, but it has been obscured. He is both clever and a great deal harder to kill than most dragons, and dragons are not easy to kill. This one can only be bespelled with gold, and only confined in adamantine."

She had quite a bit of that. The Shadow Hall relied on adamantine hardness, as well as the ductility of its joints, to survive the inevitable strain of moving all the time. Her first three attempts had jolted apart. "I have been wanting a dragon for my cauldron."

"That can be provided. But you are no match for him in physical contest."

"What are his weak points?" asked the queen. There was no point in telling the demon she'd kill this one for nothing. Merely as repayment for what he'd done to her many years of work. And the girl...well, most of those in Lyonesse would die. They might as well pay her for the killing. The cauldron took certain rare materials, and of course raising a war took gold and silver, a great deal of it.

"He does not kill intelligent life-forms."

She turned the crystal over, and a tall, dark-skinned, foxy-faced man appeared. Ah. They'd had Spathos hunting him. Cutting out the middleman, as it were. But, she admitted, it was possible they had not known that he was her lackey.

It appeared Spathos had vanished in the rebellion against Prince Maric.

It would seem that brushing up against this dragon could be unhealthy even if he did not kill.

"Is this what you pitted my other cauldron-creatures against?" she said, suddenly suspicious.

"Yes," said the creature of smokeless flame. "Or rather, his guide."

It did not even try to lie. Interesting. And it spoke of its master's master. Very high. Very powerful. "This will be very, very expensive," said the queen.

"Name your price."

Vanaheim was a place where dragons felt at home. Someone had to. Dragons liked volcanoes and jagged new mountains, and a vast blue sky feathered with thin cloud. The land, where it wasn't edging into sea cliffs, was mostly fells full of sheep. Fionn knew the other coast had a gentler slope, a warmer current and forests for Vanar's fleets. This piece of the Celtic was colored by their Nordic conquerors—a gift the islanders liked to spread around. Fionn was convinced it was the long, cold, dark winters that made them so homicidal—that or their beer. Or it could be eating slow-fermented basking sharks. Fionn had sampled this "delicacy" once.

From up here, where the Tolmen Way had brought them, they could see the fleet was on the water—every longship the islanders could find, by the look of it.

And also by the look of it, most of them were returning to the fiords of Vanaheim, because there really was a stiff onshore breeze blowing. A few determined ships were trying to row their way into it, but most had turned for home.

Besides their taste for mayhem and loot, fermented basking shark and too many salt herring dishes, the other flaw that Fionn felt the Vanar culture had was their desire to shoot dragons, and they had strong muscles, good composite bows and strong nerves that made it possible. Fionn understood fully that the desire was fueled by conflict over who would eat the coarse-haired fell sheep. But it made flying low anywhere near the coast—where the Vanar lived—quite a dangerous pastime for dragons. It took a lucky shot to kill or even seriously injure a dragon, but it could damage their wings. And killing the dog would be easy too. The air here was cold. At altitude it was winter-arctic cold. It added a layer of complications to flying to the next Tolmen Way. One forgot the flexing in time between worlds. He'd expected to fly on in the night, not to waste another day!

Díleas was already heading across the meadow, down toward the fiord below. "Where are you going, you fool dog?" asked Fionn.

"A dragon!" came a sudden shout. The Vanar warrior charged, swinging his double-bladed axe and blond plaits.

Fionn knocked him down with a swipe of the tail. Just because he wasn't supposed to kill them didn't mean that he had to put up with someone swinging an axe at him. Fionn rolled him over and sat on the warrior, as Díleas came charging to the rescue. Fionn changed his form as the stunned seat groaned. "Have you been eating those mushrooms again?" demanded Fionn. Agaric tended to make for berserker warriors...and some strange visions. And this one smelled of the mushroom. Fionn got up and rolled him over, kicking the axe away. "You just called me a dragon, tried to chop me up, and fell over my dog," he said accusingly. "What's wrong with you?"

"There was a dragon..."

"No, there wasn't. If there was, do you think either I, or the sheepdog, would be here?"

The large warrior sat up. Groaned. "I gotta go. I promised Thor Red-Axe I'd join his war band."

"Where are you going?" asked Fionn, although he suspected he already knew.

"Vleidhama, to find a ship. The völva say that the way is open to Lyonesse! We must go aviking!"

Which translated as "loot, rape and pillage and maybe even stay in a place where it isn't dark for half of the year." Fionn clipped him, hard, behind the head. He fell over again. "You were right, Díleas. Just let me relieve him of these fashion accessories, and we can walk down and join a boat."

The Vanar warrior was relieved of his mail shirt, helmet, axe and woolly breeches. Fionn looked into his travel bag. A side of salted smoked salmon, a loaf of rye bread, a bag of coarsely ground oatmeal, and yes, dried red-and-white-spotted mushrooms...a leather bag with a little money—the clumsy coinage of Vanar: iron, copper and a little gold. Díleas growled at him. "Another one of these mushrooms and he wouldn't know I relieved him of it. But you're right. I'll leave him with some of Spathos's silver. I'm not that fond of silver, but it's valued here. And his cloak. But to make you my partner in crime, I'll give you some of the salmon. It's mostly salt and smoke with a bit of fish. Consistency of leather. Keeps well and exercises the jaw. We'll leave him the bread and that flask which I think might make him see more than dragons, by the smell of it."

Disguised as a Vanar warrior—a not very rich or bright one— who came down from the sheep in the mountains, Fionn walked into the nearest crowded fishing village. Finding a place for himself and Díleas on one of the good *Skei* was not likely, but some of the bigger *Busse* were struggling to find oarsmen. Anyone who thought they were anyone wanted a place on one of the faster ships, so a slightly slow-witted shepherd who wasn't prepared to leave his smart dog behind could find a place, and be away for the shores of Lyonesse just as soon as the wind turned again. That, according to the weather-wise, would be sometime after midday, and the captains were trying to keep the oarsmen sober until then...or at least not quite paralytic.

Fionn found it amusing, seeing as his multiple livers meant he could drink their Branntwein and barley beer until it ran out of his ears without any effect. The Hákarl they were eating with it was a different matter. He'd need more than multiple livers for that. It was considered a manly thing to eat.

Fionn was glad he was a dragon, and not in need of eating ammonia-scented, fermented shark meat to prove this. Díleas, however, had embraced local behavior with gusto, eaten far too much salty smoked salmon, and was now throwing up, and needing water, along with Vanar's finest warriors. Perhaps this was why men and dogs had such a natural affinity, reflected Fionn, noting that the wind was dropping.

═ Chapter 20 ═

MEB LOOKED AT THE JAVELIN, AND AT THE GROUP OF . . . POSSIBLY people, all with more throwing spears at the ready, in the forest shadows on either side. She could see the weapons clearly enough, and their sharp stone points. The wielders . . . were a mat of hair and twigs and vine. Rather like bears that had rolled in honey and then down a steep brush slope, thought that dispassionate part of her mind. She wondered in a panic if it would do any good at all to try and "hide" Neve and herself. Probably not, thought the pragmatic part of her mind. They would throw their spears the moment she and Neve disappeared.

And then she realized that she and Neve had not walked alone into the deep woods after all. And if anyone was in trouble it would certainly also be the spearmen. Not that she and Neve would be any the better off for the fact that the muryan bit the attackers to death.

The odd spear-wielders plainly spotted the tide of muryan. They lowered their spear points warily. But how do you point a spear at thousands of foes, each smaller than a thumbnail? Quite a few spear-wielders backed off completely, vanishing into the shadows. "Are you the Wudewasa?" said Meb. "Because we were told to look for you."

"Who sent you?" said one of the hairy, twiggy people stepping out of the dense leaf-mottled shade, away from the muryan. "We have no dealing with incomers. Even ones served by the muryan." He sounded a lot more doubtful about that part.

"One of the spriggans," said Meb. "They said the Land wanted us to come to you."

"Just who are you, and where are you from?" asked the hairy man with the added leaves and twigs.

Why did they all want to know that? Did it really matter?

"She's the Defender," said Neve, proudly touching Meb, who still stood holding her axe. "Prince Medraut and Mage Aberinn didn't believe her, but she made the sea-wall window come back. And it was her, not Aberinn, that defeated the Fomoire's evil eye! The fay come to her. They look after her. Have you ever seen the muryan before? They feed us, and protect us."

"We see muryan from time to time in the woods. We leave them alone, maybe leave them some scraps of food, and they leave us alone." He looked at the ground, and at the warrior muryan there. "I'll grant I have never seen them seeming to defend anyone before. But the prince and the mage and all the rest: they mean nothing to us. We stay in our deep woods and they do nothing for us and we owe nothing to them. This is our land. Our forest."

"Yes, but we've knockers and spriggans and even the piskies helping her."

"Even the piskies! Now that would be something to see," said the hairy man, sounding faintly amused. Looking closer now, Meb could see that not all of it was growing on him, but that some of it was woven into a kind of cloth. Hairy cloth. "But it seems your friend has lost her tongue. Maybe she can talk for herself?"

Meb shrugged. "I am just me. That's all. I call myself Meb. I have been told my birth name was Anghared. I came from a place called Tasmarin, where the dragons rule. They told me here that I had magic and I must be of the House of Lyonesse. And then they decided I didn't and wasn't. They do their magic by patterns and diagrams and models and calculations and rituals. I don't even know how to start that. It comes to me sometimes, because I need it, and because I dream it. And now you see me." She concentrated hard on not being seen and walked away. He stared, blinked, rubbed his eyes. Reached out to where she'd been. Just behind him she tapped him on his shoulder, willing herself to be seen again. "And now you don't."

He turned and stared. She dug out her juggling balls, simply because they helped her think. Began tossing them one-handed, the other hand holding the axe. "If," she said, "we just wanted to go through your woods, we could. You wouldn't have even known we were there. And if I was interested in conquering and killing, I could have come unseen and sent the muryan to deal with you in your sleep."

She passed the axe to the other hand, and caught the balls with it. "But we were looking for you, because I was told you were the right people to look for. That you were, of all the humans, closest to the Land."

The hairy man nodded. "I will take you to the wisewoman and the shamans. They said . . . disaster had come. They said all the Ways were open and invaders who have no respect for our forest will be coming soon. We watched for that. Not two women."

"M'lady," said Neve, timidly. "Do you mind if I carry the axe? It's really scary when you toss it up and catch the balls. I've seen how sharp it is."

The Wudewasa man smiled and nodded. "But a woman with a big axe and balls . . . makes men nervous."

They were led through the forest, carefully skirting around several places where the trail seemed to go. Someone had plainly gone ahead, because the wisewoman who seemed to lead the tribe, as much as they had a leader, was waiting with the two shamans in their equivalent of a reception room—a huge, hollow tree set at the end of a double row of mossy rocks, with a wooden chair carved into the wood itself. It was occupied by the Wudewasa's wisewoman, with the two shamans with their drums and bones having to settle for logs.

The wisewoman's hair was white. There was a vast amount of it, and barring the addition of a willow catkin, she didn't have any twigs or leaves in it. She was tiny and frail, and attended by a young girl, because moving was obviously painful for her. Her brown eyes, peering out of a mass of wrinkles, were rheumy, and she blinked a lot. But her wits and tongue were still sharp. "I thought you said it was a woman carrying the weight of the Land. I'm seeing two girls, who couldn't carry more than a peck of dirt."

"That shows that you need look a lot more carefully, Mortha," said one of the mossy stones, unwinding itself into a spriggan. "We know, the muryan know, the knockyan know, the piskies know, and, if you look properly, you'll find you do, too. Did you think it comes with a fine horse and a coronet and troops of soldiers? You're in for a sad disappointment."

The silver-haired woman didn't move. "Those are holy rocks."

The spriggan snorted: "Then maybe you should count them more often. To not notice there was an extra one might be seen as disrespect," he said tartly, showing no deference at all for her age or the rocks. "A few minutes ago you were twittering in fear because the Vanar were coming. Wondering how best to keep them from cutting your trees for charcoal or ship timbers, like last time. Now you're fussing about the size of the help."

The wisewoman kept her dignity...barely. "We were hoping... for what is asked, that we'd get something in return. Some troops of fighting men with iron swords, against their iron axes."

"She seems to have odd ideas," said the spriggan, jerking a thumb at Meb. "Believes in giving something back in exchange for what she is given. The old kings of Lyonesse would be very shocked." He seemed to enjoy that idea.

Meb sighed. "Do you mind stopping this talking over my head? I don't know what is going on, and I think if I am going to help I will need to."

"All the Ways are open," said the wisewoman, Mortha. "All our enemies will come. And while many pass through the forest without much searching or effect, the first here, the soothsayers say, will be the Vanar. They've cut out most of their own forest. Now they want ours."

"It was the Vanar who burned my village and our boats," said Neve. "Please, m'lady. You've got to stop them."

"They burn what they can't carry away," said Mortha. "The soothsayers say the sea will be black with their dragon ships this time."

"Dragon ships?" The dragons Meb knew would make poor boats. Or even poor pullers of boats, if this was something like a donkey cart.

"Their ship's prows are carved to look like dragons or great monstrous serpents. They come from Vanaheim, where it is cold and the trees don't grow well. So they come for ours. And anything else they can find," said Neve, quite used to explaining by now. "They're not quite as big as the Fomoire, and they don't have much magic, but there are lots of them and they go berserk when they fight. You have to kill them to stop them."

"They chew mushrooms that make them mad," said Mortha.

"Where will they beach?" asked Meb. "Can we stop them getting to the land at all?"

"My Gamma Elis said that in King Angbord's day they had watchtowers along the coast and warning bonfires. The troops would ride out from Dun Tagoll, Dun Argol, Dun Telas, Dun Carfon, and fight them on the beaches. There was talk of having catapults to sink their ships while they were still at sea. But the people of Lyonesse never did it, and then the towers fell or were burned after King Geoph died."

The wisewoman sighed. "The only thing that'll hold them on land is horsemen, horsemen who fight to order, with long lances, and good massed bowmen. Our forest people... We can ambush and fight in the dark, but we cannot hold them back. And we've seen what Medraut does: fight a quick skirmish and run for Dun Tagoll, and leave those outside to feel their wrath."

The spriggan looked thoughtful. "They fear magic, though. Especially women's magic. They'd be more afraid of a woman mage than a male one. And, the truth be told, they treat us with fear and respect. That'll not keep them from the forests, and they have too much iron for us. It's a slow poison to our kind, and even being close to it in concentrated or purified form for too long weakens us. If the Lady Land asks it, tribes of piskies can mislead them for a while. And we can look very large. The muryan... well, if they slow down enough, the muryan can and will overwhelm anything. And neither iron nor anything else holds much threat to them. The knockyan, well, let's be honest, they don't really fight or do more than play jokes on those who wander underground. They have tunnels everywhere, of course."

"And they will all stand against the invaders?" asked Meb.

"If you tell them to, yes." The spriggan pulled a face. "Of course... it's not quite as easy as that."

"No," said Meb, "that would all be too simple, wouldn't it?"

"Exactly, and if life were simple, we'd all have warm palaces to live in and strawberries to eat every day, in winter too. But it isn't. See, we're yours to command, but you must command us."

"I'm telling you to resist the invaders," said Meb obligingly.

"And I will," said the spriggan. "But I'm bound to a certain area. Bound within seven miles of my place. And you've told me. But you'll have to tell each of the spriggans. We tend to live three or four together. The knockyan, well, they talk and pass it on. By now I'd guess stories about you and your juggling, and having knockyan babies on your lap, will have spread from one

end of Lyonesse to the other, and are being told to others. Other
spriggans, some human miners too. The muryan will defend you
if they are where you are, and will attack if you tell them to. But
there are tens of thousands of queens. Each only controls their
own nest. As for the piskies... well, they're family groups. And
they don't keep their mind on the task very easily. They'll enjoy
misleading and mazing the Vanar. But sooner or later the Vanar
will find out how to counter that. It's best saved for when you
need it. And by then it'll be too late, I shouldn't wonder."

Meb sighed. "The real wonder is how cheerful you are. Tell me.
Do I command anyone else? Merrows? Do you have them here?"

"Well, there are merpeople, but they live in the sea, and are
no part of the land. And they're not good to deal with."

"Even so," said Meb, "I think that's what we're going to have
to try and do, and quickly because I'd rather not have more mad
people here. Most of the ones here seem quite mad enough already."

The gilded crows gave Aberinn a wide view of Lyonesse, and a
headache. Too many images to process. He had as yet not found
any sign of the two women. They probably had not gotten very far
before falling prey to what young women roaming Lyonesse without
protectors would fall prey to. He felt Medraut's reaction to them
simply too extreme. But then Medraut alternated between believing
in the prophecy and believing, somehow, that it was all a plot against
him. Either by the mage or one of the factions of nobles who still
squabbled over Lyonesse like real crows over a corpse. Well, he'd
had his own suspicions about the girl. It appeared at most she was
adept with a knife and a few magic tricks—probably prepared by
some adept for her, to be displayed suitably.

Anyway, they were dead and gone and Lyonesse faced an influx
as she had never suffered before. As yet, the gilded crows reported
no major invasions. But they would come soon. The land would
suffer, fortresses would fall. And somehow he must work out just
what had happened to the Changer.

Meb traveled with an escort of forest people, down a wooded
valley, to the coast. They had provided her with a jacket of coarse
brown cloth, set with fresh twigs and branches, but it could not
come close to their camouflage. They could freeze and look like
trees or shrubs or just the branches of one. They were experts at

not moving suddenly, and at sticking to places where the light was broken with shadows. And for most of the journey down to the coast, that was adequate. Neither Aberinn's gilded crows nor anything else could possibly have seen them. Meb was surprised at how many other people—peasants mostly—they did see. Here a nervous group of ex-soldiers from some foreign place eking out a living, there a solitary fisherman working a stream. Lyonesse was a rich country for those needing to live off the land. It made her realize that the various fay had probably worked quite hard to get her and Neve that far without meeting anyone. She was realistic enough to realize that such a meeting would only have been an ugly experience, needing the axe and luck to survive. They crossed several open patches during the night, but the problem came the next day, when they were close enough to smell the sea, and cover was sparse.

And the gilded crow was circling.

It was probably just trying to gain height. From here in the tree shadows, Meb could see that it didn't fly as well as a real crow might.

She wished it would go away. Wished it with real urgency and irritation. Wondered if she could simply "hide" them all, and whether this would work to deceive Aberinn's magical-mechanical creatures. Just wished it would hurry up and go away, that flying should be for real birds.

And, as they watched and waited, a real bird buzzed the contrivance. And then another. Smaller than the gilded crow, of course, but far more agile. She'd seen blackbirds pack a hawk like this. And now there were more birds, mobbing the crow. The gilded crow tried to flee them, but even the sparrows were as fast as it was. And it was as if they'd realized that although the interloper might be bigger, it was fairly helpless and far from as agile as they were. Then more birds came and they mobbed it down.

It crash-landed awkwardly. The birds all flew off about their business.

The crow plainly tried to fly again. And the birds drove it down. "Good," said Meb. "It can *walk* back to Dun Tagoll, and tell Aberinn what sore feet it has."

"You're a very powerful mage," said one of her escort, fearfully.

Meb swallowed. "Birds do that to foreign interlopers from time to time." Silently, to herself, she said, "but if I made it happen...

I wish you all lots of worms, or seeds or fruit, and a safe nest for your help. I don't want them spying."

They took her to the water's edge. And she had absolutely no idea what to do. She'd had the idea that the merpeople would come to her, the way the others had.

And the waves remained ... waves.

"Is anyone listening?"

No mermaids appeared dancing on the water.

The sea just sighed against the rocks.

She reached down to it, picking up a handful and letting it dribble through her fingers, sighing back at it. She wondered how the spirit of the sea was doing with the lord of the mountains. Groblek had had no limitation to planes and places ...

"And neither does the sea," whispered a voice. "It is many seas, but it is all aspects of one Sea." The face in the foam tracery looked ... like that of someone who had forgotten to do their hair. "Forgive me. I am a little ... busy," said the sea.

"Oh dear. Groblek?"

"No, you were quite right. We've found ways ... it has been some years. But we have a child, and he is never still unless he is asleep."

Years? Fionn had said that time ran differently in some places. How was he after ... years? Was Díleas old? She swallowed. "I was hoping to negotiate for some help. We're expecting to be attacked from the sea."

"The Vanar. Good seamen. Quite respectful," said the Spirit of the Sea.

"Oh. But we can't have them here, lady. Please."

"No. They don't belong here. A few are relatively harmless. But many would upset your dragon's balance."

"He ... he still works on that?"

Lady Skay seemed amused. "Sometimes."

"Is he ... well?"

"He's a dragon. They don't usually get sick. But he, and that black-and-white dog, seemed well last time they went paddling in my water."

"Thank you. Thank you so much," said Meb, smiling tremulously.

"It seems a fair repayment. You carried similar information for me. And I will deal with the Vanar fleet. Have no fear of them. Or any further troubles with mermen. Call on me again ... I must go."

Meb could swear she heard a crash somewhere. It could have been a wave breaking.

Meb turned away from the sea, to the Wudewasa and the spriggan waiting on the shore behind her.

"They're not usually interested in talking to people," said the spriggan. "I don't know why, but they're a nasty bunch, this lot of sea-people. We'll just have to fight the Vanar on land."

"Um. Didn't you see her?" asked Meb.

"Was there a mermaid?" asked the spriggan.

If the Spirit of the Sea did not want them to see her... well, who was Meb to tell anyone about it. "We can stop worrying about the Vanar," said Meb. "Now we just need to deal with any other invaders."

"Oh. All it needed was for you to splash your hand in the water," said the Wudewasa warrior. "We could have done that."

"But you didn't," said Meb, with a sweet smile. "So it's a good thing that I did. And you never know, it might not have worked for you. Actually, I am certain it wouldn't. Now, I think we need to work out where the next threat is, and deal with that. Those soothsayers are supposed to predict these things, aren't they? Because if I have to go and ask the muryan and others for help in person, I will have to get there in time to do it. And in between I'd like to try and fit in some sleeping and some eating, which I have found make me think better, and be better tempered, too. I daresay Wudewasa and spriggans don't work like that, but we spoiled fishing village royalty do."

She'd made them laugh, which Finn had said was half the battle won. She had a feeling it might be the easy half.

— Chapter 21 —

FIONN HAD FLOWN WILD RIDES THROUGH STORM AND CHAOS ON far too many worlds. He'd been at sea and shipwrecked in more tempests than most people have days to their lives. Never had he been on such an angry sea. It was not just an angry sea, with waterspouts and waves taller than the *Busse* itself... but it was also a beautiful day, with the sun shining and not much more than a breath of wind.

They were rowing, as fast as possible, toward the fiords of Vanar. The sea was pushing them, them and all the other surviving vessels, back toward the land. Fionn was seriously weighing the possibilities of taking to the air, along with Díleas, and never mind those who saw the sailor turn into a dragon. Their chances of living to tell the story were scant. But it did seem that so far, anyway, this particular vessel had been spared the worst. Even the waterspouts had sheared away and gone to sink other, less fortunate ships. The sea did not stop its wildness inside the fiord. It seemed to be trying to spit out, or wreck, as many Vanar ships as possible. The steersman of this vessel, very sensibly, beached it on the first bit of land that wasn't cliff. It made a few holes in the ship but the fury of the waves had driven her bow well up onto the steep, rocky, grassy slope. They all scrambled off her anyway, all wanting to be away from the angry water.

"It's as if the Goddess Rán has taken against us. And we give her thralls and branntwein every year. Ai, she's a capricious one," said the steersman, looking glumly at the ship. "Come on, lads.

Let's see if we can haul her up a bit. Or the sea'll have her tail off, and we'll not be getting more timber to build another like her. Not from Lyonesse anyway."

Fionn agreed with the last part, even if he called to Díleas and then sneaked off among the boulders that had fallen from the cliffs above, rather than help with the hauling.

He was also sure that it hadn't been all Rán's—as she was called locally—idea. This was his Scrap. It had her mark of total overkill about it, he thought ruefully. She'd got on with Lady Skay of the sea, and with Groblek of the mountains.

He started walking uphill. Below, in the fiord, the water, having disgorged or sunk the fleet of Vanar, was settling back to its normal mirror-calm.

"We'll do it by flying to the island with the Tolmen Way, boy. Let's get a little distance from the shipwrecks first. I'm tired after that row, and wouldn't mind a nice easy launch. We'll need to get a fair bit of altitude, because shipwreck or no, some of these Vanar will shoot arrows at us. And your basket won't stop those."

Díleas seemed quite happy to be back on dry land, and not frantic to set off for his mistress just yet. They were both wet through and it was fairly cold this late in the afternoon. Fionn was just wondering if he ought to try drying the contents of Díleas's basket with a fire, or just take a chance on getting to the Skerry island that was their target, wet and cold, when he spotted the building.

He had excellent recall. He'd seen this angular building with its two chimneys before.

Only that had been in Annvn, not on a steep slope above a fiord in Vanaheim. And...now that he looked carefully, it was attempting to meld with the shadows of the cliffs, to look like a trick of the light. A powerful piece of spellwork, that. And it was clearly and definitely moving.

And now that he tasted the air, it smelled faintly of dead things.

It was time, Fionn decided, to go and ask some questions.

He began running up the slope. The shadowy, hard-to-see house moved faster, almost as if it knew it were being chased.

"I think we'll have to try and work it as if between two sheepdogs," he said to Díleas, who plainly did not think a building should be able to move, and probably deserved to be bitten for it. They split and Díleas raced ahead, and Fionn, in dragon form, angled away to flank it. It was a bit steep for houses here, let alone ones that were trying to run away. They cornered it in a corrie and jumped up onto the portico.

"It occurs to me that owners of moving houses may have some nasty surprises waiting inside," said Fionn to Díleas. "So behind me, dog. Dragons are a lot harder to hurt, or kill, than dogs, and I have not got this close to our human to lose you. Besides, I've become fond of you. It's probably the way you share your fleas. Very generous of you, but they can't eat me, they just irritate me."

Fionn looked carefully at the door, at its patterns of energy, and the diagram used to hold it there. The human mage who had done this was no Spathos. This was art and power. The dangerous one-every-ten-generations level of human magecraft.

So naturally Fionn scratched a break in the pattern, and added another symbol or two. The mage had thought himself clever to use an invisible ink for this. Well, invisible to human eyes . . . now he would have a little surprise as the energy in that door accumulated and spread. The break allowed Finn to push the door open.

The inside was even stranger. It was quite a bit larger inside than it appeared outside. That was a neat piece of dimensional folding. Fionn looked for traps. Found none, bar the smell of decay and various exotic chemicals, rare materials and unusual compounds for the apparent vintage of the building. They advanced cautiously along the shadowy passage. Fionn detected symbolic magic at fairly high levels behind one of the doors. He cracked it. Peered inside. It contained a planar orrery, from which a bright light shone patterns onto the floor area. That showed Vanaheim— spiky and ripped with fiords. And yes, there was a shadowy hall in miniature on it, moving slowly across the landscape on tiny muryan legs. "Hmm. 'As within, so without,' rather the classic 'as above, so below' formulation," said Fionn quietly. So that was how it moved. Dangerous, clever and tricky. Going any further into the room, Fionn realized, would be even more dangerous. He'd find himself part of the symbolism. And he was too big to survive it.

They moved on. The next door was too heavily spell-guarded to get through quickly. But his nose told him: that was where the smell of decay and exotic chemicals came from. Also there was a fire in there.

"Keep a good few paces back, Díleas. This is no hedge-wizard. This is a great adept. And there is almost bound to be a trap," he said, sotto voce, in a pitch the dog could hear, but humans would not.

He looked carefully ahead, looking for magic, looking for betraying energy patterns. They'd come to a ramp, and there was an anomaly at the bottom. He could see part of the scripts of it . . .

And then, as he stepped onto the ramp, he was caught by a purely mechanical trap. The floor—obviously a circular sheet of segments—was on some kind of castors. He barely had time to yell "BACK!" before it had cascaded him into the spell-trap. There was a sharp discharge of magic. And Fionn tumbled into the trap—a sort of box at least twenty cubits deep. There was an opening at the top . . . but it hummed with energies. Examining it, Fionn could see that it was nothing more than an illusion of an opening. The box was actually solid—barring a fingernail-width gap along the lid, and a small grating in the lowest corner. Too small a grating for a mouse.

He was aware that he was being watched, from the "gap" he'd fallen through. She was, by all appearances, a beautiful woman with flawless skin. She regarded him with a sort of clinical interest. That wouldn't help him get out, of course. He was also aware that Díleas was behind her. "I wouldn't come any closer," said Fionn, hoping sound at least carried out of here. "This is a trap."

It appeared sound did. "I know. I built it. It is a one-way portal. The walls are adamantine, and the roof is fitted to a device which magically multiplies pressure manyfold. It will shortly crush you and your tissues will flow into the holding vats for the cauldron. It appears the creatures of smokeless flame overrated your cunning and prowess."

Fionn shrugged. "I took one step further than you are standing, because of the rolling floor. It could happen to you."

"The floor is now frozen until I reset it. As you are going to die . . . Agh!! No! Dog . . ."

She tried to turn and grab, but tumbled over the edge, and into the magical discharge. Fionn caught her to stop her landing on her head.

Díleas looked down at him. "Good dog!" said Fionn, surprised himself at the pride he felt in Díl's intelligence and ability to take initiative. "Don't come any closer."

The woman struggled. Lashed out at him. He caught her hand. She was bleeding where Díleas had bitten her. "Hitting me might make me angry," said Fionn, "and I think that is all that it could achieve. So stop it. Behave yourself."

If he'd hit her he could hardly have had more effect. "Don't you dare talk to me like that!"

"Why not?" asked Fionn sardonically. "Oh, I know. You might put me in an adamantine trap and crush me to death."

She opened her mouth to scream. And then thought better of it. "You have killed me. But I will die like a queen!"

"Actually, I haven't killed anyone deliberately, yet. And we're not dead yet."

"There is no way out of here," she said with a gloomy satisfaction.

"Seems very clean for something that has no exit," said Fionn mildly.

She pointed at the grid in the lowest corner. "The remains flush through there. The muryan come up it and clean out anything that is left."

"So how long before the roof comes down?" asked Fionn. He hoped that it would not be impossible for Díleas to stop. He could of course resist considerable pressure. But it depended on how much it was.

"It won't. I did not speak the words to activate it. We will starve or die of thirst in here."

Fionn hoped not. She smelled faintly ripe already. He objected to eating carrion, and he would live a lot longer than a human. "Surely your faithful henchmen, slaves, retainers..." best to know of those to keep Díleas informed.

"There are only the muryan in this part of the house. The cauldron-men I keep confined elsewhere. And the muryan will only come here to clean every two weeks unless ordered," she said dully. "So this is how it ends, so close, but yet so far."

"So close to what?" asked Fionn. "Seeing we are both doomed, you may as well tell me, and tell me why the creatures of smoke-less flame have been telling you about me."

"Baelzeboul's master said that his master wanted you dead," she said. "Running the Cauldron of Gwalar takes a lot of resources, and they were willing to pay."

Fionn explored the trap with his vision, noting the energy flux points, thinking about the shape. "You are aware, Queen—I presume you are a queen of some sort—that the flame creature's middle name is treachery. Actually, even if it called itself Baelzeboul, its first name is treachery, middle name is treachery and all the rest are treachery too."

She raised herself up. "I am Queen Gwenhwyfach. It matters not who knows that now. And I know more about treachery than you can dream. That is why I have labored these fifty years. Lyonesse crumbles . . . and I am here."

"I am several thousand years old," said Fionn calmly, "and the flame creatures have tricked me a few times. They did you, this time. Baelzeboul—if it was the one who calls himself Baelzeboul—stands one below their great master. His master has no master, barring the First themselves. So they wanted me dead, did they? How did you know it was me?"

She drew two little crystal cubes from a pocket. Fionn looked at them, at his own visage, and that of Meb.

"Stranger and stranger," said Fionn. He hadn't seen one of those for millennia. "Me. And my Scrap of humanity. I wouldn't have thought they hated us enough, or that we mattered enough. Or that they still had First-cubes."

"Your Scrap of humanity? Dragons are now keeping people as slaves and she escaped?"

"I think I was more her babysitter," said Fionn, smiling at the thought. "But she is a human, yes. A very nice child, growing into a young woman of character and courage. The dog and I are exceptionally fond of her. I would strongly advise you against even thinking about as much as harming a hair on her head. Or you may find being trapped in an adamantine cage with a dragon is a very pleasant thing."

Something about his voice made her edge away. She caught herself doing so, and steadied her spine. "She is in Lyonesse. She will die. She is just a girl-child."

"That's what the flame creature said, was it?" said Fionn. "I suppose to flame creatures any human is fairly unimportant. But this one has the happy knack of making friends, and we don't think her unimportant. I think one of her friends smashed the fleet today. So, seeing as I am going to die of starvation, how about you tell me, Queen Gwenhwyfach, why you wish to destroy Lyonesse, and just who you are. Someone may as well hear the story." He yawned. "Sorry, it has been a long day. It's not that I find you boring."

"Lyonesse is mine. Mine to destroy for what they did to me."

"They all did something to you?" asked Fionn. "Every last one of its people, and they're all still alive, are they? You did say fifty years. Mind you, you are very well preserved."

"I am as I was seventy years ago, thanks to the Cauldron of Gwalar. And almost all of the ones who conspired against me are dust, dust or grist for the cauldron."

"So why bother then?" said Fionn, tracing patterns on the adamantine with his claws. "What did they do to you?"

"They stole my child. And that cost me my throne."

"I see," said Fionn. "Just a human girl-child, probably."

"She was a princess. My daughter! Even if she wasn't the son the king hoped for."

Fionn nodded. "A grave disappointment to kings, I have been told. No heir."

She laughed harshly. "He could have no heir. I made sure of that, but he didn't realize it. He didn't even know she was a girl."

"And her name was Anghared," said Fionn.

"How did you know?" she demanded, darkly suspicious. "No one knew. No one but the midwife. And she would never tell."

"The knowing of names is a gift of mine. I am afraid I knew your name too. I merely led you on, Gwenhwyfach. And you should never underestimate the treachery of the creatures of smokeless flame, and certainly not their masters. You see, the name of the human girl child in the crystal . . . is Anghared. I would guess by your posture that she is your daughter. There is something in the jawline that is similar, but you are otherwise not alike."

The queen of Shadow Hall shook her head. "Impossible. My daughter would be fifty-three years old, if she was still alive. And while I denied it for years, the conspirators must have killed her. I searched for her. And searched for her. I hunted for years with all my art and with all my skill. Every noble house, every hamlet. I decided they must have taken her over the Ways to hide her. I searched Annvn, Vanaheim . . . the Blessed Isles and onward."

"She was a lot further away. In a place where time moves slower," said Fionn.

"I can't believe you, dragon." said the queen, eyes narrowed.

Fionn shrugged. "Why should I lie to you? I am trapped here, too. We're both doomed. You may as well tell me the whole sad story."

She looked at him intently. He said nothing. She would talk

or she wouldn't. "It may be better for the telling," she said eventually. "I was walking back with my women. I drove them out while the babe was born, and only the midwife was in the room. But there I was, with the babe in swaddling clothes, going out of my chamber for the first time, and suddenly this great drawing magic sucked at her. As if a myriad arms, wrapped around her, pulling, pulling. I clung as hard as I could . . . I fell out of the window, trying to hold her. But I must have been stunned or . . ."

She sat in silence for a bit before obviously deciding to continue. "I woke in corpse bay, cold as death and without her. And she was not on the sand. I searched and searched. We do not drown. I couldn't go back without the child. I knew she'd been taken from me by enchantment, by my enemies from the northern parts, I thought. There was a faction that hated me. And they would claim I killed the child. I . . . I almost did when the midwife told me it was a girl. But she put the babe on my breast."

Slowly it came out. Fionn listened. Pieced parts together. She had been a powerful woman, and not afraid to make enemies. Deep in her pride and power.

Broken.

Convinced finally that it had been her husband's doing, when she had exhausted all the other foes.

"And why would that have been?" asked Fionn, keeping her talking.

"Because he was a fool. But he was the king." snapped Gwenhwyfach.

She said no more, and Fionn did not press it. But he had an inkling. The woman went on, talking of her capture of a muryan queen, and the gaining of her cauldron—which appeared to be an evasion of "murdered its guardian and stole it," and the gradual building of her forces with the device. Talking of how hard it was, as the ever-moving Ways to Lyonesse bled magic from the worlds she sought to raise against it.

She didn't explain how Lyonesse did this. But it helped Fionn to understand Díleas's changing of direction . . . and the smell of her and her creations now. And just how she administered to her own vanity in keeping herself flawless, in spite of the side effect of the smell. She herself only had the faintest taint. "Of course if they're fresher, they smell less," she said, in reply to his question. "But the cauldron merely requires the patterns of their being. I had to experiment to get the mixtures I wanted, as well as mere copies, to stir the war."

"Ah," he said. "Giants. It was very hard to kill. I presume the werewolves are yours too. Anyway, thank you for telling me so much. She is your daughter, and the magic that took her had nothing to do with Lyonesse or with politics at all. It was merely choosing the most powerful mage possible to balance out the absence of humans with that ability in Tasmarin. Tasmarin now achieves its own balance, and she has returned to where she came from. And now, I think I must leave."

"You can't. I built this trap to be inescapable."

Fionn felt that her pride and absolute self-assurance had cost many others their lives. She was Meb's mother, and he didn't kill. But she was due some retribution. "If only you were always right, then it would be. I assume the muryan will come to clean eventually. Here is a bottle of water I keep for the dog that will probably keep you alive until then. You can get them to bring you food and drink, and probably will eventually get out, at which point, if you care to, you can verify what I say. Now, I need to get on to Lyonesse. There is someone I need to find, and puzzles I still need to solve."

Fionn finished pulling back the long tendril he had transformed his tail into from the drainhole. They referred to dragons as great wyrms sometimes. The device which would press the lid of the trap down, no longer could. "Stand back, Díleas." He altered his form completely to that of the ancestral wyrm form . . . which was very well structured for pushing and was a great deal longer than twenty cubits. He used the walls to balance himself and heaved. The lid moved. And moved more, and then popped off, and like a great snake Fionn slid out, shaking the queen off as she tried to cling to him.

"I think, Díleas," said Fionn, petting the dancing dog, while down in the pit the woman screamed and cursed at him, "that we should leave this place. I understand a lot more about why some humans live in dread of their mothers-in-law."

= Chapter 22 =

VIVIEN LOOKED LANDWARDS FROM THE WALL OF THE CASTLE. Maybe that child and her maid were still alive out there. She'd seen Anghared's spatha-axe. Seen and understood just how deadly it could be. And she knew, although she was not believed, that Anghared had some powerful magical skills. Maybe she'd been taken by the Fomoire where they'd found the dead one and the blood trail. She hoped and prayed to all the Gods, not. They should never have been able to leave the castle, let alone deal with Medraut's bodyguard and nasty errand boy. And a Fomoire warrior was bigger and worse yet. And yet...they had.

She hugged herself, not daring to let herself hope again.

Meanwhile, there was a thin, broken stream of gold heading for Dun Tagoll. They'd been trickling in all day now. A stream of slightly dented gilt crows, walking slowly along the causeway, cawing at the gate to be let in. Looking as sorry for themselves as any magical-mechanical contrivance could.

Vivien could not find it in herself to feel sorry for them, just afraid. Mage Aberinn would blame it on the enchantress of Shadow Hall, no doubt. But whoever it was, it had deprived Dun Tagoll's mage of his ability to see enemies coming.

That was worrying enough.

The soothsayers had rounded it down to two immediate threats: the Angevins in the South and, closer at hand, the forces of Ys marching on Dun Calathar in the Cal valley to the north.

"It's not forest land," said the Wudewasa in a not-our-problem tone. "The settlers live there. Let them defend it."

"When they have finished with Dun Calathar, where will they go next? What happens to all the people living there? Those who do not stay and fight?" asked Neve in her quiet voice.

"They flee into the forests. And the men of Ys chase them. Then they and the men of Ys are our problem," said the Wudewasa gloomily. "But you don't understand, lady. We are not warriors. We have no armor, and we cannot stand against their iron swords and long spears. It's open moorland there. They would massacre us. And the Vanar. You say they will not come, but we cannot know."

A panting Wudewasa runner appeared. "News! News from . . . coast." he gasped out.

Meb's heart fell.

"Vanar . . . Vanar landed."

"We must go . . ."

The messenger held up his hand. "W . . . wait." He was smiling, trying to catch his breath. Finally he got it out. Holding up a finger. "One ship. One ship . . . and they were bailing . . . as fast as they . . . paddled. They, they lie on the beach, half-dead. Forty-three men!"

"No more?" asked the wisewoman, plainly delighted.

The scout runner shook his twiggy head. "No. We crept close. Could have killed them. They are too tired to even set guards. They talk, hard to understand, but a storm, I think. Many, many pieces of ship wash up. Maybe more ships, elsewhere. But not more than hundreds. Not thousands."

Meb let them celebrate for a bit. Then she held up her hands. And gradually, they were hushed. "We don't have to worry about the Vanar . . . as I promised. But if your soothsayers are right, nearly ten thousand men threaten Dun Calathar. They'll come marching and burning their way down the Cal to the fort, they will destroy the new-planted fields, chase off anyone who isn't inside the fort."

"We can't fight them until they come to the forest, so we'll have to take the forest to them," said Meb. She could steal ideas from this prophecy, too, if they had decided it applied to her anyway, no matter how she tried to tell them otherwise. One couldn't argue with ideas that people had fixed in their heads. It was better just to work around them sometimes.

✧   ✧   ✧

"Earl Simon will try to meet and weaken them here," said the man who had once been a man-at-arms, before he had stabbed his sergeant in a fight and fled to the forests, pointing at the rough map of the Cal valley. "He always does. Look, the road goes next to the river, and goes through the narrows here. He'll have his archers up on the rocks above it and his men here on the slope so they can charge downhill. He's too dumb to figure that means they'll have to retreat uphill, but it does mean they can get away over the neck and run for the Dun while the bow-men on the rocks slow them down."

"And what would you do?" asked Meb, having no idea that you shouldn't ask common men-at-arms these sorts of questions.

He wrinkled his forehead. "Make them come to me, if I could."

"How big is the river?"

"At this time of year? It's just a lot of braided streams on the gravel."

"And the other side of the river?"

"Well, it goes up to the cliff on the narrows. So the earl can't run back to the Dun from there."

"And what does it look like?"

"Dunno. Stony. Got a few scrubby trees I think."

"It might just have a small forest. I really need to see it. To see what can be done."

"It's half a day's run, and the men of Ys are through the Way and into Lyonesse. They'll be there within the day, I reckon."

Meb got up and paced. "I need a horse. I can't run like the Wudewasa. And we need to move as many spearmen as possible closer, but still in the woods. Are there any fay folk up there?" she asked the spriggan.

"They're everywhere. More waking everyday. But the Cal valley is famous for my kind. There are some choice residences in the rocks. There'll be a grundylow in the river, not that you'd want to have anything to do with it, such a big wet. And of course the muryan are everywhere, and piskies are usually where you don't want them to be."

"I really need a horse!" She visualized the lovely dun mare... hoping to translate her need into a summonsing.

She got a horse.

Just not the right horse. Instead, a furious blue-black stallion with a wild silken mane so long it almost could have reached the ground...and grass-green eyes as angry as the beautiful dun mare's had been placid. A horse that was yelling at her in what could only be swear words in mixed neighs, while gnashing its teeth and stamping.

The spriggan appeared to be choking until she realized she'd never seen a spriggan actually laugh. If this one was laughing, whatever horse she'd summonsed must be a particularly awful fate. The Wudewasa had backed away, spears ready, as the horse faced her. He reared up, flailing hooves. She held the axe in front of her and tried speaking to him. It had worked on the mare that was supposed to be a killer...Only you had use the right words for the right horse, and for this one, her step-brother's choicest fishing vocabulary definitely was right. It seemed there was a time and a place for whispering to a horse and a time and a place for yelling obscenities, because the horse stopped rearing, lashing out and stood. She finished it off by waving the axe under his nose. "See this! See this? Kick me and I'll turn you into a gelding. The grooms told me that made wild horses gentler."

The horse snorted. But not very loudly. His eyes were still wild. But whereas before there had been naked aggression in them, now it was a horse looking for a good way out.

Meb had never seen a horse quite like him.

"Do you know what you have there, Lyon lady?" said the spriggan.

"I think it's a horse. But not quite like any other horse I have ever met."

"It's a water-horse. A fay creature. They live in the waterfalls, and pools sometimes. Like to trick people up onto their backs and drown them."

The spriggan looked at the horse. "Her kind can't drown, so I wouldn't try it, water-horse." And then he turned to Meb: "They're water creatures so I am surprised it obeys you. But the river water is drawn from the land."

"Besides," said Meb to the horse, holding the gleaming axe up, "if I can call you, I can call this axe. And I am telling the axe what to do to you if you give me a moment's trouble. It'll follow you, even if I am dead, see." This was pure invention. She had no idea if she could do that, or how to even try. But the water-horse obviously believed her.

She got a leg up, up onto the horse. Then she realized that

there were no stirrups, and this was bareback...with no reins either. She'd surely gone mad. "I don't want to fall off," she said, a sudden dose of common sense coming to her head.

"Oh, you can't," said the spriggan. "Not unless he wants you to."

"Right." She tapped the horse's neck. "Unless you want to be tacked up, saddle, bridle, the lot, I hate the idea of falling off. Now, I need to go to the Cal valley. Pass me the axe, will you, goodman. I don't think I can manage the bags or a basket, but the axe is coming with me." She took it from one of the Wudewasa.

"The other thing about water-horses," said the spriggan, as this one turned, bunched its hindquarters, and took off, "is that they can fly."

If Meb hadn't been magically glued to the glossy back, she would have fallen off right then.

The Cal valley was divided by Dun Calathar. The fort stood at the top of the hill where the steep upland valley spread out into a broader, fertile dale. The point at which the earl usually attempted to hold the invasions was about two miles higher up the valley. The reason was twofold. Firstly, although the gap cut by the river was too wide and river-scoured to be blocked easily, the road could be blocked, and had been, with heavy logs, well staked in. Going past that point on a horse required that the riders get down into the hundred-yard-wide riverbed, and pick their way over the boulders, and through the deep pools and small rapids that marked the constriction, because the riverbed was wider above. Secondly, by holding the south bank and charging down—and retreating back up that—the earl's riders had a flatter upper tier to race back to the Dun, whereas the road along the river valley meandered and crisscrossed the river through various fords.

Meb was no strategist, but she could see the logic. She could also see several spriggans, a fair of piskies and a strange, squat, green, shell-coated, toadlike creature. Those were the ones curious enough to come and look when she stopped the water-horse. There was a sentry, with a horn, too, at the top of the rocky outcrop. He probably was more frightened than curious. He was still blowing his horn. It sounded rather like a sick cow, echoing down the valley.

Meb dismounted. "I suppose you'd be offended by an apple. What would you like?

The water-horse blew out through its nostrils. "Watercress," said a spriggan, behind her. "But you can't get it at this time of year up here."

Meb hoped her real desire for peppery salad leaves didn't end up with a piece of salt cod. But this time the summonsing seemed to work well...except she hadn't really meant a bushel. However, it seemed that the water-horse had. And it was very fond of watercress. "I'll need you later. You are very beautiful, you know."

He rolled an eye at her. But continued to eat.

The other fay had come closer. Even the grundylow, pond-scum green and wearing a coat spattered with freshwater mussels, was eyeing her from the undercut edge of the river bank.

"There's an army coming. I need you to help," said Meb.

"You're the juggler, aren't you?" said the biggest spriggan. "The knockyan told us about the axe."

"Not about the water-horse," said the spriggan. "And where is the second noble Lyon lady they were bragging about? We see you for what you are, but what happened to the other?"

"Neve's coming. The water-horse is new...I didn't know they flew."

That caused a snigger. She felt something nudge her elbow. It was the water-horse. He had a certain look in his eye. She had been quite good at reading Díleas. This was not dissimilar. "You can kick them if any more show you any disrespect, or I'll sort them out," said Meb, patting the nose absently. He belched watercress at her, and...went back to the bushel.

"You have a way about you," said the biggest spriggan grudgingly. "You could have taught the last Land something. He got kicked. So what do you want of us?"

"Your help in giving the army the kicking instead. A lesson. We can defeat the men of Ys. Kill every man there. The muryan can come and stick them with poison as they sleep. And next year, or the year after, they'll come back."

"That is usually what happens," said the local spriggan family head, happy in this dour wisdom.

"Which is why I don't want to do that. Finn said a frightened man is a lot more dangerous than a dead one to an army."

"Oh, that is generally true," said the spriggan. "It works for us. Humans could destroy us utterly, if we didn't frighten them witless. Which means you do have to let some survive to frighten the others still more by stretching the story. Which in turn means that they leave us alone."

"That is more or less what I had in mind."

"We could like you," said the spriggan. "Even if you didn't have the right to command. Who is this Finn?"

There seemed no harm in telling them. "A dragon. A black dragon. A . . . a friend of mine. He taught me nearly everything I know."

"Cleverer than most dragons then. Mind you, they're not all alike. Well, what do you plan?"

"I hope it includes drowning a few," said the grundylow. "My larder is nearly empty."

"I have a few ideas. Possibly involving drowning. But I was hoping for tips from the experts at frightening people witless. I want a bit of time to prepare though. Could you piskies maze them?"

"There's a lot of them, and a lot of cold iron," said a little piskie matron, dressed with decorum in two acorn caps.

"I assume they have scouts. Could you maze them? Slow them down. Panic a few."

The piskie grinned. "We can do panic. And misleading a bit. But their horses won't let us lead them over cliffs."

"We'd like them to get here in the dawn, or better, the evening. Bad light is good."

"This Finn is a fine teacher," said the biggest spriggan.

"I know you spriggans can look like giants. And I know you can look like rocks. But can you do giant rocks? Look like you fill the gap?"

"That would be easy enough," said the spriggan, thoughtfully.

"Good. We will give them talking rocks and moving forests and maybe something nasty in the river."

The pond-slime green, flattened, wide-lipped mouth of the grundylow grinned. It had lots of sharp teeth.

The forest—or at least large tree limbs and Wudewasa in their usual mix of hair and twigs, which made them look like shrubs with spears—moved past Dun Calathar in the early morning, before the gates opened. It certainly did not pass unobserved. They were only just over two thousand strong but, spread along the road, they covered a lot of road. The men-at-arms of the Dun saw them, despite the hour, and as a result, so did most of the people.

The valley of the Cal, beyond the gap, had been transformed by knockyan and muryan. The slope below where the "forest" would stand was not possible to ride. It was steeper than it used to be and carpeted with millions of small, round rocks from the riverbed, held in place by terrace after terrace of twig stakes, and woven-grass-stalk lines. A man, walking carefully, might get up. A horse on the slope would not. Every five rows was a stouter stake line to stop the entire slope cascading. And in knocker tunnels below that, ready to be pulled down, lines to remove those stakes. Piles more rocks waited at the top of the slope, ready to be pushed. The flatter "forest" area itself was a zigzag of broad trenches and narrow ridges that would channel any who rode in from further up to the valley between the trees.

And that was just the start to the preparations that had been made to meet the men of Ys. Meb had neither thought of all of them, nor had very much to do with organizing them. But the fay and the Wudewasa of Lyonesse had taken having the full cooperation of the knockers and the muryan as a chance to exercise their imagination.

They had the better part of the day to set up and prepare. The earl of Calathar did come riding up the valley at the head of his men, around midday. It had obviously taken him a lot of time, and every other ability from threat to cajolement, to get the men-at-arms to ride out from the Dun. The spriggans had not been very kind to the sentries at the gap, Meb gathered. She'd have to have words with them.

She rode up to speak to the Calathar men on the water-horse.

She hadn't really anticipated the effect of the water-horse on their nags. The stallions and geldings wanted to get back to their stables. A few of them decided to go with or without their riders. The mares had other ideas entirely.

The earl had control of his horse. Barely. Its behavior didn't sweeten him. "What are you doing on my lands?" he demanded.

Meb had expected thanks or an offer of help. Or both. "Are your wits as fat as your behind?" she demanded, entirely forgetting that she was alone and he was a noble of the realm. "The men of Ys will be here by dusk if not sooner. We're getting ready to send them home if we can. To defend the land."

"It's my right..."

At this point his horse reared, turned suddenly and tossed

him out of the saddle, and headed home as fast as it could go. The haerthman who had placed the sharp point of his lance just exactly where the horse would think it a very cheeky horsefly indeed, saluted her. "Hail, Defender. We are here to fight for you. At least, I am. Who is with me?"

Most of the men raised their lances in salute, and shouted, "Defender!"

For a brief moment it was quite heady. But then the reality of it all came back to her.

The earl sat up, groaning. "Have you rebelled against your liege? Where is your respect? I'll have you all tossed out to be landless, masterless men! Take her back to the Dun!"

The haerthman who had assisted him out of the saddle pointed his lance at him. "It's you, Earl Simon, who have not shown respect to your liege. She is the Defender. The sea-window returned, the forest walked."

"And she spoke to the sea and it destroyed the Vanar fleet for her," said the spriggan neither Meb nor the earl's men had known was there.

The men of Dun Calathar were wide-eyed. But they stood, respectful.

Earl Simon flapped his mouth, but no words came out.

"The giant should be fun," said the spriggan with morbid satisfaction.

"Giant? What giant?" asked Meb, with a sinking feeling. The spriggan looked pleased. It had been looking quite put out, and had found nothing to think of that could go wrong with the trenchwork at the forest, a sure sign that it was well prepared—and probably would go wrong. But she had no preparations for giants.

"Ach, he'll be one of the half-dead ones. They always have some half-dead marching along with them."

"Half-dead ones?" Meb was beginning to feel like one of those birds trained to repeat what was said. "What are they?"

"People, or various creatures, monsters mostly, that are not alive but aren't dead. They come with the invaders. They're often quite hard to kill," explained the spriggan.

"If they're not alive, how do you kill them?"

"They're dead but have been reanimated magically. Rebuilt, as it were," explained the spriggan. "Sometimes they have been mixed with things that are harder to kill, and they're generally not too sensitive to pain. Or very clever. A clever man knows when to be afraid and to run away. The half-dead just keep coming."

And Meb remembered Vivien speaking of her husband Cormac being seen among the forces of various other places. She understood, now, how that could be. It still made her shudder, and got her no closer to how to deal with the giant.

"Just how big is this giant?" she asked in a fading voice.

"Oh, not so big. The last one had three heads, and was terrible. This one isn't more than eighteen cubits tall. Living stone too, though, so not much use firing arrows into him. You'll deal with him, though."

"You could have told me earlier," said Meb.

"Why?" asked the spriggan.

"I could have got a better head start, running away," said Meb, bitterly. "I need to talk to the muryan."

"There is nothing like ants to bring down giants," agreed the spriggan.

"I hope you're right," said Meb. "Because that's all I can think of right now.

They came, with the sound of drums, and the tramp of the giant. It was just before sundown and a curling mist was falling over the top edge of the valley, making the upper rock walls hazy and indistinct, muting colors.

The men of Ys, in their fish-scalelike armor, each troop of horse behind its brave standard, were plainly expecting the usual trouble at the gap. They halted, just below the "forest," to tighten their formations and ready themselves. Oddly, in this light, Meb thought it really did look like a vast forest, far bigger than a mere couple of thousand branches and Wudewasa. The noise that came from it was more alarming than the drum or tread of the giant. It was a strange, deep roaring sound, pulsing, rising and falling. Meb knew the Wudewasa made the noise by whirling flat-bladed pieces of wood. Knowing full well what it was, it still made the hair on the nape of her neck want to stand on end.

Some scouts had ridden along the upper part of the valley and into the wood. None had given warning.

But now the gap was closed.

And the sound of the bullroarers in the valley was suddenly

made faint by her own yell. It was supposed to be done in unison. Supposed to echo. Somehow, with the nerves of the moment or maybe the water-horse deciding to rear and charge—which was anything but what Meb had had in mind—"Go home!" should have been a lost squeak, only fit for annoying children. Instead, it reverberated from the rocks and echoed up and down the valley—as Meb, on the runaway water-horse that wanted nothing more than to fight, charged down at them, followed by the men of Dun Calathar. The water-horse, merely walking, had had a bad effect on the normal horses. Galloping full tilt, dashing its wild mane about and somehow managing to scream horse defiance, and show itself as the biggest, most attractive, toughest stallion in existence, its effect on a horse-mounted army was...interesting.

The cavalry might largely have disintegrated, crashing through the foot soldiers, but the giant advanced. About three steps... before toppling.

Meb rode—flying—over its back. Other cavalry spilled around, driving men into the river—which was rising and full of something that pulled men under—or to scramble to the woods or just turn and run for the gateway back to Ys as if pursued by more than just nasty piskies. The giants that chased them were mere glamor, but no one stopped to check. They just ran.

As a battle it proved to be a complete rout, and fairly short.

Meb actually found herself feeling mildly guilty that she'd had the piskies dose the Ys men's water with buckthorn when they'd stopped at midday. They really didn't need stomach cramps and bowels that turned to water as well. She was glad, though, that they'd dosed the giant with arsenic and now had it tied down with cables of spider silk. It would take hammering hard steel spikes through it to kill it.

And Meb knew the heady sound of cheering.

It didn't improve the sight of dead men or horses much.

But Ys's soldiery would not be in a hurry to come back to this haunted, accursed and protected land.

Now the other armies had to get that message.

═ Chapter 23 ═

OUT ON THE OPEN MOUNTAINSIDE, FIONN SAT LOOKING DOWN on the tranquil blue sea, far below. He patted Díleas, sitting next to him. "It's good to breathe clean air again, air that has none of that scent of decay and intrigue. It's helping me to think, and we have a lot to think about. It appears our Scrap must have called in help from the Spirit of the Sea. So I thought we might try Groblek, the Lord of the Mountains, instead. He's not very fond of dogs. Do you think you could pretend to be a cat?"

Díleas turned his head away and studiously ignored Fionn.

Fionn got up. "Groblek!" he yelled. "GROBLEK!" The echo repeated it, fainter and fainter.

"I've no idea if that'll work. In the meanwhile, we may as well walk up the mountain a little further, get a good line out to the Skerries, and fly out and see if we can find that Tolmen Way."

Díleas barked. The "big trouble" bark. Fionn was getting better at telling them apart by now. Walking toward them was the reason.

A bear.

Not just any bear, but an enormous beast who must have weighed at least a thousand pounds.

And his growl was like slow thunder.

"Greetings, Groblek," said Fionn, with a wave.

"I should have guessed it would be you," rumbled the bear. "Waking the child, just when we had got it to sleep. And I do not like dogs."

233

"Congratulations! I hadn't heard," said Fionn. "You're quick about it. And that's not a dog. It's a cat."

"Time moves differently for us. And it barks like a dog, and smells like a dog. Therefore, it is a dog."

"Appearances can be deceptive," said Fionn mildly. "When did you last hear of a dog having anything to do with a dragon? Cats do. And it is very good with children. Besides, it's her cat. I am just looking after it. I wouldn't dare let it get hurt."

"You're incorrigible," said Groblek. "Very well. I suppose you can come in, you and her 'cat.' What do you want this time?"

"To talk. The last time we spoke you said she had been drawn back to where she came from."

"She told us that looking into the flame she'd seen that Tasmarin must lose either her or you. I thought her heart would break. But she was a brave little human."

"More courage than common sense," said Fionn, gruffly. "Might-be futures can be circumvented."

"Would you have taken the chance, had things been the other way around?" asked Groblek as he led them toward a cave mouth.

"I thought I asked the trick questions. No."

"So your choices are right, and hers wrong?"

Fionn sighed as they entered a vast hall. A noisy, vast hall. Groblek had not been joking about having woken someone. "You ask awkward questions. And I apologize for waking him. I really do."

"I love him dearly, nearly more dearly than anything else, but sometimes he is his mother's child. Noisy, tumultuous and restless, just like the sea," said Groblek.

Fionn was amused. "Lady Skay, of course, sees it otherwise."

"How right you are, dragon. Somehow he reminds her of avalanches, which is not inaccurate at times, I will admit."

"Well, as I imagine you have tried remedying all the usual real reasons for unhappiness, let us see if he can be distracted by juggling or by...cats," said Fionn.

"Is the...cat safe with children?" asked Groblek, to whom sheepdogs were barely a bite.

Fionn smiled reassuringly. "Children are quite dangerous to them, yes, but they're very tolerant despite that. And this one will not bite a child. Not for any provocation. Will you bite, Díleas? One bark for yes, two for no."

"Hrf hrf."

"Those are of course 'meows' in his breed," said Fionn. "My Scrap raised his intelligence somewhat, Groblek, and he's of a bright breed. Your child is safe with him."

The babe was, luckily for Díleas, not as large as his father suggested he might become. And he was distracted, almost hypnotized, by the bright balls being thrown in patterns. And Díleas's bouncing and his soft fur. "Not so tight, little one. You'll squeeze the life out of him," said Groblek. Fortunately Díleas discovered he could tickle by licking.

Between them they settled a small restless, tumultuous avalanche back to sleep.

"I had no idea," said Fionn, "just how tiring they could be. Anyway, now that you have given me a great deal to think about, can you let us out? We need to go on our way. Whatever else I do . . . she needs her cat."

"I will let you out in the mountains of Lyonesse. And I will give you your apprentice's advice to us. Talk about it."

"Your kindness wouldn't run to dinner, would it? For the cat, of course. I wouldn't trespass on your hospitality," said Fionn.

"You nearly made me laugh and wake him up again. You are a perpetual trespasser. And I am sure I could find a bowl of milk and some fish . . . I do believe the cat is baring its teeth at me," said Groblek.

"He's a very intelligent animal. And you shouldn't tease him after your child has had such pleasure trying to catch his tail and tasting his ear. Díleas thinks it may be teething causing the unrest."

So it was, well fed and without having to travel any further, that Fionn and Díleas came out into the mountains on the borders of Southern Lyonesse.

It was late afternoon here, and from the mountainside, Fionn and Díleas got a fair prospect of the land of Lyonesse stretching out to a distant sea. If they'd been conquerors, it would be the kind of view they'd have wanted to plan their campaign. From here Fionn could see a number of towns—really forts that settlements had grown up around—roads, forests, plains, and brown rivers winding their way to the coast. There in the distance was a flash of armor. It had been many centuries since Fionn was last here. The chief settlement was further north and west. Their kings lived in a sea-girt castle with only a narrow peninsula to access it. Very defensible, and a sacred site too. That would be where he'd hope to find his Scrap. She must have got to the sea to talk to it, and yes, the First-crystal image had showed her in a coracle. Well, she was safer on the sea than almost anyone else would be.

And Díleas was already starting to walk northwards. "It'll be quicker to fly," said Fionn.

Díleas turned around and pawed at the basket. And as Fionn knew he did not love flying, that said a great deal. "Let me just organize it properly. Even if she's in the very furthest corner of this place—it can't take us more than another day, as long as you know where to go. Do you?"

"Hrf." Díleas lifted a paw, and pointed. It was a little inland of where Fionn had expected. But perhaps the coast curved. He tucked the blankets in around the dog, and took to the wing. It was still warm enough to find some thermals...

They hadn't flown more than twenty yards, when something pecked at his tail tendrils as he flapped up. It was a thrush, attacking a dragon.

Then an eagle dive-bombed him—talons missing Fionn's eyes by a few hairbreadths, wings actually hitting the basket.

And that was just the start. With Díleas sitting up in the basket barking and snapping, and, it seemed, every bird from half a mile around came to peck or claw or beat at them with their wings, Fionn struggled to land a quarter of mile away from where he had taken to the air.

Díleas was not impressed by the landing. Or the flight, or the fact that he had feathers in his mouth.

But Fionn was very, very happy.

It was one thing to be told she was here. To follow the faithful dog, faithfully.

It was however much much sweeter to feel and recognize her magic.

"She's gotten even more powerful. And even more prone to cause chaos," said Fionn. "The dvergar would be proud of their work and proud of her! I am. We've walked before, Díleas. We can walk again. We're here and so is she. And it feels like she has the wherewithal to look after herself."

The air, now free of flying dragons—or any other thing that did not belong there—the birds resumed their singing, and Fionn and Díleas began picking their way down the mountain towards those forts and their towns, with Fionn choosing to appear in his normal human guise, in case they met any of the locals. The mountains were relatively bare of the things Fionn expected of mountains—sheep and bandits. There was a bear, but not even Díleas's "let's you and him fight" barking could get either Fionn or the bear, busy with fishing, interested. "It's not the same bear," said Fionn. "This one did not call you a cat, and I am not going to pick on it just because you want me to. And bears like fish. He's not catching them for you."

They walked on down, until met by a rock that turned into a spriggan. The spriggan was not expecting a dragon, not even one doing a very good shape-shift impression of a human. He didn't realize Fionn could see him, until Fionn sat down next to him and took a firm hold of his ear. "Glamor has never worked very well on me," he said, calmly but firmly. Spriggans could be decidedly nasty. In fact they usually were, unless they had reason for respect or had decided they liked you as someone trickier and nastier than themselves, or preferably, both. "Generally speaking, I find spriggans give me indigestion," said Fionn, conversationally. "But one of my fellow dragons said that if you roast them slowly enough, they become crisp and quite tasty."

"Dragons blowing in here, too, now. What is the place coming to?" said the spriggan. "I didn't recognize you. I thought dragons were more on the spiky tails and bat wings and flame-out-the-nostrils side."

"I can do that if you like," said Fionn, "but I find this so much better for nasty surprises."

"I think you might get one, coming here," said the spriggan. "We have a new Defender. I saw her birds chase you out of the sky."

"Defender, eh? I'm looking for her. She's . . . you might say a friend of mine. I want to return the dog that she left in my care. He's about to mark you as his territory, so I would lose the glamor hastily, my spriggan friend, and tell me where to find Meb. Díleas and I have searched long and far for her. And yes, we're friends of hers. I swear it on my hoard. That's a very serious oath for dragonkind."

"Your name wouldn't happen to be Finn, would it?" said the spriggan, hastily becoming less than rock in appearance. "Or something like that . . . I got it from the knockyan, and they do mangle names. And it was supposed to be a black dragon, now that I recall."

"Fionn is my name and, yes, I am called Finn among humans," said Fionn. He remembered the knockyan. Miner cousins to the dvergar. Not great artisans like the dvergar, but good miners.

"Then you could let go of my ear," said the spriggan. "I believe it's due to your ideas that the men of Ys are now back in Ys, scrubbing the insides of their armor. She frightened them near witless and sent them home with their tails firmly between their legs. Said it was your idea, I've been told."

"Can you take me to her?" asked Fionn.

The spriggan shook his head. "I'd like to, but I can't, no. We're bound to our rocks. Half a league is what I can wander."

"It seems you're quite informed for all that."

"The knockyan. They love to gossip. And now that Earl Alois has pulled nearly everyone out of the mountains and into Dun Carfon, it's quite quiet here."

"Hmm. Why don't you tell me some of the gossip. It might make travel easier. I've always preferred knowing what is happening to blundering in blindly. And if my Scrap needs help, well, best I know what help to bring."

"There's a knockyan mine a little down the hill. If you want their gossip, it might be best to get it from them," said the spriggan.

"What do they mine?" He knew he shouldn't ask, but some things were too ingrained in dragonish nature to avoid.

The spriggan grinned nastily. "You don't think I'd be stupid enough to take you to a gold mine, do you? Lead, tin and antimony as far as I know. Ask them."

"Of course they would tell me," said Fionn. "Lead on. I'll do my best not to eat you, or too many of them—as long as they're also friends of my Scrap of humanity."

"They, and we, are hers to command. But she has a way of winning loyalty, it seems."

"My dvergar friends and their little contrivances. I wonder if they had any idea what they wrought when they gave her that one," said Fionn, thoughtfully, to himself. They had accentuated certain aspects of her nature. Convinced the dvergar those powerful aspects were hers to command...which could go to her head.

From the little knockers Fionn learned much more, although

Díleas would not have agreed. The little miners were not comfortable with the dog, and all Díleas wanted was to go north. Now. But their tunnels were such tiny, narrow passages, spread across the land like some vast spiderweb. It took a week or two for the stories to travel, but if it happened in Lyonesse, the knockers got to hear about it. There were several armies still abroad in Lyonesse, and Meb had defeated two of them. And here in the south, they hoped for her. But the earl of the Southern Marches did not, because he'd tried to kill her, or so the story went.

"Where is this earl?" asked Fionn, grimly.

"Well, if he's not out with his troops, he'll be in Dun Carfon. He's much loved here in the south, dragon. He alone has managed to really keep his Marches more or less safe."

"Choosing to try and kill my Scrap is not going to help to keep him safe," said Fionn. "Is this Dun Carfon on or near to my way north?"

"It would be hard not to go past it, dragon. It lies at the end of this valley, where the river flows into the lakes."

Fionn remembered the lakes—a chain of shallow, marshy lakes just inside the foreshore dune lands. The dunes would be a good defense in themselves from seaborne attackers, and the marshes were good sources of fish and mosquitos. It was easier and faster traveling along the rolling lowlands just above the lakes than climbing up the steep montane countryside and then through the forest up to the bleak moorlands that they would cross going that way. "My thanks," he said, getting to his feet. "I'll relieve you of an impatient dog's presence. We'll stop and talk to an earl along the way."

"Be careful, dragon."

"That's difficult for me, but I'll do my best," said Fionn, with a wave, as they set off.

— Chapter 24 —

IT TOOK THEM ANOTHER TWO DAYS' HARD WALKING TO GET TO
Dun Carfon. It was enough time and distance for Fionn to see
the ravages of war on the land of Lyonesse, and that this corner
at least was doing its best to hold and somehow even to prosper.
It must have been an irritation to Queen Gwenhwyfach.

Dun Carfon itself was plainly preparing for war. The abatis on the
steep earth slope up to the wall was being repaired, a few burned
trees being pulled away. People, some with carts full of fodder and
livestock, were all heading into the Dun. Fionn joined them.

The gateway had signs of human mage-craft on it. Fionn
regarded that as hardly surprising, and besides, to turn around
now—from the one-way press of traffic—was to label himself as
someone who had something to fear.

He felt the surge of energy as he walked through. And a squad
of men-at-arms and an officer moved in very quickly to surround
him, spears at the ready, but at a respectful distance.

"We must ask you to come with us, sir. Earl Alois assures you
that no harm will come to you, and he will not attempt to stop
you leaving. He just wants to talk."

Fionn said, sotto voce in a pitch they could not hear, to Díleas:
"Stay in sight but not too close." To the officer he said: "And
where do you want to take me?"

"To see the earl, fay creature."

Fionn knew what the spell was now. Some form of working to
identify non-humans. If he'd known, he could have disguised himself

as a very big sheep and made Díleas feel important. Well, they had something that looked like a man, but wasn't. They just didn't know what they had. And Fionn was not ready to give this Earl Alois the same assurances. Some very real harm might come to him.

They found the earl in the final stages of preparing to ride out with his troops. When the officer told him what he had brought, that was put into immediate abeyance. Except that the woman he was talking to, with a girl child clinging to her knees, another baby on her hip and a sturdy young boy with far too worried an expression on his face for his age, came along. Fionn was politely taken into a large, comfortable chamber that opened onto the courtyard that, obviously by the maps and drinking horns, had served as a planning room for his staff.

"I need to talk to you about the Defender," said the earl. "Branwen. Can I ask you to leave us, my dearest?"

She looked him straight in the eye, a tear already forming on her cheek, and shook her head. "No. This concerns me and Owain," she patted the boy's shoulder, "as much too."

"Well," said Fionn, "that's why I came here. To talk to you about her."

"I had no idea who she was," said the earl. "I know now. I will pay the penalty for my error. No, Bran. Owain. It is my duty and my right."

Fionn grinned. Not an encouraging grin at all. And then there was a barking at the door. "Ah. Díleas. I'll be right back."

He moved fast. That had been quite an urgent bark.

Outside the room, a man-at-arms was attempting to spear Díleas.

Fionn snatched the spear, and snapped it like a carrot. Tossed the guard forty yards across the courtyard. Picked up Díleas, and turned on Earl Alois as other men-at-arms came running. "First you try to kill my lady, then your men try and kill her dog," he said. "Can you give me three good reasons why I shouldn't pull both your arms off and beat you with them?" Something about the way he said it told the earl and the running men-at-arms that he was not joking—that, perhaps, and the snapped spear in one hand, and the groaning man-at-arms trying to sit up on the far side of the courtyard.

"Don't you dare hurt my father." The boy had himself between Fionn and the earl. Fists up.

"That's one good reason," said Fionn.

"He's a good earl, he rules well," said his wife.

"That's a good reason for someone else." There were men with weapons in hand surrounding the doorway.

"Hold," said the earl to his haerthmen.

Fionn dropped the broken spear and reached out and calmly plucked the sword from the nearest man, without letting go of Díleas. It was not hard steel—these cultures hadn't developed that yet, so, only cheating a little, Fionn bent it double . . . and handed it back to the man-at-arms. He was showing off and knew it. But he was also hammering home the fact that his Scrap had powerful friends. "Hold that up so that your comrades can see exactly what I am going to make them sit on if I see one outside its scabbard in either my presence or my mistress's presence. Ever."

"Hrf!" said Díleas.

"Or the dog," said Fionn, his sense of humor reasserting itself. "Now go away. We're talking at the moment. I will call you if I want to fight."

It said a great deal for the earl and his men that most of them did not melt away. Not more than half had their swords back in their scabbards.

"Sheathe your weapons," the earl shouted. "Owain. Go to the kitchens and see if you can find a mutton bone for the dog."

The boy stood, hands on his hips. "You won't hurt my father." It was an ultimatum rather than a question.

"Certainly not while you're fetching a bone for Díleas," said Fionn. "And it'll improve things for him if you bring back a bowl of water for the dog, too."

"Owain," said his mother, in a tone that plainly brooked no argument. "Go. And tell Osric I said to bring food and beer, too."

"A woman of good sense," said Fionn. "A lot more sense than you, Earl Alois."

"I made a mistake. I am willing to pay for it. But not at the expense of my family. My wife and son and daughters had no part in it. I didn't know who she was. If I had, I would have been the first to bend my knee."

"The second part of that will do as the second acceptable reason," said Fionn.

The woman holding onto him said: "And I love him and I . . . don't want him to sacrifice himself for me or our children. I want Owain to have a father, spriggan lord."

Spriggan? They thought he was a spriggan. That was almost

enough to make Fionn start laughing aloud. But he was not yet ready to consider letting them off the hook.

"Hmm. That's a fairly good reason, too. Meb values loyalty and love. Now, why don't you tell me the story from your point of view, and I'll see if they're good enough reasons."

The boy returned, spilling water on the flagstones, with a shoulder of lamb, still with the meat on. "My father is worth more than a mutton bone," he said defiantly, partly to Fionn and partly to his parents.

Fionn set Díleas down and the dog walked over to the boy, waving his tail and looking hopeful. Meat was a powerful attractant. "Díleas is worth more than all the sheep in Lyonesse to his mistress. I am not joking. And one of your fool men tried to stick a spear into him."

"I was in too much of a hurry to use my sword too," said Earl Alois quietly. He told how he had conspired with some of the court to remove the regent.

"Why?" asked Fionn.

"Because the constant Changes were destroying us here in South Lyonesse," said the earl. "We'd deal with one foe by force of arms... and they'd get rid of their problem by changing the Ways. We can't... couldn't go on like that. Medraut wanted to keep the regency. He wanted the power for power's sake. We'd come so close. Lord Isadore had been killed when we dealt with the door warden. It was just me left, and nothing between me and Prince Medraut. And then... there she was. I couldn't risk her waking the castle... one woman's life against the future of Lyonesse. To be honest with you, Sir Spriggan, she looked like some... drab."

"Appearances can be deceptive," said Fionn. "He looks just like a black sheepdog. But he isn't."

"Is he also something magic?" asked the boy.

"No. Well, only in a manner of speaking. But he's black and white. I had to dye his hair."

At this point someone knocked on the door. "Food and ale, my lady," said a voice from outside.

"Good," said Fionn. "Listening to people tell me how noble their motives are always makes me hungry. It's that or be queasy."

Díleas growled at the man bearing the large tray. A nasty, deep, throbbing growl.

"Yes, Díleas. I see he's got an axe under the tray. No doubt to cut the cheese."

The man nearly dropped the tray.

"You fool, Gwalach!" said the earl, in the voice of a man much tried. "Put it down. We are trying to negotiate a peace here, help for the Southern Marches. And all my men seem to be doing is repeating my errors. My apologies, Sir Spriggan. My second-in-command. He's loyal."

"I thought I might help, Earl Alois," said the man.

"We need their help, not yours! Abalach knights and the troops of Cantre'r Gwaelod both approach. And so far we seem to be doing everything wrong. Yes, Sir Spriggan. There is a time to be honest. I had hoped to seize the regency. I hoped that my son might be king one day, if we found the anointing bowl. I have always suspected that it was the Mage Aberinn who stole it, not this imaginary enchantress of Shadow Hall who he blamed."

"Oh, she's real enough," said Fionn. "And behind many of the troubles you've had, too. She is Queen Gwenhwyfach, your last queen, I believe. But hopefully we put a stop to her meddling."

"Queen Gwenhwyfach?" The earl shook his head. "No, Sir Spriggan, she fell from the sea-window with the son and heir and was drowned."

"They never found the body of either, Alois," said his wife.

"But...but she was from Clan Carfon. She would have been my great-aunt," said Alois.

"I bet she never sent you birthday presents," said Fionn wryly. "This may be a bit too complicated for you, Earl Alois, but the young woman you nearly killed would be your cousin, the queen's daughter, out of that murky past. And now to the matter of these problems you have with the various invaders..."

The earl's eyes were half closed, as he interrupted:

> Till from the dark past, Defender comes,
>   and forests walk, the rocks talk,
> till the mountain bows to the sea,
>   Till the window returns to the sea-wall of great Dun Tagoll,
>   beware, prince, beware, Mage Aberinn, mage need.
> For only she can hold the sons of Dragon,
>   Or Lyonesse will be shredded and broken and burned.

Only she can banish the shades,
and find the bowl of kings.
Mage need, mage need.

"If it's supposed to be poetry, it doesn't scan or rhyme properly," said Fionn, disapprovingly. He had strong ideas on poetry. It was powerful stuff, not wise left unshackled by verse.

"It is the prophecy Mage Aberinn made," said the earl. "Is it not known among the fay? She does come from the dark past! I saw her restore the window to Dun Tagoll. And they say the forests walked to Dun Calathar, and the rocks shouted, and the army and the giant of Ys were destroyed."

"For what it's worth," said Fionn, "she got the sea to destroy the fleet from Vanar. And you might say it's thanks to her the mountain has bowed to the sea."

"We walk in the new age of magics. When the fay return and the land is restored," said Alois wonderingly.

"And you nearly killed your new age," said Fionn, "in which case, I would have killed you, but over several millennia. Fortunately for you, you failed."

"She is the Defender. She will return our true king to us. And we need her, to fend off the sons of the dragon."

"Yes," said Fionn, dryly. "Only she can hold them."

"I...we, the South, need to make our submission. We need her help now, and it seems we will need her even more," said the earl. "So. Do your worst, Sir Spriggan. My head if need be. But the South and my family need her."

"I think we can spare you your head. For now," said Fionn, taking a horn of ale. "I think the right answer is a suitable hostage to your ambitions. To stop you acting quickly and then telling us you regret it later."

The earl was a quick thinker. "No! Not my son!"

"I'll offer the same guarantees you offered me," said Fionn. "Your men assured me that no harm would come to me. Even if some of them carry axes under trays."

"Alois," said his wife. "I'll go. I'll go with Owain if need be. We have to trust him. We have to make her trust us."

"But he's my son. I can't."

"Alois, look how he looks after the dog. He's...not evil. And you know...you said to me yourself, the Southern Marches can't hold. Not against both of those armies. Not even one of them. Then Owain, Elana, and little Selene will die or be enslaved. We need her. And there is worse to come, the prophecy says. Only she can hold the sons of the Dragon."

The dragon said nothing. His experience with prophecies is that they were generally very profitable for the prophets, and only accidentally accurate. But he was withholding judgement on this one.

"But...but it's dangerous. She's somewhere in the north. There are bandits, deserters, pieces of armies."

"Did you notice what the spriggan did to your men's weapons?" she said, tartly. "Do you think it will be safe here? You were telling us we'd have to hide in the marshes or flee north only yesterday."

"I planned to send my bodyguards with you," said the earl.

"And who will guard you while you try to fight the men of Abalach and Cantre'r Gwaelod?" she demanded. "You will need every man."

"Oh, you can send a few along with the boy, if you're worried about bandits," said Fionn. "I won't guarantee they won't come to any harm if they carry axes under trays though. I don't know about your wife. I find traveling with other people's wives leads to trouble, and there are the little ones, and I need to move far and fast."

The earl took a deep breath. "Gwalach. Go and prepare my bodyguard to ride. The best of my horses, and spare steeds. The Lady Branwen and my family go north. Sir Spriggan. Do I have your word that you will guarantee their safety?"

"No," said Fionn. "It's dangerous out there. I will swear that I will do them no harm, and that they're safe from my lady's wrath, until you come to make your submission and she decides what is to happen to you. I know her well enough to say she will not punish your family for what you have done. You, I don't know about. But she is kinder than I am."

The earl bowed his head. Nodded. "I am content with that. I had no idea you spriggans were so strong." He gathered his family around him, holding them. "Sir Spriggan...I have never established your name."

"Spriggans don't give out their names," said Fionn, truthfully. "You can call me Finn. Some humans do."

"Sir Finn...

"Just Finn. Nobility is supposed to come with noblesse oblige and I don't have much."

"Can we provide you with a horse? You are welcome to the pick of my stables."

"Horses don't like my kind, unfortunately. But I can run as far and as fast as anyone can ride."

"How soon do you wish to go?" asked Branwen.

"How soon can you get the horses saddled?" said Fionn, helping himself to a piece of cheese.

It was rather more than an hour later that Fionn and Díleas left, complete with an escort of twenty—just enough to get into trouble and not quite enough to get out of it, in Fionn's opinion. Still, they'd eaten, and at least where Earl Alois's writ ran, would have no opposition.

Well, mostly. Fionn very soon found out why Earl Alois had been so eager to make his peace with his Scrap, besides mere invasion and fear for his family and lands. The country was alive with various fay creatures, and the piskies seemed rather prone to play nasty tricks on the earl and his people. At the first mazing, Fionn strode ahead and found the three piskies doing it. They'd already separated out Alois's son and were leading him off to a stinking bog.

Díleas ran after the piskies. Rounded them up a lot more effectively than he had done the sheep, perhaps because they were a little brighter than sheep, and perhaps because he'd been studying sheepdog tactics now, with every chance he got. It left the boy on his pony blinking at the bog, at the rest of the party, and at the little, largely naked blue-green piskies, running around in a tight circle in front of Díleas.

"Just what do you think you're doing?" asked Fionn.

One of the piskies sniffed at him, sulkily. "It's of Earl Alois's blood. He nearly killed the lady of Land. She told us."

That was the trouble with piskies. They were all too good at forgetting most of what they were told. But if they fixated on a point, well, they fixated on it. "And I am dealing with that. Do you see me for what I am?" And he let a tongue of fire lick at their underprotected nether quarters. Not enough to burn, but enough to frighten them with the smell of dragon fire. They squealed, and Díleas barked at them. Short, snappy barks. Fionn did not have to have a large imagination to hear "shut up" in that bark. The piskies obviously got it. "You tell your friends, and get them to tell their friends, or I'll send Díleas back to fetch you. And them. He's a demon dog, see," said Fionn. "Now scram. Leave them and Alois alone until she tells you otherwise."

When he thought about it logically, Fionn could understand why Earl Alois hadn't told him about it. It was one of the dubious fruits of deception: the earl assumed he knew, and that all the fay were doing it in an orchestrated fashion, and not that it was merely piskies. It hadn't seemed to him that the spriggans held this view, or the knockyan. So it was probably just the piskies. They were numerous, and so annoying that most of the others avoided them. But while Fionn knew that, most humans would not.

"Thank you, Finn," said the boy, as the piskies disappeared, leaping into the brambles that trailed over the green duckweed-covered pond.

"Think nothing of it. And thank Díleas," said Fionn. "He's the one to stay close to the boy. He's smarter than piskies and he can smell them out. They're not fond of bathing. Neither is he, but he'll tell you that's different."

Fionn noticed the boy glued himself to Díleas and spoiled him where possible, and was soon playing various games with Díleas.

"He's a very clever dog. You can't pretend to throw something. And he was throwing sticks," Owain told Fionn the next day.

"Ah. He's trying to train you to fetch them and give them back," said Fionn. "Some humans can manage that. His mistress juggles. He's fascinated by that. Watch." And he juggled as Díleas followed the balls. Fionn was amused to notice the young human and Díleas looking rather like marionettes on the same string. As they traveled, Fionn learned a great deal about Lyonesse, its ruling class and just what they'd been up to since he'd been trapped on Tasmarin. This Changer device had to go. It allowed them to leech the magic of other places into Lyonesse, but unbalanced everything—besides the socio-political effects, causing war and destruction.

Their transit across the heart of Lyonesse was relatively uneventful. Fionn was glad. It gave him a chance to think. He had an eye out for the various fay creatures, and the knockyan. A few questions kept him informed of where they'd last heard of his Scrap. She was being, as usual, a busy little lass. There were traces of her magic abroad.

She was busy fixing things. Fionn undid a few workings that were fixing things best left broken, or that hadn't been broken in the first place.

═ Chapter 25 ═

"YES," SAID THE SPRIGGAN, EVEN BEFORE FIONN HAD TO DO something like twist his ear. "She and the Lady Neve are up ahead. Half a mile or so. They're moving across to the east to deal with a mob from Finvarra's land. They've stopped at the stream to water men and beasts."

All morning Díleas had simply wanted to run on, and had been doing little forays of a few hundred yards and then running back to chivvy them on.

Now Fionn came back to the small party of Southerners. "Let me go ahead. We're just about there, and I'd rather there be no misunderstandings."

Such was the extent that they'd got used to Fionn that no one even questioned this.

So he and Díleas ran. He could run steady as a horse at a trot all day if need be. Díleas had no such systematic method. He ran too fast, panted back, and then kept just ahead.

Fionn saw her in the distance, hair flared as she turned, a face he knew every line of, and his two hearts beat faster.

Díleas must have got the scent at that point, because he deserted Fionn and sprinted.

Díleas ran up to her with little crying whimpering noises. Danced up at Meb on his hind feet, and leapt up at her, making squeaking, yipping noises and literally quivering, his fan tail threatening to beat his head to death.

"Boy, you seem pleased to see me. You look just like my Díleas, only bigger and black."

"Hrf AWHRFFF!" Díleas pawed at his neck.

"What's wrong, boy? You got something around your neck?" She knelt down on the soft green turf next to the stream and pulled away some of the rolled cloth Fionn had covered the chain with. Looked at it. And with shaking hands she uncovered the bauble on his neck while Díleas attempted to cover her face with adoring doggy kisses. She saw the red glow of it and hugged him fiercely. "Oh, Díleas. It is you. It is! Oh, my dog. Oh, my baby." Díleas sprawled himself against her, tongue hanging out, panting happiness.

She pushed him away a little bit, to look at him sternly. Still holding him with the other hand, of course. "But, Díleas, I told you to look after him. You didn't leave him, did you?"

"No," said Fionn. "He brought me along."

She looked up from where she had her arms buried in Díleas's fur. Looked at Fionn. He'd been nervous about this. Nervous about the passage of, possibly, years. He'd arranged his gleeman cloak—colors out—around himself, as he stood there.

"Finn!" she screamed and ran into his arms while an overexcited sheepdog danced and bounced and barked around them.

And for a long time, that was all, and that was enough. They stood with the dog leaning against their legs, holding each other.

Fionn was aware first of the humming. And then, looking down at Díleas, who had just decided he needed to stop for a drink at the stream, the energy flow.

He dived at the dog, grabbing for its throat, snatching the now white-hot piece of crystal there, burning hair. It seared into his hand as he ripped it away, flinging it as hard as he could. It was still not hard or far or fast enough.

It exploded midair, perhaps seventy yards away, in a column of violet and incarnadine fire. The explosion shockwave was enough to knock people down and send horses fleeing. Fionn pushed his burning hand into the stream. It steamed and the pain was savage. Díleas, shivering with fright, was in the water too.

"Finn!" screamed his Scrap, holding him. "What can I do!? Are you all right? Oh, Finn!"

"Need to keep it cold," said Finn, through gritted teeth.

The stream began to crackle with ice growing in it. "Enough, Scrap. Enough." She was a very powerful mage. And she was very frightened. He was lucky not to have the forelimb frozen off. Díleas scrambled out of the ice-sparred water. "Get a piece of ice and put it on the burn on Díl. I think I got it away from him in time, but check his throat and chest, ugh, worse than a hand."

Fionn looked into the clear icy stream water at the damage. He was going to lose part of that limb. At least two talons' worth.

But another two seconds and they would have been dead.

"What happened?" said Meb, shakily fending off the panicky ministration of another round-faced young woman. "I'm fine, Neve. Just frizzled my hair and lashes a bit. Fionn's burned. And so is Díleas. Just tell everyone I am fine. Just helping the injured."

"The tiny piece of primal fire that should have burned for several millennia was made to give up all its energy at once. Someone made it die in order to try and kill us. But the energy was limited and constrained by the crystal and the magic on it. So that had to grow hot enough to shatter before it could incandesce. Someone wanted to kill us."

"Who?"

Fionn shrugged. It sent a wave of pain up from his hand. "In my case, there is quite a list. But there are very few powerful enough to do it this way. I thought the First had gone. I did not think the creatures of smokeless flame were able to do that, and I thought it would be too holy to them."

"I'll find them, burn their homes and plow their fields with salt," said his Scrap grimly.

He could see her mother in her now. "They'd like that," he said, with as much cheerfulness as he could muster above the pain.

"What . . . ? Oh. Yes. I suppose they would. What would they fear and hate most?"

"Having known them, failure. It hurts worse than anything we could do to them."

"Won't they just try again?" she asked.

"Possibly. But doing so means admitting they've failed. Humans are quite used to failure. You admire people who keep trying. The First do not fail in their endeavors, so, gradually, they did less and less, just in case they did fail."

He could read her expressions by now. That one translated as "It's not enough." But all she said was: "What about your hand?"

He shrugged again. Regretted it again. "I'm going to have to lose part of it."

"Do you need a chirurgeon?" she asked, worriedly.

Fionn thought of the local bonesetters and what passed for medicine in Lyonesse, and how they'd deal with dragon skin and flesh. "No," he said, wincing, pulling the injured hand out. The effects of that kind of heat were grave even on dragon skin and flesh. But dragon tissue did not transmit heat well. That was how they survived brushes with dragon fire. Two fingers and part of his palm to just below the knuckle were largely carbonized. So he bit it off. That was painful. But compared to the pain from the burn damage, not so awful. He squeezed the wound closed.

"You . . . just bit off half your hand," said his Scrap, incredulously.

Fionn nodded. "Less damaging than the burn. My kind of dragon cells are toti-potent. It'll grow again eventually. Dig into my pouch and give me a piece of gold to put on it."

She did. Fionn noticed how the party with her had rapidly shifted from "with her" to "guarding her." That was good, even if it would not have stopped this. With the gold there, and some mind control exercises, the bleeding slowed, and the pain eased. "That's a bit better."

Díleas licked him. Someone had shaved away the fur on his neck and upper chest. He had a blistering of the skin there, but it did not appear to be any worse. Fionn was still worried.

"How about we bandage the hand tightly with some pieces of gold against it," said his Scrap.

"That sounds better than this," said Fionn.

So they did. "How long have you been here?" asked Fionn as she wrapped torn linen around the hand. "Time can move quite differently in different planes, and I knew that it was possible that you'd be old, or even dead, before I found you. You've grown. Well, yes, the hair, but as a person."

"I think four or five months. I missed you so badly, Finn. I really didn't keep track too well at first."

"I thought it could have been years."

"Excuse me, m'lady. But there's a party of Southerners approaching," said the little round-faced girl. "What do you want us to do?"

Meb looked up from her bandaging at Neve. Neve had proved surprisingly good at telling other people what to do, that privies were needed, to fetch water, organize fires . . . on her mistress's behalf, without her mistress having a clue what needed doing.

But there were times when she felt it was politics, and insisted on leaving it to Meb... who felt that she knew more about privies. The Southerners were led by a sturdy, worried-looking boy, a girl on a smaller pony, supremely unconcerned about everything, and a woman, quite beautiful, with a young child sitting in front of her. Behind them were what could only be men-at-arms.

"Ah, Branwen and the children. That's Owain, Elana on the horse, and little Selene with her mother. I brought them along."

Meb knew a moment of terrible jealousy. Tried to stifle it. He'd just explained it could have been years. Probably was for them. And Díleas went running up, and dancing up at the boy. She would understand. She wouldn't hate them.

"That's quite tight enough, Scrap," said Finn. "It's Earl Alois's wife and children. Officially, they're hostages. Unofficially, I brought them along to teach him a lesson about attempting to kill my favorite human."

"Oh. Um," she colored. "I thought..."

He was always quick on the uptake. He gave a shout of laughter. "No, I haven't decided to start collecting humans. Mind you, there was a farmer's wife in Annvn who wanted to collect me. And besides, I think it's been weeks rather than years, Scrap. It just felt like years, while Díleas led me to you."

"He did? He's so clever. Even though I wanted you to stay away."

"You should see him herd sheep," said Fionn. "We can talk about staying away in a while. Meanwhile, I am afraid I did give my word that they'd be as safe as I could make them."

"I don't trust Alois."

"I wouldn't too far. He is ambitious. But the boy is his life. They're very patrilineal here. That's what caused all the mess with the queen. Your mother."

"What?"

"I'll explain. But for now, maybe we need to be nice to Alois's wife. She's solid and sensible. If you get her on your side, she'll keep him there. And Díleas likes the boy."

So Meb graciously met the wife and children of the first man in Lyonesse to try and kill her. "I am sorry. We just had an attempt at assassination," said Meb. "Finn saved us, though."

"The spriggan Finn is a great warrior," said Branwen. "Defender. I... I come to ask clemency for my husband, and help for the

South. Alois wants to make his submission, but we face two great armies. And the fay seem to have risen against him."

"I think I may have dealt with that," said Finn. "But you may have to tell the piskies to stop harassing him, and to harass the invaders instead, Anghared."

Spriggan? Anghared? thought Meb.

"It's what you are, here," said Finn, winking at her.

That was enough to make her smile. He was up to his Finn tricks again! "Lady Branwen, you and your retainers are welcome here," said Meb. "This is our war band, and we are dealing with those who come in by the Ways. But that is a fair number of armies. I'll discuss it with Finn and see what we can do for the South."

"It is a part of Lyonesse, and very loyal to your mother," said the woman, looking relieved.

Her mother. They all seemed to know a great deal more about her than Meb ever had. "I will see what can be done," she repeated. "Now if you will forgive us, I'd like to finish dealing with Finn's injury."

The woman curtseyed, as did the little girl. The boy bowed. "Is Díleas all right?" he blurted, having not said a word earlier.

"We hope so," said Finn.

"You'll deal with whoever hurt him?" asked the boy, hand on his dagger. Plain that he would, if she wasn't going to.

"Oh yes," said Meb, "of that you may be sure. Even if it takes the rest of my life."

"Tell me," said Meb, once they had privacy and space again. "What brought you here, Finn? I mean, I love you..."

"Oh, mostly my feet," said Fionn, trying for insouciance. Scared of saying the wrong thing. "But then I got Díleas to stay in a basket while I flew. He knew precisely where to go, and took me to Ways between planes that I did not know of."

"You know perfectly well what I mean," said Meb, sternly. "You knew—because I asked the Sea and Groblek to tell you—what I had seen in the fireball of the creatures of smokeless flame. You knew I did this for you, Finn. To keep you alive. I saw what I saw. And I love you, and one of us will have to go away."

Fionn took her in his arms. Held her for a bit, and said, carefully, and as calmly as he could, "The being of energy probably did not lie. But the truth is complex, and they leave things out to suit themselves. Or they tell the truth in ways so that we can deceive ourselves. It seems probable that my being with you will result in my death..."

"Then, Finn, I must go. Or you must."

"Wait," said the dragon. "Let me say what I must say, and then you can decide what we must do. You made a great and loving brave choice last time. But you did not ask me what I would choose. And this is my choice: I would rather die loving and loved, than live forever without you."

She held him very tight.

"It's very hard...knowing someone you love is going to die," she said quietly.

"But my dearest," said Fionn, lifting her chin and kissing her, "I have always known that you will. In the normal course of things, dragons live far longer than humans. And humans cope with humans dying before they do, all the time. You...we love Díleas even though we will outlive him. And, there is an anchor of hope. The First have been trying to kill both of us. They just tried again, in a way that must have hurt them."

"That's...hope?" said Meb doubtfully.

"Yes. Great hope. Because if our meeting was going to cause instant death, why bother? They'd simply facilitate our getting together."

"Oh. Um, that's true enough," she said, brightening.

"And besides, there is this prophecy of yours."

"I don't think I am this marvelous Defender of theirs. I just have some dvergar help with my magic. I've been playing along a bit, Finn. They needed to believe or they'd never have had the courage."

"Maybe. But it did say that only you could hold the sons of the Dragon."

She looked at him with very wide eyes. "How is your hand?" she asked.

"Healing slowly. Not as painful as it was. Gold is good for dragons."

"Maybe we need to go for a very long, private walk," she said, with a look that was love, mischief, magic and desire all in one. "There are things that Hallgerd warned me about, that I need to find out about, firsthand."

"It looks like we have visitors," said Fionn, simply because Díleas was barking, which distracted him from kissing her and planning an immediate departure.

"Noisy cat," said Groblek.

"But our son likes him," said the Sea.

And they bowed to each other.

"We thought we would fulfil your prophecy and wish you very happy."

"And if you have a need of a quiet place in the mountains..."

"Or a noisy one by the sea..." said the two of them.

Fionn looked at his Scrap, and she at him, blushing. "Um. Tonight?"

There is a place somewhere under a warm sun where the jagged mountains meet the limpid turquoise sea in perfect scalloped bays of white sand. A week there is a day in Lyonesse. It is a place of exceptional beauty. But the two transported thence really didn't notice.

The girl kissed the dragon, and the dragon, considerably more nervous than any dragon had a right to be, carried her out of the water to the huge golden cushion that their generous host had provided. It was real cloth-of-gold, and more comfortable than a bed of coin and other treasures might have been to the girl.

The dragon would have shared even that with her. No. He would have given it all to her.

"Finn," she said, looking up at him.

"What, my dearest Scrap?"

"Nothing," she said contentedly, trailing her fingers down his chest. "Nothing more. Just Finn."

The dog, being more intelligent than most dogs, found it a good time and place to chase seagulls.

The Mountain and the Sea gave them some time—they were never sure just how long—in their secret place, which is beautiful, but not beautiful beyond human conception.

"The tricky part is not dealing with the invasions, or frightening them off. It's getting to them. Knowing where they are," said Meb, still touching him. She just liked to have a hand on him. "We head east towards Dun Telas, and they pop up in the northwest on the coast—we had ships of Blessed Isles beach themselves there. It's too many enemies at once."

"You need better communications at least," said Fionn thoughtfully. "And to pass the word among the muryan and piskies that harassment is good. Have you tried asking the knockers to pass the word along? They have extensive tunnels and a system of using their little crowdicrawn drums to talk across the length of them. They need it for the spreading of gossip and warnings and calling for help when they have ground-falls."

"No. No one tells me. They all assume I know everything," said Meb. "And what I wanted to ask, that you and half of the country seems to know, is just who my mother was?"

"Queen Gwenhywfach, the last queen of Lyonesse."

"Who was supposed to have fallen or dived or been pushed out of the sea-window at Dun Tagoll with her son."

"Yes. But she fell trying to hold you. And as for the son: she hadn't quite got around to admitting to the king or to anyone else, that the longed-for heir . . . was a girl. They're patrilineal here. Girl-children don't count much, except as trading counters in dynastic marriages. Only you've proved them wrong."

Meb pursued her line of thought relentlessly though. "So: is my mother some kind of ghost? Is this what Shadow Hall is? A place of ghosts?"

"No, she's very much alive. Has been waging and orchestrating war on the House of Lyon and every other imagined enemy in Lyonesse who stole and killed her baby. She seems to have a particular hate for Mage Aberinn."

As Meb stared at him, he said: "I hope Díleas and I put a stop to it. But I couldn't actually kill her. And she is the kind that it would take death to really stop. Shadow Hall is a real place, though. She just uses her art to hide in shadow illusions and moves it with her muryan slaves."

"You have to tell me the whole story," said Meb, snuggling up to him.

Fionn did, using his precise recall to fill in as much as he could.

At the end of it Meb sighed. "I always wanted my real mother. Dreamed she'd be everything Hallgerd wasn't when I was being lectured. Being told to concentrate, work harder, find a nice fisherman who could support me. I think . . . when I had to leave you, I dreamed that my mother would be here waiting. I never thought she might be . . . like that."

"Environment and our society shapes us. Some more than others, I suppose. You're my Scrap. The person you chose to be, that I love. Who, if I have daughters by, I would love as much as sons. You would be Scrap, not your mother."

"So my father was King Geoph, who thought I was his son."

"It's possible," said Fionn warily.

She didn't notice. "I don't feel like a princess. I'm just me."

Fionn shrugged. "What's the difference between a princess and someone else, beside politics? And sometimes money?"

"But I thought only their nobility had magical power," said Meb, puzzled.

Fionn laughed. And laughed. And eventually stopped laughing to explain. "It's a myth, Meb, to justify them being 'nobles.' At one time it must have been a rare genetic condition. That means, before you ask me, something like the color of your eyes or the tilt of your nose, that you get from your mother or father's bloodline. It gave those who had it an advantage, so they ended up as the nobility. And it might have stayed that way, if the nobility had only bedded nobility. But the nobility spread it around by exercising droit du seigneur. By now I doubt if there is a single human in Lyonesse without some of the ability. Unfortunately most of it is weak, and needs ritual and training to use. Your maid, Neve, for example, has some. I can tell. She's even managed occasional small workings. But she's never been taught, and thus doesn't know she's as much one of the overlords by blood as they are."

The First knew fear. And worse, knew uncertainty. They retreated into their councils. It would take some time to decide just what they would...or could do next. There were plenty of pawns...But their source of fears had allied themselves with powerful allies, and were hard to find or harm. And the future was uncertain.

═ Chapter 26 ═

IT HAD TAKEN QUEEN GWENHWYFACH A DAY TO GET OUT OF THE now lidless adamantine box. The black dragon had left it open, and she had at least some of the tools for symbolic magic with her. True, if it failed, she would be out of water. But she hadn't. She had flooded the trap instead and swum to the lip.

It had taken her a while to think of this, and she'd also had a period of reflection on what the black dragon had said about her daughter.

So her first reaction was not in fact to pursue revenge, but to use her seeing-basin to scan across Lyonesse. She still could not see inside Dun Tagoll, but the rest of the country was hers to overlook.

She had expected a fair proportion of it in flames by now. It did not take her long to find that this was not so. It took her a great deal longer to find the "girl-child" that Baelzeboul had tried to pass off as an irrelevant someone they wanted killed.

Gwenhwyfach followed and studied her with great care for nearly an entire day, although it had taken the queen seconds to decide the dragon was probably right and, moreover, that the child was a many-times-more-powerful magic worker than she was.

The Cauldron of Gwalar had almost finished producing the new crop with the material she had been provided with by the creatures of smokeless flame. As soon as they were ready, she set them to work. There were eight of them, and she'd made them so large that, once they emerged from the cauldron, she had to assemble them with her muryan slaves.

While this was underway, she sent orders to all of her other minions.

"What I don't understand," said Meb, "is why you came on foot through the Southern Marches at all. I mean, why didn't you fly? You were telling me you flew with Díleas in the basket."

"Because, my dearest Scrap, we couldn't. Someone," he said, kissing the top of her head, "has bespelled all the birds of the air to attack dragons. I wanted to fly to you as fast as I possibly could, but it was still wonderful to be attacked, because your magic has a distinct signature to it. I finally knew I had found you. Still, now I think it would be useful if you took it off."

"Of course," she gave him a squeeze. "I just did it for Aberinn's mechanical gilded crows. I made them walk back to him. I suppose they would be able to fly again."

"Possibly. But even if this mage wishes to find you, what he sees with the crows will probably discourage him," said Fionn. "I plan to discourage him. Permanently. Him and this Medraut. I think I already put any ideas of killing you firmly out of Alois's head. Not, to be fair, that he wanted to kill you once he had decided you were this promised Defender. But it would be nice if I could fly again at need."

"Yes. How do you think I undo something I don't even know how I did?" asked Meb, seriously.

"I'd start with calling a bird and telling it. And telling it to tell others."

So she did.

They moved against the men of Erith that afternoon—to get news that they were already fleeing. So Meb's army set up camp in a gentle valley just outside the fortress of Dun Telas.

Neve, blushing and wringing her hands, came to Meb. "M'lady, I'd like to ask leave...to go into the town. I've got family here."

Meb seemed to recall a "better not ask" zone around this. "Of course."

Neve smiled a tight little smile. "They said I'd end up a castle slut. They, they were very...unpleasant. I'm...I'm going back to rub a few noses in things."

Fionn smiled. Dug in his pouch. Handed her some silver—by the look on her face, more coined money than she'd ever seen in her life before, let alone held. "I'll bet she's never paid you either. Go and be generous. Nothing hurts more. My dearest, can you spare Neve an escort of men-at-arms? Say half a dozen of those stout fellows from Dun Calathar. Show them how important she is to you."

"Oh, Finn. You make me feel so guilty. I should have paid you, Neve... only I forget you aren't just my friend. And, uh, I didn't have any money. Never thought of getting any."

Little tears started on Neve's cheeks. "That is the greatest thing you could have done for me. But... I couldn't take your money, my lady. I want to serve you."

"It's not hers, it's mine," said Fionn. "And I have lots more, and your being lady bountiful to your kin is a small thank-you from me for looking after my lady."

"And you'll have an honor guard and a fine horse to ride. I can escort you myself."

Neve shook her head. "I'd rather you didn't see me doing this, m'lady. It's... its not very nice. But they need to learn."

Neve had not been gone for more than an hour when Fionn wished Scrap had gone with her.

He could defend her and the camp against one dragon easily enough. Two, possibly.

But the eight—flying in a rigid formation, and thus very undragonlike—were six too many. And they were carrying something beneath them in a spiderweb of lines. Had the creatures of smokeless flame gone into alliance with some of the dragons who were less than pleased about the opening up of Tasmarin?

"I think this may call for your magic, Scrap. And quite quickly. No, Díleas. You cannot see them off, or herd them."

"They're carrying white flags, Finn. And... they seem to be settling. Putting down whatever it is they're carrying."

Fionn could work out what it was, now. And that didn't make him much happier than the dragons had. Actually the dragons might be less trouble, but he did understand why they behaved so undragonishly now.

Shadow Hall began to trundle slowly toward them. It was as hard as ever to see. But the white flag was easy enough to spot. It stopped a hundred yards away, and a party of men came out escorting someone.

"Queen Gwenhwyfach," said Fionn. "And that is Shadow Hall.

And the ones escorting her I would guess are some of her cauldron-men. She makes them, as I told you, from dead tissue."

"Do you think she's come to surrender? They have a white flag."

"Let me go and find out," said Fionn.

"Not without me. And by the looks of the way Díleas is bristling, not without him, either. I don't...really think I want to meet her, Finn."

"I think you'll have to, nonetheless."

They walked forward to meet the queen of Shadow Hall. She was, Fionn noted, much better at playing the traditional part of being nobility than his Scrap could ever be. Gwenhwyfach was being carried on a palanquin of golden silk, dressed in velvet and ermine, with a crown. Meb was wearing an old skirt, a shirt that had blood on it, and her only "dressing" was an alvar comb in her hair. There was quite a lot of glamor on that ancient alvar piece, and it did make her hair exceptionally bright and flowing. Like that spatha-axe she carried...she didn't seem to realize that she called the most powerful magical artifacts to herself. The axe had been buried a long time. As Fionn recalled, it was supposed to be sharp enough to cleave stone, and she'd magically sharpened it further.

Still, his Scrap looked very ordinary compared to Gwenhwyfach's pomp. That was good in Fionn's opinion. He wasn't sure how it sat with humans. "She did plan to kill us both," he said quietly. "This may be a relatively unwise thing to do."

"Good thing that it's us doing it then," said Meb, squeezing his good hand.

The bearers set the palanquin down and a flunky gave her his arm to stand up. The queen did not appear to need it.

"It smells a bit," said Meb quietly as the queen approached.

"My darling daughter! Anghared, how I have longed to hold you! Come to your mother's arms!"

"I hear you were trying to kill me," said Meb, not moving. "I also hear you tried to kill Finn. And that you've been sending your half-dead creatures to stir up war. That stops."

Fionn wondered if his Scrap even knew that she was projecting her voice so that the entire camp, and probably the town and fortress, could hear it.

It must have got to the queen too, because she took one more step, and stood, arms outstretched. Or perhaps it was Díleas, growling with deep menace. "I never tried to kill you, child. As the dragon told me, it was the flame creatures and their masters and their treachery. I have been working on some traps for them. And Lyonesse...I merely repaid them for their treason."

"There was no treason. You were wrong, you blamed the wrong people," said Meb flatly.

The queen drew herself up. "There was much treason, even if I was wrong about who had stolen you and where you were taken to. But now you will be queen after me. Together we'll take Dun Tagoll and put that traitor Aberinn and his hireling regent onto sharpened pikes. We will find you a suitable noble from the House of Lyon to be your king. And your sons will rule. It is what I thought I would do, but I will celebrate your ascension to the throne..."

"No, thank you," said Meb. Fionn had heard that tone from her before. And he and Díleas knew it meant trouble. "I don't want you, or need you, or your dreams. I defend Lyonesse. I do not attack it, nor will I let anyone else do so. Not you, not anyone." And with that, Meb turned and began walking back to the camp.

For a moment Fionn thought the old queen would have apoplexy on the spot. She did take one angry step forward...and sank up to the knees into the earth.

"Hee hee hee," chortled the spriggan who had been doing a passable imitation of a rock. "She's the Land, old Lyon. It won't let you harm her, even if you could."

"That...that is not possible," said Queen Gwenhwyfach. "The King is the Land, and the Land is the King. It only serves the anointed king!"

Fionn could see deep energy patterns. "I'd go," he said quietly to the queen, as his Scrap turned her back and walked away. "Go and do your best to make reparations. Stop the invasions, make peace. Don't do anything else. In time she may come around, but not if you make things worse."

And then he turned and followed his human.

She had a dog and dragon for comfort, and needed them.

Fionn had been glad to see Shadow Hall—and the dragons— leave. His Scrap now of course wanted to know all about it, about the Cauldron of Gwalar, about how it moved. She could have had a guided tour, Fionn was sure. But perhaps better not.

"The cauldron appears to be a magical artifact that takes the patterns of the living creatures from dead matter and makes more, and reanimates them. She had her muryan slaves collecting corpses, and then she puts them back together and to work for her. It seems they have no free will and fairly limited intelligence."

"Slaves and prisoners should be set free," said Meb firmly.

"In the case of the muryan," said Fionn, "it raises an interesting question. The workers and soldiers are slaves to the queen, to the death, by their very nature. They are imprinted on her and cannot do anything but what she wants them to do. They adore her, and in that you might say it is a willing bondage that they would never swap. The queen, on the other hand, is their prisoner, watched and guarded every second. The soldiers assess danger to her; they will not permit her to expose herself to anything they consider even faintly risky. She will never touch the ground nor eat food that has not been tasted and waited upon for an adverse response on the health of the taster. She will never be alone. They would do anything for her but leave her to her own devices. And she would never choose otherwise. To be served, to be their prisoner, is as much part of her as being her slave is to them."

"Yes, but she is the prisoner of this woman. And that isn't right. I'm not sure about the rest, but that isn't right."

"We'll liberate the muryan queen from her somehow," said Fionn, not adding that the muryan queen would then be indebted to Meb.

Earl Alois and his troops had been hiding in ambush for the knights of Abalach when the dragons came. He thought it was the end, after their success against the troops of Cantre'r Gwaelod, who had been in disarray and piskie-led already. It had seemed that the Gods above and below might grant them victory. And now defeat, and disaster, and death.

It was ... for many of the knights of Abalach.

Afterwards, one of his men stood up from where they'd cowered in the forest brake. "Do we chase after them, my liege?"

"No." He took a deep breath. "No. We go north to meet the Defender."

There was a cheer from his men.

"How far north?" asked one of the officers. The man on whom provisioning rested, Alois realized.

"At least as far as Dun Tagoll. I think," said Alois.

✧   ✧   ✧

For the second time in her life Gwenhwyfach found herself in the pit of despair. It was worse than being in an adamantine cage with a dragon.

She had begun to dream great things of her daughter. And also realized that she was eclipsed in power by her. That was enough to make her both proud and afraid.

At first she had been inclined to blame the dragon.

But, stripped of her illusions, she realized that the dragon had firstly spared her life. Even though he could not kill, to put the lid back on the trap was not beyond him, and he had left her water, and told her she'd eventually get out, and secondly he had told her the truth. There were almost shreds of sympathy there. His kind were long-lived. And what did she have to fight for anymore? She'd hoped her daughter's son might eventually rule. She'd thought, once, that she might be the power behind the throne, but, whatever, her bloodline would rule Lyonesse. She'd never dreamed of ruling it herself. That was for men.

And now her daughter did, although she seemed unaware of it.

So Queen Gwenhwyfach took the dragon's advice and sent out her dragons, and word to any of her minions that had not already been told: stop the invaders, at any cost.

The Shadow Hall settled on a high hill in her native South while she was doing these things.

When she came to notice it, she realized that the muryan slaves were gone, and Shadow Hall would not be moving.

The Land did not like slaves, and its magic was far more powerful than hers.

So she sat in her high room and looked via the basin at Dun Tagoll.

Anghared would turn her attention there, eventually.

And that, at least, would be sweet.

Maybe she could get used to being old, and contemplating grandchildren and not plotting revenge. Then she thought of the creatures of smokeless flame and thought: maybe not.

=== Chapter 27 ===

DUN TAGOLL BASKED IN THE SPRING. THE PRINCE AND HIS TROOP rode out on local patrols, but there had been none of the deluge of foes they'd expected.

No messengers came from the other Duns. Not from the north, the center, the prince's own lands in the east, and of course not from the south.

Eventually, Prince Medraut sent out a strong party to Dun Telas. To get a message back that the men of Telas had marched south with the Defender. They were full of stories about how the Lady Anghared had dealt with the men of Ys, the Vanar, and soldiers from Erith. Even driven off the dragons of Shadow Hall.

The prince sent a message for the royal mage.

Aberinn appeared in a good mood. "I have discovered what the problem in my spells is. It appears there is now considerably more magic in Lyonesse, which has meant all our workings were miscalibrated. That's why the Changer overshot. That's why we had sufficient power so much sooner. Anyway, I have run a number of calibration spells. I can adjust the Changer so that it operates as normal."

"Why bother?" asked Prince Medraut sourly.

"Have your wits gone begging, Medraut? To allow us access to fresh magical energy. To allow us to escape our enemies." said the elderly mage.

Medraut shrugged, insolently. "You've just said there is considerably more magical energy in Lyonesse. And that young woman, it appears, is not dead. She is this Defender that you prophesied."

"Don't be stupider than you have to be, Prince Medraut."

"I've just had my messengers return from Dun Telas. She's defeated Ys, Vanar, Erith and your Shadow Hall. And she will want my head. Yours, too, I would think."

The mage rolled his eyes and said in a voice of severely tried patience, "She is not this legendary Defender, whoever she is. If she has defeated Shadow Hall, my crows can fly. I will test that, but I doubt it. Shadow Hall merely waits. The enchantress has that kind of patience, that long view. The Vanar were destroyed by a storm. We saw wreckage. As for the rest, Ys under Dahut is dissolute..."

"How do you know that she's not this Defender? It was prophesied..."

Aberinn drew himself up. Shook his head. "Because I made it up, Medraut. I made it up so it would be easy enough for me to arrange if my son returns. I did it so it would be easy to get rid of the likes of you."

And he turned on his heel and walked out, leaving Medraut without a word to say. He was still standing staring at the door when Lady Cardun came bustling in. "Those crows fly again from Aberinn's tower. What's this story we're getting via the men-at-arms, Prince?"

"How is your scrubbing, Cardun?" he asked. "Kitchen floors, I would say, would be the best you can hope for."

She looked at him as if he'd gone mad. "What are you talking about, Prince Medraut?"

"The news from Dun Telas is that that girl Anghared has been hailed as the Defender. She's defeated our worst foes, even Shadow Hall. Aberinn says it is impossible, but that he'd test it with his gilded crows. You say they fly out. So, therefore, that at least is true."

The chatelaine's face went white under the face paint. "It can't be."

"That's what Aberinn said. He said the entire prophecy was a fraud set up so that he could claim the throne for his son," said Prince Medraut.

"But...he doesn't even like women. He has no son...Let me go and speak to Vivien. There was gossip. But it can't be true."

"You'll be scrubbing and I'll be at the whipping posts before I lose my head," said Prince Medraut, glumly. But his aunt had not stayed. She'd gone in search of Vivien.

✧   ✧   ✧

Lady Vivien was out on the battlements, looking at the distant golden flashes. "It seems you were wrong, and I should have been braver. I was afraid of Aberinn and afraid for my boys."

"Hmph. What do you mean, Vivien?" demand Lady Cardun, unable to leave go of her hectoring tone, even now.

Vivien shrugged. "Just what I say. She was the Defender. And I was too weak to go with her when she asked me for help, to leave. I told her to fit in here. She went, with just a maid to support her. Now, Lyonesse itself is changing, and we are not part of it."

"Not while Prince Medraut holds Dun Tagoll, it is not. Is it true that Aberinn has a son?"

"Not that I know of. He uses women sometimes, so he could have, I suppose." The younger woman turned. "I see that some of the golden crows are coming back already. Why don't you ask him yourself?"

And she walked away.

Vivien had taken herself to the wizard's tower, a little later, unable to not know. It was possible to do this in a way which did not make it easy to overlook, as she knew all too well.

The inner door was open. It was never open. She tiptoed in. She could hear them now—Aberinn, Medraut, Cardun. Voices raised. Aberinn: "The neyfs are even plowing again."

"Where is she?" asked Medraut.

"South of Dun Telas, dealing with a handful of knights under the banners of Brocéliande. The crows show that they've made a peace with them and the knights are being taken back to the Way, under escort."

"Is it definitely this Anghared?" asked Cardun.

The sarcasm in Aberinn's voice was thick. "It was a woman who looks as like her as two peas in a pod, mounted on a warhorse, with that silver axe Vivien told me of. She is accompanied by that maid of hers or someone who looks exactly like her, but other than that, no, I am not certain."

"Can we...you, kill her?" Medraut asked. "With your art, perhaps."

"You tried and failed. I used my art to shoot at her with the model-bow. And somehow...that failed. I made two other attempts. She is defended in some way. She is now accompanied by what I take to be her master. He must be a mage of considerable power."

"So what are we going to do?" asked Cardun.

"We hold Dun Tagoll. If she could act against it, she would have while she was here," said Medraut.

"It is defended and provisioned," said Aberinn. "And we control the Changer."

"What good will that do?" asked the chatelaine.

Vivien tiptoed away, not waiting, going back to the women's quarters. For a long time she stood in the passage outside the bower. She went in. It was empty. She took a deep breath and looked among the embroidery frames. Found the one she was looking for. Marveled at the stitches. And got up and did what no castle lady would do: she went down to the barracks. It was in a ferment, a cheerful happy hubbub. It also hushed the moment she walked in. She had two sons here. Likely lads, good squires, walking in a famous father's footsteps. It could have been worse, because they assumed she'd come to see them.

They were desperately embarrassed to see her there. "Mother, you shouldn't be here," said the older, Cadoc. Melehan just stared at his mother, as if he could make her go away by eyes alone.

"I need to speak to you," she said.

"Come, we'll escort you back to the bower," said Cadoc, taking her elbow.

She found her courage. "No. What I need to say to you may as well be heard by everyone. We need to leave Dun Tagoll. The mage's gilded crows bring word that our foes are banished. The Defender has won, Lyonesse is at peace. Prince Medraut and Mage Aberinn have decided to keep the gate of Dun Tagoll closed on the Defender. To keep things as they are. I should have taken you and gone with her the first time, when she wanted to leave. I will not make that mistake again. We leave now."

There was a silence.

Then one of the grizzled veterans spoke. "How do you know this, Lady Vivien?"

"I have just heard it with my own ears. Do you doubt me? The gilded crows brought the mage news and sight of the land. You saw them fly and you've seen some return. Our foes are gone. Out there the peasants plow again. They've come out of the woods. Left the shelter of Telas and the other forts. They know it's over. Do you think I would risk my sons' lives for nothing? It's over. The Defender has come. There will be a new king. But those who rule here do not wish it to be over."

"It's true enough," said one of the men-at-arms who had ridden to Dun Telas. "I saw some of the neyfs on the ride. No beast so they'd yoked two of them to the plow."

He stood up. "I'm not one to stand against my sworn liege. But I'll not hold Dun Tagoll against her. She's a good lass, that one. I saw her at the queen's window, and I saw her put that axe in front of her face and face down the Fomoire. I'm for leaving."

"Aye," said the veteran. "Me too." And then another... A little later they spilled out of the barracks. Some went to the kitchens, to their peculiars, and others to the stables to get horses, Vivien among them. The grooms had liked Anghared, it seemed. They provided horses, and were mounting themselves. The men-at-arms had gone to the gate guard, and the gate was opened.

A few minutes later the entire courtyard was full. The gate was wide and people had already begun to walk and ride out.

The noise brought Prince Medraut and the Mage Aberinn and Lady Cardun out of the wizard's tower.

"What is happening here?" demanded Prince Medraut.

On the causeway, Vivien could hear his voice.

"Keep riding," she said to her sons. The causeway was no place to gallop, or she would have told them to do that.

"We're going to join the Defender, Prince Medraut," shouted someone.

"Close those gates! Get within, all of you! I command here! You will follow my orders."

"Ach. We'll take orders from her instead," shouted someone else. "You cannot stop us, Medraut."

"Go then. Be masterless, landless men. When the next invasions come, Dun Tagoll will be closed to those who leave. There will be no fortress whose walls cannot be breached to shelter you. There will be no magical multiplication of scant rations. You will starve or be killed."

"I can stop you," said Aberinn's cold voice, carrying above the noise.

Vivien knew how dangerous the narrow causeway was. "Run," she yelled.

They did, the press of people all scrambling for the headland.

And behind them the gates of Dun Tagoll swung closed, crushing the last few who tried to force their way out of the gates.

But they'd won free to the headland. "We will gallop now," said Vivien.

Then felt the blow and then, as she fell from the horse, the pain.

Someone yelled: "Run. They're firing the scorpios at us."

The next Vivien knew, she was surfacing as someone bathed her face. She looked up into the tear-filled face of her younger son. "Don't die, Mother, please don't die."

She was not sure she would be able to do that for him. "In the...little bag...on the saddle. Tapestry. With black dragon. Give it to her. Ask kindness to you...my sake. Cormac..." she whispered. Maybe she would be with him now.

"It would seem," said Finn, "that the last of Lyonesse's foes has retreated in some disarray. Now all that remains is Dun Tagoll itself."

"Do we have to do anything about it?" asked Meb. "I've seen Aberinn's crows. He knows what has happened."

"I think it is necessary to deal with this Changer device. The levels of magical energy it has caused to flow into Lyonesse... are not good. Some of it must run back to where it came from, Scrap. And then I think things can return to normal here."

Meb sighed. "I don't really want to go back. But let us go down there and see what we can do."

"Let's not use more magic than you have to, Scrap. It's quite unstable as it is. And every time you summons something...it has knock-ons. They use magic too freely here anyway."

"My magic is quite different from theirs, though."

"Part of it is. The part with fertility and life, yes. The rest is very human magic. They just draw and chant to achieve their visualization of the symbols. They complete things they have a little of, physically. You do the same, but the entire image is within you, and that part of the the thing—its essence, as it were—is also within you. But it should be used with caution, because it draws from within you, and, of course, makes work for me."

"Lady Anghared," said a respectful man-at-arms. "There are people here from Dun Tagoll. Shall I bring them?"

She smiled at him. Nodded. All she really had to give was a smile, but they seemed happy with that. She felt faintly guilty. By virtue of fighting the invaders, she had somehow ended up largely running the country and had absolutely no idea how to do so. Fortunately, she had Finn, and, oddly, Neve, who was proving very good at telling others what to do. "Maybe it has all resolved itself," she said hopefully.

A few minutes later she realized it hadn't. And that it would have to be dealt with, right now.

They were Vivien's sons. She recognized them although they were white-faced and plainly had been crying. The older one bowed and handed her a piece of tapestry. It was her own work. A black dragon . . . and it had blood on it. "My mother asked that we give this to you. Just before she died," said the older boy, his voice tight. "It has her blood on it. They shot her in the back from the walls as we fled." He started crying. Tried to control himself. "She brought most . . . of Dun Tagoll to your banner, Defender. She asked a kindness . . . for my brother and me, for her sake."

Meb found it hard to talk past the lump in her throat. She nodded. "What I can do, I will. She was good to me."

"I just ask that I . . ."

"*We!*" interrupted the younger boy.

"We can have a part in bringing down Dun Tagoll, in the downfall of Medraut and Aberinn."

"We go to achieve that end," said Meb. "And . . . I know your mother worried about you being provided for. Having a place was important to her. I will see that you have one. I promise."

So by afternoon the greater part of Meb's raggle-taggle army was heading west. And Meb had put a stop to the flying of the gilded crows again.

"There is no point in going to the headland. Dun Tagoll will stand any siege and its walls repair themselves," said Meb. "They have scorpios and catapults, and hot pitch. But there is a little hidden door at the back of the zawn to the south. The knockers said that leads to the tide engines and up to the wizard's tower. If Neve's count of those who left is right, then there can't be more than seventy people still inside Dun Tagoll, and very few of those are soldiers. Courtiers, a few servants. Medraut and his inner circle of haerthmen."

"I'll go and scout it then," said Finn. "Before you, or Díleas, argue or try and come with me, I can swim across, transformed into a seal at high tide. The knockers will tell us if there are any guards outside the cave, and I can swim right in and have a look at the spellcraft. I promise I will go no further. And you can think about crossing the gully in the meanwhile. I'd suggest making a pontoon-way of small boats and planks. I'll interfere with the weather a little. A bit of energy adjustment and we'll have a sea mist tonight."

By dark Fionn was back, pleased with himself. "It was a bolt-hole, I think. A neat piece of spellwork, but rubbed out now. I had words with the knockers to stop them going in before us, in case there are other alarms and defenses. How is the pontoon-bridge?"

"We've had some of the Lyonesse nobility exercise their magic," said Meb. "We took the coracle apart, gave a fragment to each of them and had them apply their magic. We've got planks to put across the top. Now all we need is low tide."

"That comes, as does the mist," said Fionn.

And it did. At dusk a column of men came down. A few paddled across in a coracle with the ropes and soon the floating bridge was in place. There were a good two thousand men there.

"They'll have to be deaf up there if they don't realize something is going on," said Fionn, grumpily.

The little door proved no match for Fionn. But the narrow passage beyond was going to be something of an impediment to the invaders. Getting thousands up was going to take time. Fionn went ahead. He knew better than to tell Meb—or Díleas—to stay back more than a few paces. The narrow passage brought them out into huge caverns. The knockers provided light, showing the great iron chains and sluices and a waterwheel that drove the engines far above.

The stairwell led upwards and upwards. Fionn looked and listened intently and, when he got to a certain point, called a knocker miner out from the crowd following. "There's a hollow just behind this wall."

"That'll be the wine cellar. We used to visit it. There are a few of our passages into it," said the chief Jack, with a toothy smile.

"Send a few of your lads in there to see if it is empty. Not of wine. Of people. And if it is, we'll have this wall down and send some men that way."

About a minute later the knocker was back. "Just the chief steward. Drunk. He's locked himself in. By what he's muttering, the murdering bastards upstairs will have no more wine even if he can't get out. The wine is dreadful. My lads will have that little wall down in no time at all. And quietly too."

"Good. We'll go on up while you do that."

They did. Another two flights of stairs and Díleas growled.

Fionn could hear him now, too. The dog had keen ears and a keener sense of smell. They advanced slowly on the human they could hear snoring on the other side of the door.

Then there were shouts and yells and the sound of swordplay in the distance. Fionn pulled the door open. The men coming in through the cellars must have encountered some resistance.

The door opened onto the courtyard, at the foot of Aberinn's tower. The guard who had been asleep at the tower door was still trying to wake up when a sheepdog bit him, and rough hands grabbed him and threw him down as more men spilled up out into the moonlight.

Fionn and Meb had not waited. The key here was not the castle. It was the mage's tower. And the iron-studded door was locked. Meb swung her axe at it, the magical blade cut through the bolts, and they were into Aberinn's tower.

There were signs that the mage had left in haste. Part of a machine was scattered onto the floor, in contrast to the neatness of the other tables.

Outside there was screaming and shouting.

Here, only a gilded crow looked at them from its cage.

"Upstairs!"

So they ran up towards them. "Stop!" shouted Fionn.

They did and he disarmed the little cross-bow miniature set to fire across the passage. Disarmed two other trap-spells.

They advanced cautiously. There was a great creaking sound. The next room was a mass of cogs and interlocking wheels—a great driver for the planar orrery above.

And that was where they found Aberinn. Behind a phalanx of forty-nine armed and fully armored men that advanced as one.

Meb looked at the small army that faced them. "They're not real! It's a broomstick and some tin."

"Curse you," screamed Aberinn, pulling a lever down. Machinery began to clank, and he took the long lever and ran to the stair up to the roof, Díleas tearing his robe.

And there on the roof, they cornered him, standing on the edge of the parapet.

"Come any closer and I will throw the key to the Changer. I may get it into the sea from here."

"Give up, Mage. The Defender has come," said one of the men who had come up with them. Everyone wanted to be there with her.

"Defender!" spat Aberinn. "You fools! I made that prophecy up. I invented it. I did it so that when my son returns I could use some stupid woman to get rid of the regent easily. So I could avoid the silly plots in the meantime. Lyonesse needed me. I preserved it. And my son still lives and only he, because he is my blood, will be able to find the ancient font. Without it Lyonesse will never have a king who is the Land. It will never be able to defeat the invaders."

When the black dragon had opened the castle, he had broken Aberinn's circle of protection. Queen Gwenhwyfach, sitting peering into her basin, had at last been able to see into Dun Tagoll. She'd seen how Medraut fled to the women's quarters and was dragged out by two young squires.

She'd seen surrender and the bloodshed she'd dreamed of.

She was quite empty of emotion now, as her daughter and the black dragon faced her former lover across the roof of the tower.

And now she understood what had driven him.

He'd never known that she'd given birth to a daughter.

When she'd found out about King Geoph's little pleasures with her chambermaid Elis, when Gwenhwyfach herself could not fall pregnant... She'd gone to Aberinn, and the magics they'd worked had made sure the king would sire no more bastards.

Then she'd needed a lover to see to that herself.

His spells on cord-blood told him their child lived.

It did not tell Aberinn the sex of that child.

Fionn could feel the build of energies. It worried him. These humans had no idea what forces they dealt with messing about as they did with the planes and subplanes. "Let us stop your Changer. I think I may be able to solve the mystery of this son you wait for. I saw the workings you had below. They're centered on your blood."

"All is made for my blood and my son. And I will destroy you now, woman!" screamed Aberinn. "It's too late. The Changer is set so it will try to change... when there are no Ways to open! All that energy will pour in here, and the tower will burn. I just had to hold you for a few more minutes. I have the key." And he threw it, out into the darkness. "And now no one does! You will all die with me."

"You fool," said Fionn. "You've probably destroyed Lyonesse, let alone this tower. And it should have been obvious to you who your child was. Díleas, NO!"

The sheepdog had been edging forward quietly. He took a nip at a skinny calf. Just as he might have worried a recalcitrant sheep into moving.

The sheep would have pulled away too.

But it probably would not have been standing on a narrow parapet eighty cubits above a stone-flagged courtyard.

And from below them in the tower, there was a horrible scream and a grating noise.

Silence. And another scream from inside the tower.

They ran down.

It was Alois's son, Owain, his hand trapped in the cogs. Whatever he'd done, the Changer would not change anything anymore. Pieces of spring and little brass cogs lay scattered about.

"Axe," said Fionn grimly, holding out his hand for the ancient and magical alvar blade.

It would cut steel.

It cut brass.

The alternative would have been to cut the arm off.

"I . . . heard what the mage said," said the boy. "I squirmed between the legs, back down here. Stabbed it. It . . . drew my hand in," he said through gritted teeth. "Mother . . . said I wasn't to come. But I wanted to do something for the Lady Anghared. So . . . so she would pardon my father. Not have his head . . . I was too scared already when I thought he was dead last time."

"Whatever else you've done by this deed," said Meb, "I promise that I am not going to have your father's head. I was never planning to."

"Tell my mother I am sorry . . . I disobeyed," he said faintly and slumped in Fionn's arms.

There was cheering and shouting down the stairs.

But Fionn only had space for the small sorrow in his arms. "He's a brave lad. We must see if we can save the arm. But he saved all of us. I think the castle has been taken. You'd better send for his mother, Scrap."

✧　　　✧　　　✧

It was only a few hours until morning. When the sun came up that day, the gates of Dun Tagoll were open. The bodies had been dragged away. People came and went. Messengers rode north and south.

And the dragon, dog, and the daughter of Queen Gwenhwyfach and Mage Aberinn stood together in a little oasis of quiet by the outer wall, where the water trickled through the now luxuriant ferns and tiny star lilies and into the stone basin.

"This is my favorite place here. About the only place I like here, actually. I didn't like this castle when I came to it. And now I like it even less," said Meb. "I always wondered just who my parents were. Daydreamed I might be a princess or the daughter of a great magician. Did I make that happen?" she said, touching the dragon pendant at her throat.

"No," said the dragon. "It's common enough, I gather, for humans to dream such things, especially when they know little of them, or the price of them. Would you have dreamed them as they were?"

Meb shook her head. "No. I...I didn't like either of them. I should have loved them. They were my parents."

"If you had, Scrap, I would be worried about you," said the dragon. "They had their strengths. Even, oddly, good points. But they were not strong enough to rise above their upbringing and society."

"It's not a society I want. Not for the sons of the Dragon," she said, twisting her fingers in his. "So what do we do now?"

"Eat breakfast, I would think. Ruling is what they expect of you, though."

"Me?"

"It seems you have found their holy puddle. Díleas is drinking from it, which probably makes him the king dog. I wouldn't tell him, because he gets insufferable enough anyway."

Meb looked at the rock-bowl. "This is the font? I thought it was a horse trough. No one ever comes near it."

Fionn shrugged. "Because they can't see it. It looks like a rock to them. Aberinn hid it so only his bloodline could see it, the same as his other illusions. The question now is what you are going to do with it."

"But I thought it was for kings. I drank from it. Washed my face in it."

"Some of the best kings have clean faces, at least once in a lifetime," said Fionn.

"So what do you think I should do?"

"That you must decide. I can't decide for you," said Fionn, hoping he hid his nervousness.

"I'd make a slightly worse king than Neve."

"In the way they see matters, in terms of bloodlines anyway, she has a better claim," said Fionn. "She's the king's granddaughter; you are not actually more than the queen's daughter. And of course there are any number of others. Getting this society to accept that may be difficult, though. They have gotten used to the idea of you."

"I think I would make the worst possible queen or king or ..."

"Dragon partner? Troublemaker? Provider of breakfast to faithful sheepdogs?"

She smiled and kissed him. "I think those sound more like what I wish to be good at."

And, thought Fionn, will be, even possibly without help from a dragon pendant. "I hear Earl Alois has arrived. I think we need to go and give him greeting."

Meb winced. "We'd better."

They found the earl with his son.

He knelt when he saw Meb. "Lady Anghared. Defender of Lyonesse."

Meb looked at him. Looked at the boy, pale and drugged by Fionn. Looked at his wife, holding him by the shoulder. "He's a very fine son, Earl Alois. He did this for you. And even if I had wanted your head as much as I wanted Medraut's or Aberinn's, I would have forgiven you, for his sake."

"I failed you, too, Alois," said Fionn. "I did not keep him safe."

The earl stood. "My son has taught me honor. And they tell me that he would have lost his arm completely if it were not for you, Sir Spriggan. That you were the one who set the bones and sewed the skin. I cannot blame you for his actions."

"Then you'd blame me for his courage too. And that, I think he learned from his father," said Fionn. "And actually, I'm a dragon, not a spriggan."

"Oh, I'd say his mother, too," said his Scrap, as Alois stared at him.

Fionn could see it in her face. She reached her decision. "Earl

Alois. Pick him up. I know he is sore, but this is important. Lady Branwen, please bring your daughters. I've learned that the land doesn't care what sex its kings are. They might have to find a better word than 'king.'"

They walked out into the courtyard, to the outer wall, with, by now, a large following.

Meb came to what everyone else there perceived as a protruding piece of rock.

She told it to be what she could see. Then she made Earl Alois come forward and took a handful of water from the stone bowl. Bathed Owain's forehead in it. "And your daughters. The land is a heavy burden, best shared. One guardian for the South, one for the North, one for the East."

So she bathed their foreheads too.

"But you are the Defender. You are the Land," said Earl Alois.

"The Land does not belong to any one person," said Meb. "Lyonesse belongs to the people of Lyonesse, and they belong to it. But you will be the regent for it."

"But you..."

"I came to change it, not rule it. I am going to hold the sons of the Dragon, not Lyonesse. However, I do need two favors of you."

"You will always command whatever I or mine can do, Lady Anghared," he said earnestly.

"My Neve is to be chatelaine of Dun Tagoll. And a place of honor and lands must go to Vivien's sons."

Earl Alois nodded. "My word on it."

Meb smiled at them. Patted Owain's head. Took a firm hold of Finn and called Díleas to her.

It was easy to vanish.

And it was also easier to vanish from their sight, to leave them with an event that would grow in song and story, than to try and leave in any normal manner.

"Where now?" asked Fionn, enjoying sitting watching the confusion.

"We can still see you," said the spriggan. "And they'll make a mess of it. Just you wait."

"Probably," said Meb, smiling at the grey-faced fay. "But that'll make you happy. Anyway, this is not our place. And Finn would make a worse ruler than I would."

Fionn nodded. "I can't think of anything I'd like less. My work still needs doing, and if the First are going to meddle ... it may need more. There are some travelers out there we can quietly fit in with. We can come back from time to time. When they least expect us. I will make you and Díleas a home somewhere, but this is not it."

She put her arms around them, dog and dragon. "Home is not one place. It's where we are together."

"So let's go home," said the dragon.

⸺ Appendix ⸺

Afanc	A monster with a tail like a beaver and a crocodile head.
Cauldron of Gwalar	A magical artifact in which the enchantress of Shadow Hall cooks apart dead tissue and then grows her reanimated creatures.
Dun	A fortress. The principal fortresses in Lyonesse are Dun Tagoll (center West Coast), Dun Argol (Northwest), Dun Telas (East), Dun Carfon (South), Dun Calathar (North).
Haerthmen	Knights directly loyal to the earl of the Dun.
Muryan	Fay creatures rather like ants and ruled by a tiny human-looking queen.
Neyfs	Serfs.
Knockers/knockyan	Dwarflike miners.
Piskies	Field and woodland fay, mischievious, not too bright, about ten to twelve inches high. Live in family clans or tribes.

Spriggans	Larger, generally malevolent (by repute) fay, masters of glamor, and bound to rocky outcrops.
Shadow Hall	Queen Gwenhywfach's moving home.
Water-horse	Kelpie.
Wudewasa	Forest people.
Soul traps	made of human hair with the souls of drowned sailors inside.
Yenfar	large island ruled by Zuamar that Meb lives on.

CELTIC CYCLE SUBPLANES:

Cantre'r Gwaelod	The land below.
Ys	Ruled by Queen Dahut.
Mag Mell	Fomoire land beneath the waves.
Finvarra's kingdom	A wild Irish place.
Vanaheim	A mythical Iceland/Shetlands.
The Blessed Isles	
Brocéliande	A forested land with a large population of magical beasts.
Annvn	One of the least magical, where things are very regimented.
Albar	
Carmarthen	Great for sheep.
Abalach	Good for apples.
The Angevin Empire	Unmagical, but technologically advanced.